A VINEYARD WEDDING

A VINEYARD WEDDING

JEAN STONE

THORNDIKE PRESS
A part of Gale, a Cengage Company

LIBRARY OF CONGRESS CIP DATA ON FILE.
CATALOGUING IN PUBLICATION FOR THIS BOOK
IS AVAILABLE FROM THE LIBRARY OF CONGRESS.

ISBN-13: 978-1-4328-9774-1 (hardcover alk. paper)

Published in 2022 by arrangement with Kensington Books, an imprint
of Kensington Publishing Corp.

Printed in Mexico
Print Number : 2   Print Year : 2022

For my mom,
who would have loved this series,
and for my dad,
who would have been proud
to quietly show my books to
everyone he ever met

CHAPTER 1

Tuesday, November 23
Two Days Before Thanksgiving

It was the ugliest wedding dress Annie had ever seen. Which she knew was ridiculous, because all wedding dresses were beautiful, weren't they? Like newborn babies and puppies and kittens?

She stepped back from the full-length mirror to see if the image improved. It did not.

"How is it?" Claire called from the living room, where she no doubt was wringing her arthritic hands, anticipating the verdict from her soon-to-be daughter-in-law. Originally, the dress had been made for Mabel Lyons, grandmother of John, Annie's fiancé. But that wedding had been in 1941, when heavy fabric, big shoulder pads, and a bodice tufted as if made for a Victorian settee may very well have been the height of fashion. Claire hadn't worn it at her own wedding to Earl because she was too short, and the

7

"bottom line," Earl later confided to Annie, was that it was two or three sizes too small.

But Annie couldn't use size as an excuse.

"You're slender enough not to strain the satin buttons that cascade down the back," Claire had told her when she'd suggested that if Annie wore it, the gesture would be special for all of them, especially for John, who'd been close to his grandmother Mabel. "And you're taller than she was, so on you it will be tea length. Which will be lovely." Thankfully, she hadn't noted that the dress was ivory, which would be more "appropriate" than white, as this would be Annie Sutton's third wedding. Which Annie was trying not to think about now.

"Annie?"

She realized she had to come up with an answer that wouldn't hurt Claire's feelings. "John's grandmother must have been a beautiful bride" was all she could utter in spite of the fact that, as a best-selling author of mystery novels, she might be expected to have "the perfect words" at hand on any occasion.

"Come, come!" Claire clapped her hands. "Step out here and let's take a look."

"One second," Annie said, stalling. "Let me find shoes. Dresses always look better with the right heels." She knew, however,

8

that heels were not the answer. Maybe a large burlap sack . . .

"Judy said it's in wonderful condition," Claire affirmed. Judy worked at the dry cleaners in Vineyard Haven, where, according to Claire, they'd given it a thorough going-over.

"She's right," Annie replied. "It's hard to believe it's so old." She pushed aside sandals, sneakers, and flip-flops in an attempt to locate the lone pair of heels she'd salvaged from the life she'd left in Boston when she moved to Martha's Vineyard a few years earlier. In addition to writing novels, she now co-owned and managed the Vineyard Inn on Chappaquiddick and also spent time gathering berries and wildflowers for the soaps she crafted — activities that hardly required four-inch high-heeled Manolo Blahniks.

Finally she found the comfortable black pumps and slipped them on. Even the mirror seemed to grimace. Luckily, the wedding wasn't until Christmas Eve, so Annie had time to buy proper shoes and a more suitable dress.

Right now, however, she needed to say something that wouldn't make her seem ungrateful. As she put her hand on the doorknob, she tried to imagine how she would feel if the wedding dress had been her grandmother's, instead of John's. Annie had known only one grandmother — her father's mother — and she'd been kind and loving. Turning the knob and opening the door, she willed herself to believe she was wearing Grandma Sutton's dress.

As she stepped into the living room and onto the rug that had actually been braided by her softhearted grandma, Annie looked at Claire.

"What do you think?"

The only parts of Claire that moved were her pearl-gray eyes as she scanned Annie from the hemline to the bulbous shoulders.

"Well," Claire said.

Just as Annie was about to smile and say, "It's a bit much, don't you think?" Claire said, "You look so beautiful, Annie. Oh, yes, this is going to make Earl and John so happy." She wiped away a tear. Then another.

There was little doubt that Claire wasn't crying for the same reason Annie wanted to. What made it worse was that Claire had insisted they not tell John about the dress because it would be a wonderful surprise. Which meant Annie couldn't enlist his help to convey the news that she did not want to be caught dead, let alone married, in it.

She stifled a groan. "I'll get matching shoes, of course."

With an enthusiastic nod, Claire said, "Turn around. Let me see the back."

While Annie was doing a one-eighty, she wondered if there was some other way to convince herself that the dress would be fine. But when she turned back to face her again, Claire was frowning.

"You don't seem excited." The woman's flyaway white hair was nailed down with a headband that day, causing her seventy-five-year-old face to look more intense than usual.

"Well," Annie said, "it's amazing how the quality of the fabric has held up all these years. But the style . . ."

Claire chuckled. "Right! You probably never had shoulder pads. I think they were last popular in the eighties."

Not wanting to correct her by saying the fad had lingered into the nineties and that she'd had more than one outfit with two padded triangles stitched at the shoulders, Annie reluctantly replied, "The dress does fit. You were right about that." Then she checked the clock over the sink. "I'll adjust the rest later. Right now, I'd better change so we can start making our Thanksgiving pies."

11

But as she started to retreat to the bedroom, the door to the cottage swung open, and Lucy, John's younger daughter, the delightful designated maid of honor, walked in. After a quick look at Annie, Lucy halted.

"Wow," she said matter-of-factly, "that's the ugliest wedding dress I've ever seen."

An awkward pause gave way to Claire's resounding sigh. She dropped into the rocking chair, brushed back a lock of hair that had escaped the headband, and said, "I might be an old lady, but I've always thought tradition never goes out of style." She sighed again. "Let's go make the pies. And worry about this later."

Claire and Lucy headed up the small hill to the Inn to begin the annual baking extravaganza. Annie stepped out of the dress, put it in the garment bag, and hung it on the back of her bedroom door. Then she changed into her jeans, long-sleeved T-shirt, and sneakers, and added a light wool jacket. She mused that people on the island wouldn't be startled if a bride showed up at the altar wearing this outfit instead of traditional wedding attire.

Stepping outside onto her porch, Annie breathed in the stillness, the soothing calm of off-season. It was one of those late-fall afternoons when the sky and the water merged into the same color — gunmetal gray. But the leaves were not yet done falling from the scrub oaks and the cedars, so splotches of autumn's red and gold glowed in the air. In the distance, a small fishing trawler chugged into the still water of Edgartown Harbor, no doubt carrying the last of the striped bass and bluefin tuna of the season.

Earl had taught her that kind of trivia when he'd been the caretaker of the small place she'd rented long before she'd known the difference between a fishing trawler and a yacht. And before she could have imagined he would become her foremost teacher of the rhythm of the island as well as a supportive friend and, soon, a father-in-law. And now, she had no idea how to tell him that his mother Mabel's wedding dress wasn't going to be the catch of Annie's wedding day. But as she watched another boat bob in the harbor, she wondered if it would be kinder if she simply wore it. Would it serve as a symbol to the family that she was accepting love from all of them?

Of course it would. That would be Murphy speaking. Although her old college friend had died several years ago, Annie occasionally still heard her friend's voice and sage advice.

"Even though it looks like something I picked up at a flea market?" Annie asked.

John will think you're beautiful no matter what you wear. Of course, there is one sensible alternative . . .

"Which is . . . ?"

Have it altered. A good dressmaker can work miracles.

"There isn't time. The wedding's a month away, and with the holidays coming, the seamstresses here must be busy. I'd be better off going over to the Cape and buying my own dress. One I actually like."

Don't you have soaps to pack?

Murphy was referring to the inventory Annie had amassed a month ago so it would be cured and ready for wrapping in time for the Christmas in Edgartown Holiday Fair. For the past couple of years, Annie had a booth; this year, Lucy was going to help. Annie had lost precious time in the early fall thanks to her latest book tour, so she'd need to work nonstop from the day after Thanksgiving for the two weeks until the Fair, which would be another two weeks before her wedding.

She closed her eyes and wrapped her jacket more tightly to ward off a sudden chill. "So I have to wear the dress?"

Like I said. Have it altered.

Annie shoved her hands into her pockets. "Thanks, Murph. And like *I* said, there isn't time."

It's all in whom you know.

Claire, of course, was the first person who came to Annie's mind. In spite of the pain in her aging hands, the woman remained adept at knitting sweaters and making doll clothes. She also knew more about sewing than Annie, who could barely thread a needle. "But Claire thinks it's great the way it is."

I'm not talking about Claire. I'm talking about her granddaughter.

Annie flinched. She knew that Murphy didn't mean Lucy but the other one, the older one. Abigail.

What have you got to lose? You know she's good at fashion stuff. It's her college major, for God's sake. What more do you want?

"It would help if she liked me." As hard as Annie had tried, Abigail, unlike Lucy, hadn't been receptive to her father's fiancée.

You're the adult. You can do something about that. But first, get yourself up to the Inn. I don't eat much these days, but the aromas of Thanksgiving still make me happy.

If Murphy were a real ghost and not a figment of Annie's overactive writer's imagination (the jury was still out on which of those things was true), she might have formed a cloud of wispy, white smoke, spun around a few times, then swirled up to the sky. As it was, Murphy's aura merely vanished, leaving Annie with the uneasy prospect of trying to enlist self-centered, eighteen-year-old Abigail's help. Or not.

CHAPTER 2

"Apple-cranberry and pumpkin," Claire said as she stood at the long marble counter, rolling out piecrust.

"No pecan?" Lucy whined. "And no chocolate cream?" She pouted as if she were five instead of fifteen.

Claire looked at Annie. "Please explain to my granddaughter that four grown adults do not require two pies, let alone one apiece."

Like Annie, Claire was probably a little sad that this Thanksgiving only Earl, Claire, John, and Annie would sit at the big table. The others in their world were, or would be, off island, except for Rose Atkins, their quiet and shy retired winter tenant.

"I hate that I can't be here," Lucy said. This year, John's daughters had "switched parental schedules," as Lucy expressed it, and would be performing "mother duty" in Plymouth over the long weekend. That way, they could be on the Vineyard for Christmas Eve and attend their father's wedding to the woman who did not want to wear their great-grandmother's dress.

"I wish you could be here, too," Annie said, then perused the kitchen. "But we'll have fun making pies. How can I help?" She was about as adept at baking as she was at sewing, but Claire and Lucy never seemed to mind.

"The pumpkin's in the oven, starting to roast, and Gramma's working on the crust for the apple-cranberry," Lucy said. "Do you want to peel and slice apples?"

"Don't use the machine," Claire interjected. "They come out nicer when we do them by hand, don't you think?" From oven roasting sugar pumpkins for pies to preparing apples by hand, Claire, like her husband, usually preferred to stick with the old ways. Annie could not disagree, especially since pumpkins and apples had been grown and harvested right there on Chappy without pesticides, organic before organic had become a household word.

As for the cranberries, they, too, were local, having been harvested from the bog in Vineyard Haven. Annie had learned that the bogs in Massachusetts yielded the best berries because, eons ago, glaciers had formed them; they were not man-made. The island was lucky to have one. It was one of those facts that Annie-the-writer loved learning.

"I'll help you pick out the best apples in the root cellar," Lucy said, as if the amount of apples needed for a single pie required a two-person team.

Once they were outside, however, Lucy whispered, "That wedding dress really is gross."

Annie tried not to smile. She opened the bulkhead and went down the half flight of wooden stairs. The root cellar was well stocked; it emitted a scent of autumn's sweetness, though the chill felt more like winter.

"What are you going to do?" Lucy asked, carefully selecting a combination of McIntosh, Cortland, and Granny Smith apples and setting them in a canvas bag that Annie held open.

"I don't know, honey. But I love that it was your great-grandmother's — and don't tell your father that. It's supposed to be a surprise." She examined a McIntosh. "So I do want to wear it. I might ask your sister if she'll help . . . uh, *renovate* it."

Lucy made a face. "Knowing Abigail, she'll probably tie-dye it or turn it orange."

"But if we can convince her to keep its

original color, it will look nice with your powder blue." Instead of traditional holiday red and green, Annie wanted the wedding décor in shades of winter white, silver, and powder blue — with Lucy's dress accented by an overlay of tiny glittering stars. The colors would blend with the sea-glass shades of the great room at the Inn where the wedding was going to take place. Claire had noted that she could remove the wintry sparkles from Lucy's dress afterward so she'd be all set for the spring prom.

Lucy stared into the canvas bag. "My sister has a new boyfriend. She's bringing him to Mom's for Thanksgiving. And the weekend."

"Oh. But at least Abigail will be out of your hair, right?"

"It's not fair. Kyle's been my boyfriend since last summer, but I'm not allowed to bring him even for dinner. Abigail meets some guy on the boat a couple of months ago and suddenly he's moving in, like he's part of the family."

"Is he an island boy?"

"He's in college in New Hampshire. I guess he lives there, too."

"But you'll bring Kyle to the wedding, right?"

"Absolutely."

20

"Well, I think that's more important." Annie smiled. "Now, do we have enough apples?"

"More than."

As they headed out of the cellar, Annie's phone rang: it was her brother, Kevin, who'd gone to Minnesota to spend the holiday with part of their mismatched island family — "the troops," Kevin liked to call them. She handed the bag of apples to Lucy, then stepped outside and answered.

"Whatcha doin'?" Kevin asked nonchalantly.

"Lucy and I were foraging for apples."

"If they're for Thanksgiving pies, you'd better forage a few more. Taylor and I will be home tomorrow. And we might have a few tagalong troops if we can get enough plane reservations."

"They're coming back?" Claire asked after Lucy scampered into the kitchen ahead of Annie, dumped the bag of apples on the counter, and blurted out the news about the pending arrivals from the Midwest. "And more importantly, why?"

"Kevin and Taylor will be home tomorrow," Annie said. "He's trying to find more seats on a plane, so I don't know who all will be with them. As for why they're coming, I have no idea. Maybe they're afraid of missing out on your cooking." Her smile widened; she was pleased that her brother would be there, even though his sometimes-crabby wife, Taylor, would be with him.

"So Francine and Jonas are going to come?" Claire asked, wiping her hands on her bib apron. "Will Bella be with them?" Once a stranger, Francine had become much beloved; Jonas, her boyfriend, was Taylor's son; and Bella was Francine's adorable little sister. None of which mattered, because they all now felt like blood relations.

Lucy looked at Annie. "Gramma wants answers."

Annie forced a laugh. "Sorry. All I know is that Kevin and Taylor will be on the three forty-five boat tomorrow, so I'll be there at four thirty to get them." It went without saying that the travelers would fly into Boston and take the bus down to the ferry terminal. It also was taken for granted that when mentioning the boat's schedule, islanders rarely referred to the boat by when it was due to pull into Vineyard Haven but by when it departed from Woods Hole on the Cape — in this case, three forty-five.

It was an island quirk; Annie had learned there were a lot of those.

"I wonder if Francine's aunt and uncle will be with them?" Claire asked, as if Annie hadn't already clarified what she knew.

"I have no idea," Annie replied. She secretly hoped not; she'd met them only once, briefly, and though they'd seemed nice enough, their presence would shift the comfy dynamics of the group Annie loved.

Don't be greedy, Annie would swear she heard Murphy say.

"No matter what," Lucy interjected, "if more than Kevin and Taylor show up, you're going to need more than your Jeep to haul them and their stuff back to Chappy." Then she pressed a forefinger to her chin as if she were in deep thought. "Hmm . . . As it happens, my dad is supposed to bring me and my sister to the noon boat tomorrow . . ."

"Abigail and me," her grandmother corrected.

"Right," Lucy said. "Anyway, if everybody comes in at four thirty, won't it make more sense for my sister and me to take the five o'clock boat? Then my dad would be right there in Vineyard Haven to help."

Lucy's agenda was transparent to Annie: by taking the five o'clock boat instead of the one at noon, Lucy would spend less time in Plymouth with her mother and sister. And her sister's new boyfriend.

"Let's see who winds up coming, and what your dad says," Annie said. "For now, we need to think about pies. And turkey. And everything else! What do you think, Claire? What will we need if more of them come?"

Claire pulled her iPad from her purse. (It always surprised Annie that old-fashioned Claire never went anywhere now without her tablet.) Ever the matriarch, she quickly calculated that if five to seven additional people showed up, they would need more potatoes and butternut squash, but that they had plenty of those in the root cellar. She added that the turkey would work for dinner, but there wouldn't be leftovers. "Earl says leftovers are the best part of the meal," she said. "So he can battle the crowd at Stop and Shop and pick up another turkey, if there's one left in the meat case. And extra stuffing." She figured they could take green beans and Brussels sprouts that they'd canned in September out of the pantry. "And Earl should get more cream for whipping. And vanilla ice cream. And cheese, because Kevin would rather have cheese with apple-cranberry pie. And Bella loves chocolate cream pie, so we should make one of those. And maybe everyone would like a sample of pecan."

Annie wasn't surprised that Claire had a quick grasp on the essentials. She'd gladly feed the whole island if she were asked.

Lucy checked to see if they had enough chocolate for pie (they did) and enough pecans for a fourth pie (they did not). They also decided to make an extra pumpkin pie, which Claire calculated they could have underway by the time Earl returned from the store. Five pies for a total of eight to ten adults and one toddler ought to be enough for both dinner and leftovers.

Lucy got her grandfather on the phone, filled him in on what was happening, and rattled off the shopping instructions.

Annie knew that everything would not be as befuddling as it seemed right then; she'd learned that, on the Vineyard, a little confusion was part of the fun. She was curious, however, as to what had triggered the wish to return to the Vineyard. After all, Francine was currently in college in Minnesota; she also was pregnant with Jonas's baby. Along with Bella, the young couple had been living with Francine's aunt and uncle in their home. If something was wrong, Annie hoped that it wasn't about the new baby.

As Lucy hung up from talking to her grandfather, her eyes filled with tears. She put both hands on her slim hips and looked at Annie and Claire. "Everyone's going to be here but me. I'm even more bummed now about having to go to stupid Plymouth."

Claire patted the top of her granddaughter's head. "Plymouth is not stupid, dear. Some of our ancestors landed there." She straightened the bronze-colored plait that stretched halfway down Lucy's back. Though Lucy's childhood freckles had faded and her tomboy ways had been morphing into softer femininity, she was still a child at heart. "And your sister won't be here, either."

"I'm sorry, Lucy," Annie said, not giving Lucy a chance to offer a comment about Abigail. "Maybe they'll still be here when you come home. And maybe only Kevin and Taylor will show up. It's such a busy time for air travel."

But the teenager's tears slipped out, glistening on the remnants of her freckles. She pulled a large stainless steel bowl and a colander from a cabinet and began scrubbing the apples in the sink with more vigor than necessary.

Annie's phone rang again; this time, caller ID read: BRIGHTON, TRISH. Annie let the call go to voice mail. Trish was the editor of Annie's best-selling mysteries. But with Annie's last book successfully released and a new one underway, chances were, whatever the call was about could wait.

CHAPTER 3

The following morning, Kevin texted Annie from the airport. They were coming on two separate planes: Kevin and Taylor on one; Francine, Jonas, and Bella on the other. That was all. Francine's aunt and uncle were not with them.

Annie grinned and tried not to feel guilty.

John agreed that Lucy and Abigail would leave on the later boat. And Annie and Claire went into high gear, rearranging the feast and everything to go with it, including making sure that the plates, glasses, silverware, and serving dishes were "holiday clean."

Earl had procured an extra turkey; it would make for great leftovers — sandwiches, soup, Claire's famous potpie. Thankfully, Claire and Lucy had made lots of cranberry sauce after the harvest at the bog in October.

The organizing, planning, and the timing

of dinner weren't done until after two o'clock. Annie was in the great room, touching up a few wrinkles in the linen tablecloth, when John came up behind her and slipped his arms around her waist.

"Put down that iron," he ordered, "or I'll have to arrest you."

Annie set down the iron, not because she always did as she was told, which she did not, but because his arms enveloped her body. She tipped her head back and rested it below his shoulder. "Yes, sir, Officer."

"That's detective sergeant," he said.

She turned and yielded to a lingering kiss. "How silly of me to forget," she said when they at last pulled away.

"The same way that, like my mother, you've probably forgotten to eat today. Which is why I brought vittles. Cheese-and-avocado paninis. Not exactly Thanksgiving food, but I figured one will keep your taste buds hankering for turkey tomorrow."

"Hankering," she said. "What a great word."

He rolled his pearl-gray eyes the way Lucy rolled hers. And as Earl often did, too, though his eyes were brown, while John's and Lucy's were clones of Claire's.

Annie followed him into the kitchen, where Claire was sitting at the island, relishing a sandwich.

"Here's the deal," John said after he poured glasses of water. "I'll bring the girls to the boat and meet you in the lot. Do you still have the car seat for Bella?"

"I do. It's even still hooked up in the back seat." She bit into the sandwich and slowly chewed.

"Good. You'll be able to pick up Francine, Jonas, and Bella. I'll have room for Kevin and Taylor and all the suitcases. Then we'll meet at Taylor's. I assume that's where Francine and Jonas will stay?"

Gesturing that she had no idea, Annie said, "Unless something's changed since they left."

"Changed how?" Claire interrupted. "Is something wrong?" Claire was a fussbudget who was always concerned about those she called family.

"Not that I know of," Annie replied. "So, yes, I expect they'll stay at Taylor's."

"Oh, please," Claire said, setting down her sandwich and folding her hands as if in prayer. "Please let everyone be all right."

"Stop it, Mom," John said. "Everyone's fine. Except Abigail, who's pissed about having to wait until the five o'clock boat, because it cuts into the time she'll have with her boyfriend. Like that's my fault. Anyway, she said she hates me and stomped out of the house."

"She'll get over it," Claire said as she resumed chewing. "As I recall, you hated me plenty of times when you were young."

"No, I didn't, Mom. And at eighteen, I sure as hell didn't bring home a girl and expect that you and Dad would let us have a sleepover."

Annie ate in silence, listening to the lighthearted chatter and wondering if it was going to be possible for her to be a patient stepmother to willful Abigail.

The parking lot at the boat was Thanksgiving holiday crazy. Both vehicle check-in booths were open, with the ticket checkers hollering "Lane six," "Lane three," "Lane eight" over the din, directing cars and trucks to the pre-boarding queues that were rapidly filling up. Suitcases ground across the pavement as people walked every which way, clutching bags of last-minute snacks from the Black Dog Bakery next door or the Stop & Shop across the street. Dogs barked, children shrieked, gulls dive-bombed the crowd, hunting for scraps of anything edible. It reminded Annie of summer, except that the mob now wore down jackets and hats with earflaps, as if they were expecting a nor'easter.

The three forty-five hadn't yet arrived from across the sound.

Inching the Jeep through the narrow pickup, drop-off area, Annie could not find an open slot. She drove out to Water Street, but the few parallel-parking spaces were taken, as were those in the public lot. She turned onto Union and went up to Main Street; if there wasn't room there, she'd swing onto State Road, head up to Park-n-Ride, and take the shuttle back to the boat.

As she considered her options, an SUV miraculously backed out of a spot in front of Rainy Day gift shop. Annie gave a thumbs-up to the driver, then slid between the white lines.

"Hallelujah," she said as she checked the time on her phone: 4:21. She texted John: PARKING IS HIDEOUS. I'M ON MAIN. YOU MIGHT NEED P-N-R. Then she grabbed her purse, jumped out, and headed back down the hill on foot, texting Kevin as she went, alerting him she'd be at the terminal entrance.

By the time she crossed the street and stepped onto the sidewalk, the *Island Home* had rounded the jetty and was gliding into the harbor, its massive size and stark white beauty evoking detectable awe through the crowd. It was clear that Annie wasn't alone in thinking that the sight of the "lifeline to the island," as it was called, was somewhat magical.

Finally, the big boat docked and the de-boarding process began. Like Annie, those who were there to pick up friends or relatives stood first on one foot, then the other, their necks craned, their eyes darting around, searching for familiar faces.

Her mane of vibrant auburn hair made Kevin's wife, Taylor, easy to spot. Annie waved both arms and, within seconds, she was greeting the four adults and holding Bella.

Then John called. He said he'd dropped off the girls and Restless, his dog, and parked at the Tisbury Police Station, across the street. Annie hadn't realized that, of course, he could park there. She also hadn't been aware that the sweet black, white, and brown, part Bernese mountain dog, part something anonymous, would be going to Plymouth, too.

Leaving Kevin and Taylor to wait for the luggage cart to roll off the freight deck, Annie told them to stay put until John crossed the street to help convey the bags, while she, Francine, Jonas, and Bella buckled up and headed to Chappy.

33

Finally, they broke free from the dance of holiday revelers, and life began to feel almost normal again.

The sun was fully set by the time Annie reached Edgartown Road, and her passengers had settled in for the twenty-odd-minute drive to the Chappy Ferry — the *On Time.* Bella had fallen asleep in her car seat; Jonas sat quietly beside her with one hand protectively positioned on the armrest. Francine was in the front passenger seat, rambling on about the flights, the wait in Philadelphia, the bus trip from Logan.

"We're exhausted," she said.

Annie still didn't know why they'd come back to the Vineyard. Or if Francine's aunt and uncle hadn't joined them merely because of a lack of available reservations. Perhaps there had been a falling-out between the aunt and uncle and Taylor, which would not be surprising, at least not to Annie. Kevin's wife could be irritating, no doubt especially to people who did not know her well.

She tossed a side glance to Francine. "I'm so happy to see you. We're all so glad you're here. But —"

"But . . ." Francine cut in, "it seems like a lot of trouble and expense for some turkey and apple-cranberry pie — especially since Kevin and Taylor only came to Minneapolis three days ago. Is that what you're thinking?"

Annie laughed. "Now that you mention it, yes."

Francine sighed.

"Tell her," Jonas said from the back seat. "That was our agreement."

Francine began to weave her gloved fingers together.

The uneasy feeling that something was wrong returned with a vengeance.

"It's no big deal," Francine said. "I've just been nervous lately. A lot."

Annie reached across the console and touched her shoulder. "Is the baby okay?"

She nodded. "The doctor says the baby's fine. And I'm fine. Sometimes I feel a little sick, you know? But then it passes. He says it's normal. And that everything will be fine."

Because Francine had used the word *fine* three times in her short sentences, Annie now knew for sure that things were not fine. They fell into silence until they reached the roundabout, when Annie gently asked, "What are you not telling me?"

Francine didn't reply right away. Then she simply said, "See? That's why I had to come . . . home. I know my aunt and uncle care about me — about us — but I'd rather be here with all of you."

Her words hung in the air a moment before Jonas added, "She's scared, Annie."

"About what? That something will happen to the baby?"

Francine cleared her throat. "A little. But I'm more scared that something will happen to me."

"But, honey," Annie said, "you're healthy. You take good care of yourself . . ."

Francine shook her head. "Remember I told you that after Bella was born, my mother got an infection?"

Annie remembered that. The woman had died within days of giving birth. "But that won't happen to you. For one thing, your mom was over forty, wasn't she? You're not quite twenty-two."

She nodded. "I know."

"Besides," Annie said with a crooked smile, "we're not going to let anything bad happen. You have my word. So you can stop worrying."

"I'm trying not to. Honest I am. But it's really hard." She started to cry.

Jonas reached over the top of the seat and rested his hand on her shoulder. "Which is why I asked her if she wanted to come home."

A tiny lump rose in Annie's throat. "What about school?" As much as she wanted her on the island, Francine had been working so hard toward a degree in hospitality and tourism management . . . .

"I can work remotely. And my adviser said I can get extra on-site credits if I get an internship at one of the hotels. Which I think would be fun."

"So . . ." Annie started to relax. "You want to stay here until the baby's born?"

"That's the plan. If you'll have us."

"Marty and Bill are upset that we left," Jonas said. "They're pretty attached to Bella. And to Francine, too." Marty and Bill were the aunt and uncle; Marty had been Francine's late mother's sister.

"We're pretty attached, too," Annie added, then lightly patted Francine's knee. "It's going to be okay, honey. We're here for you. And you have a doctor here that you like, right?"

She nodded again and wiped her tears. "Yeah," she said. "Which is another reason I want to be here."

"Well, then," Annie said with a tender smile, "welcome home."

CHAPTER 4

I don't know anything about fate. Or destiny.

I only know that life had been going okay, and the future seemed pretty solid. Until, in a heartbeat, everything changed.

And though it's too late to undo what's been done, if I don't do something now, I'll wind up with nothing but doubts about how things would have been, could have been different, if only I'd had the courage to act. If only I'd had the courage to try and make things right.

So I'm going to do it.

And I'm excited as hell.

I don't know yet how to make it happen. Or when. But I'll do it. Because this is not a coincidence. This is my chance.

And the little baby will finally be where she belongs.

CHAPTER 5

By the time they were back on Chappy, Annie felt as if she were the one who was exhausted. Throughout the drive, she'd kept flashing back to the first time she'd seen Francine. It had been at the Holiday Fair, and a young woman with sad, soulful dark eyes approached Annie's table of hand-crafted soaps. She was carrying a woven basket; at the time, Annie didn't notice that a baby — Bella — was inside. Nor could she have guessed that, days later, the baby would be left on her doorstep. Or that Francine and Bella would become so important to her.

Francine had been through so much anguish and sorrow. And now that her life seemed to be on a happy, positive track, Annie was determined to be supportive and reassuring. To make certain Francine knew that she and Bella were protected. And loved.

With sunset and twilight long gone, the sky was pitch dark as expected, what with winter looming and the fact that the island wasn't known for its streetlights.

Taylor's — and *Kevin's,* Annie had to keep reminding herself — Cape-style house was tucked away, as houses there tended to be; it was off a bumpy, unlit dirt road, down an equally bumpy, unlit dirt driveway, which was lined on both sides with tall pine trees that cast dancing shadows as Annie's headlights bounced past them. When she at last pulled up to the house, she was surprised to see a light in the kitchen window. Maybe Taylor had left it on for safety, though Chappy had fewer interlopers than streetlights.

But just as Annie started to open the car door, the figure of a man walked out the back door and stood stock-still on the deck. He was tall and bulky; from where Annie was sitting, she couldn't tell if his size was due to muscle or fat. Both his hands were crammed into the pockets of what looked like saggy jeans; the kitchen light behind him silhouetted his large frame and camouflaged his features.

"Either of you know this guy?" she asked her passengers.

Francine shook her head.

Jonas put his window down a few inches. "Never seen him before."

Annie unbuckled her seat belt and opened the door. "Wait here," she instructed her passengers, as if she were her fiancé and not merely a civilian with an unfortunate tendency to find trouble.

"Excuse me, but who are you?" Annie asked as she stood by the Jeep and purposely didn't approach him.

"Bigger question," a gruff voice replied. "Who the hell are you?"

She wondered if she might be in the wrong place. But the garage was in the back and the flower beds were in need of tending, and it looked like Jonas's car was there as well, right where he had left it before they'd driven Francine's to Minnesota. So yes, Annie thought. This was the place.

Jonas began to get out of the Jeep, but Annie motioned to him to stay inside. She didn't want him leaving Bella or attempting anything heroic with Francine still in the front.

"I'm Annie Sutton," she said. "My brother, Kevin MacNeish, lives here."

The gruff voice snorted. "Lady, I don't know who he is, either, but this is not his house." He pulled his hands out of his pockets and folded his arms. In the process, he shifted enough so that Annie could see past him into a sliver of the kitchen. The cabinets were pale blue . . . exactly as Kevin had painted them when he'd moved in with Taylor at the end of last summer.

Of course this was the right house, she thought. For starters, Jonas had lived there a while now. Surely he would have known if Annie had turned into the wrong driveway.

"If this isn't Kevin and Taylor's place, then whose is it?"

"I didn't say Taylor doesn't live here."

"Well, my brother, Kevin, is married to her. So who are you?" It had begun to feel like a childish game.

"Rex."

"Rex. Okay. Would you care to elaborate?"

He snorted again. "I didn't know Taylor got married. My invitation must have been lost in the mail." He readjusted his stance. "I'm her brother."

Annie knew that Chappaquiddick was known for being quiet. Away from the water, the few sounds anyone might hear after dark would be a couple of chipmunks scuttling through underbrush or a raccoon poking around in search of food. Skunks sort of wandered here and there, but mostly they stayed in the woods. And there were deer, though the only noise connected to them came during hunting season — and in the daytime — when gunshots were common and residents needed to remember to don neon outerwear when venturing outside. An owl or two hooted at night and bats did whatever bats did, but otherwise, there was quiet.

The silence that fell after the man's last remark, however, landed with a thud that could have come from one of the World War II ordnance bombs that occasionally surfaced on East Beach. To date, as far as Annie knew, none had exploded accidentally, but the anticipation could be nerve-racking.

After more than a few seconds, Jonas got out of the Jeep and gently closed the door so that he wouldn't disturb Bella.

"As far as I know," he said, "I don't have an uncle."

The large man guffawed. "Well, I sure as hell didn't know I had a nephew. Not one that would be here, anyway."

Annie's mind raced back to the clash of events when Jonas learned the truth about his heritage and was confronted by the evils of his grandparents. She held out an arm now as if to stop him from getting closer to the deck that he and Kevin had finished building last summer.

Then the man — Rex — jerked his chin

toward the Jeep. "Who's the girl? And who's the kid in the back? More relatives no one told me about?"

Annie realized he had the advantage of enough light leaking from the house out into the driveway so that he could clearly see not only them but also inside the car. And though she could not see him well, she noticed that no other vehicle was in the driveway. It wasn't exactly walking distance from the *On Time* to Taylor's, so someone must have dropped him off.

"I need to see an ID," Jonas suddenly said. "This is my house. I live here. With my mother."

The big man scowled. "I should be asking for your ID, kid. Except that your red hair is a dead giveaway that you came from my sister. So what's your pleasure? My driver's license? Passport? Birth certificate?"

Jonas shrugged, his courage now slipping, thanks to his innate shyness. "Whatever you have."

"I'll go get it. You can come inside or wait out here in the pitch dark and the cold. Up to you."

"We'll wait here," Annie said.

As soon as Rex lumbered back into the kitchen, Annie turned to Jonas. "Get in the car. Now. For all we know, he isn't alone.

And he could come back with a gun." She supposed she'd been writing too many mysteries, but she knew that life could be surprising, even on peaceful Chappaquiddick.

They hurried into the Jeep. Annie started the engine, then deftly backed down the driveway while connecting to Bluetooth and directing it to "Call John." After the usual struggle of Chappy's cell service to wake up, John answered. Annie quickly filled him in.

"Bring the kids to my parents," he said, his voice grave and insistent.

"But who's Rex? Is he really Taylor's brother?"

"Yeah. Probably. But it's good that you left. I'll take care of it. And I'll meet you at your place later." He disconnected abruptly, leaving Annie stumped.

"So, that guy's for real?" Jonas asked.

"Apparently."

"What a strange man," Francine said.

Annie could have said, "No kidding," but, once again, her better judgment told her to keep her skewed sense of impending conflict to herself.

"Hell and tarnation," Earl commented when they piled into the Lyonses' house and told him that a guy named Rex, claiming to be Taylor's brother, was on the island.

Claire was now home — Annie deduced that the pies were finished. But after the woman waved her hands in what looked like a spasm of exasperation, she sputtered and disappeared into Earl's study.

Their reactions, combined with John's words, heightened Annie's concern about the new man in town. "Can you give us some details?" she asked.

Earl huffed. "Sit down. Francine, take Bella in to Claire. No sense having the little one hear this."

Annie doubted that the two-year-old would be able to grasp whatever Earl was about to say, but she took a chair at the table and did not challenge him.

He scratched at his stubbly white whiskers, sat across from Jonas, and waited for Francine to return. Then he huffed some more.

"The suspense is killing us, Earl," Annie said.

"Okay. There are some blanks, but I can fill in a few. It's true that Rex Winsted is Taylor's brother. As I recall, he's older than she is by about a decade. He left the island a long time ago, long before you were born, Jonas." He nodded kindly at Jonas, as if trying to reassure him he did not need to feel responsible for his uncle, whatever he'd done. "I don't think anyone really knows why he left, but to my knowledge, nobody mourned his absence. He was a surly kid, a real scrapper. Stealing vegetables out of people's gardens for fun, chasing squirrels and throwing the acorns they collected into Poucha Pond, racing his beat-up old Ford up and down Chappy Road like he owned the place. Getting into fights with anyone who wanted to fight, and some who didn't. The only thing he was good for was cooking. In his teens he started a business catering gourmet picnics to rich summer people. Folks said he dreamed of opening his own restaurant on the island. But God knew his family didn't have a dime to do that."

Yes, Annie thought, she'd heard the story that the family had been strapped financially, especially after Taylor's father, who had been a fisherman, became ill. Which was why Taylor had returned from Boston after Jonas was born and she'd given him to his grandparents to raise, after she'd gone on to college and had been earning a living as a cellist with the symphony and tutoring kids. She'd come back to the island because her father was unable to work, and someone — she — had to support her parents. But that must have been long after Rex left.

"Rumor had it that Rex had a falling-out with old man Winsted — over money, or the lack of it," Earl continued. "Apparently he expected his dad to get a second mortgage on the house in order to finance his dream." Earl chuckled. "Anybody who knew old man Winsted knew that wouldn't go over too well. Anyway, Rex took off, and later we heard he'd opened a restaurant in Boston. A nice one, or so the rumor went. No one knew — or probably cared — how that happened, but I don't think he set foot on the Vineyard again. Not even for either of his parents' funerals."

"Well, he's here now," Annie said.

"Lucky us," Earl replied.

Then Claire stepped back into the kitchen. "Anyone want tea?"

They shook their heads in unison.

"John's on his way with Kevin and Taylor," Annie said, "so I'm sure they'll straighten this out. In the meantime, if you wouldn't mind if Francine and Jonas stay here tonight . . ."

"It will be our pleasure," Claire said. "Francine and Bella can have their old room upstairs, and, Jonas, you're welcome to the study. It's small, but comfortable." Though Earl and Claire knew — and were thrilled

48

— that Francine was expecting Jonas's baby, proper old Yankee protocol of young people not sharing a bed until they were married needed to be followed under the Lyonses' roof.

"I'd be grateful with whatever," Jonas said. "That guy is creepy."

"That guy is your uncle," Earl said. "No reflection on you. Or on your mother. As I remember, Rex wasn't only a ratty son, he wasn't the nicest brother to your mother."

Though Annie would have loved to hear details about that — if only to perhaps learn some unique character flaws that she might use in one of her novels — she knew this was neither the time nor the place. She also knew that Earl typically wasn't inclined to squeal on a neighbor by spilling too many stories that weren't his to spill. So Annie stood up and said she needed to go home. "We have a busy day tomorrow. Someone told me it's Thanksgiving."

"Pies are done and veggies are prepped," Claire said. Then she looked across the counter at Earl. "I suppose we have to invite Rex to join us?"

"And open that can of worms?"

"It's only right, Earl. He was nothing but a nuisance when he was a boy, but he's lost his parents since then, and if he's here alone on Thanksgiving, he must not have a family of his own."

"We'll talk about this later."

"I'd like to talk about it now."

Annie's, Francine's, and Jonas's eyes ping-ponged between the bickering elders.

"Seems to me you weren't too thrilled ten minutes ago when you heard he was back."

"He's still one of ours, Earl. One of Chappy's."

"And what good did that ever do this place?"

"Maybe he's changed. Maybe he's come back to make up for a few things."

Under his spikey eyebrows, Earl's blue eyes narrowed. "And if he hasn't?"

"Then maybe he can at least contribute some of his fine cooking skills to our dinner tomorrow. He must have been a great chef to own that fancy restaurant he had."

"As I recall, his mother was the only one who called it a 'fancy' restaurant."

Claire sputtered again and disappeared back into the study. The outcome of their discussion would be hard to predict.

Jonas went outside and returned with their bags, while Annie said her good-byes and reiterated to Francine how happy she was they were home. Then she left the house and headed back to her cottage, her distress

50

over how to help Francine momentarily superseded by wondering if Rex Winsted had returned to upend Kevin's life. After all, Annie was protective of her brother, too, no matter that he was a grown man.

CHAPTER 6

"Winsted's up to something," John said later when he arrived at Annie's, kissed her quickly, then ran his hand through his buzz cut. "I can tell."

"Wow," Annie said, "you sound like your father." She didn't say that she, too, was worried about Rex's presence.

"But, unlike my dad, I tend not to hold grudges."

Annie didn't know what to say because she hadn't noticed that Earl did that. She believed he was kind to everyone he'd ever met or had known.

"Winsted's older than me," John went on, "so I don't remember him well. It's true he was the neighborhood thug, but I guess he didn't bother with me because I was too young. What matters now is that Taylor didn't seem afraid of him when she saw him. Not that she was overly happy. But she told him he could sleep in the house tonight and move into the garage apartment if he plans to stay."

"Will he stay?"

"Don't know. Still don't know why he's here."

"Did you ask?"

He laughed again. "Actually, I did. You might remember I am a detective. I've been trained to ask questions."

She smirked. "Very funny."

"I asked if he'd come back to the island for business, but he said, 'No business, bro. It's home. You know?' I couldn't argue with that."

"Is he alone? I only saw Jonas's car . . ."

John put his arms around her. "You are so perceptive. No wonder I'm going to marry you. But, yes, he's alone. He said he took the bus from the boat into town, then walked to the house from the *On Time* when it was still daylight. He said he doesn't have a car because he didn't need one in the city."

Annie supposed it added up. And chances were, Rex Winsted had walked the route from the Chappy Ferry hundreds of times, so he certainly would have known the way.

"I am suspicious as to why he's here, but until he shows any clear indication that he's up to no good, we have to give the guy a chance. It's called 'innocent until proven guilty,' okay?"

"Sure," she replied. "But I think we should keep Francine and Bella away from him. Jonas can do whatever he wants."

"And my bet is that Jonas would rather be wherever those girls are."

She smiled. "I agree."

"If it makes you feel better, when I left, I brought Kevin outside and told him to let me know right away if he learns anything of consequence. I gave him some of Rex's back-story, so he's prepared. With any luck, it's ancient history."

"With any luck," Annie repeated.

Then John drew his arms more tightly around her, looked at her with the eyes she found so captivating . . . and let him steer her into the bedroom. "In the meantime," he added, "in case you've forgotten, my girls are with their mother, so I'll be here through the weekend. Shall I get my pack out of my truck?"

"Oh, Detective, there's plenty of time for that." Then she kicked the door shut.

Which was when John spotted the garment bag hanging over the full-length mirror.

"Whoa. What's this? A wedding dress?"

Annie laughed. "What makes you say that?"

"A little birdie named Judy. From the dry cleaners."

"Not fair! It's a secret."

"Well . . . Judy is married to Lou Simpson, who's a retired cop and volunteers for traffic duty during Christmas in Edgartown, and he was at the station yesterday going over the schedule . . . and it doesn't matter, does it? It's not like I know anything about the dress. Except it's supposed to be special."

"It's special, all right. But if you know what's good for you, you won't look at it yet. And please, don't say anything about it to your mother. She's excited that you'll be surprised."

"Mum's the word. No pun intended."

She swatted his arm. "And you have to promise you won't sneak a peek while I'm asleep."

He held up two fingers. "Scout's honor."

Grabbing his hand, Annie led him to the bed. "Besides," she added, "it needs a few alterations."

"So do I," he replied. "My heart is beating very fast, and I think it needs some attention."

They fell onto the bed, laughing, and Rex Winsted fled from Annie's mind as quickly as the squirrels he'd once purportedly chased.

The only reason Annie ever ate green beans was because she'd been told they were good for her. On Thanksgiving, her mother had always re-created a recipe she'd found in a popular women's magazine. It was a sad casserole, whose only touch of flavor came from a can of cream of mushroom soup and a few fried onion rings, also canned. (Years later, when Annie first tried fried onion rings in a Boston pub, she'd been startled that they weren't tiny and limp and laced with aluminum essence.) She was fairly sure that her mother had never heard of a tomato-almond pesto dressing for the legumes. But on this Vineyard Thanksgiving morning — with the turkeys in the ovens, the root veggies ready for slicing and dicing, and the pies lined up in the chef's room, where Francine was busily shaping fresh dinner rolls — Annie watched Rex prepare a mysterious dish of lightly roasted green beans, and she was enticed by the aromas.

"My mother was a *Mayflower* descendant," she told him. "But her old Yankee recipes looked nothing like this." She was trying to rise above their tenuous encounter the previous evening, hoping there might be a way they could connect, which might please her brother. She hadn't yet talked to Kevin about his unexpected houseguest, but family was family, and, like it or not, he was Kevin's brother-in-law. Knowing Kevin, he'd make it work.

Rex emitted a coarse half laugh as he steadily sautéed the beans on the Inn's ten-burner gas stove. "I don't suppose the Pilgrims arrived with sacks of garlic, paprika, and olive oil," he remarked. "More likely they boiled them to death over an open fire or ate them raw from the garden — once they had gardens."

Glancing around the Inn's kitchen, Annie wondered how it measured up to whatever a top-notch chef like Rex Winsted — and it was starting to appear as if he, indeed, was one — was accustomed to. Designed with help from things Francine had been learning in culinary classes, the room was a modern blend of white marble and stainless steel, accented by the bank of windows that provided a spectacular view of Edgartown Harbor and the town on the opposite side. The kitchen had been intended to enable efficient preparation for breakfast making and baking while establishing the Inn's positive brand with clean lines and professionalism in a comfortable setting that showcased the ambiance of the island.

"And my ancestors sure didn't have a kitchen like this one," Annie said. "Though it must pale in comparison with the one in your restaurant. Or other places you've worked." She was fishing for information about him, as he might have guessed. But it was hard to believe that such a lumberjack of a man would create such delicate food. Of course, people often told her that she didn't look like a mystery writer, as if they expected her to have shifty eyes, a trench coat, and a .22-caliber pistol in her handbag. She knew that whatever "look" she had came straight from her birth mother: tall and lean, with hazel eyes and Scottish black hair that Annie wore cropped just below her ears and refused to dye despite the silver strands that were increasing in number since she'd turned fifty.

Because Rex continued to prepare the pesto and had not replied, she asked him outright if he'd attended culinary school.

He responded with a roar. "Not unless you'd call Cedar Hollow Road a culinary school."

It took Annie a moment to remember that Cedar Hollow Road was the name of the street where the family home was, where

Taylor and Rex had been raised, and where Taylor and Kevin now lived. With Rex.

"Your mother taught you?"

"No. But when I brought home berries and mushrooms and whatever herbs I could find, she showed me what was good and what might be poisonous, and I went from there. Never poisoned anyone. Not that I know of." His voice was as gruff as it had been the night before; Annie wondered if it was not an attempt to intimidate but was simply the post-puberty tone he'd wound up with.

She supposed he might be an interesting, if not very sociable, man, but not quite as scary as she'd first presumed. He was indeed large — well over six feet and extremely broad — and if he'd ever had Taylor's auburn hair, it was no longer visible, thanks to the bald head he presumably shaved. It also seemed that his bulk was due not to fat but to muscle, as if he were a bodybuilder. But though that day Rex was acting friendly enough, Annie would not want to encounter him at night on one of Chappy's remote roads. Then she remembered she'd once thought the same thing about Taylor.

Just then, their tenant Rose Atkins padded silently into the kitchen, holding a bone china cup, as if in search of tea. Dressed in a long, plain wool skirt and what looked like a hand-crocheted cardigan sweater, she smiled at Annie, then turned her head toward the stove. But when she spotted Rex, she stopped. She blinked. Once. Twice. The teacup rattled in its saucer. She took a step back; perhaps the man's size had frightened her. She was, after all, fragile, "a mere slip of a woman," as Earl had noted when she'd first moved in.

Rex glanced at her for a second, nodded once, then resumed his task.

Rose twittered, spun around, and dashed from the room.

Annie looked at Rex. Did he know Rose — or did she know him? But he was engaged with the green beans again, as if the woman's presence had been inconsequential.

"Excuse me," Annie said. "I need to check on the table settings." Grabbing a selection of tea bags from the cabinet, she tossed them into a small basket. Rose had once said that she had a passion for tea that must have come from her British ancestors. Since she'd become a tenant, it was the most she'd revealed about her life, past or present.

Until now. When something had definitely prompted the mere slip of a woman to flee.

60

■ ■ ■ ■

Six guest rooms with private baths and a small suite perpetually reserved for Francine and Bella — or anyone who might need emergency shelter when they weren't there — graced the second floor of the Inn. As Annie climbed the sweeping staircase in the two-story foyer, she tried to determine a reason for Rose's reaction. It was clear that Rex's presence had startled her. But Rose looked a lot older than he was, so it wasn't as if they'd been in school together — if Rose had ever lived on the Vineyard, which Annie had no reason to believe she had. She didn't even know if the woman had ever visited the island until now. Still, something about Rex had scared her.

When Annie reached room 2, she knocked.

"Rose? It's Annie." No sounds of the television or radio came from within, not even the click-click of a keyboard.

Clearing her throat, Annie spoke louder. "I've brought tea." The guest rooms did not have kitchenettes, but every morning Rose typically filled a thermos of boiling water in the kitchen and brought it to her room so that she'd always be prepared for a "cuppa."

61

The door opened slowly, exposing small brown eyes that were rimmed red. "Yes?"

"Are you all right?" Annie asked. "Would you like to talk?"

The woman shook her head tenuously, as if she feared that her fine gray curls might be disturbed or that she might wrench her neck.

Annie reminded herself that in a way Rose, as a tenant, was under her care.

She held out the basket of tea bags. "Please? I could tell Rex's presence upset you. I'm so sorry. He's Kevin's brother-in-law. Perhaps you didn't know that . . ."

Pursing her thin lips, Rose took the basket from Annie. In order to do that, she'd opened the door a little wider, affording Annie a quick peek inside and revealing something surprising: a large dollhouse sitting on top of the desk.

A *dollhouse*?

Next to that was the window that had a lovely, deep window seat. Which seemed to be covered with . . . rocks.

Rocks?

Annie was baffled. She managed to quickly avert her gaze and offered Rose her best effort at a warm smile. "Maybe I misunderstood. But I hope you can join us for dinner. I meant to invite you earlier, but we got caught up in the preparations." She inhaled deeply. "You can smell the turkey roasting up here, can't you? We have quite a spread — too much food, of course — but we'd love to have you with us. You can sit between Kevin and Taylor and keep them from spatting. Or sparring. Or whatever it is that they seem to enjoy doing." She'd tried to be humorous, but Rose didn't change her bland expression.

"Thank you for the offer," she said in a hushed tone. "But I have correspondence to catch up on."

Without a doubt, it was a veiled excuse. "It will just be us."

"And a stranger," she blurted out.

"Well, Rex has helped a little with the cooking, but I'm not sure if he'll stay to eat. Do you know him, Rose?" She knew she shouldn't pry, but how could she help if she didn't know what the problem was?

With eyes turned downward, Rose seemed to quiver. "H-he . . . ," she stuttered, "he reminds me of someone I once knew. That's all."

Annie's writer's imagination supposed that the person Rose "once knew" had either disappointed or betrayed her. Or maybe died. Any of those explanations would make her reaction understandable.

"Well, if having him around bothers you," Annie said, "Kevin will watch out for you." And she knew that Kevin especially would. Because he was a sweet, gentle man. And the best brother ever.

"What time?"

Annie was surprised at the about-face. "We actually had a conference about that last night — sometimes we make a big deal out of things that don't really matter." She hoped she sounded upbeat and carefree. "Anyway, we decided on two thirty. I have no idea how we came up with that. When I'm in the same room with Kevin and Earl, I easily get confused." None of that was true; Claire had been the one who'd suggested the time long before they'd known that all the troops — except John's girls — would be there. But the image seemed to please Rose, who appeared to relax a little. "You're really most welcome to join us."

Then Rose paused and rubbed her hands over her forehead, and her expression went back to being bland. "I'm sorry, but I have a Zoom event then. But thank you." She paused, then decisively shut the door.

Annie stood there a moment, trying to discern what on earth had happened. She didn't want anyone to be anxious about living at the Inn. Maybe she shouldn't have meddled. "I'll put a tray at your door," she said, elevating her voice. "If you don't want it, leave it. But if your plans change, please come downstairs. I think you'll especially enjoy Francine and little Bella."

That time, Rose didn't reply, so Annie headed back to the stairs, deciding that if Rose had wanted her to know more, she would have told her. Besides, if Annie felt that any trouble was brewing with her tenant on account of Rex, she could always ask Claire, who pretty much knew everything that had happened, or might happen, on Chappy.

Then again, maybe Rose was just painfully shy — an outdated term Annie had learned in grad school in a class on the psychology of children.

Stop poking into other people's lives, Murphy suddenly whispered. *This is not one of your books. And, frankly, my dear, Rose Atkins is not one of your characters.*

Despite the admonition, Murphy laughed, so Annie did, too. Then she skipped back down the staircase. A turkey dinner, after all, awaited.

CHAPTER 7

Merriment lit up the great room like the luminous swath of the Milky Way when it painted the night sky over Edgartown Harbor. Kevin and John tossed witty barbs at each other throughout the meal; Claire admonished them as if they were ten and should "know better"; Earl chuckled and asked Francine to please pass the sweet potatoes. As the curious writer in residence, Annie was content to sit back and quietly celebrate the antics of these wonderful people that she'd both inherited and welcomed into her life. Taylor and Rex — the Winsted siblings — were quieter than the others, but they commented on occasion, and for the most part they answered questions directed at them. Annie wondered if brother and sister had made a pact to maintain a congenial decorum, at least in front of the others.

Bella looked adorable in a pumpkin-colored dress and matching tights, her black eyes shining, her ebony hair having grown into thick, dark curls. However, if there were awards to give out, she would have received one for being the loudest, as every so often she let out a squeal that prevented anyone from forgetting she was there. Finally, Francine took her into the kitchen to peruse the cupboard in the chef's room where the toddler's toys were conveniently stashed. Bella toted one of the yarn-haired dolls Claire had made for her back to the table. Then she climbed into her high chair and proceeded to feed it a full meal that ended up on the authentic hardwood planks that Kevin had insisted on and had spent many days and nights on his knees hammering into place.

Annie was glad that before they were seated, she'd fixed Rose a plate and left it at her door. Even if Rex's presence hadn't put her off, the boisterous partying would most likely have overwhelmed the woman.

All in all, the company was amenable, the food was five-star (thanks not only to Rex's green beans but also to several innovative tweaks he'd applied to other dishes), and no one had room left for pie.

After dinner, Claire and Taylor cleared the table; Claire informed the men that they were in charge of the cleanup (including the dishes) and that the ladies would go for a walk.

Annie didn't object. She figured it was probably wiser for her to leave the Inn than go upstairs, snoop to see if Rose had brought the tray into her room, and subsequently stick her nose once again where it did not belong. Or, as old islanders called it, to "stick her oar in someone else's water." Then Annie wondered if being patient and simply letting things happen would forever challenge her.

That time, Murphy did not throw in her two cents.

Outside, it was a perfect late-autumn day, with the fading sun beginning to yield to a dusky sky. As they turned onto a walking path off North Neck Road, Annie reveled in the beauty of the now-naked scrub oaks and the jumbled vines of bittersweet, their bounty of red-orange berries a well-known harbinger of winter. The stillness of off-season was evident, punctuated only by the crisp brown leaves crunching beneath their footsteps and the churning wheels of the stroller.

Claire and Taylor lagged behind, talking about who knew what.

Bella fell asleep. Francine reached down and tucked a blanket — one of Claire's hand-knit creations — around the girl's little legs.

"I need your opinion about something," Francine asked Annie as she straightened up but kept her eyes on the stroller.

"Anything. You know that."

"You might not like this one. I want to know what you think about the future."

Stifling a laugh, Annie asked, "Are you asking if I have a crystal ball?"

Shaking her head, Francine said, "Okay. My future."

Annie paused. "I think you have a fabulous future. You're a natural mother. You're about to have two children — because, let's face it, Bella is more like your daughter than your sister, and you're going to have a new baby. Jonas is a wonderful guy, and you seem to have a great relationship with him. And you've been working very hard to get the education and skills that will give you a solid career." She stopped and took a breath. "Is that what you wanted to know?"

"Thanks, but not really. The truth is, my aunt and uncle think my life will be limited here on the island. That the kids' lives will be too sheltered here, and not in a good way." She hesitated, then added, "Please don't tell anyone, okay?"

A boulder the size of the meteor that some people thought had crashed on Chappy eons ago and had carved out Cape Pogue felt as if it had landed in Annie's stomach.

"Oh," she said. "Well. Of course, I won't tell anyone."

They walked a few more feet.

"Is that the real reason you wanted to come back?" Annie asked. "To say good-bye to us?"

Francine stopped. "No. I told you — I'm nervous about having the baby. I want to be here where I feel like I belong. And Jonas . . . I don't want to take him away from his heritage, especially since his mother hopes he'll live here year-round while she and Kevin spend winters in Hawaii."

That last part, her brother and his wife had been "kicking around," or so he'd hinted to Annie. She didn't yet know if it was a sure thing. Something Annie did know, however, was that, unbeknownst to Francine and Jonas, after they'd left the Vineyard for Minnesota at the end of August, Kevin had begun to reconfigure the outbuilding on the grounds of the Inn that had been a workshop for Kevin and a soap-making space for her. He was turning it into a house for Francine and Jonas. And Bella.

And for the baby that was due at the beginning of May. The house would be a cozy nest for the young family — and, like Annie's wedding dress, a surprise. Annie and Earl had agreed it would be a wonderful use of the property; it would be their gift to the young couple to celebrate the baby's birth. When it was finished, Kevin planned to build a separate outbuilding for his workshop and Annie's little boutique business, over by the meadow, so that Francine and Jonas would have plenty of privacy.

"How does Jonas feel about this? Assuming you plan to raise the baby together?"

Francine started walking again. "I haven't told him yet."

"Do you think the idea has merit? Is that why you're conflicted?"

"I don't know." She scuffed at a small pile of leaves. "Without my aunt and uncle, I wouldn't have been able to go to college. I know that technically I don't 'owe' them for that, but they never had kids. Bella and I are my aunt's only relatives. We're all they have. And the baby, of course."

Annie paused, then said, "If you don't mind my asking, how committed are you to Jonas?" Even when Francine had told Annie she was pregnant, she hadn't addressed the couple's future. "Do you think you might get married one day?"

Shaking her head again, Francine said, "I don't know that, either. Everything's happened so fast."

Annie knew that knowing someone all of six months wasn't much time to decide if the person would be a "forever" mate. Still, she didn't ask whether or not Francine thought they would still be together if a baby wasn't imminent. The question was too abstract for a realistic answer.

"I told my aunt and uncle I was afraid that what happened to my mother might happen to me. And that I was worried if I'm too scared, I'll harm the baby. I said it was why I wanted to come back here now. Because it's quieter. Less stressful. I didn't add that I'm more comfortable here. Or that you're depending on me. To help with the Inn come summer."

Annie stopped and took one of Francine's hands. "Listen to me, honey. You do not 'owe' me — or any of us — anything, either. So please put that out of your head, okay? I'm thrilled that you've come home to have the baby. So, get ready, because if you're planning to be here for the next five months, I intend to totally spoil you and Ms. Bella. After that, we'll see, okay? But at some point you might want to discuss this with Jonas.

He's kind of important to the what-ifs, right?"

She nodded, and they resumed walking.

Kevin, of course, would be crushed if Francine and Bella moved away permanently, and not solely because of the house he was building for them. Earl and Claire would be heart-broken. And Annie would be, too. Especially because as often as she'd told Francine she'd become a wonderful mother to Bella, Annie had tried to be a substitute mom to Francine, and a designated, alternate caregiver for sweet little Bella. Annie pulled her wool scarf more tightly around her neck, not for warmth, but with hope that the fiddling would help her keep her opinion — and her real feelings — in check.

The best part about having too many irons in the fire was that when Annie's hopes and dreams clashed with reality, at least she had something to do. A distraction or two (or three or ten) tended to keep her productive and preoccupied and prevented her brain from imploding or her mouth from blah-blahing, especially about people and situations she had no control over. Which, of course, meant *all* people. And most situations, unless they were of her making.

She and John spent a wonderful night together. He teased her several times, pretending to unzip the garment bag that held the ugly wedding dress, then feigning despair when she wouldn't relent. Mostly they slept, because they both were tired, and John had to work on Friday, and Annie had to finish preparing the many bars of soap she'd need for the Holiday Fair.

Which was what she was doing in the morning, standing at her workbench in the corner of the workshop, surrounded by several dozen rectangular molds, the size of containers for small loaves of bread, where her batches of soap had firmed up weeks ago. She'd since transferred the loaves to trays and, using a stainless steel cutter, sliced them into generous-sized bars, then cured the bars on racks in the open air for thirty days. Now their time was up; they were ready for market. Adding to the clutter were rolls and sheets of packing and wrapping materials: pastel mesh, colorful wire ribbon, and stacks of empty plastic totes to fill with finished products.

Annie examined large chunks of what she called snowdrops and winterberries, the latter being bright red fruits that she'd first thought were bittersweet. Until Earl had corrected her.

"Bittersweet grows on vines; winterberries on stems," he'd said. Then he'd shown her how to find winterberries around the ponds on Chappy. "They're always in wet soil. Not like bittersweet, which couldn't care less where it grows."

Earl must have taught Francine a lot as well when she and Bella lived with him and Claire for nearly a year. And though Annie often lightly referred to them as an "island family," for Francine, the connection must be stronger: she'd lost her father to suicide when she'd been quite young, and her mother died when Francine was nineteen and Bella was just an infant. Earl, Claire, and the rest of them had become much more than an island family to Francine. It almost seemed unfortunate that her aunt and uncle had suddenly surfaced, paid her college tuition, and now offered to change her future.

With a long sigh, Annie raised her eyes and looked around the room that was supposed to be Francine's kitchen, once Kevin's work was done. He'd assured Annie that he wouldn't gut the first floor until she was done prepping for the Fair — which also meant that now Francine wouldn't hear any hammering or power-sawing and start asking questions for the next two weeks.

In the meantime, Annie worried that she might leak Francine's secret news about the potential move back to Minneapolis after the baby came; she worried that Francine would be unhappy there; she worried that Jonas would, too. And though Minneapolis was a vibrant city, Jonas's paintings of the Vineyard, exquisite as they were, might not sell as well in the Midwest as they did in island galleries.

Annie also worried how she would cope if she lost the little family.

And she worried that she was worrying too much.

So she turned on the radio, and went back to work.

Once she finished inspecting two dozen bars of snowdrops and winterberries, she began to wrap each piece in plain white beeswax paper — biodegradable, non-toxic, plastic-free, recyclable — after which she'd add an outer wrap of red netting, then tie the package with red wire ribbon and add the tag that read *Soaps by Sutton.* She was building her brand, just as Trish and her team kept building the brand for Annie's books.

As with writing mysteries, the business of soapmaking was time-consuming and labor intensive. If Francine stopped by this morning, maybe Annie could enlist her help. And when Lucy and Abigail returned from Plymouth, maybe she would ask Abigail to help out with the dress.

Creasing and folding another sheet of beeswax paper, Annie thought about her first wedding dress, an elaborate gown. It was the late 1980s, so the shoulders weren't only padded but also pouffed, as if small helium balloons would lift her toward the altar. The gown itself was of pure white satin and lace with a sweetheart neckline, a very full, floor-length skirt, and tapered long sleeves with twice as many tiny buttons from shoulder to wrist than the ones that John's grandmother's dress had running up the back.

"Are you going to keep this?" Annie's mother asked a year or so after Brian had been killed in a car accident. Mother and daughter had been cleaning the attic because Annie's father had died by then, too, and Ellen Sutton wanted to sell the house and buy a condominium.

"Of course I'm going to keep it," Annie responded. Parting with her wedding gown had been as unimaginable as losing Brian once had been. She hadn't yet learned that the only memories that mattered were the ones she kept inside her heart.

Later, when she made the mistake of marrying Mark, she brought the gown to the thrift shop, hoping a young bride would cherish it as much as she had. A few years after that, however, she heard that a costume shop bought it for thirty dollars, and that it probably wound up as a Halloween costume or in the wardrobe room at a community theater in case a script featured a 1980s wedding. Annie had been upset, but by then she also was distracted by making plans for her second wedding, her new beginning. She and Mark wound up tying the knot in Las Vegas, of all places; she'd worn a shimmering black sheath that had a single slit halfway up her thigh and a deep V-neck, and made her feel like someone she didn't know.

But that was the past.

And Annie now had an amazing present and a promising future with a wonderful new man. It didn't matter that she'd long ago vowed to herself that she'd never marry again. It didn't matter that marrying John meant she would live on the Vineyard until death did them part. That's what she wanted. Wasn't it?

Snipping a few lengths of ribbon, Annie decided she would absolutely contact Abigail as soon as the girls returned from

Plymouth. Maybe once the semester ended, Abigail wouldn't mind stepping up for her family — unless, of course, she moved to New Hampshire to be with the new *boy-friend.*

"Stop it this instant!" she admonished herself for being sarcastic, just as the door opened and her brother appeared.

"Oh, my God," Kevin said, "you're talking to yourself."

She wiped her brow. "Yes. I enjoy that on occasion."

"Does the groom know?"

"Not that I'm aware of."

He looked around at the mess. "Looks like you have work to do."

"Two weeks until the Fair. Two weeks after that until my wedding. Yup. You might say I have work to do. I think I'll ask Francine to help. It might take her mind off worrying about the baby."

"Asking her to help sounds like a good idea," Kevin said. "But just because I won't be hammering, when she comes in here, she'll probably wonder why there's a bath-tub in the middle of the floor and crates of kitchen cabinets all over the place."

"Oh. Right." Annie scanned the evidence that a major construction project was nearly underway.

It was the perfect time to tell him about Francine's possible change of plans. And that it wasn't even yet decided if she and Jonas would wind up as a couple, married or otherwise. But though Annie wished she could prepare her brother, she couldn't betray Francine's confidence.

Thankfully, Kevin interrupted before temptation overruled Annie's better judgment.

"I'm on my way to Vineyard Haven to pick out bath fixtures," he said.

As far as she could tell, he wouldn't need those for a while. "A little early for that, isn't it?"

"I wanted you to come with me. I was going to treat you to lunch at the Barn. But I can tell you're busy."

Annie always seemed to be the one in need; Kevin rarely asked for anything. So, without hesitation, she wiped her hands on her apron, unknotted the tie, and set it on the workbench.

"Your timing is perfect," she said. "I need a break."

"Thanks. Because otherwise you might be forced to watch me explode."

That's when Annie noticed he looked bleary-eyed, as if he hadn't slept, and that his usually cheerful face was anything but.

As he turned and went out the door, she snapped off the radio, grabbed her phone, purse, and jacket, and was right behind him.

CHAPTER 8

This place is perfect. It has a nice big room with a fireplace and a little kitchen, plus two small bedrooms and a bathroom. It's furnished with things that are old but look okay: a plaid couch and matching chair, a worn leather recliner, a small table. There are sheets and towels in a closet, so whoever owns it must rent it in summer.

Best of all, there are woods all around. The land is thick with pine trees and some other things that haven't lost their leaves, so the cabin's well hidden. And the other driveways I saw on my way in look like they lead to summer cottages, so I don't think anybody else will come down the road this time of year.

Not that it matters. I won't be here very long. And then I won't ever have to come back.

CHAPTER 9

"Talk to me," Annie said.

They sat in a large booth in the busy restaurant; since they'd climbed into his pickup, Kevin still hadn't told her what was bugging him. They'd gone to Vineyard Haven first; he loaded the truck bed with lots of boxes and more crates. Then they backtracked to the big brown barn in Oak Bluffs that was also a bowling alley and bistro, hence its official name, the Barn Bowl & Bistro.

Through the wall of glass behind her brother now, Annie had a bird's-eye view of the bowling lanes. She knew that before Kevin had hooked up with Taylor, he'd spent a lot of evenings there, often finding someone to play a string or two with him. On Monday nights, especially in winter, he seemed to like going for board game night. Kevin loved to be around people; he liked both working hard and having fun. Unlike

Annie, who leaned toward overthinking almost everything, Kevin had inherited their mother's optimistic outlook and usually took life as it came. Which was another reason why the fact that he still hadn't shared his problem was puzzling.

He sipped his beer. He set down the bottle, picked up his spoon, and made swirl designs in the bowl of chili parked in front of him. The longer he stalled, the more unnerving Annie found it. Then the table started to shimmy; she knew he must be jiggling his leg. She pressed her palms on either side of her place setting to try to stop her French onion soup from slopping out of its crock. She prayed for patience.

"We were gone four days," he said suddenly, finally. "Counting two for travel. Sunday. Monday. Tuesday. Wednesday. Now we're back on the Vineyard, and I'm living with a stranger."

The fact that Taylor could be defined as strange wasn't news to Annie. Then she realized maybe he meant Taylor's brother.

"Rex?"

Kevin harrumphed as if he were an old man. "His name is Theodore Whitcomb Winsted. The Whitcomb was his mother's maiden name."

"And the Rex came from . . . ?"

"He was a giant kid. You might have noticed he's a big guy now."

"Well. Yes." She grew annoyed at how Kevin continued to stir his chili, and at the way he was making the table wobble. He did not, however, seem aware he was doing either.

"Taylor said he was so much bigger than the other kids in elementary school, some of them called him 'T Rex,' like the dinosaur, you know?"

Yes, Annie knew.

"The Rex part stuck."

"Oh." She doubted that the etymology of Rex's name was why Kevin was upset. "So . . . is he living in the garage apartment now? Is he planning to stay?"

"He's in the spare bedroom and refuses to go to the garage. I have no idea how long he intends to stay. In fact, my wife hasn't told me much of anything, except the bit about his name."

"Oh," Annie said for what felt like the hundredth time.

"They talk, but if I walk into the room, they both shut up. Do you know how that makes me feel?"

She said she imagined it would be disturbing.

"Disturbing?" He harrumphed again.

"Yeah, it's like I've walked in on my wife cavorting with another man."

Cavorting? She suppressed a smile at her brother's word choice. Under other circumstances, she might have asked if he'd become part Victorian.

"Have you talked to Taylor about it?" Was something in the air preventing people from talking to their partners? Annie understood Francine's reluctance to tell Jonas about her aunt and uncle's request; after all, they were young and inexperienced. But Kevin? Good grief. What was stopping him from talking to his wife?

"I tried," he said. "She said she and Rex have a few things to work out, and she doesn't need my help. I asked, 'My help?' Like I'm not her husband and don't want to know if she has a problem with her dinosaur brother?"

Annie tasted the soup not because she was hungry but because tasting, chewing, swallowing gave her something to do.

Then Kevin dived into his chili as if he'd just noticed it. Or maybe he felt as if he'd said all there was to say.

And Annie was reminded that even the happiest couples couldn't always avoid troubled waters. She wondered if, at some point, that would happen to John and her.

Dismissing the thought, she asked if there was some way she could help. Kevin just shook his head.

"Okay," she added. "But that's a standing offer, in case you change your mind."

He nodded, and they went back to eating their lunches, and did not talk again on the whole way back to Chappy.

Later that night, John stoked the woodstove. They turned off the lights and curled up on the love seat, their wineglasses forgotten on the end tables. Then, as if they were a longtime married couple, they shared the news about their days.

John had taken care of three minor traffic accidents — no injuries. He'd also followed up on a resident's complaint that her neighbor's chickens persistently kept wandering into her yard and making a mess. And he'd checked out a summer home where the front door was ajar though the owners lived in Sacramento and no one seemed to be around. His investigation didn't turn up mischief — apparently the wind had blown the door open.

"Another exciting day in law enforcement," he added.

Annie knew that though John was a detective sergeant, he did whatever was needed, especially in winter, when little was going on.

She told him she was making progress on getting her soaps ready for the Fair and that she'd gone to Vineyard Haven with Kevin and had lunch at the Barn. Once again, she refrained from mentioning Francine's dilemma. She also failed to mention Kevin's conundrum over his newly acquired brother-in-law. Though John might have been able to add some insight to both situations, Annie didn't like gossipy natter. Besides, it was too nice to be together to bring other people's problems into the mix.

But once John's breath slowed into sleep, her mind slid back to Francine.

To Kevin-Taylor-Rex.

Even to Rose, whose reaction to Rex had been bizarre. At least the tray Annie had left showed up in the kitchen the morning after. No leftovers were on the dishes, so maybe Rose had enjoyed a Thanksgiving dinner and a slice of pumpkin pie.

Annie mused that she barely knew the older woman. When she'd signed the lease for the October-through-May "winter" rental, Rose had said she was from Maine, which would explain the license plates on her little Fiat and the fact that her rental check was drawn on a bank in Kennebunk.

She'd also said she was retired, but had not elaborated.

Annie did notice that she went for long walks every day, often returning with her knitted handbag bulging. Annie had supposed there might be a book or two inside, something from the shelves at the Chappy Community Center. Or maybe a scone, a muffin, or one of Lucy's cookies that Rose had snitched at breakfast. But now Annie wondered if the bag had been filled with rocks like those on the window seat. The act might have seemed more than a little odd, but on the island, few people bothered with "odd." Instead, most things and most people were simply accepted.

Quirks aside, however, it was apparent that Rex Winsted had triggered a knee-jerk reaction in Rose. Annie knew there could be an emptiness, a dark side to being alone. Maybe she could help Rose overcome whatever was bothering her.

Drama, drama, drama, Murphy suddenly chimed in from somewhere up in the ceiling. *You've been writing fiction far too long.*

Annie's eyes darted to John to make sure Murphy hadn't woken him up . . . as if anyone but Annie could actually hear her.

As usual, Murphy remained undaunted. *Do you think if you can learn the secrets of real people, you'll create a more interesting story?*

"Sssh," Annie whispered. "Go away. Go to sleep."

Murphy's happy Irish laughter filled the room, and Annie dropped her chin, wondering if, indeed, she was confusing compassion for self-serving snooping.

Annie should have spent Saturday returning to her priority of wrapping and packing. Instead, she stayed in bed with John, who was off duty until Monday. He offered to help her cut soaps or pack them or whatever she needed, but Annie said if she couldn't take a day off to be with him, what was the point in living?

He laughed and pulled the comforter over their heads, which Annie told him made her miss Restless, his furry dog, who no doubt was protecting Lucy up in Plymouth.

Though their busy schedules made leisure days practically nonexistent, they were the ones that Annie cherished most. Somehow rigid, coplike John brought out a playful side in her that she never wanted to let go of.

Annie had amassed enough Thanksgiving leftovers to hold them through the weekend, and, best of all, no one bothered them. No calls, no texts, no knocks on the cottage door. And though her mind often wandered to how the troops could possibly be handling things at the Inn without her, she was having too much fun to get up, get dressed, and go looking for trouble. Until Sunday afternoon when she no longer could stand being so content.

"I have to find Francine," she announced when they sat at the tiny kitchen table, finishing the turkey potpie that Claire had made on Friday before they'd gone into seclusion.

John laughed. "Tomorrow, right?"

She shook her head and tried to look coquettish, though she doubted she was succeeding. "I'm worried about her, John. She's afraid she's going to die of an infection after the baby's born — the way her mother did. I need to try and nip that in the bud because she still has five months to go."

"You've become such a mother hen. And I mean that in a good sense."

"I grew up in the city, John, where people kept to themselves. I only had my parents and one grandmother. I had an Aunt Sally, but she and her husband moved away — which is another story I'll share with you someday. We had neighbors and friends, but not like here. I like having people to watch out for."

He shook his head that time, as if he'd spent his whole life doing that, and that it wasn't quite the fantasy that she imagined. "Were you a lonely kid?"

"No. I didn't know the difference." She wasn't going to tell him that loneliness had consumed her after Brian died. That was her other life — one of them, anyway. John knew the basics, but she saw no need to weigh him down with gloomy details. She smiled and brought the dishes to the sink; she'd had enough turkey for another year. "Before I track her down, I'd better take a shower."

"And I suppose I could go back to Edgartown and rest up for my Monday-morning shift."

Then, suddenly, he was behind her, urging the tie of her thick terry robe to come undone and slide to the floor.

And Annie didn't get to see Francine, and John didn't leave for Edgartown, until dinnertime.

"We're having Chinese tonight," Francine announced when Annie found her later in the kitchen of the Inn. "Jonas went to pick it up. Do you and John want to join us? I think we ordered too much."

Annie patted her stomach. "Not all of us are eating for two," she said with a gentle smile. "And, to be honest, I'm fooded out."

"Fooded? Is that a word?"

"It is now. I make up new ones whenever possible." She glanced into the chef's room. "Where's Bella?"

"Upstairs napping. I put the baby monitor on. I think she's confused about all the changes in the past few days. We went from Minnesota to Earl's and now we're at the Inn. The poor kid probably wakes up without a clue where she is."

"And you?" She pulled out one of the high stools at the island in the center of the room. "Are you doing okay?"

Francine told her she'd decided to stay at the Inn because she wanted to sleep in the same bed as Jonas, which they couldn't do at Earl and Claire's.

"I missed him," she said. "So I thought we'd stay here while you and John were in the cottage. We'll go back to Earl's tomorrow." She folded her hands across her tiny baby bump and raised her big, dark eyes. "And before you ask, no, I haven't told Jonas about my aunt's request. Not yet."

"It's up to you, honey. Whatever makes you comfortable."

Then John arrived, even though he'd just left, and his reappearance put an end to the conversation. "Guess who I ran into at the ferry," he said. Behind him came Jonas, carrying two large bags that scented the room with something unmistakably sweet and sour. Or fried rice. Maybe dumplings.

"Join us?" Jonas asked.

John said he hadn't had Chinese in ages, so before Annie knew it, the four of them sat down to yet another meal. Being with Francine and Jonas — hearing them laugh, watching loving glances crisscross from one to the other — dispelled Annie's worries about them. Or at least it did until she felt familiar arms suddenly reach out and softly hug her. They did not feel like John's arms but Murphy's.

CHAPTER 10

In the morning, Annie and John bumped against each other while they hurried to get ready for the day; Annie had told Francine to sleep in as long as Bella did, that she'd tend to breakfast for their tenants, which was far easier off-season than in summer, with oatmeal, yogurt, and muffins replacing Francine's elaborate brunchlike casseroles and quiches, served with heaps of ham or bacon and thick slices of homemade toast slathered with butter.

John had to get to the station for his eight-to-four shift, which was nicer than the double shifts that greeted him in season. Annie was glad he'd stayed; it was still hard to believe that soon they'd be sleeping side by side every night, night after night. Except, of course, when he worked midnight to eight. Or eight to eight. Or when Annie was off island on book business — which reminded her she had another novel to finish. Her manuscript had been derailed by the lengthy book tour earlier that fall, and now by the holiday and the wedding planning. She hoped her editor would give her an extension.

Trish!

Annie suddenly remembered she hadn't called Trish back, hadn't even listened to her message. She'd sent a wedding e-vite, but Trish hadn't yet replied; maybe that's what the voice mail was about. Annie didn't expect her editor to journey from Manhattan, especially at Christmas. But they hadn't seen each other in a long time, and she missed their lively banter, which often sparked the concept for her next mystery.

"You're an idiot," she admonished herself and vowed to call Trish as soon as her current mission was complete.

With John off to work and breakfast set out for the tenants, Annie was driving to the boat — the big boat, not the little Chappy Ferry. Before they'd fallen asleep the night before, she'd offered to pick up his daughters on their trip back from Plymouth.

"Sure," he'd said. "If you can make it to the eight fifteen."

Which would be easy, thanks to the abbreviated breakfast. And worth it if Annie could begin her concerted effort to befriend Abigail.

The eight fifteen was pretty much guaranteed to arrive in Vineyard Haven at nine o'clock. The trip across the sound took exactly forty-five minutes: encounters with rogue waves, runaway jet skis, or great white sharks were merely the stuff of movies. If the schedule went awry, it most likely was because the boat hadn't left the Cape due to high winds, nor'easters, or mechanical issues.

Annie had no idea why she was thinking about that when she should have been strategizing a "let's be friends" approach for Abigail, whose ego sometimes seemed as big as the rocklike tower at Lucy Vincent Beach before it had collapsed. Abigail was a polar opposite of Lucy, so Annie knew she faced a major challenge.

With the long weekend's holiday traffic mostly gone, she arrived at the boat in record time. But because she'd spent too much time daydreaming, she was mentally unprepared.

She sat in the drop-off, pickup lot and stared at the empty berth, waiting for inspiration. She could start the conversation by asking the girls if they'd had a good time. She could say they'd been missed at dinner at the Inn. Lucy would likely do most of the talking, so Annie would need to find a way around that. Maybe she should jump right in and mention that their great-grandmother's wedding dress was still hanging on her bedroom door. Then Lucy would laugh and tell Abigail it was ugly, and Abigail would remain mute until Annie could smile and say, "Abigail? Do you think you could help? I don't want to ruin the surprise for your dad. Or disappoint your grandmother."

Yes, she thought now, Abigail might be more receptive to doing something for Claire than for her father, whom she hated living with because, though she was eighteen, he still had rules.

As Annie was congratulating herself on her brilliant idea, the big white boat inched between the pilings. In the several minutes it would take for the docking and winching and whatever else was needed to secure the vessel, Annie speculated how she'd respond if Abigail snapped questions at her — or if the girl didn't speak to her at all.

At last, passengers and vehicles began to disembark. Soon Annie spotted Lucy's prancing gait and her hair, which was not plaited that morning, but flowing in grown-up waves over her shoulders. Maneuvering her suitcase with the ease most islanders had with the ferry routine, Lucy quickly spotted the Jeep and offered a big wave. Annie got out and returned the greeting, her gaze flitting across the crowd.

But, unlike Lucy, Abigail was not in sight.

"She stayed on the Cape," Lucy said once their seat belts were buckled up, and Annie asked where her sister was. "She has classes today."

Annie had forgotten that Abigail would be in school. She must have picked up the car John had bought and left at the Steamship Authority lot on the "other side," driven it to Plymouth, then back to Woods Hole and dropped Lucy off. Annie had to admit that having a vehicle on the Cape made sense: Abigail could easily commute to the college in West Barnstable from the boat, and go back and forth to the island as a walk-on passenger. It saved the need for reservations and money on ferry rates.

"Well," Annie said, hiding her disappointment, "how did everything go? Starting with your Thanksgiving meal?"

"I can start before that. Like on the boat, when I realized I didn't have my phone. That was fun. And then when we got to Plymouth, Abigail's boyfriend was already there and my mother had been feeding him beer and he was drunk. That was fun, too." Her ridicule was obvious from her signature eye roll. "But things got better the next day, because he was hungover, and Abigail walked around pouting, so at least nobody was yelling. My mom has always liked yelling."

Annie hadn't known that and wished she didn't know it now. "And dinner?"

Lucy shrugged. "It was okay. Mom's latest guy is okay. I don't know why Abigail hates him."

"And did your sister pout the whole time?"

"Once Cal — her boyfriend, whose real name must be Calvin, 'cuz he's cute, but sometimes acts ludicrous, like that old cartoon — anyway, once Cal recuperated, Abigail was, like, glued to him and paid no attention to the rest of us, so that was good. And the food was okay. Not like Grandma's, though. The rest of the weekend, I was wicked bored." Her voice dropped. "I'm glad I don't have to go back for Christmas."

Pausing a few seconds, Annie said, "Me, too. I'm going to need my maid of honor."

The girl brightened again. "I can't wait. What's even better is that my stupid sister will hardly be on the island between now and then."

Annie navigated through the five corners while trying to decide what to say next. Should she ask Lucy why her sister was going to be absent? Or should she just ask John? But if he already knew, wouldn't he have told her?

Not necessarily, either Murphy or Annie's smarter self commented in her ear.

Wishing she had the ability to slow down her brain, she glanced over at Lucy. "What do you mean she'll 'hardly be on the island'?"

"Dad didn't tell you? Abigail met a girl who lives with her parents, not far from the college. She's going to sleep in their garage apartment when she's there during the week."

"Your dad's okay with that?"

"Well, duh, yeah. He's paying them."

Annie hadn't expected that. The fact that Abigail wouldn't be on the island very often for the next few weeks was one thing, but renting the apartment seemed more . . . important. But even though Annie had just spent more than four days with him, he hadn't mentioned it. Sure, they'd agreed that after they were married, he'd remain in charge of his girls and their financial needs, but Annie would have thought . . .

Stop, Murphy chided. *He's a man. When it comes to communicating, you know they usually suck.*

Annie would have responded if Lucy wasn't in the car.

"Well, living there should give Abigail more time for her schoolwork." She tried to sound unfazed, but didn't dare look at her passenger again for fear of revealing her real feelings. Wanting, needing to change the subject, Annie asked, "Did you know Taylor has a brother?"

"What?"

"Taylor. You know. Kevin's wife. Jonas's mother?"

Lucy laughed. "Nope. I didn't know she has a brother. Is he as weird as she is?" Then she deftly wound her hair into a knot and pinned it atop her head, as if she'd been to a hairdressing academy. Perhaps she'd read a how-to article online when she'd been bored at her mother's.

"You do know that calling someone 'weird' isn't a nice way to describe someone, don't you? I mean, you're not five years old anymore, are you?" Annie said it in a joking manner so Lucy would get the message without being offended.

"I don't say it about anyone but them. And maybe about Abigail. But only to you."

102

Annie patted Lucy's arm. "Well, okay, then, between you and me, you're right. Taylor's brother is a little . . . let's call it 'unusual.' "

Lucy laughed. "How?"

"He's older than she is. He used to own a fancy restaurant in Boston. And he's a really good cook."

"What's 'unusual' about all that?"

"I only know no one was enthusiastic when he showed up unannounced. He's probably fine."

"Where's he living?"

"With them. Taylor and Kevin."

"What about Francine and Jonas?"

"They went to Earl's."

"*Geeez.* The Vineyard shuffle."

"I guess." Then Annie told her that Francine and Jonas were going to stay on the island so that Francine could have the baby there, which they agreed would be awesome. It was easier to talk about happy things than to think about how, if Abigail wasn't available, Annie might end up being the ugliest bride the Vineyard had ever seen.

That will never happen, Murphy said. *Not even on your worst day.*

Which was easy for her to say.

But what if someone took ugly pictures and posted them all over social media? Or what if Trish showed up with a PR person?

Trish! she thought again. She really must get back to her. Which was why, after depositing Lucy at John's town house, Annie finally listened to her voice mail.

"Call me back ASAP," her editor had said. "In other words, *now.*"

The "now" had been almost a week ago.

So as Annie headed to the *On Time* pier, she turned in to the parking lot at Memorial Wharf, stopped, turned off the Jeep, and returned the call.

But, as Trish's had, Annie's connection went to voice mail.

CHAPTER 11

Sometimes, when Annie had too much of her own muddle to think about, she resolved nothing. So the following day, she decided to take action on behalf of someone else: her brother. She began by hunting down Francine after breakfast, which wasn't hard, as she was in the kitchen.

Bella was on her play mat, busy with her yarn-haired dolls and a new teddy bear that had made the trip from Minnesota. Perhaps Francine's aunt had bought it.

Annie squatted down and touched the bear. "What's this? You have a teddy bear! He is very handsome, isn't he?" The bear was mocha colored and sported a bright turquoise bow.

"It's Mr. Bear," Bella replied with her sweet smile. She handed him to Annie. "Say 'hello, Ammie,' " she instructed him.

Annie hoped it would be years before Bella learned that Ammie wasn't the right way to pronounce her name. The little girl had come up with that pronunciation on her own, and each time she said it, Annie wanted to hug her.

Fluffing the bear's ears, she said, "Hello to you, Mr. Bear. It's very nice to meet you." She paused, then handed him back. "He says he'd rather play with you right now, okay?"

Bella nodded; Annie kissed her forehead and stood up.

"I need a favor," she said as she carried a few plates from the counter to where Francine was loading the dishwasher.

"Oh, no!" Francine said with a laugh. "Not another favor!" She was kidding, of course, because Annie rarely needed her to do anything. The young woman always was a step ahead.

"It's about Bella. May I take her up-island to Winnie's today?"

"Don't you have soap to pack? A book to write? A wedding to plan?"

"Yes, yes. And yes. But I need a break. Please?"

"Winnie plays with clay," Bella announced.

"Do you want to play at Winnie's today?" Francine asked and Bella nodded several times. "Okay, then. Be off with both of you!

Leave the pregnant lady all alone, I don't mind."

"We're going to leave you with some peace and quiet."

Francine grinned. "Since you put it that way . . . Jonas is going to paint at Katama Bay today, so maybe I'll hang out here and look for baby stuff online."

"Great," Annie replied, and gave Francine a hug. "While you're at it, you might want to register somewhere for gifts." She went into the mudroom and fished out Bella's quilted jacket and her hat and mittens; it reminded her of when Bella had been an infant and Annie had lugged her up-island to Winnie's along with a heap of diapers, formula, and blankets. Thankfully, that added baggage was no longer needed.

"While you're gone," Francine said, "maybe I'll ask Rex if he has any suggestions for your wedding food. I don't know what you're planning, but because there's a real chef at our disposal, maybe we should pick his brain."

Annie and Claire had contemplated a menu, but they'd decided to wait until after Thanksgiving to nail one down. The reception wouldn't be extravagant — no more than sixty or seventy guests. Annie had invited Murphy's husband, Stan, and their twin boys, but they'd be spending the holidays in Pasadena, where Danny, the older twin, was at Caltech, finishing his PhD in astrophysics. Annie's agent, Louisa, and Trish were the only others from Annie's off-island world whom she'd invited. Louisa had already replied that she'd attend, so if Annie's editor couldn't make it, at least her agent would.

But as for Taylor's brother contributing menu ideas, Annie didn't know what to tell Francine. If he was still on the Vineyard at Christmas, she supposed they should invite him, at least.

"Let's wait, okay?" she said. "I'm not sure how Kevin will feel about that. As it is, I think he'd be happier if Rex went back to Boston. Today."

Francine's large, soulful eyes narrowed. "Really? Why?"

Annie gave a half laugh. "Let's just say my brother isn't too thrilled about the man. He still doesn't know why Rex is here, or if Taylor wants him hanging around. I'm trying to stay out of it." Which Annie thought sounded rather noble.

Closing the dishwasher, Francine said, "Maybe you should ask Winnie about him. She knows pretty much everything about the island people, doesn't she?" Then she scooped Cheerios into a small baggie, put string cheese in another, and took a juice box and a container of water from the refrigerator. She gathered a few crayons and a workbook with stickers, a yarn-haired doll and Mr. Bear, and zipped everything into Bella's pink backpack.

"Good idea," Annie replied, as if she hadn't already thought about that, as if that hadn't been one of the main reasons she wanted to drive up-island. "If Winnie didn't know Rex when he lived here, she might have heard something about him. If there was anything to hear." She'd also decided to ask Winnie if she knew Rose. And if she knew of any connection Rose might have to someone who reminded her of Rex.

What would be the harm in that?

Winnie was busy doing what Annie should have been doing — preparing her wares for the Holiday Fair. She mostly showcased her pottery for Christmas; she'd once told Annie that spending time at the kiln helped keep her warm when the days began to cool, and it gave her a chance to shore up her inventory. She also offered her authentic wampum jewelry — bracelets, earrings, and stunning necklaces — crafted from the white-and-purple interiors of true quahog shells that she, then her children, and now her grandchildren collected on the beaches of Aquinnah. Winnie's wonderful art represented one of the many ways she adhered to Wampanoag traditions.

"Tell me if you know anything about Rex Winsted," Annie said after Winnie took a break and they sat down at the long table in Winnie's family kitchen, which was nearly as big as the house in Boston in which Annie had grown up. Annie had lost track of how many of Winnie's extended clan lived in the rambling, homey place.

Bella was on a booster seat next to Annie, her little brow scrunched as she quietly shaped a ball of clay, its bright striations of red, bronze, and gold reminiscent of the clay once harvested from the Gay Head Cliffs. The toddler had, however, learned it was not a good idea to eat the clay — she'd attempted to do that last summer.

"What about Rex?" Winnie asked. "Has the rascal returned?"

Rascal was an interesting word.

"Indeed he has." Annie sat back and relaxed while Winnie mused, sipped her tea, then let out a sardonic laugh.

"Rex was one of the 'bad boys' that every mother warned her daughters to stay clear of. As I recall, my sister-in-law got caught

110

in his net for a short while."

"Barbara?" That was a surprise. Barbara was a nurse, a strong family woman. Then again, Annie supposed most people might be surprised to learn that she, too, had had a bout with a bad boy. The guy she'd married after Brian had been killed.

"Yes, dear Barbara," Winnie continued. "But she recovered quickly once she met Orrin, which, needless to say, I'm glad she did."

"What was Rex like?"

"Full of himself. A bit of a scrapper. He thought he could get away with anything, which I guess, for the most part, he did. Nothing major, but annoying. His parents pretty much ignored his evil ways, but his father wouldn't fund his crazy idea to open a restaurant. Rex was just a kid. And his father was tight with a dollar. He had to be — he was a fisherman."

"You do know that Rex opened a nice restaurant in Boston?"

Winnie nodded. "So rumor had it." Then she paused. "Why is he back?"

Annie told her the story and filled her in on Kevin's distress.

"Maybe Rex was successful," Winnie said, "but you know what they say about leopards and their spots. Chances are, he wants something."

In all the time Annie had known Winnie, she hadn't heard her so cautious about anyone.

Just then Winnie's nephew, Lucas — Orrin and Barbara's son — came into the kitchen with two of Winnie's young grandkids in tow.

"Look who's here!" he exclaimed to the kids.

"Bella!" the little boy shouted. Annie thought his name was Harry, but she could not remember his position on the family tree.

"Hi, Annie," Lucas said. "I saw your Jeep outside. Does Bella want to come into the big room and play with the kids? I'm on babysitting duty this morning."

Lucas was a nice young man, about twenty-one now, Annie calculated. In the summer, when he either was fishing with his dad to earn a living (the way Rex apparently had not done with his), or working at the shops up at the cliffs and running programs for kids at the tribal center, Lucas also helped organize the annual Wampanoag Powwow in September and Cranberry Day on the second Tuesday in October. Offseason, he was enrolled at a state university and was studying remotely to become a teacher. Lucas was not a bad boy as Taylor's brother had been.

Once he'd steered the kids — and Bella — out of the kitchen, Annie turned back to Winnie.

"Do you think Rex is dangerous?" she asked.

Winnie shrugged. "I don't think he ever physically harmed anyone, not that he couldn't have. He was a big kid. Built like a giant, you know? Good looking, though, and he turned more than his share of girls' heads. Beyond that, I think he was mostly irritating. Of course, it's anybody's guess what he did in Boston. Or how he managed to raise the money to open his restaurant in the first place."

"What about Rose? Do you know anything about her?"

"Who?"

"Rose Atkins. One of our winter tenants."

"I don't know anyone named Rose. Is she from the island?"

Annie shook her head. "I don't think so. She doesn't seem to know anyone here."

"Is she connected to Rex?"

Annie laughed. "Doubtful. She's quite a bit older. And extremely timid." She then told Winnie how Rose had fled back to her room when she'd seen him.

Winnie smiled. "Maybe his size scared her half to death."

"Right. Well, she did say he reminded her of someone. Maybe it's as simple as that." Finishing her tea, she decided it was time to take Rose at her word. Because Annie really needed to pay attention to her own life and everything she had to do.

Which was, of course, a ridiculous thought. Most writers she knew had a tough time focusing on their responsibilities when something curious was looming. Even if it turned out to be nothing.

But she did know of another possible way to learn more about Rex, and it didn't involve grilling anyone else. On the drive back from Aquinnah, she could stop at the *Vineyard Gazette.* Hilary, the newspaper's librarian, had helped Annie with other research — maybe she could point her in the right direction again.

With her thoughts spinning like an eddy in a tidal pool during stormy, high-tide waves, Annie collected Bella and her things and hugged Winnie good-bye.

Then she drove with extra caution and made it to Edgartown with her precious passenger intact.

Having been established in 1846 —

"Around the time newsprint was invented," Earl had explained when he'd acquainted her with the historic publication — the *Gazette* housed both the editorial and production departments on School Street in a gray-shingled house that had been built in 1760. "Even before my time," he'd said. "And the word on the street is that a ghost still roams the halls dressed as a Revolutionary soldier." Earl did not, however, specify if the soldier was a Brit or part of the militia.

Thanks to the fact that it wasn't summer and it was a weekday between the holidays, Annie easily found a parking spot and unbuckled her seat belt and Bella, Mr. Bear, and the lump of clay Winnie had given her. Then they went inside.

Hilary was upstairs in the archives, right off the busy newsroom. It was a small, quiet room, a welcoming respite. Annie wondered how many people over the years had stepped inside for furtive investigations.

Not that Annie's intention could be considered furtive. Unless the definition of *furtive* was spying on one's neighbors.

"How long ago?" Hilary asked after Annie said she wanted to research an old islander.

"Eighties? Seventies?"

The young woman smiled. "Great! You'll get to look through the envelopes. Before digitizing was available, our librarian cut out every article, sorted them by topic or a name — sometimes both — and filed them in manila envelopes. The clippings are yellowed and pretty brittle, but I know you'll be careful."

A tingle of excitement fluttered through Annie, as she supposed it would in any writer, historian, or person who loved all things Martha's Vineyard. To literally touch the past and be able to weave it into the present was extraordinary.

That day, however, her task wasn't about weaving her efforts into anything, but no one would know that, because doors were often open to writers to learn all kinds of things under the pretext of research.

Spreading her jacket on the floor, she set Bella down on it; Hilary provided a fistful of crayons and a few sheets of blank newsprint.

Then Annie plunged into the journalistic gems from the weekly — twice-weekly in summers — editions, starting with the name Winsted.

She found one envelope. Only a few clippings were inside it. As Hilary had cautioned, they were yellowed and brittle, but clearly had been handled with care.

The largest article was dated 1949 — the

year the elder Winsted won the fishing derby. His prize was a building lot in Gay Head (now Aquinnah), which at that time, Annie knew, must have seemed like the other side of the ocean for someone who lived on Chappaquiddick.

A smaller, more recent article from 1978 included a grainy photo reproduction of a woman named Bertha Blaine Winsted, who apparently was Rex and Taylor's mother. The picture showed her on a small stage holding a flute; the caption noted she had performed for the island nursing home's holiday party. Annie remembered being told that the woman — whom Annie had only heard called "Mother" Winsted — had once played at the Metropolitan Opera in New York City. Why she'd left all that for a fisherman on the Vineyard was a mystery to Annie.

But that wasn't the mystery she'd come to the archives to unravel.

After scanning the obituaries for the elder Winsteds, Annie turned to a voluminous batch of envelopes marked *Court Appearances,* hoping to find Rex mentioned in one. She worked slowly and thoroughly. But, after more than an hour, Annie had found nothing. She groaned.

Bella, who seemed absorbed in drawing

117

something that might have been balloons, mimicked Annie's sound with a guttural one of her own.

Across the room, Hilary grinned. "As much as we sometimes romanticize the old ways of doing things, sometimes it's easier to ask Google to search for you. Then all you need to do is click."

"No kidding," Annie said.

She moved on to high school graduations. And there was Rex, class of 1982. He wasn't listed among those who'd attained honors, nor was there mention that he was headed for college.

Overall, her mission seemed to have proved pointless.

Before leaving, however, she thought about Rose. Was she connected to Rex? Or to the island? Had she kept such a low profile that no one remembered her? Fumbling through the packets of graduations, Annie turned to the sixties. But Rose Atkins's name was not among the students or underclassmen. Then Annie checked the seventies in case Rose looked older than she was. But if she'd grown up on the Vineyard, it didn't seem she'd attended local schools.

As long as Annie was perusing, she decided to simply look up the surname Atkins; maybe she'd stumble on a clue. Within a few minutes, she'd found three envelopes.

Atkins, Warren, warranted several clippings, all from the 1940s, when he'd served on a few Edgartown committees until his death in 1953. There was no mention of a family.

Atkins, Genevieve, was a scientist, a Nobel Prize winner in the 1960s, recognized for her work on what sounded like some thing akin to global warming, which back then was called the greenhouse effect. She traveled the world, but her home was in Tisbury. Annie recognized the name, but hadn't known of her island roots. The contents of the envelope documented a number of events when Ms. Atkins was a featured speaker at the Tabernacle. Annie skimmed the articles, but saw no mention of the woman's personal life.

Atkins, Clive, had been a cemetery caretaker for four of the six island towns, the exceptions being Chilmark and Gay Head. Several articles reported various cemetery situations — upkeep and gravestone-cleaning records, bits of history, names of young people he'd run off for partying among the plots. There was also an obituary. Clive Atkins of West Tisbury died in 1984. Though no wife, children, or siblings were mentioned, the article noted that he left a niece, Mary Rose, of Kennebunk, Maine.

If this were a Friday evening in the late 1970s, when Annie sometimes went with her mother to their church's parish hall, she would have shouted *Bingo!* and stepped forward to collect her prize: two jars of strawberry preserves; a loaf of banana nut bread; potholders made on a square metal loom. Various church ladies would have made them all.

Yelling *Bingo!*, however, did not feel appropriate within the confines of the historic *Gazette* library, especially since Bella would probably echo her in a loud, screeching voice.

After putting everything back neatly, Annie thanked Hilary, packed up Bella (again) and carted her, her coloring masterpieces, Mr. Bear, and the lump of clay down the narrow staircase and out the front door, all the while thinking the stop had been well worth her time, after all, as she now knew that Rex Winsted was not a hardened criminal — or, at least, not on the Vineyard — and that Mary Rose Atkins could quite possibly be her Rose . . . and have an island tie. Which was (hopefully) enough to satisfy Annie's curiosity so that she could put her nosiness to rest and let everyone just be themselves.

Besides, if she wanted to know more about Rex, she could go straight to the one person who would know him best — Taylor. It might give her another shot at befriending Taylor, a consolation prize for having struck out with Abigail. And if it worked, maybe in the process Annie would ease Kevin's situation with his wife.

But as she opened the back door to the Jeep, Annie thought she heard Murphy whisper, *Tread lightly, my friend.*

Or perhaps she'd only imagined it.

CHAPTER 12

The car is a rental, a nondescript thing with Oklahoma plates so most people on the island will figure it came from the airport. It's a compact gray one, which was a brainstorm on my part because it would hardly stick out among the few people who trek over to Chappaquiddick in November unless they belong there.

I decided to go over and look around the place to see what I could find. Just look, you know? No harm, no foul.

So I went today. I kept a camera on the front seat. If anybody tried to make conversation, I was going to say I'm a freelance wildlife photographer. Who'd argue with that?

Anyway, nobody asked, not even the captain of the On Time.

I found my way around without a problem. I even parked the car a couple of times and took a few pictures in case anyone was watching. It wasn't hard. But it was a little scary.

And yet, I think it was a good trial run.

Sometimes, though, I wonder what I'm doing here and why I feel so compelled to do this.

CHAPTER 13

Annie's minor success at the *Gazette* gave her the boost she needed to get back to work on her inventory for the Fair. Which was great, because she not only loved creating the soaps and the artistic packaging, she also loved having a booth at local events, getting to know her fellow islanders better, and meeting happy shoppers who wanted island-made creations.

The boost also helped because it was already Wednesday, and she needed to be ready by a week from Friday. Ten days, really nine. Not much time. So she put everything else on the back burner of her imagination, except trying to improve her relationship with Taylor. Because helping her brother had to be a top priority.

But first, Annie called Trish again because she still hadn't heard back and she was getting concerned. "ASAP," Trish had said. "In other words, now." But again, Annie was diverted to voice mail. Hoping that whatever had been urgent a week ago had either been resolved or no longer mattered, Annie — recharged and refreshed — left a quick message, saying she'd understand if Trish couldn't make the wedding. Then she got back to work.

It was after eleven o'clock before she got around to calling Taylor. Four rings later, the woman answered. She sounded winded, as if it were the old days when people had to run to the phone from somewhere else because they didn't have the luxury of a cell phone in their pocket.

Annie asked if she wanted to have lunch tomorrow at the cottage. "I don't know what we'll have, but I'll come up with something."

"What's the occasion?" Taylor asked. As with many of her sister-in-law's comments, it came out sounding caustic.

"I just thought it would give us the chance to talk without the gang around," Annie said. "And I'd really like to ask your opinion about a few things for the wedding." Until that moment, Annie had no intention of saying that — maybe Murphy had swung by unannounced and dropped the idea into her mind.

They agreed on one o'clock. Then Annie

decided to walk up to the Inn and see what she could cobble together for lunch the next day; she hoped she wouldn't have to go to Edgartown to shop.

She went in the back door, through the mudroom, past the laundry room, and into the *House Beautiful*–worthy kitchen. All was eerily off-season quiet, when year-round tenants and winter renters were all at work. Or had gone wherever they went, which would apply to Rose. Niece of the late Clive Atkins of West Tisbury. Or so it seemed.

Opening the door to the big refrigerator and staring inside, trying to will an appropriate gastronomical choice to step forward, Annie suddenly heard a small sound — a scurrying? — coming from the chef's room.

She glanced in that direction; the door was closed.

Rationalizing that the subtle noise was due to either the heating system kicking on or by someone — Francine? A tenant? — crossing the upstairs hallway above the kitchen, Annie decided to ignore it.

Until she heard it again.

Then she felt certain that, yes, it was coming from inside the chef's room. The door to which Francine kept closed only when she wasn't there.

Like a young girl with a proclivity to listening at doorways (she'd done that many times when her parents had spoken in voices low and muffled), instead of being the adult Annie Sutton, she tiptoed to the chef's room door. Then, forgoing a polite knock, she quickly turned the handle and pushed the door open.

And there stood — or rather, there crouched — Rose. She jumped as if she'd been shot by a BB gun, like the one Earl kept on hand to scare off skunks and raccoons when new guests were en route to the Inn.

"Annie!" Rose exclaimed, as if shocked to see Annie in her own kitchen.

"Rose," Annie replied calmly. "May I help you with something?"

The older woman twittered; she stood up and smoothed her long woolen skirt. That's when Annie realized that Rose had been rifling through the cupboard where they stored Bella's toys. "I thought I saw a mouse run in here," Rose gibbered some more. Then she added, "Guess not. Sorry."

Annie didn't know why Rose had added the "Sorry." As the woman began to leave, Annie remarked that she'd have Kevin take care of any critter that might have sneaked inside.

But Rose paid no attention; she brushed past Annie, then darted from the chef's room into the kitchen, skittered into the great room, and headed toward the staircase almost as quickly as a mouse would, if a mouse had been there at all.

One of the many wonderful things about living on the Vineyard was its notorious hodgepodge of personalities — from the highest-profile celebrities (the list was lengthy) to introverts like Rose Atkins (there was a healthy roster of them, too). Each person was seen as a thread in the giant tapestry that, when woven together, became the fabric of the island.

Annie filed an unwritten "ask Kevin to check for mice" memo in her brain and continued with her mission to concoct a decent lunch for Taylor. Maybe another time she'd have a chance to talk with Rose and ask if she had a history on the island without sounding as if she were prying.

Luckily, she located a frozen salmon filet, fresh greens, and couscous; she mused at how much better the food choices were when Francine was home. Yes, Annie thought, this was Francine's home. Chappaquiddick, not Minneapolis. The Vineyard, not Minnesota. Not wanting to dwell on Francine's dilemma (or, for that matter, on

Rose), Annie loaded the goods into her arms, left the Inn, and went back to her cottage.

After stashing the food for tomorrow's lunch, she grabbed a protein bar and made her way back to the workshop, determined not to let anything else sidetrack her intentions to get her soap ready for market.

Of course, even Annie's most ardent plans could be thwarted by her brother. Especially when she stepped into the workshop and he was standing in the middle of the room, glaring at the cartons of cabinets and the new bathtub as if they were mortal enemies.

"What's up?" Annie asked. "Are you praying for the installation gods to show up and get it done?"

He scratched his chin, one of Earl's traits that Kevin had adopted. "I'm trying to decide when I'm going to get these in with Francine and Jonas here."

Annie recognized it as a lame reply. "The Fair is a little more than a week away. You're not going to touch this mess until then, remember?" She'd had enough of her brother's addictive penchant for hammering — loudly — when the Inn was being built.

"Right," he said.

"After that, you can build to your heart's content. You can tell Francine you're finally going to finish the interior. I doubt she'll guess you're converting it into a house, let alone into one for them." Now wasn't the time to tell him that Francine might never live there, anyway. Life, Annie thought, was exactly like the tides, coming and going, ebbing and flowing. Someone who was a far better writer than she was surely must have said that more beautifully.

Kevin pulled off his knit cap and rubbed one side of his head.

She recognized the gesture as one of bewilderment.

Zigzagging through the clutter, Annie made it to her workbench, where bars of soap sat patiently, waiting to be made ready for packing into the remaining totes that were messing up the workshop as badly as Kevin's cabinets. She sat on the high stool and looked around. "We're a couple of slobs," she said with a laugh. "It's clear that neither one of us inherited Mom's genes for organization."

"I used to be organized. When I had my construction business." Apparently he had not recognized her comment as humorous.

"Then blame it on the island," Annie added. "Maybe it's something in the water." She was trying to get him to loosen up; she knew he was troubled because, most of all,

Annie had learned that when her brother was upset, he wanted — needed — to hammer. "Are you going to tell me what's bothering you?"

He jockeyed his shoulders back and forth, as if trying to get them to relax. "I have a lot on my mind."

Because they were half siblings from the same birth mother whom Annie had found the courage to contact only a few years ago, she was still learning how Kevin ticked. But it did not take a lifetime of experience to recognize that he wasn't the same jovial guy who'd come back from Minneapolis only a week ago. If Annie were a betting woman, she'd say it was due to Rex. And she was pretty sure she'd win.

Rather than ask him outright, which he might misinterpret as her trying to control his life, she said, "I invited Taylor to lunch tomorrow."

He squinted. "My wife?"

She dropped her gaze to the workbench, plucked a bar from the curing rack, and studied it for imperfections, unattractive little glitches that she hadn't been able to smooth out. Unfixable bars went into the scrap pile either to be reworked at another time or set aside as "seconds" for a later fair.

"Um, yes," she said. "That Taylor." As if there were more than one Taylor they both knew. "I'd like to get her input on my wedding plans."

Kevin looked at her blankly — yes, Annie thought, blankly was the perfect word. Then he zipped up his parka, pulled on his gloves, and said, "I've got to hit the hardware store and pick up some stuff."

He turned and left the workshop, forgetting to say good-bye or even wave.

Annie sighed. She tried not to feel guilty that she hadn't pressed him into telling her what was wrong. She knew that sometimes Kevin needed prodding, a gentle or a not-so-gentle nudge to help him peel back the top layer of his anxiety so he'd be able to expose what was sizzling beneath.

But Annie had too much to do; the time it would take trying to solve his problems would be better spent talking with Taylor the next day. In the meantime, she would wrap and pack, even if it meant staying up all night. So she texted John and said she was chained to her soap stool. He answered by saying she'd better get cracking because if people stopped reading books, he was pretty sure the two of them would need her soapmaking industry to fund their retirement. He added a laughing emoji, which made her smile.

Then Annie remembered she should have told Kevin about the mouse. So she texted him, too. But he did not respond.

After going to bed just before dawn, Annie stood at the window over her kitchen sink a few hours later, nursing a mug of hot tea, allowing her mind to grasp that three weeks from tomorrow she and John were going to get married. They'd be standing at the big fireplace in the great room at the Inn. Lucy would be on her left, holding Annie's bouquet; Earl would be on John's right, because John had said his dad was the best man he knew. It had brought Earl to tears, which he'd tried unsuccessfully to hide. The room would be filled with the fragrance of lavender and freesia ("Not local, but imported?" Earl had asked in mock horror because neither flower bloomed on the island in December). Soft music would drift in from somewhere, while love and joy would radiate from family and friends . . . .

Oh, God, Annie thought. She'd forgotten to arrange for some music. And to order the flowers. When she'd called the florist a few weeks ago and relayed what she thought she'd want, the woman cautioned her that they might have to come from outside the

Northeast, unless she could find them at a greenhouse, which would be a long shot.

Annie knew she had to hurry. Hopefully, the florist knew someone who could provide music. Unless . . .

An outburst of laughter from Murphy at that moment was not appreciated. Especially since, dear God, it was eleven thirty, which didn't leave much time for Annie to shower, dress, and make her tiny kitchen ready for her sister-in-law.

Then she had a better idea.

She grabbed her phone and texted Taylor. CHANGE OF VENUE. COME TO THE FLORIST WITH ME? LUNCH AT THE BLACK DOG? MY TREAT?

By the time Annie was out of the shower, Taylor had replied: WHY NOT. Annie took that as a halfhearted yes.

Taylor showed up early. She said that should give them enough time at the florist and get to the Black Dog before they starved to death. Annie had intended to put on a little makeup, but having Taylor wait would not be worth the effort.

The florist was wonderful and had done some homework since Annie's first call.

"Freesia is native to South Africa," she explained. "But a grower in upstate New

134

York cultivates blooms year round." It turned out that the same grower could provide lavender. And — *huzzah!* — hydrangea blossoms.

When Annie explained her "color scheme" — which actually was only her off-white dress (she didn't mention she might not be wearing it) and Lucy's powder blue, the woman suggested blue hydrangeas to blend with cream-and-lavender freesia. And fresh sprigs of lavender, too.

Annie signed on the dotted line and prayed that a December storm wouldn't arrive while the flowers were in transit from New York.

She didn't ask about the music.

The Black Dog Tavern down by the harbor was crowded, which wasn't unexpected on a Thursday afternoon, as more people seemed to live year-round on the island now. They sat in captain's chairs by the fireplace instead of on benches by the windows, which was fine with Annie, as she saw the harbor and the ferries often enough.

"So what's up?" Taylor asked once they'd both ordered crab cakes and she dug into the loaf of bread that was still warm from the oven.

"I really appreciated your input with the flowers," Annie said. "I'd almost forgotten I needed to get that done."

"It was obvious you already knew what you wanted. So what's the real reason for the lunch invite?" Taylor wasn't stupid, nor did she mince words.

"Nothing, really. I just realized I hadn't been focusing on the wedding plans, and I thought if I could sit down and talk to someone — to you — maybe it would help me get organized."

"Uh-huh," came the reply, as if Annie's companion clearly wasn't buying her convoluted elucidation.

"Actually . . ." She had no idea why this was so difficult to ask. Was she afraid her sister-in-law would laugh at her? Or turn her down? Annie squared her shoulders and willed herself to stop acting childish. "I was wondering if you'd be willing to play the cello. At the service. Christmas Eve." She gulped her water while waiting for the answer.

"Why not," Taylor said flatly and rather quickly. "Kevin made it clear we won't be going to Hawaii for the winter until after your nuptials. And until he's done with the house for the kids."

Annie toyed with the napkin, which by then was in her lap. "Thank you," she said with genuine relief. "It means a lot to me that you'll be part of the service."

"What else?" Taylor asked. "I mean, you could have texted me about that. You didn't need to spring for lunch."

There would be no fooling Taylor, no dodging the fact that a greater question loomed, no beating around the bittersweet vines.

"Okay," Annie confessed. "I'm also worried about Kevin. He seems upset about your brother — not because Rex is here, but because Kevin doesn't know what's going on. I don't want to butt in, but . . . well, all he said is that when he walks in on you when you're with Rex, both of you stop talking."

There. She'd said too much, of course she had. For which she'd probably have hell to pay with Kevin. She'd probably made Taylor defensive, and she wouldn't blame her. So Annie looked down at the bread and said, "I'm so sorry, Taylor. I shouldn't have said anything. I've been trying to find a way for us to be better friends, but I suppose I just blew my chances. Just because I'm over fifty now, doesn't mean I know when to shut my mouth. And if you want to change your mind about playing at my wedding, I'll understand."

Taylor said nothing. She did, however,

tuck her auburn mane behind her ears and stare out the window. And then teardrops spilled over her lower lashes.

"My bully of a brother," she said quietly, "is trying to steal my house."

CHAPTER 14

The trademark mugs and the crab cakes arrived. The server set them down and, with a pleasant smile, asked if they needed anything else. When they said no, thanks, he sauntered away.

Annie was glad for the momentary intrusion, as it gave her time to try to process the latest glut of information. And though she wanted details, she didn't want to antagonize her sister-in-law. So she simply said, "I don't understand how Rex thinks he can steal your house."

"Neither did I. But he lost his restaurant in the height of the pandemic. He claimed that few people wanted 'takeout flambé,' which I suppose makes sense." She raised her head and stretched her neck but didn't wipe the tears from her dark amber eyes. Maybe she thought Annie hadn't noticed; maybe she thought she should appear unflappable, rather than as a weeping woman.

"After a while," Taylor continued, "Rex had to turn his restaurant back to the bank. Next went his waterfront condo. I expect he'd made tons of money over the years, but material things were important to him. He once told me if you look successful, people will think you are. He said it was a big part of why his business had taken off. He let people think he was a great business-man as well as an amazing chef. Turns out he was one but not the other."

Annie wanted to interject that few small businesses had been prepared for the on-slaught of COVID-19, but she didn't think defending Rex would be a good idea.

"What about your house?" Years ago, An-nie had been on the hamster wheel of hav-ing a lot of money, needing more, getting more, needing more. Thinking about that still put her at risk of developing a migraine. She decided to swing the conversation back to the issue at hand. "He can't just 'steal' it, can he?"

Taylor resumed a small interest in lunch. She lifted her fork, picking at a crab cake, then at the greens around it. "Yes," she said. "He can."

"But it's your home. Wasn't it your mother's? Didn't you grow up there?" Kevin seemed to enjoy living there, not far from the Inn, with plenty of space for family and friends, especially Francine and Jonas. Maybe he even dreamed of having grandkids race around the lawn, the screen door slapping behind them in summer.

"I grew up in that house," Taylor answered. "But so did Rex."

"Can you find a compromise?" Maybe Rex wanted to sell it so he could take half the money and start over again. Maybe, somehow, Kevin could buy him out. Then maybe Rex would move away and leave Chappy — and everyone on it — intact. Maybe, maybe, maybe.

Taylor shook her head. "He insists that it's already his."

His? Annie scowled. "But you've lived there for years. You gave up your career to come back to the island and take care of your father when he got sick. Am I right?"

Taylor stopped stirring and looked at her curiously, as if Annie had said more than she should have known. Annie swiftly searched her mind, wondering if, indeed, she'd been told those things in confidence. By Kevin. Or maybe by Claire.

"It's true that while Rex was busy making a name for himself and his restaurant, I gave

141

up my life and came back here. I was a good cellist. I played with the symphony." Taylor's voice was louder, stronger. But beneath the surface, a small waver indicated that the teardrops were about to make a comeback.

"Your family was more important to you," Annie said gently. "There's nothing wrong with that."

Taylor's eyebrows lifted, then lowered as if in a shrug. "You know the story about Jonas. How his father died before we could get married. How Jonas went to live with his father's parents."

Yes, Annie knew that story. She nodded.

"The truth is," Taylor continued, "I came home to try and 'atone for my sins,' which is what my mother called it. My father didn't call it anything. In fact, he hardly spoke to me. He died still hating me for what had happened. Even though I'd done as he'd demanded — I left the island, went to Boston, had my baby, my Jonas, in secret." She sat, staring into the fireplace, her eyes glistening, the orange flames reflected in them. "All that time, my father refused to support me. He claimed he didn't have any money. So I moved in with Rex."

"But I thought Jonas's grandfather gave you money . . ."

"That came later. After I gave them Jonas.

I'd planned to keep him. I wanted to stay in Boston, get a job, and raise my baby. I never wanted to see the Vineyard again. Back then, Rex worked a hundred hours a week trying to save money to start his own restaurant. He paid my doctor bills. And the hospital bill. I have to give him credit for that. But a couple of weeks later, he said he was done giving me a free ride and that he wasn't going to support my kid as well. Plus, he had a girlfriend who wanted to move in. So I had to leave."

Annie lowered her head. "Were you in a position to be a single mother?" She was reminded how, even twenty-five years ago, society still frowned on that, still made it difficult for a young woman who wasn't lucky enough to have a family helping out.

Taylor snorted. "I didn't have a dime to my name or a place to live. That's why I turned to Derek's parents. Derek, you might remember, was Jonas's father, who drowned before Jonas was born. Anyway, I figured they'd love Jonas. And keep him safe. They were rich summer people who had a ton of money, but I didn't 'sell' him to them. A little while after that, Jonas's grandfather — Roger Flanagan — gave me a big check. I was stunned. I felt guilty for taking it, but I had little choice. I still can't believe I told people that Roger offered to keep me — and my family — financially solvent forever. I guess in my teenager's brain it sounded more acceptable to say that instead of admitting I gave Jonas to them."

"Where did you live after Rex booted you out and before you got the check?"

"In a homeless shelter."

Annie stifled a gasp.

"I got a housekeeping job at a hotel. But it wasn't enough to live on, even by myself."

Annie wanted to ask, "Your brother let you give up your baby and go to a shelter?" But she knew better than to come between siblings.

"I paid Rex back with the Flanagans' money. I paid off the mortgage on my parents' house. I got a studio apartment and put myself through Berklee. I was amazed that they accepted me. For a few years I was okay. I loved playing in the symphony. But when my father got sick, my mother found me and, well, here I am. I thought my father would forgive me if I took care of him. But he said I owed him more than that for the shame I'd put them through."

Annie ate a forkful of salad, trying to think of the right words to say next. It was true that the story sounded as if it took place in the fifties, not in the late nineties. She

144

wondered how much had changed since then when it came to the dynamics in some families.

"My plan didn't work," Taylor added. "Or, at least, my father died before he forgave me. And it wasn't long before the big check from Roger Flanagan was long gone."

After a quick swallow, Annie said, "I'm so sorry, Taylor."

The auburn eyebrows elevated again. "After my father died, my mother and I became friends again. So it wasn't such a bad thing. And because I'd already paid off the house, I was able to support the two of us with my caretaking jobs on Chappy."

Annie was reminded of the first time she'd seen Taylor. It had been a cold, wintry night; Annie and Earl had been combing Chappaquiddick, hoping to find the mother of the baby that had been left on Annie's doorstep. As Earl turned his pickup down a narrow dirt road, they came across the caretaker of a seasonal estate. He was dressed in a heavy knit cap and an L.L.Bean parka, not unlike the one that Earl wore. Thankfully, Bella was tucked warmly and safely in her basket, which sat between Annie's feet on the floor of Earl's truck. Then, as the caretaker moved closer to Earl's truck, he removed his cap and a mass of auburn hair tumbled out. As it happened, it was not a man but Taylor.

Pushing her plate away now, Taylor continued. "I didn't know that my father changed his will, that he left the house to Rex. And only Rex. The old man really did hate me. I'll never know if my mother had known about it. And if she'd agreed."

Annie was stunned. "Oh, my God, are you sure?"

She nodded. "I never saw any paperwork — or the will. When my mother died, I just kept living there and paying the bills. The property taxes still have my father's name on them; I guess no one at the town hall thought to fix it. And I never said anything because, in my mind, nothing had changed. Yesterday Rex called a lawyer, Sophie Johnson — the daughter of our parents' original attorney, who's dead now, too. Rex put Sophie on speaker and she confirmed it. Of course, Rex has known the truth all along. So I guess it's true that most of us never get everything we want out of life." She sighed again. "Please, don't tell Kevin. I don't want him to know yet."

Annie did not want the responsibility of keeping something so important from her brother. But she also wanted to be friends with Taylor, so she said, "I won't tell him if you don't want me to." She hoped it wasn't a mistake.

It was Taylor who hesitated that time, perhaps weighing her losses. "Thanks. I was hoping Jonas would know he had a place on the Vineyard where his father had been happy. At least there's the house on Maui. It's run down now, but it was Derek's, so Rex can't get his big mitts on it."

"And Jonas will have the house at the Inn, too," Annie said. "As long as he and Francine stay here and don't wander back to Minnesota." As soon as she'd said it, Annie wished she could hit "delete." She had no idea why that information had popped out of her mouth.

"Jonas and Francine won't wander anywhere. Unless you know something I don't."

Annie returned to toying with her napkin. "No," she said, forcing a smile. "I'm just so glad they're here, I'm afraid they won't want to stay forever." She had no idea if that made sense.

Then she wondered that if the house on Chappy went to Rex, would Taylor and Kevin move to Hawaii . . . for good? Not just for the winters? And what about Jonas and Francine? Would they decide to live there, too? For someone who, until moving to the island, had always lived her life within five miles of the house where she'd grown up in Southie — South Boston — it was strange that housing concerns now occupied so much real estate in her brain.

It's the Vineyard, Murphy whispered. *Where housing drama is a tradition. Especially for single mothers like Taylor had been. And Francine.*

Annie shushed her spirit friend. Then an idea begin to take shape — not a book idea, but a very different one. It was small in scope but might help spread a little cheer. And, more important, some hope to those who might need some.

Signaling the server for the check, Annie wasn't trying to dismiss Taylor; instead she wanted to mull over her new thought.

In the twenty or so minutes it took to get from the Black Dog to the triangle in Edgartown, Annie decided that her new idea had merit. She told Taylor she needed to make a quick stop for a gift, then she ran into Granite — the "everything" store that was a seventy-five-year-old island staple — where she bought a dozen woven baskets with handles — about the same size as the one in which Bella had arrived when she'd been not much bigger than an infant.

Once they were back on Chappy, Taylor

climbed into her old pickup and headed home. And Annie quickly ducked into her cottage and powered up her laptop. She knew she should be in the workshop tending to her soaps, but her new project now felt more important.

She clicked on the file that listed participants in the Holiday Fair. Scrolling through it, she noted at least a dozen who might like to contribute to Annie's "baskets" with their beeswax emollient bars, soy candles, all-natural healing balms, and more. Anything to help the recipients feel pampered. Annie would include a couple of her soaps, a gift certificate for a mani-pedi or a facial at an island spa of their choice, and a pretty, handmade alpaca scarf. Maybe there would also be room for extra treats: a jar of raw honey, a bag of locally roasted coffee, some fabulous sea salts, and, of course, Vineyard chocolates. She would contact the island support services for women and let them distribute the baskets anonymously to whomever they felt could benefit from some unexpected joy. Then Annie thought that, because her book sales had been good this year, she might donate the profits of her Holiday Fair soap sales to the support services. Yes, she thought with a small smile. And she'd do it all in honor of her dad.

She couldn't believe she hadn't thought of it sooner.

Annie's dad, Bob Sutton, had owned a small insurance company that he liked to say "specialized in helping families." And he'd meant it. He'd been a kind man, often generous beyond his means, according to her mother. But her dad told Annie that some of the best Christmas fun was to be one of Santa's Helpers, a local charity whose members collected gifts and donations from individuals and businesses and secretly distributed them on the Sunday night before Christmas to neighbors in need.

Starting when Annie was six years old, she'd gone with her dad on his rounds. By the time she was ten, she figured out that he'd been slipping extra gifts into his sack, and that he sometimes went to houses that weren't on the official list.

"Don't tell your mother," he said with an impish twinkle when Annie questioned him.

That was the year they went to the tenement where Frankie Longworth lived, down by the railroad roundhouse, where the trains from Albany and Providence turned around before heading north or south or west, because the only thing left to the east was Boston Harbor.

Frankie and Annie were in the same classroom, grade four, Miss Topor. Some kids made fun of him because he had few clothes. In the fall, he wore a red plaid shirt; once the temperature dropped, on top of the shirt he wore a dark blue sweater that had red diamond shapes around the chest. Day after day, Frankie showed up at school wearing the same things. Annie remembered feeling sorry for him.

After they left the tenement that Sunday before Christmas, she told her dad about Frankie's shirt and sweater. The next night after supper, her dad announced that he needed to shop for the three girls in his office; he asked Annie to come along. They bought small bottles of Shalimar cologne and Isotoner gloves. But while the clerk was gift-wrapping the purchases, Annie's dad steered her to the boys' department.

"How big a fellow do you suppose your friend Frankie is?"

They bought a dark green sweater with three horizontal stripes — one yellow, two white — and a green turtleneck like the ones skiers wore. They also bought a light blue sweater and a white collared shirt. They had those wrapped as well, then added a tag that read: *Especially for Frankie, Merry Christmas from Santa's Helper.*

They left them at the family's door on Christmas Eve.

Frankie wore the clothes to school, and Annie swore he smiled more than before. Every time she saw him, she felt proud of her dad, and she felt special, too, because she was the only one in grade four who knew Frankie's secret.

Like her dad's Santa's Helpers, Annie decided to make small acts of charity her Christmas tradition; she also suspected that Lucy would be happy if Annie asked her to help.

When John called and interrupted her thoughts, Annie made up a story about why she sounded as if she had been crying.

"Do you have a cold?" he asked.

"No, I'm fine. I inhaled too much bayberry." Luckily for her, he wouldn't argue because he'd never made soap and probably never would. And because he didn't know she was in her cottage and not the workshop.

"Good. I don't want my bride sick on our wedding night."

It sounded so corny that she laughed.

Then he said, "What's your schedule for the weekend?"

"Please tell me you need to work. I'm so busy trying to get things finished . . ."

"I'm working Saturday, but I'm off Sunday. I was thinking about going Christmas shopping for the girls. Wanna come? Unless you're too busy?"

Annie thought about his daughters, who might appreciate a woman's opinion about their presents from their dad. She'd also love to tell him about the baskets and about her father. "Will Christmas shopping include lunch? I'll even pay."

"Are you trying to bribe a police officer?"

"Yes." She could take him to Town Bar and Grill, because he loved their marinated flank steak and bacon mashed potatoes.

He laughed. "You're on. And thanks. My daughters will be grateful."

"Speaking of daughters, do you want me to pick Abigail up at the boat tomorrow?" It was a spontaneous thought that Annie credited to full immersion in the holiday spirit.

"Thanks," he said, "but there's no need. She's done with classes but still has to do a final project that she can do here, so she's bringing her car over for winter break. And I won't spend unnecessary money on rent."

Annie congratulated herself for not commenting on "the rent."

"And," John added, "her boyfriend's coming over with her for the weekend. I arranged a bed at the hostel for him." He snickered. "Maybe I'll even get to meet him."

Annie pushed down her disappointment. If she'd been able to pick up Abigail, it would have been a perfect opportunity to ask her to rework the wedding dress. And a chance to reach out to her. Reaching out, after all, seemed to be working well with Taylor.

"Well," she replied in a neutral tone, "that will be nice for Abigail."

"Right," he said, sarcastically. "In the meantime, do you want to come for supper tomorrow night? I have no idea how many of us will be here, so I thought we'd get pizza."

"Sounds great," she said.

They agreed on six tomorrow, did the "love you" bits, and then rang off.

Annie printed out the list of artisans she hoped would donate products for the baskets, then she put her jacket on and walked over to the workshop. It was time to get back to work, time to try to forget that, with Abigail's boyfriend around over the weekend, the hours would be shrinking for Annie to expect that the wedding dress could be fixed. So she would, indeed, be an ugly bride. Or at least a bride in an ugly dress.

But she could feel good, thanks to her Christmas surprise for a dozen deserving Vineyard women.

Oh, and she'd feel good that she and John were getting married.

She felt a little guilty that that had been an afterthought.

CHAPTER 15

Pizza night at John's was fun, a delightful change from being trapped in the workshop until late Thursday night and all day Friday. Abigail, however, wasn't there; she was out with "the boyfriend," as Lucy still called him. Best of all, that gave Annie a chance to share her idea with John and Lucy, who was thrilled about helping out, starting with how she knew almost everyone on Annie's list of artisans and said she'd contact them about donating their products.

"Everybody who lives here is generous," she asserted. "Which is why few people have much money."

The three of them laughed, but Annie knew that what Lucy said was true. It was part of what Annie loved about living on the Vineyard.

"Speaking of money," Annie said, "I've also decided to give the profits of my sales at the Fair to island support services for women. It might not be much, but I think that every little bit must help."

"Oh," John said, feigning distress, "there goes our retirement fund."

They laughed again, and Lucy rolled her eyes. Then, with her priorities in order and the clock ticking, Annie gave John a kiss, Lucy a hug, and Restless a scratch behind his ears, and was home by nine o'clock.

And now, Saturday morning, she was showered, dressed, and back in the workshop before eight in the morning, determined to use her time wisely. After all, setup for the Fair would be Friday — less than a week away. The Fair itself was only open from 10:00 a.m. to 4:00 p.m. on Saturday.

She worked in veritable silence for a couple of hours. Then Earl appeared with coffee and cinnamon rolls that he admitted he'd stolen from Annie's freezer. "Couldn't help it," he said. "You make the best."

He pulled a stool up to her workbench and made himself comfortable. "How's it going? Think you'll be done in time?"

"I will if I don't keep finding other things to do." Then she told him her plan for the baskets.

Earl got emotional because that was Earl. He lowered his head and bit into the cinnamon roll.

"Do you think Claire would like to con- tribute something?" Annie asked. "My hope is that several recipients will be single moth- ers. Do you think Claire would like to donate a small doll for each basket — maybe like the yarn-haired ones she made for Bella? With a Christmas theme? I want to keep this as confidential as possible, just among the contributors."

The comment made Earl laugh. "My wife is good at keeping things, as you say, confi- dential, when it's for a good cause. And, by the way, it's a mighty nice idea you have."

"I just want to be able to show a few people that others care." She decided not to mention donating her profits from the Fair. She wasn't, after all, doing all this to receive pats on the back.

Earl nodded. "You tell John?"

"I did." She didn't add that he'd bitten into his pizza the same way Earl had just tackled the pastry. "Lucy's going to help me. And I know it's short notice, so please tell Claire she's welcome to decline."

"You have my word that she'll say yes. Not that I can speak for her, of course." He grinned.

Annie took a quick sip of coffee, then went back to wrapping soaps. "I should have asked her directly, but, well, here you are, and it came to mind, and . . ."

"I shall be honored to be your messenger." With that, he finished his morning treat, said he now had an important mission and that he'd leave Annie alone. So he did.

And she went back to work.

Until almost noon.

When she realized she'd run out of ribbon.

"Noooo," she groaned. She decided to call Lucy and ask if she could bike over to Granite, grab a few spools of red, green, and silver wire ribbon, and get them over to Chappy. She'd offer to pay her handsomely, which Lucy would decline.

But then Annie remembered that Lucy and Kyle had plans to ride their bikes to Polly Hill Arboretum before it got too cold out for a picnic. But because Lucy might be one of the few teenagers left on the planet who still listened to voice mail, Annie said, "I forgot to ask if you'll still be able to help me at the Fair. I hope you're having a fun day. Last night was nice." She rang off, then checked in with Francine to see if she needed anything from Edgartown (she did not), then hightailed it to the *On Time.* With any luck, people hadn't yet started wrapping gifts, so the store would have plenty of ribbon.

■ ■ ■ ■

Overnight, the town had been transformed into a holiday village: the white sea captain's houses were exquisitely decorated with lush greens and bright reds. Annie knew that members of Claire's garden club made their services available to seasonal residents whose homes were vacant this time of year but needed to be "properly dressed" for Christmas in Edgartown. Adding to the ambiance, white lights twinkled everywhere, as if Santa himself were spreading cheer up and down the narrow streets and brick sidewalks where smiling shoppers sauntered in and out of stores with lots of bundles in their arms. It felt magical.

At Granite, the parking lot was crowded; shopping locally was not a request but a Vineyard tradition.

After three tries around the lot, Annie finally saw a space open near the bank; she wasted no time sliding the Jeep into it.

She expected the store to be packed.

It was.

Inside, the skinny aisles were skinnier than usual, thanks to myriad extra merchandise.

As she gingerly made her way toward the sewing section, a voice called out, "Annie!

Merry Christmas!" It was Myrna, from Sweetwater Farm in Chilmark, who had taught Annie about making honey a couple of summers earlier. They did a how-are-you, what-are-you-doing-for-the-holidays exchange, then parted, just as Annie spotted Lottie from the Chappaquiddick Community Center.

She asked Lottie how she was, and they chatted about the upcoming Christmas Eve party at the center, which had been postponed until the day after Christmas because the timing conflicted with Annie and John's wedding, which several residents would be attending.

At last, she reached the aisle of ribbons when, from the corner of her eye, she saw someone she thought she recognized. A double take confirmed that she was right; it was Abigail. She was standing in the housewares department with a tall, dark-haired boy with a neatly trimmed beard. The boyfriend, Annie supposed.

Because she was so darned curious, she tried to squint without getting caught. The boy, too, looked like someone she'd seen before, but Annie reasoned that, sooner or later, most year-round islanders looked familiar. Though Annie doubted that she knew him, one thing for certain was that he was standing close to Abigail. And they were giggling.

Annie ducked down the aisle before Abigail could notice her.

Moving straight to the ribbons, she quickly found three large rolls of what she needed. Ribbon was sold by the yard, but before taking them to be measured, she knew her behavior about Abigail had been ridiculous. Saying hello and having a chance to meet her boyfriend might be a good way to connect. But when Annie turned back toward housewares, they were no longer there.

Rather than look for them and lose time, she had the ribbon measured, then moved quickly to the checkout counter line. She kept an eye out but didn't see them. She did, however, see Monsieur LeChance, a pleasant older man, an accomplished violinist who lived on Fuller Street and was in a quartet that Taylor had joined with her cello. The group played at several venues every summer.

Finally, Annie paid for her purchases and left the store. But when she crossed the lot toward the Jeep and started to open the driver's door, she quickly saw something disturbing: the left front tire was completely flat.

She studied it a moment, trying to figure

out what happened. But she wasn't pleased with the thought that came to mind. She took a deep, slow breath.

Tires go flat all on their own, she tried to convince herself while standing on the asphalt, shopping bag in hand. It wasn't as if Abigail would have punctured the tire. She was not a malicious girl.

Was she?

Just because she and Annie hadn't meshed, it didn't mean the girl would do something so . . . juvenile.

After staring at the tire for a couple of minutes — as if staring could inflate it back to life — Annie tossed her things inside and knew she'd have to change it. At least she'd developed some survival skills since moving to the island. But as she went to remove the spare from the rear cargo space, she remembered what she'd find: before she'd left the island for her book tour in September, she'd run over a nail on her way home from Winnie's. Grateful that her spare tire was full-sized and not one of those doughnut things, she'd changed it on the side of the State Road, put the damaged one in the cargo space, and gone on her merry way, knowing she should have it fixed before she left. But Annie had run out of time. And she'd since forgotten, what with everything else.

So she had no spare tire.

She didn't want to call John because he was on duty and this wasn't a police emergency. She didn't want to call Francine because she'd said she had schoolwork. She could have called Jonas, but he was probably babysitting for Bella or outside somewhere painting on Chappy. So Annie called Earl, the go-to guy. He told her to sit tight and that he'd be right over.

If Annie had known the kind of vehicle John had bought for Abigail, she would have strolled around the lot to check out the cars while she waited for Earl. She could have called Lucy and asked, but that would seem more than a little obvious. So, with the afternoon growing chilly, she went back into Granite and browsed for the twenty minutes it took for Earl to arrive and call to say he was outside in the lot.

"Sliced clean through," he said when Annie joined him. "Looks like you ran over something with an agenda. Like a ferocious knife."

It took all the self-talk Annie could muster not to tell him that she'd seen his granddaughter just before the tire met "something with an agenda."

"I'll get you home," he added. "I already called John, and he'll take care of this when

164

he's done with his shift. He'll get a new tire on and a spare in the back that actually works. He'll leave the Jeep at his place; you can get it tomorrow when you two go shopping or whatever you're going to do." He scratched his chin. "There's nothing better than having a couple of men around to look after a fair damsel, is there?"

Annie groaned and got into his pickup before she had a chance to hear him chuckle.

And on the way back to Chappy, she no longer paid attention to how lovely the village looked in its finery: the town hall, the small cinema marquee, the cheery window at Edgartown Books — and the traditional white canvas banner strung between the rooftops across Main Street that heralded the upcoming weekend.

Instead, Annie was saying a silent prayer that the tire slicer had not been Abigail.

CHAPTER 16

I've thought about her lots of times, even though I was warned not to.

"What's done is done," they said, as if Bella didn't exist. As if she weren't family.

They'd be pissed if they knew what I'm going to do. But I don't have to worry about that now.

I should have brought her a gift, something that might get her to like me. Maybe books or puzzles or something frilly for a girl. I could get her a musical toy, like a little keyboard or something where she can punch buttons and listen to kids' songs. She might like that better.

If anyone asks, I'll say I'm buying Christmas presents for a long-lost relative.

I suppose I should get a car seat, too, in case she wants to go for a ride. I can't believe I didn't think of that sooner.

But I'm getting ahead of things.

I've spent these past days thinking a lot

about it. My plan is coming together now. And when I think about seeing her again, hearing her voice, my heart starts beating fast. Because deep down I know this is what I'm supposed to do.

No matter what anyone else will think.

CHAPTER 17

Annie told John she'd be at his place at
eleven o'clock Sunday morning to begin
their shopping trip. She dressed in a mid-
length, gray wool skirt, black boots, and a
powder-blue cowl neck sweater because she
wanted to look nice. With their busy lives,
they rarely had time for simple dating anymore.

She'd just finished doing her hair when
her phone rang. It was Trish.

"I'm sorry I took so long to get back to
you," Annie said before Trish had a chance.
"But it was two days before Thanksgiving
and I'd just learned that my brother and his
family were coming back to the island and
we had to get pies baked and . . ."

"Stop apologizing," Trish interrupted. "I
did what I needed to do without waiting for
your blessing." She sounded more chipper
than all-business Trish typically did.

Annie pulled out a chair at her tiny kitchen

table and sat. "Would you care to share the details?"

"Funny you should ask."

Picking up a pen that she kept on the table, Annie pulled a nearby pad of paper toward her in case she needed to take notes. "Okay. Tell me."

After pausing, Trish said, "I've been in L.A."

"California?"

"Well. Yes." She said it as if there were no other, as if Louisiana weren't abbreviated with the same initials. "I flew back to the city last night."

"Well. Good," Annie said, though she couldn't imagine what this had to do with her. Or with RSVPing to the wedding.

"We finalized the deal."

Huh?

"Trish, you are my favorite editor in the whole world. But I'm missing something here. What deal are you talking about?"

A robust laugh came through the phone. "*Your* deal, my dear. Your Museum Girls Mysteries are going network. Not even cable, mind you, but a full-fledged network series. How about that?"

Annie set down her pen. "What?"

"I doubt that you've gone deaf since we last talked. I went to the West Coast to iron out the details. And I succeeded; it will be a blockbuster. And you, Annie Sutton, are going to be very busy. And, I might add, very rich."

Then Trish rattled off specifics that Annie was too stunned to digest. All she heard was the part about becoming very busy and very rich. Didn't Trish know she was already busy? Didn't she know that being rich wasn't high on Annie's list of goals?

By the time Trish finished prattling, Annie was flushed. Her long wool skirt was now too warm, and her cowl-neck sweater was clinging to the perspiration on her back.

"Hello?" Trish insisted. "Have you heard a word I've said?"

"Yes, yes," Annie managed. "But how . . . when . . . did this happen? Has my agent been involved?"

"Of course she has. Louisa wanted to be with me, but she and her husband were in Brazil with her parents, so she couldn't get away. But we were on the phone three or four times a day hammering out a deal you won't be able to turn down. Your agent's very sharp, you know. And, as your publisher, we retained your dramatic rights, which I had to keep reminding her." Then she laughed. "But we made a good team. All for you, my dear. Well, less my company's cut. And Louisa's commission."

"I wish you'd contacted me . . ." Even as she said it, she remembered dismissing Trish's voice mail for a week.

"I did. I asked you to call me ASAP. I'm not sure how a person can be so busy living on an island. And this kind of proposition can never wait. But believe me, we secured top dollar. No one's making this much in Hollywood right now. Of course, we also got them to agree that you'll consult on the scripts . . ." She laughed again. "You'll work side by side with the screenwriter, which means you can make sure they stick to your style and character development . . . ."

She was prattling again.

"Trish, I have to go. I'm meeting someone in Edgartown. Can we pick this up tomorrow?"

"Seriously? I thought you'd be elated."

Annie paused. "I am. I think. But I need time to process it. To think about whatever questions I might have. Like, what do you mean I'll work 'side by side'? How will this affect the manuscript I'm working on? I have other commitments . . ."

"We all do, Annie. This one needs to move front and center. Most authors can only dream of a deal one-tenth as good as this." Her chipper attitude turned back to all-business.

"I'm sure. But please. Can we talk tomorrow morning?"

Annie heard a slight huff. Then Trish said, "As long as you aren't going to tell me you need to leave it up to your fiancé. That would be so last century, don't you think?"

Forcing a laugh, Annie said, "I think you know me better than that."

"All right, then. We'll talk tomorrow. But I'm booked all morning, so let's make it three o'clock. I'll call then. Don't let it go to voice mail this time or I'll think you disappeared, and we won't know where to send your contracts."

Trish didn't say good-bye but simply disconnected, the way Taylor often did.

Annie sat for a few minutes, staring into space, her space, the little cottage that she called her own, where she'd been so happy. She still didn't know what this news would entail. She only knew she had to change out of her date-worthy outfit and put on something that wouldn't make her sweat as if she'd just received a blockbuster TV network series offer that she'd have to tell John about.

She settled on a short black skirt, leggings, a red-and-white striped shirt, and chunky red jewelry — the same outfit she'd worn for the Christmas Eve party at the community center the previous year. Though no one had had the nerve to say so, she'd thought it made her look like a middle-aged woman trying to mimic a candy cane.

At breakfast that morning, she'd asked if anyone could give her a lift down to the ferry as her car was in Edgartown at John's. Harlin, one of their year-round renters, whose day job was a restaurant server and whose night job was leading a marimba band, offered. He told her he was heading over to work, that he wanted to grab as many hours as he could while some tourists wandered back for the holidays before they headed south for the winter. He was a nice young man who'd had his eye on Francine when he'd first met her. But with his erratic schedule, Annie knew it had been just as well that Francine had chosen Jonas; besides, Harlin seemed to have his pick of many girls, judging on the frequency with which he was out late, often missing the last *On Time* and staying who knew where.

As they rode across the channel, Annie couldn't believe she was thinking about her tenant and not about the deal that Trish had just unloaded on her.

Harlin brought her straight to John's door,

which was nice of him, especially since her legs had been a little numb since she'd received the call.

Restless greeted her with his usual enthusiasm, dispersing puffs of white fur all over her leggings.

Neither of John's daughters was around.

John, however, trundled down the stairs, looking far too handsome in his Sunday, off-duty attire, which included jeans and the pearl-gray sweater that she'd given him last Christmas because it matched his eyes.

He kissed her sweetly, perhaps not noticing that they both looked like they were stuck in last year, which might not have been such a bad place to be stuck, given their latest challenges.

"Do you have a list?" she asked once their embrace seemed it might lead to more, which would have meant the shopping list would be forgotten.

He tapped his temple. "It's all up here."

She laughed. "Are we shopping in Edgartown?"

"Later, maybe. First, let's go to Vineyard Haven. I think the girls like a couple of the shops there."

They buttoned their jackets, put on gloves and hats as the wind was picking up, and went on their way.

Rainy Day, Green Room, Bunch of Grapes, and more. In each store, they found perfect things for Abigail and Lucy, though John admitted he probably would not have chosen them.

"Teenage girls are easier to buy for if you've actually been one," Annie said as she leaned against him when he pulled out his debit card — again — to ring up another purchase, that one a book on archaeology, which had become Lucy's favorite topic since skeletal remains had washed up on the beach at the Inn the year before.

They even found a buffalo-plaid jacket for Restless, which they decided Earl would have a thing or two to say about because he had a shirt with the same design. They found a polished slab of island stone for Earl and Claire that had one-of-a-kind striations and would make a unique trivet for their dining table now that so many people were eating there again.

As they made their way in and out of stores, they found lots of baby things for Francine and Jonas; a pretty silver necklace with aqua sea glass for Francine; a collection of acrylic paints for Jonas; pink leggings for Bella with a pink parka that matched and had a fuzzy hood, and a couple of winter outfits because she'd outgrown last year's. Best of all, Annie knew that she was practically glowing because she was with John, having fun together before their married life began.

He told her he'd also ordered Lucy a new laptop to help make up for buying Abigail the car; he asked if he'd forgotten to tell her about that. Annie decided it would be childish of her to feel slighted.

Up and down Main Street, small brass bells rang at Salvation Army stands, and all the people on the sidewalks seemed to be smiling. They ran into so many who knew one or both of them (mostly John) that Annie could not keep track. It crossed her mind that Vineyard Haven was definitely not L.A., but she quickly buried the thought.

Before she knew it, it was three o'clock.

"Are we done?" she asked as they juggled more bags than they could carry and had laughed more often than Annie had ever laughed while Christmas shopping.

"We'd better be," John said, "because I'm hungry, and I think my card's about to pull the plug on my account. Can we go back to Edgartown to eat?"

"I already planned to. How about the Town Bar and Grill?"

He did not disagree.

On the way back to Edgartown, they sat in the truck and held hands as if they were the teenagers in the family. But when they reached the restaurant, he asked her to go in and get a table; he said he needed to make a quick stop at the station and that he'd be right back.

His request seemed strange, but Annie was alone inside the vestibule almost before she knew it. The host escorted her to a table for two.

While waiting, she perused the menu that she already knew. Anyone who'd lived on the island very long knew most of the selections at the restaurants, especially the year-round ones. She set it down and wondered if lunch would be the right time to share Trish's news. They'd had such a happy day. Would it add to the magic? Or break the spell? She wished she knew how he would react. Then again, she still wasn't sure how *she* would react once the reality set in, once she figured out how the deal would change her life, and if that's what she wanted. Or not.

If she was very rich, she could do lots of things. Didn't everyone wonder what they'd do if they won the lottery? She'd start by giving Kevin the money to either buy the house from Rex or build a new one. She could invest in turning the Inn into a wedding venue, which they'd talked about. It would require expansion, marketing, and a whole lot more, but it might be exciting. She could create college funds for Bella and the new baby. She would pay for Abigail and Lucy to go to college, too, if John would let her.

But her daydreams were abruptly interrupted when John sat down next to her.

"Hi," he said.

"Hi, yourself. That was fast."

He smiled.

The server brought champagne.

Annie adjusted herself in the chair, pulling her thoughts back to reality. "What's this?" she asked as the bubbly was being poured.

John shrugged. "I thought it was as good a time as any for our own Christmas celebration."

She smiled back. She'd been with John long enough to know that he had a romantic side, but he didn't usually show it while in public.

The server left, and John raised a glass. "To us."

They clinked.

He took a sip, set down the flute, then reached into his pocket. And presented Annie with a small box.

"For you," he said. "Merry Christmas."

She laughed. "It isn't Christmas yet."

He shook his head. "But this is overdue. Open it."

The box was wrapped in glossy red paper and tied with a white satin bow. She undid the ribbon and removed the wrapping. A leather cube stared back at her, the kind that jewelry — nice jewelry — came in. She looked at him again, smiled quizzically, and then opened it. Inside was a marquis-cut diamond. Not a huge one, but a gorgeous one. Surrounded by several small diamonds. And set in what looked like platinum. She sucked in her breath.

"Will you marry me?" he asked.

She stared at the ring. "But . . ." They had decided she would forgo an engagement ring. Rings were expensive. Rings were ostentatious. And yet . . . and yet . . . this one was so beautiful. "John . . . ," she uttered.

"It isn't new," he said. "Well, the big stone isn't new. It was my grandmother's. My mother's mother. I had it reset with a few extra diamonds for you. Try it on."

She raised her eyes. "The box is from Claudia's. Is that where you just went?"

He smiled. "I can't put anything over on you, can I? And yup, she reset it. I confess that I ran down the street to pick it up. I did not go to the station." He took the ring. Annie held out her hand, he slipped it on her finger. It was a perfect fit — of course it was. Annie had taken one of her birth mother's rings to Claudia's to be fitted to her last year; the jeweler must have kept the order and known Annie's exact size.

The almost newlyweds sat in the Grill, both of them fixated on Annie's hand. Then John leaned over and kissed her. And she kissed him back. And the servers and the other patrons erupted in applause because, in Edgartown, in winter, everyone knew John. And now they knew Annie, too.

CHAPTER 18

After leaving the restaurant, they went to John's to show Lucy and Abigail the ring. Lucy was home; Abigail, however, had brought her boyfriend to the boat, which perhaps was just as well. Lucy was nearly delirious at the sight of Annie's "swag," as she called it.

Once back on Chappy, she climbed into bed. In less than ten minutes she began tossing and turning, like the lyrics of an old record her mother used to play. She held up her hand and watched the diamonds twinkle like starlight; she wondered how she'd been so lucky to be loved by such an awesome man. Then she tossed again, this time staring at the ceiling, worrying about the conversation she'd have with Trish, and, furthermore, the one she needed to have with awesome John. She didn't think that being very rich was a priority for him, either, and the fact that Annie would be very busy would likely be upsetting.

Most of all, she was apprehensive about the phone call, because she had no idea what she should say to her editor. She tried to sort out the facts she already knew.

Fact one: If she could push away her utter panic long enough to write down every tidbit Trish could provide, at least Annie would be better equipped to list the pros and cons.

Fact two: The more she knew, the better chance she'd have to make a decision she'd want to live with.

Fact three: The better she felt about her decision, the easier it would be to tell John.

She thought about what to ask.

When would she be expected to start?

Should she finish the manuscript she'd already started?

How much time would she need to spend in California — and, as important — when? If it was in the summer, the Vineyard's crazy season, Annie would have to decline. She couldn't abandon Kevin, Francine, Earl, and everyone who depended on her to help make things happen. They were a team. They were the troops. And they needed one another.

She knew it was possible that she was merely too afraid of getting caught up in

182

that other world again, the one across Vineyard Sound, over in America. Where there were big stores and all kinds of businesses and high-rise apartments and planes and trains and traffic lights and streets with lots of lanes, some coming, some going. Where there were too many people. Most of whom called it the real world.

If Murphy weren't sleeping, she'd probably berate Annie for obsessing.

Annie sighed. She got out of bed, went to the kitchen, and made tea. She sat at her small table and wrote down her questions because she'd learned that middle-of-the-night thoughts often had a way of vanishing once the sun rose.

She thought she'd finalized her list when another idea surfaced: What if the series was expanded beyond a first season?

And then: What about her future ideas? Would they wind up being forty-five-minute episodes instead of three-hundred-page books? If so, was that what she really wanted?

She wrote those things down, too.

Then she went back to bed.

Morning came too early, as mornings often did. But now that Annie knew what to ask, and now that there would be eight hours before Trish called, she knew she needed to stop thinking about it. Wrapping and packing soap wouldn't help distract her, because she'd be in the workshop alone, tediously working, with nothing to do with her mind except let it wander. Instead, she needed to do something completely different.

It seemed like the perfect time to relocate the mouse, if there really was one, from the chef's room at the Inn. Dressed in old jeans and a sweater that her mother would have labeled "threadbare," she went to the workshop where she knew Kevin kept a few no-kill mousetraps. To date, Annie didn't think they'd needed them, but with the fields and woods and the beautiful meadow on the grounds, being prepared was a wise idea. After all, not all their guests would appreciate the Inn's theme of "Vineyard Natural" in that kind of natural state.

She wondered how her brother was doing, and if he'd pre tend to be speechless that Annie was tackling such a "manly" job as tracking down wildlife.

Then she laughed, because Kevin always made her laugh. Made her happy. Made her feel like she belonged.

She wondered what he'd have to say about Trish's offer.

"Stop!" she cried aloud, as she often did

when Murphy was not available.

Plucking two traps from the cabinet, she grabbed a pair of gloves and walked up to the Inn, went in the back door, and ran smack into Rex.

"Oh!" she eeked.

"Oh, yourself," he replied, then brushed past her and went outside.

Annie supposed she should have asked what he was doing on the property. But when she went into the kitchen, Rose was standing there, looking bereft.

"Rose," Annie said, "are you okay? Why was Rex here?"

Shaking her head a little, Rose simply slipped out of the room. For all Annie knew, they'd been having a romp upstairs in Rose's room.

Annie sighed. She wondered if all writers had problems reining in their imaginations.

Turning to the task at hand, she went into the chef's room, put on the gloves, then opened the door to the cabinet where Bella's things were stored. She removed the play mat and the dolls and the Fisher-Price stove that Earl had bought last Christmas; she reached up, grabbed a jar of peanut butter, and baited the traps. Then she stooped and set them inside the cabinet. Dread snaked through her body, as rodents weren't her favorite things. Quickly closing the door, she knew she should find a way to tape it shut so Bella couldn't open it. And she should post a notice that Bella's things had been moved to the reading room. Deciding to get a sheet of paper from the reception desk, she stood up. But Rose had returned. And she was standing in the way.

"He looks just like him," Rose said. "I know it isn't him, but he looks just like him. And I don't know what to do."

Annie quickly figured that the "he" referred to Rex, but whom he looked like remained a mystery. Though Annie no longer had the mental fortitude or, frankly, the interest to get involved, she knew that, as Rose's landlord, she should probably try to help.

So she pulled off the disposable gloves, tucked her hair behind her ears, and asked, "Shall we have a cup of tea?"

But Rose shook her head. "I don't want to see him, that's all. If he's going to spend time here at the Inn, I'll go back to Maine."

Annie leaned against the cabinet. She thought about Rose — a sweet woman, almost childlike. How many women her age (sixty-five? seventy?) who seemed to have few clothes and fewer belongings rented a room for the winter, played with a dollhouse, and collected rocks? Annie would have liked to help, but she really could not. Her list of priorities no longer had room for Rose — whom Annie would most likely never see again after her lease ended in May.

"I'm sorry you feel that way," Annie said. "I love having you here. You're a nice addition to the Inn. But Rex is my brother's brother-in-law. In a sense, he's family, so I'm afraid he might be around. It upsets me that he makes you uncomfortable. But even if I knew why, I don't know how I could help." She paused. "Are you sure you won't have tea?"

But Rose shook her head and darted toward the great room and upstairs to her room, which, sadly, was the response Annie expected.

It wasn't until she was headed down the hill back to her cottage that Annie realized she still didn't know why Rex had been at the Inn.

But as with Rose's decision to stay or go, Annie decided if it mattered, sooner or later she'd find out. Whether she wanted to or not.

Oddly, Annie's reaction to the situation left her feeling lighter. She knew she needed to set healthy boundaries more often, to avoid getting too involved with tenants' problems. It was against her nature, but ultimately would make her a better landlord. And she'd be able to save her energy for the people in her essential family.

She wondered if she should write that on a Post-it and stick it on her forehead: BRAIN SPACE RESERVED FOR ISLAND FAMILY ONLY.

Shaking off those thoughts, she knew that before forcing herself to go into the workshop to try and squeeze two weeks' worth of soap preparation into four days now, she had to review her list of questions for Trish. The woman would expect Annie to be prepared and professional. Which would be easier to do if each time she thought about it, a flock of butterflies didn't swarm inside her stomach.

She wished she knew what a blockbuster deal should include, and how other authors handled them. If only she had a Christmas angel like George Bailey had in *It's a Wonderful Life.* Then she could see what would happen to her and to those she loved if she took the deal or turned it down.

Most of all, Annie wished Kevin hadn't knocked on her door at exactly five minutes before three.

"Can't talk right now," she told him

quickly. "My editor's about to call. I need to be on my game."

His eyebrows elevated. "Anything wrong?"

She shook her head in a nervous way, the way that Rose had shaken hers. "I can't get into it right now. But I promise I will if you scram. Right. *Now.*" She gently pushed against him, defying his instinct to remain where he was. "Honest, Kevin, this is important."

"Maybe I'll wait outside and listen at the door."

"Kevin. Brother. Please. It's business." She pushed some more until he had one foot on her front porch and the other still in the living room. He was playing a game, but Annie was getting irritated.

"Just answer me one question. Please."

Her phone rang.

"No!" she squealed as if he'd stepped on her toes. She gave another push, that one not so gentle. And she slammed the door after him.

Sucking in a long breath, she returned to the table, picked up her notepad, and scanned her questions. On the fourth ring, she picked up the phone just before it clicked to voice mail.

"It's about time," Trish said.

"Sorry. I was fending off my brother."

Trish laughed. "I know what that can feel like. I have three of those."

"Brothers?" How strange, Annie thought, that she'd been working with Trish all this time and hadn't known she had siblings. They always seemed to have too many work-related topics to discuss.

"Yes. Three brothers. And two sisters. But on to you. Do we have a decision?"

"I have questions." She sat down and reviewed her list. One at a time, she posed them.

As usual, Trish did not mince words.

Annie would need to leave for L.A. right after the holidays. How long she would be there would depend on how quickly the script writing progressed and could be approved. "Six to eight weeks," Trish suggested.

Annie didn't comment that it was a long time for a newlywed to be separated from her husband. Trish might remind her that Annie wasn't twenty-five and this wasn't her first bridal rodeo.

"You said I'd have input on the choice of actors."

"Input, yes. And your opinion will be seriously considered. Like with a book cover, you won't get the final say, but if you make a solid case against someone, you might get your way."

Which probably meant she would not, because the sales and marketing teams were more adept at those things.

"What about final edits?"

"Those are up to the director. Though your opinion will be —"

"Seriously considered," Annie added, not holding back her sarcasm.

"Sorry, but that's how it is with film deals. What sets you apart is not only the hefty advance but also that you'll receive a nice percentage on reruns. I can't imagine why you — or any author — would pass this up, Annie."

Trish was right. Annie had been in the business of writing long enough to know that.

"I need to talk about my books," she said. "What will you want from me going forward?"

"You've just started another two-book contract. Naturally, we'll expect you to keep to those deadlines, though I think we can tag an extra month or two on to give you a breather."

"But what about the content? Should I write what I'd planned? Or will the series direct the way the plots go?"

There was no easy answer to that, and Annie knew it. But she and Trish went back and forth, bantering ideas of what might play well in print versus on camera. After an hour, Annie was exhausted.

"Okay," she said. "If you ask one more question I won't be able to think straight. Just tell me if there's a timeline to give them an answer. And do they know I'm about to get married?"

"They need to know no later than Christmas Eve."

"Seriously? Like anyone actually works between Christmas and New Year's?"

"It's a budget thing."

"I'll need to speak with Louisa," Annie said. "And show the contract to my attorney."

"Of course. I think Louisa will be back in town later this week if you want a face-to-face. But along with your attorney, I'm sure she'll give you the same answers. Like I said, we did this together. We both know I know my side of the business, and she's a cracker-jack at making sure legal issues are covered."

Annie couldn't very well zip off to Manhattan for a meeting with her agent. Not this week. Or next. But she'd settle for a phone call. So she promised Trish that she'd have her answer before Christmas. Then they rang off and Annie sat, musing, until

Kevin knocked again and stepped back into the living room and said he really had been listening at the door and that he didn't know what the hell was going on but he figured by the tone of things that she might need her brother.

He was right.

So she stood up and let him hug her, and then they sat, and she explained it all to him.

Kevin said "Jesus" about fifty times.

When Annie was finished he asked, "So. What are you going to do?"

"It's four thirty," she said. "I'm going to bed. I think better in a dark room with my eyes closed. In the meantime, promise me you won't breathe a word about this to anyone, okay? Not to Taylor, not to Earl, and, most of all, not to John. I have to think about how I'm going to tell him." It wasn't until then that she realized she should have told John first, the way he should have told her about the car for Abigail and about her weekly rental on the Cape. She supposed it would take time for both of them to know how to act like a married couple.

"Okay," Kevin said as he stood up from the table. "But make sure you understand this could be a one-shot deal. A chance to earn yourself a healthy stash for the future.

You might have some crazy months, but it might be worth it. The worst part is," he added with a wink, "only you can decide." He gave her a half a wave, then pointed to her left hand and said, "By the way, nice ring."

She glanced down at it, too, and smiled. When she looked up again, Kevin was gone.

And Annie went to bed to try and nap.

First thing in the morning, she would call Louisa.

CHAPTER 19

"I knew I'd hear from you when you were ready," Louisa said the next morning.

They talked for a while. Trish had been right; Louisa confirmed the fine points of the deal and encouraged Annie to say yes. "We don't know what the future holds," her agent said, "but this is very much a bird in hand. A very nice bird, I might add."

Her comments mirrored Kevin's. It's here. Take it. Because tomorrow — or ever — might not be as lucrative.

Before ending the call, Louisa said she was looking forward to the wedding. Originally, Annie had been pleased when Louisa accepted the invitation. But now she wondered how on earth she'd be able to focus on her marriage vows with thoughts of Hollywood in the room.

Skipping breakfast, she retreated to the workshop, where she wrapped and packed until mid-afternoon, when Lucy showed up.

"School's out," she said. "I figured you could use my artsy-craftsy talents." She held up her hands and wiggled her fingers.

Annie laughed. "You're an angel. But first, I need lunch."

Ten minutes later they were sitting at Annie's table, Lucy nibbling on a cookie, while Annie made do with a cheese sandwich, to which she added a few sprigs of fresh spinach so she could tell herself that she was eating healthy.

"I've been thinking," Lucy said. "Now that Francine and Bella are home, can Bella be the flower girl? My grandmother can make her a dress that looks like mine . . ."

Annie brushed a bread crumb from her lip. "Lucy, you're a genius! What a great idea."

Lucy grinned and rolled her eyes. "It's not like I invented the internet or anything. It seems pretty natural. Bella's kind of your granddaughter, isn't she?"

If she'd had a mouthful of sandwich, Annie might have choked. "Kind of," she replied, not mentioning that she preferred to be thought of as a kindly aunt, "if you don't take DNA into consideration. But, really, Lucy, it's a terrific idea. I can't believe I didn't think of it."

"Well, I know you weren't sure if they'd

be here, what with Francine's . . . condition."

There was never a moment when Annie didn't love having Lucy for company. "I was more concerned about a blizzard that would ground the planes. But, hooray, everyone is here. And I think Bella will adore being the flower girl. And she'll make the ceremony extra special."

"And she'll love the sparkles on her dress." Lucy set down the cookie, picked out a couple of chocolate chips, and popped them into her mouth. "Speaking of the wedding, I know you must be bummed because you wanted Abigail to redesign your dress. Her boyfriend's left the island, but she has to work on a final project for the semester . . ."

"Let's see how it plays out," Annie said, though in truth she was beginning to resign herself to looking ugly. Mostly because right then it just seemed easier.

"And before I forget," Lucy said, chattering on, "Gramma wants us to come to dinner tomorrow. My dad, too. They're dying to see your ring. She said she wants to try out recipes for the reception. She knows you're busy, but she said you have to eat anyway, so you might as well kill two birds with one stone, not that she'd want anyone to kill anything. I think the real reason she wants to do it is because she doesn't want Rex to upstage her cuisine."

Annie put her elbows on the table and rested her face in her palms. With a wedding that was supposed to be low key, she feared it was on its way to getting out of hand. Especially if a feud developed over the stainless-steel, ten-burner gas stove. But no matter how many gastronomic stars Rex had collected, she would not allow Claire to be slighted. Also, if Annie went to the house for dinner, maybe she could grab some time with John and tell him about Trish's deal. And get that resolved. Which, of course, sounded way more simple than she knew it would be.

"Tomorrow will be great," she told Lucy. "By then I'll need a break." She wolfed down the last of the sandwich. "But for now, let's think about soap. As long as you're here, I'm going to work you like a dog."

"Don't ever say that in front of Restless. You know he'd rather be sleeping than working."

By Wednesday night, thanks to Lucy's help, Annie was almost ready for the Fair. Dinner at Earl and Claire's turned into a merry event, with Lucy and John and Jonas and Francine. (Bella had an early supper, had said "Good night, everyone," and been put to bed.) Claire's "potential recipes" for the wedding turned out fantastic: roasted Camembert with an orange-cranberry compote; a spinach salad with feta cheese, pomegranates, and figs; garlic butter and herb seared scallops on riced cauliflower. And a hot chocolate bar, which was Lucy's idea. Everything was now neatly copied and pasted into Claire's iPad for safekeeping.

"I've made a two-part decision," Annie said after they feasted. "The first part is that I'm going to announce the second part without having consulted my groom. The second part is that Claire, I want you to decide on the menu. I want you to surprise us. I know whatever you do will be wonderful." Then she added, "As long as it isn't too much pressure on you."

Claire's cheeks turned pink and her eyes widened with . . . surprise? Happiness? Hesitation?

"Well, my goodness," she said. "I didn't expect that. I was only trying to . . ."

"To make our wedding special," Annie said. "And you will. I am absolutely confident."

John leaned back and rested his arm around Annie's shoulders. "I agree, Mom. This stuff is great. And if you do the food, it will take a lot off our minds."

Lucy said, "Seriously, Dad?" and everyone laughed because they all knew John's involvement with menus was limited to pasta and pizza, fish chowder, and beef stew, all of which were delicious but would be rather understated as a memorable wedding meal.

"You don't think Rex's creations would be more delectable?" Claire asked.

"Huh," John said. "I didn't even know he was invited. Did you invite him, Annie?"

She love-slapped his leg. "If he's here, of course he'll be invited. But he'll sit on a chair in the great room like everyone else. He will not be hovering in the kitchen."

Claire smiled.

Mission accomplished, Annie thought. And now she could check one more to-do off her list.

"Another thing," Annie added, "Lucy came up with a wonderful idea. Lucy, why don't you ask Francine if it will be okay? You remember, the thing with the sparkles?"

Lucy nodded fervently. "Bella! Can Bella be the flower girl? Annie wasn't sure if you guys would get here, but you are, so wouldn't it be fun? Gramma can make her a dress just like mine, can't you, Gramma?"

"In between shucking scallops and roasting cheese?" John asked.

"Oh, yes, it will be fun!" Francine said. "Bella will love it. And I can help you, Claire."

"You have classes, Francine," Claire said.

"The semester ends this week. I'll have lots of time." Then she turned back to Annie. "Which reminds me, I have a doctor's appointment Friday. I got in fast thanks to Claire's connections." Between everything else she did, Claire volunteered at the hospital two mornings a week. She said it kept her fit and healthy.

"So it's good news all around," Annie said. "Do you want me to watch Bella?" Annie did not — would never — let on that she hoped Francine would say no. Friday was setup day, so Annie would be traipsing to Edgartown with her plastic tubs and decorations for her booth. But Francine — and Bella — needed to come first.

"You'll be busy with the Fair stuff, won't you?" Jonas asked. "I can watch her. I need to come to the Inn and take a few of my paintings off the walls so, hopefully, the gallery can sell them this weekend. And while I'm there, can I finish framing a few more for Old Sculpin Gallery if I promise not to make a mess? There's lots of space for me to spread out in the great room. And Bella's never in the way."

"It's fine with me," Annie said. "You'll be doing us a favor, too, because I hate to leave the Inn unsupervised for long. I have no idea how long I'll be in Edgartown — I have so much more soap this year."

"That sounds perfect, Jonas," Francine added. "But I might be late. After my appointment I want to stop at the Kelley House to ask about doing an intern project for next term. Seeing as how we'll be here."

Earl's spikey eyebrows shot up. "So it's official? You're not going back to Minnesota?"

Francine laughed. "The baby's due the first week of May. The season starts three weeks later. As long as you still want me here to work this summer, I see no point in going to Minneapolis for a few weeks, then moving back."

Everyone smiled, even Annie, who was the only one who knew that the young couple's presence on the Vineyard might not be forever.

It was a lively evening, but Annie had no chance to talk to John about the TV series. After dinner, she brought Lucy and John back to the *On Time;* he suggested that Lucy come back after school the next day, stay overnight, and skip school Friday so that she could help Annie cart her wares over to set up at the Fair. He added, "If you want."

"Skip school?" Lucy cried. "Seriously, Dad? Wow. Isn't that an arrestable offense? If *arrestable* is a word?"

"It's a word," Annie chimed in, "and under the circumstances, it's an excellent one."

John said, "If it makes you feel better, I'll arrest both of you. Lucy for skipping, Annie for aiding and abetting. Or I could just turn my head and pretend I didn't know."

"Turn your head, Dad," Lucy said.

"Yes," Annie added. "Please do."

So it was settled. And Annie felt better that Lucy would be there to help pull her bit together, because right now she felt as if she were hauling around a huge weight made up of her career, her future, and her life. Which might even be an understatement.

In the morning, when she slogged into the workshop, Annie was reminded that she wasn't the only one whose mind was feeling heavy; Kevin sat on a stool by the soap-wrapping counter, his face set in a grim expression, his hazel eyes downcast and troubled.

"I'll wrap; you pack," she told him.

"Huh?"

"If you need to talk, I promise to listen. Lucy will be here after school, but in the meantime, I have to keep moving or I'll never be finished in time."

"Right. I'll pack."

Annie nodded and pointed to several stacks of soap she'd already wrapped and then to the plastic totes. "Cranberries and cream in the pink tubs; Scotch pine and vanilla in green ones; snowdrops and winterberries in red ones. They're the holiday ones, so they're the most important. Whatever I can finish in my regular line will go in the clear totes."

He shrugged. "Sure."

She slid a stack of bars that were already wrapped toward him. "And make sure they stand up nice and straight. If the edges bump, they become seconds. And then they go in a cardboard carton."

"Because cardboard's cheaper?"

"No. Because I ran out of colors for the totes." She thought that might make her brother laugh, but it did not.

Annie took a large sheet of beeswax, spread it on the counter, and, using a T-square, sliced the precise measurement needed to wrap each bar tightly. Kevin dragged a few cartons of kitchen cabinets near Annie's worktable, set the totes on top, and carefully began to place the soaps into their color-coordinated bins.

Annie smiled. Leave it to her brother to make the chore easier by constructing a waist-high addition — no bending required — to the assembly line.

"Okay," she said. "What's going on?"

"Not much. Except that my wife and I are going to be homeless."

So Taylor had finally told him. Annie hoped she also hadn't mentioned that she'd told Annie.

"Because?" she asked.

"Because Father Winsted left the house to Rex. It's all buttoned up and legal in the old man's will. And because, technically, Taylor has been trespassing for years."

"Wow."

"No kidding. When she told me, I got pissed at Rex. I figured he was trying to pull a fast one. But . . ." He grabbed four more bars and aligned them in their proper spots.

"Sounds like a bit of a pickle. What's going to happen?"

"Rex wants to sell. He wants to open another restaurant, and he needs the money."

Annie secured another piece of cranberries and cream in the beeswax, then wrapped it in a sheet of red netting. "Can you buy him out?" She knew that her brother had assets. Apparently, unlike his wife.

Kevin was silent for a moment. Then he emitted a short snort, like a bull before he charged. "Hardly. He wants a million four. I've fixed lots of things to make the place livable, and it has a little acreage, but a million four?" He snorted again.

"You have assets. Your condos in the city. Can't you make a deal with him? Like offer him one in a trade — assuming he plans to move back to Boston? Or can you sell a couple and buy another house on Chappy?" Annie hadn't seen Kevin's condos, but she thought he had three that he rented. Knowing her brother, she assumed they would be worth something substantial.

He plunked a bar into a tub a little too hard. He removed it, held it up, then tossed it into the cardboard carton. "Sorry," he muttered. "I appreciate your thought, but I don't own them anymore."

"What?" Annie knew that when he'd sold his business, he'd given the money to his former wife. But as for the condos . . .

"I gave them to Meghan," he said.

Annie was startled. "What?" she asked again.

He waved a hand. "I didn't tell you, but

my sweet ex-wife decided to sue me for negligence in her accident. She said she'd settle for the condos. I didn't want to bother you about it, because it happened when you were on your book tour, and I knew you and John were planning your wedding, and I didn't want to be Mr. Wet Blanket."

Stopping what she was doing, Annie moved around the worktable and leaned against it, facing her brother. She folded her arms. "God, Kevin, I wish you'd told me."

"You couldn't have done a damn thing. Neither of us could. I didn't have the head-space to fight her. I couldn't go through all that guilt again. And I have Taylor. I have a new life. I felt bad that Meghan doesn't . . . or, rather, didn't. After I signed over the condos, I found out she has a boyfriend. An attorney. The one who talked her into suing me." He snapped the lid onto a tub he'd filled. "I guess it goes without saying that I'm a schmuck."

"Kevin," Annie said in what she hoped were soothing tones, "you are not even close to being a schmuck."

He shrugged, snorted again. "Well, it's done. Taylor and I were left with nothing but her house, or so I thought."

"Does she know?"

"Sure. She told me it wasn't worth the

fight. That we can find a place to rent. She said at some point we'll all start getting some profits from the Inn, and in the meantime, she'll go back to work as a caretaker. She said she kind of misses doing that." He laughed. "I guess she didn't marry me for my money, huh?"

Annie waved a hand around the workshop. "Maybe you can turn this place into a two-family; one level for you and Taylor, one for Francine and Jonas."

"It's kind of small for that, isn't it? Besides, I don't think the selectmen would allow it. It was hard enough to get them to agree we could convert it from an outbuilding to residential space. And they made it clear that once I put together our new workshop over by the meadow, we've maxed out the buildings for a three-acre parcel."

She wanted to be able to tell him not to worry. She wanted to say she could help. But Annie had only recently been able to start saving money from her book sales, and she didn't have enough to buy her brother a house on the Vineyard. Unless she signed the deal for the TV series. Then there would be plenty.

By the time Lucy arrived, Kevin was long gone. He'd said that he'd keep Annie posted and asked her not to tell Taylor that he'd shared the Rex crisis with her.

Annie vowed to herself to wait until after the Fair to think about her problems — and everyone else's. At least the wedding wouldn't be a problem. She hoped.

Fortunately, Lucy often helped with Annie's soapmaking venture, including the fairs, so she didn't need instructions. While they worked, she chatted about school and her boyfriend, Kyle, and the cool classes she'd have next term (specifically, "Principles of Green Engineering" because, in addition to her interest in archaeology and genealogy, she wanted to become part of "framing the earth for the future"). Annie was awed by Lucy's confidence to try new things. It was going to be great fun to see what vocation she eventually landed in.

Francine and Bella stopped by at dinnertime with veggie burgers on homemade rolls; Annie made a bow out of red ribbon and tied it in Bella's hair.

"One for new baby, too," Bella said. "Please, Ammie?" She added a small giggle, which got them all laughing because since Bella had begun talking in short sentences, she seemed to love sharing everything her little brain was thinking.

As Francine started to leave, Annie said,

"I wish I could go with you tomorrow. But the doctor will take good care of you."

Francine nodded with what Annie hoped was assurance.

"And good luck at the Kelley House," she added.

They shared good-night hugs, then Annie and Lucy worked until each bar of soap was wrapped, packed, and ready to go. Finally, Annie declared it was time for bed; in the morning, they'd record their inventory, load the Jeep, then go to Edgartown.

They turned off the lights in the workshop and went to the cottage.

Annie tucked Lucy in on the sofa, then retreated to the bedroom. But as she crawled under the comforter, her text alert dinged. It was Trish. Again.

TWO WEEKS FROM TOMORROW! the message read.

Annie smiled, until she realized that chances were, Trish wasn't referring to Annie's wedding: two weeks from tomorrow also was the deadline to sign the contracts for the blockbuster deal.

She pulled the comforter over her head and waited for sleep to come.

CHAPTER 20

It's time. I've waited long enough.

I'm nervous and excited, but I have everything I need.

I have no idea what's going to happen. Maybe everything. Maybe nothing.

I only know it's time for me to try.

CHAPTER 21

Friday, December 10
Christmas in Edgartown

The sky was soft pewter with a low layer of clouds, but the weather folks promised it would clear up by evening. They also said that tomorrow would be brisk but sunny, perfect for the traditional Main Street parade, for the festive open houses throughout the village, and for shoppers to flock to the Holiday Fair.

At the school gymnasium, a flurry of motion and commotion had already begun: artisans bustled in all directions, some wheeling dollies loaded with cartons, bags, and all kinds of totes; others set up racks and stacks of their exquisite handmade crafts. Chatter and clatter echoed off the concrete walls, buoyed by a classic rendition of "Jingle Bells" that scratched through the old PA system. Annie loved the merriment and energy that the weekend brought to the island.

Carrying a tote of her special Christmas soaps, she followed the chart and located her booth. But when she turned to direct Lucy to follow, the teenager wasn't behind her. With a bevy of friends, Lucy's lively social skills mirrored those of her grandfather and her father, which meant she was often sidetracked at events such as this.

Annie set down her purse and opened the tote; light scents of Scotch pine and vanilla wafted out. She smiled with determination to put all the drama in her life aside and concentrate on doing her part to make sure the Fair was successful and fun.

"Look what I found!" Lucy's voice broke into Annie's thoughts. The girl wielded a dolly that she'd either borrowed or swiped; the rest of the totes they'd stuffed into the Jeep were piled on it.

Setting down a small bundle of freshly clipped evergreen boughs — a last-minute decorating idea Annie had when they'd been dashing out the door to her cottage — she helped Lucy unload the array of goods. When the totes were empty, they slid them under the cloth-draped tables, and Lucy maneuvered the dolly back through the crowd, presumably returning it to wherever she'd found it.

Then Annie started to create small displays of her fragrant treasures so that they'd look inviting and gift-worthy. She stacked the Scotch pine and vanilla in the shape of a Christmas tree and adorned it with a few of the greens. Then she grouped the snowdrops and winterberries into three pillars of varying heights to resemble large candles and sprinkled deep red berries around the bases. She was nearly finished when Lucy came running back toward the booth, her long braid bobbing over her shoulder. Surprisingly, Jonas was sprinting alongside her. His face was ashen, his expression, panicked.

"Where's Bella?" he shouted to Annie above the noise.

Annie frowned. Wasn't Jonas supposed to be on Chappy, babysitting for Bella? "She's with you." Annie paused. "Isn't she?"

His eyes squeezed shut, his shoulders dropped. "One minute she was next to me . . . ," he cried, shaking his head. "The next minute she was . . . gone."

Annie thought the noise in the gym must have prevented her from hearing him correctly. But as she studied his face, she knew that something was very wrong. The hubbub around her swooned into slow motion; she leaned against the table of snowdrops and winterberries.

"What do you mean, she's 'gone'?" Her voice was softer than she had expected.

"It's true," Lucy said, folding her arms, tightening her stance as if she, too, had lost her footing.

"I can't find her," he cried, and slumped onto a folding chair in the booth.

"Tell me what happened," Annie said. "And make it fast." In order to think straight, she needed facts.

"It's not like she could walk away." Lucy jabbered because that's how she reacted when she was nervous or scared. "Bella's a toddler. She toddles. She doesn't walk." She'd planted her hands to her hips and swayed back and forth now, her jaw stiff, her eyes wide.

Annie regained her bearings, pulled a bottle of water from her bag, and handed it to Jonas. "Drink," she said. "Then take a breath." She thought she sounded relatively calm for someone whose heart was racing as if she were the captain of the leading keelboat in the Edgartown Regatta.

Jonas drank. He breathed.

"Did she come to Edgartown with you? Did she slip away from you here at the school?" If Bella was there, she should not be hard to find. Maybe someone would recognize her. Or maybe she'd ask a friendly face if she knew *Ammie* and Lucy.

He shook his head.

"At the Inn," he croaked. "I was in the great room, framing. She was on her play mat at the other end, talking to her dolls like she likes to do." He stopped. He struggled for another breath. He drank again. "I'd put her down there to make sure she wouldn't get near the knife I use to cut the canvasses."

Annie crouched in front of him and put a hand on his knee.

"I was busy," he continued. "I went into the media room to change a couple of pictures and I wound up reframing them in there . . . . I left her for maybe ten minutes . . . . Oh. God. I'm such a jerk." His voice cracked. His chin dropped to his chest, reminding Annie of the sensitive young man he'd been when she'd first met him and he'd apologized that his grandfather was making her move out of her rental house because of him.

"What happened next?" She pressed her hand against his knee more firmly.

"I realized she was awfully quiet. She likes talking to her dolls, you know? But she'd stopped." He put his face in his hands. "I went back to the great room. And she was gone."

"How hard did you look?" Lucy demanded. "Did you check her room upstairs?" Much to Francine's terror, Bella now knew how to navigate the big staircase on her own.

"It's the first place I went. She wasn't under the bed. Or in the closets."

An alarm went off in Annie's mind. "Did you look in the chef's room, where her toys used to be?" she asked. Could Bella have peeled off the tape and opened the cabinet? Did a mousetrap snap down on her fingers? But if so, wouldn't Jonas have heard her cry?

"I checked. The cabinet's sealed. I even looked where you moved her stuff, which was lame because it's not like she could read the note you left."

"Did you call my grandmother?" Lucy asked. "Maybe she picked her up?"

"I did. She didn't. I didn't say that Bella's missing. I just asked if Francine asked her to pick her up. Claire said no but offered to come and get her. I said it was no problem, that I only called because I couldn't remember if Francine had asked." His eyes pleaded for help. And forgiveness. "I didn't want to upset Claire. I didn't tell her that Francine has my car. That hers is still in Minnesota."

Even in shock, Jonas had thought of others.

"How did you get here?" Annie asked.

"I ran to the *On Time*. Then up here from the pier."

They stood and sat, not speaking as, overhead, "Jingle Bells" persisted.

"I can't call Francine," he added quietly. "She's pregnant."

That's when Annie knew they had to act.

She stood up, grabbed her purse, and told Jonas to get up. "We're going to find her," she said, and turned to Lucy. "Run over to Winnie's booth. See if someone's there. Ask if they can unpack for us. We should be back before the gym closes. Then come outside. And hurry."

Clutching Jonas's arm, Annie zigzagged around people, cartons, and dollies until they reached the side door. As soon as they stepped outside, she called John.

"Bella's lost," she said, then spewed out the news. "She must be at the Inn. But we don't know where. I'm sure she's okay, but can you help?"

John replied in the authoritative voice she'd often heard when he was on duty. "When a two-year-old's missing," he said, "we take it seriously. Especially in this case, with the Inn so close to the water."

Annie wished he hadn't said that. She hadn't yet thought about the path that led straight from the patio down to the beach. She hadn't thought about how Bella had trailed Francine and Annie and probably Jonas, too, down that path countless times to walk along the shore or have a picnic on the beach. She hadn't thought about how every time they'd gone there, they'd had to remind Bella to keep a safe distance from the water.

And she didn't want to think about those things now, either.

"Point taken," she replied curtly. "We're heading to Chappy. Lucy's with us. I'll keep you posted." She rang off before he could say anything else she didn't want to hear.

They reached the Jeep; Annie started it and let it run to get the heat cranked up and circulating. A damp chill blanketed the afternoon; the sky had grown grayer since they'd been in the school. It would be dark soon; it was, after all, almost winter solstice, the shortest day of the year. Chappaquiddick was farther east than Boston, so darkness came even sooner there. In reality, Annie knew it was only a couple of minutes sooner, but at this time of year, she often felt as if she lived in Iceland, where the longest amount of daylight was something like four hours.

Tapping her fingers on the steering wheel, she stared out the windshield. She saw two women dressed as elves with pointed ears, green felt hats, and strings of multicolored, mini flashing lights dangling around their necks rush past while singing "Santa Claus Is Coming to Town."

Annie turned her head away. She put the gearshift in drive, wheeled over to the exit, and parked, blocking access. The engine idled, her foot twitching with impatience to step down on the gas. Next to her, Jonas rubbed his hands together. Over and over.

"There's an extra pair of mittens in the glove box," she said.

He opened the latch and slipped them on. He must have been too upset to think of gloves when he'd raced over from Edgartown.

Finally, Lucy sprinted out the doors and jumped into the back seat. She announced that Winnie's sister-in-law, Barbara, would finish setting up the booth.

Annie barely heard her as she slalomed the Jeep around cars and SUVs and pickups, then fishtailed off the school grounds, aimed for the *On Time,* and hoped that the little ferry was in its berth on this side of the channel, because she had no patience for that, either.

Once out of the lot, she stomped down on the gas pedal. The three of them stayed silent, as if speaking might slow them down. But as soon as Annie reached Main Street, where she needed to turn right, the traffic was backed up. Of course it was. The fact that Christmas in Edgartown had begun gave rise to flashbacks of July and August.

"Crap," Lucy expelled from the back seat.

After only a minute, her blood pressure surely rising, Annie saw a chance to sneak between a Volvo SUV and a station wagon dressed up as a reindeer with antlers on either side of the roof and a big plastic nose on the grill that was lit up bright red. A speaker from the passenger window blasted the old Gene Autry tune, "Rudolph, the Red-Nosed Reindeer." Annie wondered if anyone celebrated the holiday like ordinary people anymore.

Then she wondered if Bella would be there to celebrate Christmas with them this year . . . to open piles of presents from her island family beneath the tree. A tiny lump rose in Annie's throat. She prayed that Bella was at the Inn, that she was warm, that she wasn't hungry. Maybe she'd been hiding from Jonas, thinking she was playing a game.

Yes, Annie thought. *I'm going to believe that. For now.*

After inching the few feet to Peases Point Way North, Annie took a quick left toward the shortcut to the *On Time.* But traffic was backed up there, too, as the driver of an oversized van was attempting to parallel park.

"Jonas and I should make a run for it," Lucy said. "We'll get to the ferry before you will."

"Go," Annie replied. "Maybe someone on the other side can bring you to the Inn."

Both Lucy and Jonas were out of the vehicle before Annie finished her sentence. And she was left to continue drumming her fingers on the steering wheel, trying to stop her thoughts from going into overdrive.

222

CHAPTER 22

As Annie rounded the corner and tore into the clamshell driveway, she was greeted by an eerie glow of floodlights permeating the darkness, filtered by a veil of fog that had rolled in.

She turned off the engine, not knowing in which direction to head first. Four police vehicles were already at the Inn — one from Massachusetts State, one from Oak Bluffs, and two from Edgartown, one of which was the one John most often used. She took a deep breath and dropped her forehead onto the steering wheel. Thank God *he* hadn't been held up in traffic.

Then a thought swept over her like beach sand on a windy day: if the cops were there and the floodlights were on, that meant they hadn't found Bella yet. She started to tremble.

Stop it, Murphy's voice bellowed through the haze. *Get the hell out of the car and find out what's going on.*

Annie closed her eyes. Tried to compose herself. Then she grabbed her phone, got out of the Jeep, and hotfooted it toward the back door of the Inn, praying for strength of mind and body, then praying that she wouldn't need to keep praying, because everything was going to be fine.

But as she stepped onto the patio that led to the back door, she nearly bumped into a poster board standing on an easel. *BELLA,* the thick black marker letters read. AGE: 2 YRS. 4 MOS. H: 32.5" WT: 21.8 LBS. LAST SEEN: PALE BLUE HOODIE SWEATER, DARK BLUE PANTS.

The information had come quickly; John must have contacted Bella's pediatrician. But as disturbing as the poster board read, it was the reference to the sweater Claire had made that made Annie feel as if hands had clamped tightly around her throat. The sweater, and the omissions: mittens. Claire had knit matching mittens that she'd attached to the cuffs with a thin braid of yarn. Had they become detached? Or had whoever scribed the poster simply not known that they were there? Annie loosened the collar of her parka. And then, her text alert went off. Her eyes shot to the small screen.

It was from Francine.

Oh, God, Annie cried inside. *Oh, God, oh, God, oh, God.*

Where was Francine? Did she already know?

Annie squinted at the text.

WHAT'S GOING ON? Francine had typed. I'M AT EARL AND CLAIRE'S. NOBODY'S HERE. LOOKS LIKE CLAIRE WAS MAKING DINNER? HALF-MADE STUFF IS ON THE COUNTER. JONAS ISN'T ANSWERING HIS PHONE. IS ALL OK?

Annie shoved the phone into her pocket. She knew she needed information before she could respond.

"Annie?" It was John's voice, coming from behind.

She turned. "Did you . . . is she . . . ?"

He went to her, hugged her, kissed her cheek. Then he stepped back and put his hands on her shoulders. "We'll find her. So far, we don't see any signs that she went down to the water, so that's good. We've got a team there, just to be sure. And a pack of volunteers is on the way."

Her angst began to settle. "Things are happening fast . . ."

"Bella's a little kid," he said with a small smile.

Which, of course, said it all. Annie had lived on the Vineyard long enough to know that neighbors watched out for neighbors. And when anyone needed anyone . . . well, more than once, she'd witnessed islanders gathering to help. Especially when a child was involved.

"My mom's in the kitchen making food," John continued. "No surprise, right? A couple of the OB cops are combing every nook and cranny inside the Inn. Lucy's with them. My dad put together a team to search the meadow. Your year-round tenants are part of it. Two single guys and a couple, right?"

Annie nodded, grateful that the tenants had joined in.

"Linc's outlining the grid search for them," John added.

Annie knew that "Linc" was Lincoln Butterfield, an Edgartown detective, like John. Linc and his wife were good friends, too. She also knew that Earl would have known that the meadow was a prime spot to search, because Bella loved to walk among the flowers and was too young to understand that they weren't blooming in December. "Where's Kevin?"

"One of the cops said he saw Kevin and Taylor walking into the Wharf. You want me to text him?"

She wrapped her arms around herself. Her

226

brother and Taylor would no longer care about being out for dinner once they heard the news. "Yes. Please. They'll want to help. And Francine just texted me from your parents'. I have to answer her before she shows up here and gets even more scared than she'll already be."

"Jonas told me he didn't tell her."

"He's worried about the baby. And Francine, too . . . ." She stared at John's black leather boots, their typical high polish now scraped and dusty from the sand down at the beach. Where he'd been looking for Bella.

"Go to my folks' house," he said. "Tell Francine what's going on. Bring her back here. She needs to be part of this, or she'll never forgive us."

Annie knew he was right. She lifted her eyes to him. "I love you," she said. "In case I don't say it often enough."

He hugged her again, kissed her forehead that time. "I love you, too. So much." He pulled away. "Now go. If we find her while you're gone, I'll text you right away."

She nodded and trotted back to the Jeep, aware of the sound of John's boots jogging away, most likely heading back toward the water. Quickly, she texted Francine: ON MY WAY TO YOU. BEEN A LONG DAY SETTING

UP AT THE FAIR, SO MAKE TEA! Annie had no intention of having tea, but she thought the text might deflect any worry Francine might be having.

She felt strong now, able to face her. But as soon as Annie backed out of the driveway, she paused to let another vehicle pull in: it was the pickup that the police kept at the station on Chappy. And it was towing the rescue boat.

Her heart dropped to her gut.

Somehow, Annie made it to Earl and Claire's with her game face in place.

As she pulled into the driveway, she called up to the sky. "Murphy, if you're there, I need a good dose of your courage."

I've got your back, my friend, came the reply.

Which was exactly what Annie needed to hear. What she didn't need, however, was when she drew close to the house and saw Francine standing outside on the deck. Suddenly Annie felt sick.

As Francine quick-stepped toward the vehicle, Annie braked and turned off the engine. She wanted to be outside, facing her, so that the first thing she could do would be to give Francine a hug. It wasn't much of a plan, but it would be a start.

"What the heck's going on?" Francine asked, her petite body rigid, visibly braced for bad news. "I know something's wrong. Is it Earl? Is it Claire? Are they okay?"

"Oh, honey, they're fine," Annie replied and took her into her arms. "I'm sorry if you were worried."

"Of course I was. There's food on the counter, but no one's here. Not even Jonas and Bella." She paused. "And where are *they*, by the way?"

Annie rubbed Francine's shoulders the way that John had rubbed hers. "Let's go in the house. I hate talking outside when it's dark. I'm always afraid of getting dive-bombed by bats." She knew her comment wasn't funny, but, again, if she kept things light, it might soften the blow she was about to deal.

Once they were in the kitchen, neither of them made a move to sit down.

"So what's up?" Francine asked. "And don't tell me 'nothing.' Look at this place."

She was right. Claire had left what looked like the makings of eggplant Parmesan strewn everywhere: eggplant, already sliced; a canning jar of marinara sauce already opened; slices of mozzarella already shredded; a hunk of Parmesan cheese partially shaved into a pile. Yes, Annie thought, the mess was out of character for Claire, who no doubt had flown out the door.

Annie tried not to glance at Francine's rounded belly. Her information would be harder to deliver if she thought about the new baby in there.

"We don't really know if anything's wrong," she started slowly. The next line was going to be the toughest. If only John had texted to say they'd found her. If only . . .

But Annie knew she couldn't wait any longer. She tried to keep her voice steady as she looked directly into Francine's eyes and took Francine's hands in hers. "But we can't seem to find Bella."

Francine must have taken off her coat when she'd first arrived at the house; the white alpaca scarf that Annie had bought for her birthday last year was still looped around her neck; she still wore the matching beret.

Annie stepped closer as if the young woman might need steadying.

"What do you mean? She's with Jonas. Isn't she?"

"She was, honey. Come on, let's sit at the table." Annie reached out to guide Francine to a chair.

Francine shook off Annie's hand. "No!

Where's Bella? For God's sake, be straight with me!" Her cheeks flared Merlot red, her large eyes narrowed.

"She's . . ." And then Annie had no idea what to say. Why couldn't she — the great wordsmith, the one who made up stories about people and lives, good and bad, every single goddamn day — why couldn't she come up with the right words when they really were needed? She stared at the counter instead of Francine. "It seems she wandered off. She was at the Inn with Jonas . . . well, you know that part . . ."

Francine shook a finger at Annie's face. "Are you saying Jonas *lost* her?"

Before Annie could explain that he'd gone into the media room for just a few minutes and when he came back Bella was gone, Francine stormed into Earl's study and returned with her coat, shoving first one arm, then the other, into the sleeves as she tromped out the back door. "I'm going over there. *Now.*"

"I'll drive," Annie said, grateful that she didn't get pushback.

On the way to the Inn, Annie realized she'd never seen Francine angry; the young woman seemed to hold her anger inside, perhaps letting it fester, perhaps not. For as well and as long as Annie had known her, she couldn't be sure. Then again, after their friendship had blossomed, Francine often said she hadn't been as happy as she was now since before her mother died. Until she'd come to the Vineyard, she'd gone through an empty, lonely time, which had been complicated by toting a baby in a basket.

After settling in on the island, maybe she'd been too happy to be angry about anything.

Annie would have bet that Francine was angry now. Irate, furious, livid at Jonas, the father of her unborn baby. She didn't speak on the short trip. She simply sat as rigid as when she'd been standing, as if she were afraid that, if she moved a muscle, she would erupt, a volcano on Chappaquiddick, splaying boiling lava across the dunes and the meadows and the ponds.

Before turning onto North Neck Road, Annie eyed her phone; still no text from John. She remembered when Murphy's twins had disappeared; they'd been around four years old. Texting was in its infancy back then; neither Murphy nor her husband, Stan, had cell phones that provided it or software that could have tracked them. A few neighbors had gathered to help in the search; Annie had been the one who'd found them. It was springtime; they were under the forsythia bush, "camping out," as the older twin, Danny, expressed it. The branches of full, yellow blossoms had grown straight up, then arced down to the ground, creating a near perfect dome that left plenty of space underneath for two small boys to disappear into with their Matchbox cars and a bag of Skittles. "We weren't hiding," Danny, who now, amazingly, was about to become the astrophysicist, had explained matter-of-factly.

It had been a happy ending. But it had been in the daytime, not in the dark. And the suburban home in Brookline didn't have the ocean in the backyard.

In the distance, the floodlights smoldered through the fog. "Lots of people are looking for her," she said softly. "I think John called every police officer and every islander he knows."

Francine didn't respond.

And then the road curved and the vehicles appeared: scores of pickups, SUVs, and vans were parked willy-nilly on both sides of the one-lane dirt road, as if it were August and this was the ferry queue.

Beside her, Francine shifted ever so slightly.

Annie aimed the Jeep toward a small aisle

between the vehicles.

"Stop the car," Francine suddenly said. "I can walk faster than you can drive."

Annie stopped and let her out.

Francine crossed in front of the Jeep, her head straight, her legs fast-clipping in mechanical motion, a soldier advancing to the front line, propelled by determination.

Annie wilted. She puffed out her cheeks and started to cry the pent up emotion that had been building since Jonas arrived at the school and asked if Bella was with her.

"Oh, God," she said to no one in particular, not to Murphy, not even to God, really. Then she knew that she, too, must propel herself forward. But while Francine was moving on adrenaline, Annie needed to march ahead with common sense. A level head. With a priority to support Francine . . . no matter what.

So she continued to drive on to the Inn. There were no spaces left in which to park the Jeep, so she stopped in the middle of the road. Let the others figure out how to get around her. She had work to do.

CHAPTER 23

It was so easy, it's sick.

But it happened fast. Like I was dreaming.

How was I supposed to know she'd be right there — sitting all alone, playing with her dolls — with no one else around?

Is it any wonder I couldn't resist?

I'd left the toys and stuff in the car. I wanted to see if she was there before I brought them to her.

"Bella!" I whispered as I bent down, all the while grinning, not believing she was really there. "I've been looking for you." Then, before I knew I was going to say it, I said, "We're going for a little ride! Okay?"

She didn't say no. To be honest, she didn't say anything. She looked at me as if she were a little confused, but then she held her arms out, so I picked her up.

Then I spotted what I figured must be her jacket and hat and stuff hanging up near the back door, so I grabbed them, and off we went!

I didn't get a car seat because I really just wanted to see her. I thought that would be enough. Until I walked into the Inn, and there she was . . . mine for the taking.

When we got into the van, I snapped the regular seat belt around her and gave her one of the books I bought her. And she was fine. I went slow so she wouldn't be scared, and, anyway, once you're outside Edgartown, there's not much traffic in December.

And, like I said, it felt like I was dreaming.

I didn't notice till we got to the cabin that she'd brought her teddy bear. I was glad because it would be nice for her to have.

Wow. This day turned into such a surprise. I'm not sure what to do next. I only wish that she'd stop asking me where Mommy is.

CHAPTER 24

The number of vehicles seemed to have doubled in the few minutes Annie was gone. She hoofed from the street to the back door of the Inn again, assuming — correctly — that Francine had gone there first. She was standing, still rigid, at the marble-topped island, where a large platter now sat. She'd no doubt seen the poster on the patio; perhaps it had added to her trancelike demeanor.

Fixings for sandwiches were on the counters along with various rolls of wax paper, plastic, and foil, all of which must have arrived from numerous refrigerators in numerous households on Chappy because they'd shown up so fast.

Claire stood with one arm over Francine's shoulders, holding her close. Annie glanced around: two large urns perked aromatic coffee; a couple of stainless-steel pots gently bubbled on the stove, frothing from long strings of spaghetti. A small gaggle of women bustled about, stirring pasta, pouring cream into small pitchers, slicing bread. She recognized Georgia Nelson, the hospice nurse, and Georgia's sister, Lottie, from the community center. Dot was there, too, along with Judy, Ellen, and Sami — all Chappy ladies, essential strands of the fabric that made up the community. They shuttled back and forth to the great room, carrying plates and napkins, mugs and utensils to the expansive dining table, making ready for the searchers, an unofficial army of Vineyard volunteers, comprising anyone who arrived.

"Where's Jonas?" Francine — her jaw stiff, her teeth gritted — asked Claire.

"I don't know. But Lucy's upstairs with two police officers from Oak Bluffs. They're going through every nook and cranny, honey. They'll find her." Claire must have needed to believe that Bella was somewhere inside the Inn, safely under cover, not lost in the fog or out on the water.

Annie looked away; she could not bear the fear exuding from Francine. It was difficult enough to maintain her own self-control.

"Why don't you text him, honey?" Claire said. "He's awfully upset."

Francine neither nodded nor shook her

head. She simply said, "I'm going to the beach."

"I'm right behind you," Annie said. Then she asked Claire if anyone had checked the cottage. "Bella knows the way. She might have gone there looking for Francine. Or for me."

"Even if they did, you might as well check it again. Is it open?"

"Probably. We were hauling stuff out of the workshop for the Fair, and God knows I'm not the greatest at locking up. So . . ." She didn't finish her thought; they had to get moving.

Claire let go of Francine and said to pass the word that coffee and hot food would be ready soon and to come get it whenever they wanted. Then she got back to work shucking scallops.

Annie grabbed a flashlight from a cabinet by the back door and led Francine outside.

"If anything happens to Bella," Francine said, her voice husky with anger, "I will never forgive Jonas."

There was no need to ask why she blamed him. Annie was trying not to, but . . .

They headed toward the cottage with purpose, stepping blindly through the fog, the flashlight of little use, so Annie shut it off. Spotlights had been added in the direction of the meadow, but it was like peering through a sheet of the wax paper in the kitchen — the scene was hazy, surreal, Stephen King–ish. She suddenly remembered her grandmother complaining of hazy vision when she'd had cataracts; Annie wondered if this was how Gram had been seeing the world.

Next to her, Francine shuddered. Annie resisted the urge to reach out to stabilize her. She did not want to be overly protective and have Francine pull away from her again.

More than anything, Annie wanted to tell her that she hoped, no matter what, that Francine would forgive Jonas. She wanted to tell her there was no need to speculate on what he had or hadn't done, and that not being able to forgive a loved one only made life harder, heavier. But Annie couldn't say those things right then, because she knew too well it would take time for her to forgive him, too, despite the desperate, vulnerable look he'd had when he'd run into the gym.

If Francine had seen that look, surely she could forgive him. But she had not. And so there they were.

When an outline of her front porch was at

last visible, Annie picked up the pace. It was time to stop worrying — again — and get to work.

"If she's in here, we'll find her," Annie said, as if Francine didn't know how compact the cottage was. "If not," Annie added, "we'll go down to the beach." She quickly wished she hadn't said that.

Pushing open the door that, indeed, hadn't been locked, she let Francine go in first. Then, as Annie raised one foot to step in behind her, something caught her eye. Something that did not belong. Sticking out from under the planter on the porch was what looked like a piece of paper. Unless the fog was playing tricks on her eyesight. She bent down, lifted the edge of the planter, and extracted an unlined Post-it Note. She turned the flashlight back on and saw a message printed in block letters. It simply read:

THE GIRL IS FINE. SHE'S SAFE WITH ME.

Annie's breath caught in her throat. She blinked; she read it again. Her first instinct was to smile. Her lips parted; she almost called out to Francine until she realized that the note hadn't been signed. Was it an oversight? Or intentional? Could it be a signal of something . . . sinister?

She stared at it again, trying to read

between the lines.

The girl is fine. She's safe with me.

Short. To the point. Nothing was between those lines.

Despite the chill of the December night, a thin line of perspiration formed on her brow. She was still standing on the porch, trying to decide what to do, when Francine reappeared in the doorway.

"She's not here," she said. Then she brushed past Annie and headed toward the beach, plowing through the fog as if, like Bella, it wasn't there.

Annie caught up with Francine before the young woman dissolved into the shroud.

Muffled sounds of footsteps, voices, and shouts of Bella's name — to which there were no audible replies — greeted Annie and Francine when they stepped onto the sand.

"No sign of her yet?" Annie asked the first person she saw, a man. The patch on his uniform identified him as a West Tisbury police officer. He did not look familiar.

He shook his head.

"Where's Detective Lyons?" Annie continued, determined not to show anguish or to let on that her right hand was clenched around the Post-it in her pocket.

"Don't know," came the reply. "Maybe he's on the boat?" He pointed toward blurry red lights that blinked on and off through the layer of haze that topped the water.

Apparently, they'd wasted no time hauling the rescue boat down the path.

She walked a few feet to the shoreline and began to cup her hands to yell for John. Then she knew that would be futile; the ambient sounds of the engine and distant voices along with the slap-slap of the incoming tide would surely drown her plea.

Incoming tide, she thought, and quickly squelched the idea of what that could mean to a small girl, wobbly on her little feet, unfamiliar with being alone in the dark — or, in fact, with being alone at all.

She tried to swallow but could not.

The West Tisbury officer was suddenly beside her; Francine was next to him. "I can get Sergeant Lyons on the radio," he said.

Annie clutched the Post-it more tightly. "Please do. Tell him I've thought of something important. I'm Annie, his fiancée." She needed to show John the note before she told Francine about it.

The officer stepped aside, clicked on the radio on his shoulder, and called to John.

With her free hand, Annie reached over

and cupped Francine's arm. They stood motionless until the officer signed off.

"He'll be right in," he said.

"Thanks. Do you know Earl Lyons? Is he still up in the meadow?"

Motioning away from the beach, he said, "Last I knew, he was. He's with Linc Butterfield. And the boy."

Francine stiffened. "Jonas," she said, spitting out the word.

Ignoring the retort, Annie told the officer, "This is Francine. Bella's mother." She turned back to her. "If you don't want to see Jonas, at least go talk to Earl. More than anyone, he'll be on top of this. He loves her as much as we do." She unlatched her hand.

"If you want, I'll take you to him," the cop suggested.

Francine hesitated.

"Go," Annie said.

Francine's big eyes darted from side to side, searching for an answer that wasn't there. And Annie's heart broke a little more.

Then Francine quickly spun and headed back up the small dune toward the path; the officer from West Tisbury followed closely behind, his flashlight beamed straight down at the path, which Annie realized must afford a clearer view. It probably wasn't the first time the officer had needed to search for something — or someone — in the island fog.

Annie watched until they were out of sight, then allowed soft tears to form.

A minute later, John was in front of her, his arms around her.

"We'll find her," he said, the way he had before.

But still, they had not.

She closed her eyes a moment, letting his strength infuse her. Annie had spent so many years learning to be independent, sometimes it was hard to turn over control.

When she felt strong enough, she pulled the note from her pocket and handed it to him.

"This was on the doorstep of my cottage." Her words then spurred a memory of the handwoven basket that had been placed on her doorstep two years ago at Christmas: the basket that had cradled the infant Bella.

Then she folded her arms across her chest and tried to stop her heart from shattering.

"Shit," John said after he'd read and reread the note. "Who the hell wrote it?"

Annie cleared her throat. "I believe the saying is 'your guess is as good as mine.' "

"Did you show it to Francine?"

"No."

"Good. It could be a nutjob playing a sick

prank. Even on the island, that kind of stuff can happen."

Annie hated to think that, but supposed John was probably right.

"Where is she now?" he asked.

"The West Tisbury cop brought her to see Earl. And Jonas, if she'll speak to him. She's really angry that he didn't watch Bella more closely."

As any good police officer would do, John said nothing. He'd once explained that when it came to a situation, an officer did not comment on emotions: facts were what mattered, not feelings. But Annie knew that he'd filed the information that Jonas hadn't watched Bella more closely, that she'd gone missing on his watch.

"Kevin and Taylor are on their way back from Edgartown," he said. "He's going to check with the *On Time* captain; maybe he saw Bella in a vehicle with someone. When your brother gets here, I'll have Taylor and him search the woods across the street from the Inn. When the OB team's done inside, I'll send them to the woods, too. It's probably a long shot that Bella would go there, but right now we can't rule anything out."

"So you're going to keep searching?"

"I'm not about to cancel the search because of a lame note that's not even signed.

We'll ramp things up as best we can. A few more officers are on their way from Chilmark and Aquinnah — along with more volunteers. I'll turn the beach over to them and join Kevin and Taylor."

Just then a small wave lapped Annie's foot, a reminder that the tide was coming in. She took a step back. "Until then you'll go back out on the water?"

"For now."

"What can I do? I want to do something, John. I need to do something."

"You can go to the meadow and be there for Francine. She probably needs you. Or go help Lucy. The Inn's a big place with lots of places for a little one to hide." Then he paused and pulled her close. "Are you doing okay?"

"Sure." She didn't really mean it, and she knew he knew that.

"Go up to the Inn. If Francine gets into it with Jonas, my dad will sort them out. You might be better off helping my mother in the kitchen. Or seeing how Lucy's doing."

"I already saw your mother. She has a team that's preparing to feed the entire Vineyard."

He let out a small laugh.

"And, by the way, she wanted everyone to know the food is almost ready when they need a break." She glanced at him; he was looking at the note again. Then she had a disturbing thought. "Oh, God. I should have put it in a baggie. You might have been able to get prints. Of all people, I should have known to do that." She stared at the note, then dropped her eyes down to her boots, the tips of which were now wet. "I was only thinking that I didn't want Francine to see it. Not until you did."

He shrugged. "Maybe we can still get something. But don't go back to the cottage until I can get someone to dust the porch. In case something's there."

She winced. "Of course. I hadn't thought of that, either. Sorry."

He gave her another hug, that time a quick one. "Most important, don't tell anyone about the note. Especially not Francine. I'll be up there in a while. I need to figure out our next steps. In the meantime, I'll let you know if anything shows up."

Then, as Francine had done before him, John disappeared into the fog.

Annie remained standing, trying to decide which direction to go in. She sensed John was right: Francine might need her, but it might be better to leave her with Jonas. Maybe she'd be able to forgive him if they searched side by side, sharing their pain. If a rift developed, well, again John was right: Earl was there. Unlike Annie, he wouldn't become a hovering mother figure.

If she went into the kitchen, she wouldn't bother to ask Claire if she needed help. As always, the woman would have the food prep under control. Every island crisis, especially those on Chappy, relied on a competent person to tend to the needs of the volunteers: Claire had been blessed with that role.

A breeze kicked up, chilling Annie's cheeks, reminding her she was standing on the beach, wearing only her jeans, a cotton top, and a light wool jacket, hardly smart attire for a cold, wintry night. And she certainly wasn't doing any good at all by just standing there, a sandcastle of confusion. After all, there was a whole lot to do. And Bella to find.

"Bella," she whispered into the fog. "Where are you, my sweet girl?"

Ignoring a shiver, Annie turned and headed up the path, her flashlight bobbing back and forth close to the dunes, her determination to be the one to find her growing with each step.

She was beginning to feel confident about the outcome until she reached the lawn that led up to the Inn and saw a tall, bulky figure standing off to one side, silently watching the action at the bottom of the hill. As Annie got closer, the fog thinned a little, enough for her to make out whose figure it was.

Rex.

If he saw Annie, he did not acknowledge her.

CHAPTER 25

Annie trudged toward the Inn, passing the workshop and her cottage on the way, wondering how soon John could get someone there to cordon off the porch with tape that warned intruders not to cross. Had Tyrannosaurus Rex been there? Was he the one who left the Post-it? But why? It seemed that he was going to get what he'd come to Chappy for — the house. Still, the thought of the big man carrying Bella off somewhere launched somersaults inside her.

There were more people at the Inn than there were a short time ago: men, women, teenagers. In the kitchen, Annie stopped to tell Claire that John would be there soon. Claire acknowledged her but kept a stiff composure and did not pause her rapid pace of layering ham and cheese into sandwiches for searchers to take outside while they worked.

Keeping her anguish likewise buried, Annie moved into the great room, where volunteers were lined up at the urns, waiting to fill thermoses before beginning or returning to comb the grounds. After all her time on the island, Annie was surprised at how many faces she still didn't recognize.

"Remember when Mason Beachem's kid went missing?" she heard an older man ask. He was dressed in a well-worn Navy peacoat, his white-bearded face rimmed by a plaid wool scarf; he was addressing a woman of a similar age whose knit cap was pulled down around her ears. She wore a full-length, quilted coat that might have been acquired at the nearby thrift shop. Annie knew that the attire in no way indicated whether either of them was rich or poor, but exemplified Yankee frugality in which many lifelong Vineyarders took pride.

"Found him in the dog pen, didn't they?" the woman replied.

"Yep. Sound asleep, while Mason's two beagles were keeping watch."

A man behind the woman tapped her on the shoulder. "And Liza Watkins? The waitress? We looked for her for days. When was that? Nineteen ninety-something?"

Turning from the group, Annie didn't want to hear more. She wondered how it happened that when tragedy appeared, people often felt a need to revisit other misfortunes. Car accident? Right! Remember when what's-her-name ran off the bridge? Cancer? What kind? I heard Mr. So-and-So had it even worse.

She headed for the front reception area, ducked around the corner, and slipped into the reading room. She couldn't stand to think that Bella's story would be future fodder for island gossip, another anecdote passed down for years to come.

Sitting quietly without turning on a light, Annie tried to think about what she'd do next if she were John. Which, of course, she wasn't, never having had police training or been certified in tactics and strategies. "But you think like a cop, Annie," her editor often reminded her. "That's why you're a good mystery writer." It was easy for Trish to say; Annie wasn't sure John would agree. He'd praised her instincts on occasion, but even Annie knew that her hunches often clashed with the legal system. She also knew that once she and John were married — two weeks nearly to the hour — she'd have to back off from getting involved with anything the police needed to handle. She wouldn't want to get her new husband into trouble.

But they weren't married yet, and this was about Bella, and Annie knew she'd do whatever it took to find her. She also knew that time was of the essence — a cliché that, like most of them, had been invented for a reason.

The word cliché, however, reminded her of Trish, and that time was also of the essence for her to come to a decision about her career. But because she tended to feel more comfortable creating stories than dealing with real-life issues, Annie decided that her time would be better spent right then if she examined Bella's disappearance as if it were a plot line for one of her novels. After all, in her books, characters had been known to disappear — some for legitimate reasons, some because they had something to hide, others because they'd met with something evil. Bella didn't fit into the first two categories. Which, unless she was merely lost, suggested that she'd met with something evil.

But how could that have happened on picture-perfect Martha's Vineyard?

Rex Winsted seemed the obvious culprit. But the more Annie obsessed about him, the less plausible he was. Rex simply didn't have a motive. At least not one that Annie was aware of. Any more than she knew the real reason Rose was afraid of him.

Still, he was a curious addition to the island, especially on Chappy. So she decided not to rule him out.

Who else?

Annie knew pretty much everyone who had regular contact with Bella or Francine. The year-round tenants were wonderful and had added vibrancy to the Inn. In the year and a half since the grand opening, the tenants were both compatible and companionable, and hadn't posed a single problem. She wasn't surprised that they were helping now.

Then, there were this year's winter renters. One was Charlie, a middle-aged man who worked for the Steamship Authority. He stayed on the island only during the week, returning to his wife and two kids in Fairhaven on weekends. So far, he'd been no trouble, either. Because it was Friday, his workweek would have ended with a trip on a late-afternoon boat to Woods Hole. He would not have been available to come back to Chappy and steal Bella, which he'd have no reason to do, anyway.

A second winter renter was a nurse named Jenna who was maybe in her forties and worked ten to ten at the hospital; more than once she'd commented how grateful she was to have found the Inn. When high season arrived, she'd move into a small apartment with other nurses until she could return to the Inn in October. No, Annie thought, Jenna didn't seem to have a reason to bring evil into Bella's life. Besides, as far as Annie knew, she'd left for work before Bella had gone missing, and wouldn't return until close to eleven.

And then there was Rose. The woman certainly was curious, but Annie had doubted she was capable of wrongdoing . . . until a bolt of imaginary lightning — Murphy's doing, perhaps — reminded Annie that she'd found Rose in the chef's room, where she'd claimed a mouse had run into the cupboard where Bella's toys were kept. If this had happened in one of Annie's manuscripts, would Trish call the coincidence a red herring . . . or a viable clue? Would she delete "Rose Atkins" as a possible suspect if a crime had been committed?

John hadn't mentioned if Rose was among the tenants who were helping, which most likely meant nothing. Rose was no doubt in her room, where she spent each evening alone, as far as Annie knew. Besides, where would she have hidden Bella when Lucy and the OB cops had been searching her room?

And there was Abigail, though even considering her a suspect made Annie feel disloyal. John's daughter would have no reason to be mean to Bella. Any more than she'd had cause to slash Annie's tire. She might not like Annie, but if she were prone to being vindictive, surely Lucy would have told Annie by now.

Though she had no answers, Annie was reassured that at least her brain was working again. Her thought process felt sensible and logical and had quieted her innards. Until light suddenly flooded the reading room, and Annie was no longer alone.

She blinked.

"There you are." The intruder was Earl. He held a large mug that emitted an aroma of hot chocolate. "My son's on his way. He has a list of things for us to do." He pulled out a chair and sat opposite her at the small table. "Are you okay?"

"Holding my own. How 'bout you?"

He sighed one of his heavy, weary sighs. He rubbed his spikey eyebrows and scratched at the stubble on his chin. "Esau Gibbons wanted to haul over a couple of his old haying rakes — the kind on wheels. He said we could pull 'em by hand, like they were wagons. He thought they'd comb a wider swath in the meadow than what we can do by walking slow. He was all revved up about it, until I pointed out that the rakes might hurt Bella along the way, not to mention scare the bejeepers out of her . . . ." He choked up. "He meant well, though." He bowed his head and scratched his chin again.

"It's okay," Annie said, "it's early yet."

"No, it's not okay. It's been hours since our little one disappeared. It's cold outside now. And really dark."

She looked at the clock. He was right. It had been hours. But though it felt as if things had been happening in snail'space motion, the time had somehow sped by. And every hour that passed portended an outcome that would not be positive.

"How's Jonas?" she asked. "And how was Francine with him?"

He snorted. "Best as I can tell, she doesn't want to talk to him. Other than when she told him to go home to his mother's, that she doesn't want him around the Inn or anywhere near her, that he's already done enough damage."

Annie's heart began to ache. "Did he leave?"

"They're not done in the meadow, so he's still out there. But he's staying clear of her."

Annie nodded without commenting. She couldn't get involved in the young couple's discord; right then, on the scale of importance, it needed to be low.

Then Claire and Francine appeared. Francine's cheeks were red, either from being out in the cold or from crying.

A minute later, John arrived. Lucy was with him. And another Edgartown police officer whom Annie didn't know.

Everyone except John and the other cop sat on one of the barrel chairs.

"I brought Jeremy along," John said, "to take your fingerprints."

Annie supposed the others were as surprised as she was.

"Sorry, but that way we'll be able to quickly dismiss them if they show up where we dust — which they likely will."

No one challenged John. So Jeremy opened a leather valise and began the process.

"We'll get Kevin and Taylor's later," John added. He didn't mention Jonas. Maybe they'd already taken his.

While Jeremy was busy, John turned to Annie. "Can you get some paper and pens? Sometimes it's good to do things the old-fashioned way."

She stood and quickly went out to the reception area, where she grabbed a few pencils and small notepads that read *The Vineyard Inn — Chappaquiddick's Finest Re-*

sort. The tagline had been a joke that Earl had come up with, as the Inn was the only one on Chappy.

Back in the reading room, she distributed the materials, returned to her chair, and waited in silence until the process of the fingerprinting was complete. She was glad John was in charge. And that she didn't have to be.

When Jeremy left, John continued. "Mom," he said to Claire, "I'll start with you. The food on the table looks fabulous. But a lot of folks won't want to stop to come inside. I need you to figure out how much coffee, cream, sugar, hot chocolate — whatever you think they're going to need. That includes paper towels, toilet paper, paper cups, and small bags for sandwiches. Plan to have enough to last a few days, just in case. Once you're done, I'll call Stop and Shop. They'll get the order to the *On Time.*"

He turned to Earl. "Dad, I'll let you know what time to go to the ferry and pick it up. For now we're concentrating on searching the grounds at the Inn, up and down both sides of North Neck Road, and on the shore from the Gut to the *On Time.*"

Annie knew that the Gut was the channel this side of the Cape Poge Lighthouse, which was on the northernmost tip of

Chappy. She also knew that it seemed like an awfully large area in which to find a 21.8-pound little girl.

"By dawn I hope to have volunteers spread north through the Gut and into the bay," John was saying, "then east past the burying ground and out to Pease Pond, west by land between here and Chappy Road down to the ferry, and south as far as we need to go. I'll keep you updated so you can bring supplies out to them. They might need fresh hats and gloves, too, so find out how and where to get some. Maybe Lucy can help with that. And Abigail, if she ever shows up."

Annie blinked twice at the sound of Abigail's name. John did not seem pleased that his other daughter wasn't there. But where was she? And why wasn't she helping? Annie steadied her gaze on him, hoping no one had noticed her reaction.

Then John scanned the room. "Where's Jonas?"

Francine went into lockjaw mode. Her mouth went tight, her shoulders squared, her gaze moved to the wall.

"Francine?" he asked.

Without looking at him, she shrugged.

"Lucy," John continued without skipping a beat, "I also need you to figure out what

261

to do about Annie's booth at the Fair, okay?"

For a second, Annie was startled. She'd forgotten about the Fair. The same way, she supposed, that she'd repressed the need to talk to John about Trish's "blockbuster" deal. Those things now seemed — no, those things now *were* — inconsequential.

"I already called Winnie, Dad," Lucy said. "They set the soap out this afternoon; Winnie's daughter-in-law, Barbara, and Barbara's son, Lucas, will take turns manning the booth. Winnie and I figured that even if we find Bella soon, Annie and I will be too tired to work it."

Annie closed her eyes. She was grateful, so grateful, for Lucy. And Winnie. And Winnie's entire clan.

"Ms. Lucy, you are your father's daughter," Earl added with a tender smile. "Always on top of things."

"Okay, that's good," John said. "So maybe you can make some cookies. And work on getting extra hats and gloves and maybe some socks, too." There was no need for him to repeat the possibility that they might be searching for a few days.

"I'll start at the homeless shelter. And the thrift store," Lucy said, and John nodded in agreement.

"What about me?" Francine suddenly asked. "Don't you have a job for me?"

"I do," John said. "I know that Lucy and the OB officers have looked for her upstairs, but I need you to go through your room inch by inch to see if anything is out of place — or missing. You're the only one who can tell if something's different. And please write even the smallest detail down. It's hard to know what might turn out to be significant."

"But we haven't been staying here."

"They've mostly been with us," Claire said.

"Then go there, too," John said to Francine. "Go anywhere Bella has been. Except Annie's cottage. Stay away from there."

Silence hung over the room. Until Earl broke it.

"What's wrong with the cottage?"

John hesitated a heartbeat. Maybe two. "Just a precaution."

"I already looked," Francine said. "Bella's not there."

"Right," John said. "And I'll have Annie check it again once she's done with the other thing I need her to do."

"Which is what?" Annie asked, her pencil poised over the notepad on the table in front of her.

"Make a list of anyone who's been acting strangely. Or anyone else who's missing that you usually see around here. A delivery person. One of your tenants' visitors. A cleaning person. Anyone. Take your time and really think about it. I know you'll be good at it."

He had no way of knowing that she'd already considered a few suspects. Including Abigail.

"When you're done with that, come to me. I'll let you know when it's okay to go back into the cottage."

"I have a question," Earl piped up. "If the cottage is off limits, why not the Inn as well? Bella was here when she . . . disappeared. Not there."

John nodded, and Annie recognized it as a ploy for him to buy a few seconds of time to try and come up with an answer. "A lot of people come and go from here on a daily basis. It would take weeks for us to sort through fingerprints, if we could even find clean ones. The back door alone would be nearly impossible to test."

Annie didn't know if Earl was buying the explanation, but at least he didn't ask if they were lifting prints from Annie's cottage and, if so, why, when that's not where Bella was when she went missing. Maybe he knew when to be quiet and let his son do his job.

"A couple of other things," John said. "Do *not* talk to anyone from the media. Some of them must be here by now. In fact, do not talk to *anyone* about what might have happened to Bella or say anything about her. Don't even talk about her to one of the volunteers. Okay, that's enough for now. Does everyone understand what to do?"

Heads nodded, voices murmured around the room.

"Okay," he added. "If she hasn't turned up yet, we'll meet back here tomorrow morning at ten. In the meantime, if you have any news or any questions, you all have my number. Call me or text me right away."

Heads nodded again.

John went to the door, stopped, and turned around. "Most of all, remember that time is of the essence."

Lucky for him, Trish wasn't his editor. Annie knew she surely would have killed his cliché.

CHAPTER 26

After the group dispersed to tend to their tasks, Annie closed the door behind them and moved to the small table where the brass banker's lamp with the green glass shade stood. It was her favorite spot. She'd discovered the iconic lamps at the Boston Public Library when she'd been young; sitting at one of the tables there became a comfortable, quiet place for her — the kind of comfort and quiet Annie needed now to think about the list John wanted her to make.

The note on her doorstep, if it was not a prank, should convince her that someone had taken Bella, that she hadn't "wandered off." But who? Anyone on the island who knew, or knew of, Bella most likely knew her story: that her mother had died a few days after giving birth to her; that Francine had been unable to support her and had felt she needed to give her up. Bella's little life had seemed to be on the path to a bleak future, until the people of the Vineyard embraced Francine and her. Why would someone want to cause her harm now when she'd already been through so much turmoil?

Aside from Annie's obvious suspects — Rex, Rose, and Abigail — who else could there be? Who else would have a motive? Even Bella's biological father, Stephen Thurman, a house painter from Edgartown who'd first denied his culpability by claiming that either of his sons could as easily be Bella's father, finally admitted that he was. But Francine hadn't wanted to pursue getting child support from him, so Annie highly doubted that Thurman would have the need, the desire, or the chutzpah to kidnap her now. Especially since, not long after his admission, he'd packed up his family and slithered away from the island.

She tapped the pencil on the edge of the table. Who else? *Think, think, think,* she commanded her brain, which felt too wrung out now to be able to.

Then another idea began to form, slowly at first, until she realized it honestly might be possible: *Francine's aunt and uncle.*

Annie didn't know them, but they certainly knew Bella. Maybe they felt entitled

to have her. Maybe they were angry that
Francine hadn't agreed to move to Minnesota permanently. Maybe that was the
real reason Francine had wanted to come
back to the Vineyard to have her baby —
because they'd been pressuring her. Marty
and Bill could have secretly come to the
island in the past week, for the sole purpose
of taking Bella back. Or maybe they'd
stayed home and paid someone to snatch
Bella away. In which case, it was possible
that she was now in Minneapolis. With
them.

Annie tried to sort out the possibility. If
she were right, how would it make Francine
feel? Maybe Bella mattered more to them
than Francine did. Maybe they planned to
try to get custody of Bella, basing their actions on Francine's behavior by being
pregnant and unmarried to a boy whose
father had died under mysterious circumstances and whose grandmother was currently in jail for reckless assault and battery.
Hadn't Francine told Annie that Marty and
Bill had no children? And that Marty was
the only sibling of Francine's late mother
— which made Francine and Bella her only
blood relatives?

The possibility grew stronger.

But would they really have abducted her?

Taking a long breath, Annie knew she needed to reel in her thoughts.

"Oh, Murphy," she said, "this is such a mess." She ran a hand through her hair, waiting for a reply. But apparently, Murphy was unavailable.

So Annie needed to continue. But for the thousandth time since Jonas had raced into the school gymnasium that afternoon (*My God,* she thought, *had that only happened today?*), her thoughts went back to Bella. She could almost hear her infectious giggle and see the way she spread her little arms wide open and cried "Ammie!" whenever Annie walked into the room. She could envision Bella's tiny face aglow at the simplest things: picking blueberries, helping Francine snap fresh green beans for dinner, talking to her dolls — the yarn-topped cast of characters that Claire had made, and that Bella brought to life in her budding imagination. It was hard to push away those sounds and images and concentrate on the task at hand. Especially because of the note that claimed she was safe. It reminded Annie of the other note — the one that had arrived when Bella first came into Annie's life.

HER NAME IS BELLA, that one read. Annie had found it in the handwoven basket where the swaddled infant had been tucked.

Outside, a nor'easter had roared across Chappaquiddick, snow was piling high against the thin walls of the cottage, wind whistled down the vent of the woodstove where sputtering logs of ash and cedar struggled to warm the room.

PLEASE TAKE CARE OF HER . . .

So Annie had.

But the baby cried. It was a tiny cry, soft and forlorn. She was in Annie's arms by then, this innocent creature with a perfect little pink mouth and shining black eyes that gazed squarely up at Annie, pleading.

Annie had sat down in the antique rocking chair in front of the woodstove. She'd leaned back and slowly began to rock. Baby Bella stopped crying. And Annie had melted.

Suddenly, footsteps in the reception area jostled Annie back to the present. She sat up straight and turned off the green-glass-shaded brass lamp. And realized she'd been crying. She quickly wiped the traces of her memories. The footsteps stopped. She waited for the door to open. But it did not. She did not hear anyone go up the staircase. And no one spoke.

Annie clenched her teeth. Then she heard a light tapping on the door.

"Who is it?" she asked, her voice small

and tentative, as if it belonged to Rose.

"Jonas," came the response.

Her face, her shoulders, her spine relaxed. She sighed. "Come in."

The door opened. Standing in the doorway, Jonas looked like a frightened boy instead of a twenty-five-year-old almost-man, an almost-new-father, an almost-highly-successful-artist with a following most artists would not achieve, even in their dreams.

"I can't find her," he said quietly. He crossed the room, sat down, and then he cried, too.

And Annie's heart broke for the thousandth time that day.

"I've lost them both, haven't I?" he said in a low voice after he stopped crying. "I've lost Bella. And I've lost Francine."

Annie didn't know what to say. As with Bella, Jonas had come into her life unexpectedly, a victim of other people's misguided actions. Also, as with Bella, he had won her heart, especially since she'd witnessed how much he cared about Francine and Bella, and how much they loved him back.

She was mindful not to sound accusing. "Jonas, please don't say that. We don't know if it's true."

"We know the first part is. I lost Bella.

Me. And only me."

"Not if someone's taken her." She'd blurted out the words before she'd thought them through.

"No one's taken her, Annie. Why would anybody do that?" He might have been convinced that he was right, but his glazed blue eyes then widened, as if she'd set off an alarm.

"You're right," she responded. "We don't know anything. Yet. We have to have faith that everything will work out. Take a look around at all the people who are helping. They'll find her, Jonas. They will." She didn't know if she sounded believable. She wasn't even sure that she believed herself. The fantasy of Martha's Vineyard as a safe and wondrous place to live seemed to be crumbling with every hour that passed.

He unzipped his parka and pulled off his woolen hat, allowing his thick, ginger-colored hair — so much like his mother's — to escape. He exhaled a puff of air; he did not wipe his tears, which were now drying on his winter-weathered cheeks. Even in this state, Jonas was a good-looking young man. Strangers would not have guessed the anguish that had racked his life before these recent, happy months.

"She should have listened to her aunt and

uncle," he said.

Annie winced. "What about them?" She sensed that Jonas would tell her everything he knew. And she needed to hear it all. For John, of course. Because this was his case, not hers.

His cheeks puffed out again. "They don't like me," he said.

Annie's eyebrows shot up. "You're kidding, right?"

"No. They think I'm going to hold her back. From making the most out of her life."

"Because of the baby?"

"Because of me. Of who I am. Of where I came from. My grandparents aren't exactly upstanding citizens, remember?"

Annie leaned across the table, carefully covering Marty's and Bill's names with her forearms. "That is them, Jonas, not you. You are a successful young artist. You have a good head on your shoulders. You are dependable and responsible . . ."

He stood up, shoved his hands into the pockets of his jacket, and began to pace. "Seriously? Did you really just say that?"

"You made one small mistake . . ." She paused, unsure of what words should follow.

"Francine doesn't know it, but just before we left Minnesota, I overheard her aunt talking to her. Marty said, 'That boy will cause you pain, Francine. And, mark my words, he'll cause Bella pain. And your new baby, too. He's a dreamer. The kind your mother always got tangled up with.' " With that, Jonas zipped his parka and put his hat back on. "I gotta go back outside. I really only came up here to get coffee refills for the volunteers. If you see Francine, please tell her I'm sorry. And that I love her." He turned and left the room.

Annie sat in silence again. She looked back at the notepad. She knew she needed to find John and tell him about Francine's aunt and uncle and not wait until tomorrow.

As soon as she opened the back door of the Inn, Annie saw that, halfway down the hill, her cottage was lit up like Fenway Park when the Yankees were in town. On a different, happier day, Earl would have chuckled at that analogy.

However, neither Earl nor anyone would be chuckling at the sight that greeted Annie as she drew closer. The entire cottage — not just the porch — was now cordoned off with yellow tape, the kind Annie had seen too often: POLICE LINE. DO NOT CROSS.

It was one thing to be told not to go home and quite another to be barricaded from it.

A gust of wind blew across her face as if mocking her.

"John?" she called out as she reached the porch. The door was open; people were in her living room. They were dressed in blue paper garb from head to toe, with plastic shields covering their faces, as if the full-blown pandemic had returned. She wanted to duck under the tape, go inside, and ask why they were in her house when the note had been left outside on the porch. But Annie knew better than to interrupt the investigation. Or at least she knew where to draw the line.

So she kept her distance and hollered for John again.

It took only a few seconds for a large man to fill the doorway and slide down his mask. "Hey, Annie," he said. It was Linc. He seemed to be everywhere that night, John's fellow detective and right hand, especially when John was too close to a situation to be totally objective.

"How's it going?" she began, unsure how to continue. "Have you found anything?" She longed to ask him to move his bulk out of her line of vision so that she could see what they were doing in her home. *To* her home.

"Sorry," he said, "can't say. But I guess

275

you know that."

"Right." He didn't have to explain police protocol to her. Still, she craned her neck, trying to peek around him. "Are they dusting for prints? The note was on the porch, Linc. I don't think anyone went inside." She wasn't exactly prying. Well, maybe a little.

"All I can tell you is that we're checking everything."

She wondered if that included the ugly wedding dress, which, as far as she knew, was still hanging on the back of her bedroom door. If they impounded it, at least she'd have a good reason to wear something else.

"What about the Inn?" she asked, aware that she sounded irritated, but could not seem to do otherwise. "Bella was last seen in the great room."

"There will be too many prints from too many people up there." His answer was the same one John had given Earl. As if the cops had studied the same manual. Or were in cahoots.

Annie recognized that her thoughts had turned ridiculous. She shifted on one foot and discovered that her toes were cold, despite her fleece-lined boots. "I need to talk to John," she said. "Do you know where he is?"

"He's back out on the rescue boat. With a couple of up-island cops."

Annie started to reach into her pocket when she discovered she'd left her purse and phone . . . somewhere. In the Jeep? At the Inn? *Oh,* she thought, *who cares?* "How far out are they?"

"Can't say for sure."

"Can you reach him?"

"Yup."

"Will you? Please? It's important, Linc."

He shuffled his blue paper–clad feet back and forth. "If it's about Bella, you can tell me, Annie. John asked me to take the lead. He's too close to it, you know?"

Believe me, I know, she thought. But Linc was one of the good guys, so she didn't want to get snarky with him. Still, she couldn't bring herself to tell him about Francine's aunt and uncle: she didn't want him to question Francine and upset her more.

"It's more of a personal matter," she lied. "But an important one."

Linc kind of smiled. "Did you call him? Text him?"

"No. I forgot my phone." Which was true. After all, she hadn't known she'd need it. Her only mission had been to find John, tell him what Jonas had told her, and let him do whatever he wanted with the information. She also knew she now needed to tell him Francine's aunt's opinion about the "limitations" of the Vineyard.

"Never mind," Annie said. "I'll go down to the beach and see if I can flag them down." Hopefully, the rescue boat was cruising close to shore, looking for whatever they could see in the spotlights' sweeping arcs.

"I'll let him know you're headed down," Linc said. "So they can beach the boat if he's in range."

Without waiting for her reply, he fished through his garb and produced his phone. His thumbs skittered across the face of it, texting rapidly as if he were a teenager.

Five seconds later the phone rang.

Linc answered. "Hey, bud. Yeah. Annie's here. She needs to talk to you." He paused. "Nope. Something personal." He paused again, that time longer. And longer. He wiped his brow. He turned sideways, as if trying to avoid her gaze. "Shit," he said. "Seriously?"

And Annie felt as if someone had stabbed her in the heart.

She wanted to cry, "What?" and "Tell me!" But she was afraid of what he would say.

Linc kept listening. Then he said, "Yeah.

Bag it. Tag it. Bring it up here."

Annie pressed a hand against her stomach. Then she ran around the corner of the cottage and threw up on the grass.

And then Linc was behind her. "Sorry you had to hear that, Annie. They haven't found her. But they found a doll. John said it has yarn for hair. Like the kind of dolls his mom has made for Bella."

CHAPTER 27

Later, much later, between darkness and dawn, it occurred to Annie that she was slogging through the night in a heavy fog of fear, where sight and sound had become ethereal, as if she were in a netherworld, having an out-of-body experience. Murphy once told her those kinds of things were more common than most people knew, when God, or nature, or whatever one called it provided a full-body pillow to absorb the shock, when the real world stepped aside but allowed lungs to keep breathing and hearts to keep beating when the pain was so intense that the mere act to "go on" did not seem possible.

Annie wondered where Murphy was right now and why she had abandoned her in this time of anguish. Then again, Annie wasn't sure she could handle hearing *Hang in there, Annie,* or *Stay positive, my friend* right then.

Lying in her bed, she stared up at, yet did

not really see, the ceiling of the cottage. John had allowed her to come home last night and sleep in her own bed, but only with him next to her. And now Annie had just one thought:

How will I tell Francine about the doll?

It had been the one with the orange hair made from the same yarn that Claire had used to knit a sweater for Francine last Christmas, because by then Francine was in Minneapolis, where the winters were bone cold, colder even than the Vineyard got in January, when the wind often whipped off the water and spun around the island like a cyclone in a deep freeze.

As far as Annie knew, Bella hadn't yet named the trio of dolls that Claire had made, though she'd assigned each of them chores: the brunette was in charge of picking blueberries for dinner; the blonde mopped the floor; the orange-haired one shopped for groceries and toys.

Closing her eyes, Annie tried not to think about what now seemed inevitable: that Bella had, indeed, made her way down to the beach, that she'd wandered into the water, that she'd been swept off her feet by what might have been a gentle wave, but she was so small that even a gentle wave could have pulled her out to sea. She could have been caught in an undertow or stumbled on some pebbles and fallen face-first into the water.

Annie stopped herself from crying out, though fresh tears formed in her eyes. She understood why Francine didn't want to see or speak to Jonas. Ever again. Even if they found Bella safe and sound, the trauma of last night would not be easy to erase. How could Francine ever trust him again?

And what about the new baby? Was it too late for Francine to change her mind and have an abortion? Annie didn't know what the laws were anymore; she'd had no need to until now. She wouldn't blame Francine if she decided it would hurt too much to raise Jonas's baby when he'd been the one who'd caused Bella to disappear . . . and never come back.

Still, Annie wondered if she could convince Francine that the way she felt right then might not be how she'd feel forever, that having an abortion would always be with her, nagging at her for years, the way that Annie's had. The way she'd never forgiven herself for having had it, even though the baby would have been a constant reminder of her good-for-nothing husband Mark. But Annie also would have had a lovely child who would have been part of her.

She wondered if she should share that with Francine now.

Next to her, John began to stir. Annie snuggled closer, letting his strong, steady pulse thrum against her shoulder, his arm around her where it had been when he'd made her go to bed, the heat of his body the only reason Annie supposed that she'd been warm. And had been able to sleep at all.

Last night, he'd wanted to tell Francine about the discovery of the doll. But Annie had hesitated, partly because she'd nearly been immobilized by the shock, partly because of Francine and Jonas's unborn baby. If Francine miscarried, Annie might feel it was her fault. So she convinced John to wait until he knew if the note revealed any fingerprints or other identifying marks.

Someone from the State Police Crime Lab would be on the early boat in the morning to collect whatever evidence they could and take whatever John's team had already gathered. They'd bring it back to the main lab, which was west of Boston, to be tested. As Annie recalled from having done research, the process could take three to five days. Maybe they'd tighten the time frame because a child was at stake. If she was still alive.

As daylight began its slow rise over the Atlantic, over East Beach on Chappy, Annie decided to let John sleep as long as possible. She wanted to check on Francine, who typically rose early. She might even be in the kitchen at the Inn, preparing breakfast for the tenants and for everyone and anyone who'd shown up during the night to help with the search. Thank God John had corralled the officers who'd found the doll and sworn them to secrecy.

Annie hadn't always done well at keeping secrets. Especially like now, when holding back did not feel fair. Maybe John was right, that Francine should know. If that was true, Annie should be the one to tell her.

Sliding out from under John's loving arm, she tiptoed to the bathroom, where she quickly showered and pulled on yesterday's clothes. When brushing her teeth, she decided not to check her face in the mirror. She already felt as awful as she must look. Out in the living room, she put on her down parka and woolen accessories and slipped her phone into a pocket, glad that she'd retrieved it from the Jeep last night. Then she raised her chin — as if the small act would give her confidence — and stepped outside onto the porch, where she nearly tripped over Kevin, who sat, one hand gripping a coffee mug, the other one resting on his head, as if he were thinking. Or crying, like Jonas had.

Sitting on the wide-board plank, Annie curled her arm through his.

"Hey, brother. Did you get any sleep?"

"Not really. I kept hoping she'd turn up. She's been out all night, you know."

Yes, Annie knew.

"Nothing's going to be right until we find her," he said.

She rested her head against his shoulder, which, though not quite as muscular or as strong as John's, was as comforting. Her brother, she knew, would always be there for her. There was little risk that something — or someone — would ever come between them, like a prickly stepdaughter who, if she hadn't kidnapped Bella, seemed to want her father and Annie to split up. Or a creepy brother-in-law who wanted to steal the house and might have already stolen Bella. Kevin would always be there for Annie, and she would be there for him, just as their mother had planned, before either of them had known it.

"How are you doing?" she asked.

His shoulders raised a little, then came

down. "Same as you, I expect."

"Still no news?" It was a preposterous question, as Annie knew that John would have been the first to be alerted.

He shook his head, and she snuggled closer, the brisk morning air brushing her cheeks.

"We'll find her," she whispered. She longed to tell him about the note and the doll but she couldn't. Not until Francine knew. Then she asked, "Have you seen Francine?"

"She's in the kitchen. Claire showed up early, and they're moving like robots, not talking, just doing stuff. Baking pumpkin bread. Making coffee." He gestured toward his mug as if only now remembering that he was holding it. He took a sip and wiped his brow. "I don't know how they're functioning."

"What about Jonas?"

"He's with Taylor. They walked from here to the ferry, walked back, then retraced their steps. They went past the Inn all the way out to the point. And back. Now they're in the woods." He sipped again. "Tide's coming in again."

She tried not to think about that or about any evidence that might be washed away. "It got dark so early yesterday," she said.

286

"But soon we'll have full light. It will be easier for everyone to see." She hadn't wanted to check the weather report. If the temperature was going to drop, if the wind was going to pick up, if snow was on the way, Annie didn't want to know.

"Reinforcements showed up around midnight. At least two dozen drove in from Aquinnah."

Winnie's people, Annie thought. Her dear friend no doubt had quickly spread the word around the tribe.

She felt a twinge of guilt that she'd slept for a few hours. "What about Rex?" she asked. "Has he joined the search?" She felt an urge to ask if Kevin could get his hands on a piece of Rex's handwriting. Though she'd turned the note over to John, the image of it was imprinted on her mind.

"Don't know," Kevin replied. "Haven't seen him."

She wanted to pry some more, to ask if he knew where Rex had been the afternoon before, and if so, what he had been doing. But Annie stopped herself. This was no time for idle accusations: she must keep her thoughts on Bella. And on helping Francine get through this, whatever "this" turned out to be. Maybe that way she'd be able to get through it, too.

Slipping her arm from Kevin's, she patted his knee. "I need to see Francine. You want to walk up to the Inn with me? Get a refill on that coffee?" It would be nice if Kevin went with her. Not that she'd need or even want him in the same room when she gave Francine the news, but it would be nice to know that she had backup right outside the door.

They began a slow trek through the pastels of dawn, through the far-off sounds of footsteps treading in unison through the meadow and the mingle of voices drifting up from the boats down on the water. The reinforcements were clearly still at work, while no doubt praying that Bella would be found, that Bella was all right.

Francine was sitting on a stool in the kitchen, hugging her small self and staring out the window that stretched the entire width of the big room. Across the channel, the beacon in the lighthouse on the Edgartown side winked red, pause, red.

Annie bit her lip. "Hi, honey," she said quietly. There was no sign of Claire, only collective murmurs coming from the great room.

Francine hugged herself more tightly and nodded in response.

Annie stepped away from Kevin and went to her. "They'll find her soon," she whispered. "Now come with me into the reading room. Just the two of us."

Francine slid off the stool and walked out of the kitchen, her gaze having shifted from the window to the floor in front of her. She headed toward the shortcut through the hallway that ran under the staircase between the chef's room and the laundry room, most likely to avoid the volunteers who were gathered in the great room. Assuming that her thoughts were functioning well enough to think to do that.

Kevin and Annie exchanged painful glances, then Annie asked him to give her a couple of minutes, then bring them coffee.

By the time she reached the reading room, Francine was seated in one of the cozy barrel chairs, staring at the wall of bookshelves just as she had stared out at the lighthouse, then at the floor.

"Can you stand up for a second?" Annie asked.

Francine's long-lashed eyelids blinked, but she didn't move.

"Please?"

She stood.

Annie went to her and wrapped her arms around her. In her embrace, Annie felt the robot start to weaken. Then tremble. *Please cry,* Annie wanted to say. *Please let it out right here, right now, just the two of us.* She moved one hand to the back of Francine's head and threaded her fingers through the girl's pixie-cut black hair.

"It's okay," Annie whispered. "She's going to be okay."

It seemed to take forever before small heaves began, followed, at last, by subtle shudders and, finally, tears.

"She'll be okay," Annie whispered over and over.

"But I can't . . . ," Francine sniffled.

"Sssh. Yes, you can. You can stay strong and positive. And know that we aren't going to give up. Not until they find her."

But Francine shook her head. "I can't go on without her."

Annie's heart felt as if it were swelling and about to leap out of her chest. She wanted to reassure Francine that the worst was not going to happen, but she kept seeing the image of the doll, her soggy orange hair matted against the round cotton face that Claire had painted with pink circles for her cheeks, round black eyes like Bella's, and a perfect little mouth. "I think she's still on the property," Annie said. "Come on, let's sit."

Francine whisked some of her tears away, then dropped onto the barrel chair again. Annie pulled a matching one close to her. She sat, then reached out and took both of Francine's hands in hers. And prayed for the right words to come.

"They found Bella's doll, Francine. The one with the orange hair. She must have dropped it." There was no need to say that the doll was on the beach, that the tide had been coming in again, that there was a chance Bella had walked into the surf and been carried away. Instead she said, "So it must mean she's here. Somewhere." With that, she offered a small smile that she hoped looked optimistic.

Francine didn't respond.

Annie kept holding her hands, hoping to transfer any courage she might have. She'd do anything if it meant taking Francine's pain away, the way she supposed a mother would want to do for her hurting child.

Suddenly, Francine lifted her eyes and said, "She lost it last week."

It took a couple of seconds for Annie to realize what she'd said. "The doll? Bella lost the doll last week?"

"The orange-haired one. Yes."

Annie let go of Francine's hands. She

wasn't sure if the revelation was good news. Or not.

Then Francine jerked her head toward Annie as if her senses had just awoken. "The bear my aunt gave her is missing, though. The teddy bear. I didn't tell John I couldn't find it, because if it's with Bella, it would mean they're both lost, wouldn't it?"

Not knowing what to say to that deduction, Annie simply said, "Yes, I guess it would." She made a mental note, however, to mention it to John, if for no other reason than to prevent him from thinking she was keeping anything from him.

"Coffee?" The question came from the doorway. Kevin was standing there, holding two steaming mugs.

Francine stood up and said, "I didn't sleep last night. I think I'll go to bed." She walked past Kevin as if he weren't there and departed from the room, leaving a cloud of melancholy in her wake.

And all the air rushed out of Annie, as if her lungs were big balloons and someone had pricked them with a pin.

Kevin gulped the coffee that he'd brought for Francine. "Speaking of which, I'm going to go find Taylor. She's been outside all night. I need to convince her to get some sleep."

"And Jonas," Annie said. "He needs rest, too." No matter what had happened, Jonas also needed to be taken care of.

She told her brother that she'd see him later, that there was someone else she needed to check on. She waited until he left, then grabbed her phone and went out to the reception area. Once at the massive staircase, she took the steps two at a time.

When Annie reached Rose's room, she paused. And said a quick prayer that Rose would come to the door, invite Annie inside, and tell her she'd been too upset to join the others in the search and hoped Annie would forgive her.

But when Annie knocked, there was no reply.

So she knocked again.

And again.

She called out Rose's name.

No answer.

And no sounds were coming from within.

Chapter 28

She cries a lot. I wish she wouldn't. Doesn't she know I'm trying my best to keep her happy? When she isn't crying, she holds her teddy bear and looks at me but doesn't talk.

She doesn't eat much, either. I throw out most of the food I bought. No surprise. It's not like I knew she'd be with me. But I can't go shopping again. For all I know, the police are looking for me.

Today we went for a walk in the woods. I thought the fresh air would be good for her and tire her out so she'd sleep better at night and wouldn't wake up crying. But when we were outside, I heard a noise. It could have been a deer or maybe a squirrel, but it's hunting season, so I realized it was dangerous for us to be out walking around. Aside from the risk of being shot, what if someone saw us?

We came back inside, and she sat in the corner of the plaid chair again, holding her bear, looking at me. At least she ate a little chicken noodle soup and a few saltines. And she didn't cry. Then she fell asleep.

I like watching her sleep. She's so perfect, so innocent. It reminds me of the first time I saw her, when she was curled up in a basket on the kitchen table. Though I have no idea why, I even remember what I had on that day — torn jeans and a plain blue flannel shirt. I'd been in the basement playing video games.

But suddenly I was in the kitchen and the baby was there. Earl Lyons was there, too. And Annie Sutton — the woman who was going to marry Abigail's father now.

Sometimes the world is really small.

CHAPTER 29

Annie gave up. She decided she shouldn't read anything into Rose's not being home. There could be a million reasons why she wasn't there, none of them mysterious. None of them pointing to her as the guilty party.

Leaving the Inn, Annie went down to her cottage and ducked beneath the yellow tape again. She heard John before she saw him. He was still in the bedroom, and he was talking on the phone.

"I don't care," he sniped, his voice so loud she might have heard it down by the water. "Get your butt over here."

At first Annie thought he was talking to Linc and that his voice was raised because Linc was out on the water, and between the engine rumbling in the rescue boat and the wind blowing around, Linc couldn't hear him unless he shouted. However, telling his friend and fellow officer to get his butt over there wasn't John's m.o.

If Annie were in a better mood, she would have laughed at herself for thinking about John in police-speak — m.o. being cop talk for "modus operandi." Instead, she stood in the living room and waited until he came out of the bedroom. She wondered if he wished he'd been able to slam down a receiver, the way anger could be vented in phone calls of yesteryear.

He was dressed. He walked to the rocking chair, sat down, and started to lace up his boots.

"Bella lost the doll last week, not last night," Annie blurted out.

She was startled by the chill in the room; she knew he hadn't lit a fire to avoid moving around too much and possibly disrupting evidence. It was bad enough that they had slept there. She quickly shared what Francine had told her about the orange-haired cloth doll.

"Crap," he said.

Annie didn't mention that it actually might be good news; the fact that Bella had lost it a week ago meant there was a chance she hadn't gone down to the beach, strolled into the harbor, and . . .

"Abigail's on her way," John said. "She finally answered her phone."

Annie pressed her lips together. So he'd been talking to . . . her.

He stood up; he always seemed taller when he was in uniform. "I told her the least she could do was help out in the kitchen, so her grandmother could go home and rest. I reminded her that the woman might seem immortal, but she's almost seventy-six."

Biting her tongue was something Annie rarely did. But Annie was not going to comment about Abigail. Not then, anyway. Maybe never.

"I've gotta get down to the water and relieve Linc. He needs some shut-eye, too. You don't mind if he camps out in here, do you?"

She shook her head. "Of course not. But before you go, I need to tell you something else. Jonas said that Francine's aunt and uncle want her to live in Minneapolis with Bella and the new baby."

John frowned. "What?"

She repeated the news.

"When did he tell you that?"

"Last night. I was going to tell you, but then I saw Linc, and he called you, and you'd just found the doll, and, later, I forgot about that . . ."

He held up a hand. "Stop. I'm not interrogating you."

She lowered her eyes. "There's more. Her aunt and uncle don't think Bella should be raised here on the island. They said something about it being too limited for a child. And for Francine. Don't forget that both the girls are Marty's nieces."

He studied Annie, as if his pearl-gray eyes were soaking in her words.

"What do you think?" she asked. "Would they have taken her? Left the note? But how could they have? They're in Minneapolis."

"I have no idea. But we can't rule anything out. I wish I'd found out sooner." His jaw tightened, as if he were trying not to be angry with her the way he was angry with his older daughter.

"I'm sorry, John. It honestly didn't occur to me that they'd want to scare Francine. Or harm Bella. And then there was the doll . . . ."

He checked his phone. "Forget it. Right now, I've got to find Linc. If the note's for real, we'll find her. Maybe we'll get a ransom call this morning. They typically come within the first twenty-four hours of a kidnapping."

"A ransom . . . ?" She'd thought of that, of course. But having it flit through her psyche and hearing John say it out loud

299

were two very different things.

He headed toward the door. "Go back to the Inn until we meet at ten. I don't want you hanging around in here alone. Work on your list. And if you hear anything else, let me know right away. Okay?"

She watched him leave, knowing he wasn't angry with her but rather at the huge responsibility that had crash-landed on his shoulders. And the fact that so many people were counting on him.

As Annie walked up the hill, she decided that before putting the names Rex and Rose on her list, she should make sure that every closet, every corner, even under every bed of the Inn had been inspected. Besides, right now, moving around suited her far better than sitting in a chair and trying to think. As she reached the patio, she heard a rustle in the shrubbery; maybe a raccoon was running late to get back to its den now that the sun was up. She didn't see a raccoon, a skunk, or any other creature. But she did spot the bulkhead that led down to the root cellar.

The root cellar.

She stopped.

Had anyone looked for Bella down there? Bella knew that the fruit "lived" there; she'd often gone with Francine to pick out veggies and things they'd canned the year before and the sweet apples that she loved. It was possible that Lucy — or the OB cops — might not have thought to look there.

Suddenly feeling skittish, Annie glanced around. She didn't see anyone she could enlist to go down with her; everyone must be searching or in the kitchen prepping food or catching a little sleep. She told herself it didn't matter, that it would be better if she did this alone. If Bella was there, being held captive by someone, maybe Annie could talk to that person. And at least Bella would see someone she knew who loved her.

Or . . . maybe Bella had wandered down there alone and was too scared of the dark to find her way out. Maybe John had been right the first time when he'd suggested that the note had been a prank. Maybe Bella had been sitting in the cellar, eating her fill of apples, and then fallen asleep. Maybe she was awake and confused right now, waiting for someone to come and get her.

Annie prayed that it was true.

Taking her phone out of her pocket, she turned on the flashlight app. She also clicked on the screen with the red circle, the one that was the Emergency SOS. Not that there would be a problem, she tried to convince herself. But it would be better to be prepared.

Watch your head, came a voice, Murphy's voice, from above. *And don't worry. I've got your back.*

For the first time since the afternoon before, Annie smiled. As long as Murphy was with her in spirit, yes, Annie would not feel alone. As she opened the bulkhead door, she felt an unexpected twinge of sorrow that Murphy — or Stan and the boys — couldn't be there for the wedding. She hoped this wasn't the start of Murphy's family growing farther away, more distant — geographically, emotionally — with time.

Ducking under the low clearance, Annie crept down the first one, two, three steps, and was met with the dank aroma of a root cellar close to the sea, partly veiled by the fresh scent of fruit from nearby orchards and veggies from local gardens. It was a special, welcoming place, not at all like the basement of her Boston apartment that she'd only once dared to venture into.

When she made it to the bottom, she reached for the chain attached to the overhead light, her pulse racing a little, anxious now about other possibilities of what she'd see. Would Bella be there motionless, lying in a wood-slatted bushel basket? Would whoever had written the note be standing guard, a gun poised at Bella's heart? Her neck? Her head?

Annie's hands grew clammy; she gripped her phone to keep it from sliding to the dirt floor. With her eyes wide open, she pulled the chain; the single lightbulb glared. And there it was: the twelve-by-sixteen space, packed with stores for the winter — squashes, potatoes, parsnips, beets, and buckets of carrots. And, of course, the apples. And shelves that lined two of the concrete walls and were filled with Claire and Francine's canning creations from last summer — jars of everything from green beans to strawberry jam and Earl's grandmother's recipe for chutney, which he claimed had originated in India and made its way to the Vineyard by way of the shipping trade during British colonization.

But Bella was not resting in an apple basket, and there was no hulking figure (had Annie assumed it would be Rex?) hovering over her. She exhaled but nonetheless moved gingerly around baskets and barrels and through the room, looking behind things, under things, above things.

"Bella?" Annie whispered. "It's Ammie. I'm here." She told herself she was whispering so she wouldn't frighten Bella. But although writing her mysteries often brought her to darker, more menacing places, most of those were in her mind, occasionally formed by photos or glimpses of real people and places that would fit her imaginary plot. A few times a police officer had brought her to the scene of an old crime she'd read about, and the officer had described what it had looked like then and explained the accuracy with which they'd tracked down the bad guys. Those crimes, however, had taken place years earlier. And this time she was not writing fiction; she was trying to find Bella. And it was happening right there. Right now.

And suddenly . . . a clatter. Annie's eyes darted from corner to corner. Then something dashed past her. She yelped . . . just as a tiny chipmunk ran up the steps and escaped outside.

"You okay down there, whoever you are?" Earl's voice called down.

Annie dropped her face into her hands. "It's me, Earl. Annie. I'll be right up."

I sent him to find you, Murphy said. *Before you scared yourself to death.*

"Thanks. You're a pal," Annie replied. Then she moved toward the bulkhead, tugged the chain, extinguishing the bulb, and went back upstairs out toward the daylight.

"It's almost ten," Earl said. He led her to the patio; they sat on the low stone wall before going into the Inn. His skin was pale, his face was drawn; he looked older and grayer since she'd seen him the night before. She supposed they all did. "John will be here any minute to make sure we did as we were told. Half of which, by the way, I think he dreamed up to keep us out of his hair. And to keep us from losing ours."

"Sometimes distraction is a good thing," Annie replied.

Earl didn't answer. He looked down at his hands, studied his fingernails. "What do you think, Annie? Where is she?"

She wanted to tell him about the note. Though she understood why John wanted to keep it confidential until they determined whether or not it was a prank, Annie thought the others might see it as good news. And they could use some good news, couldn't they?

But as she stared down toward the harbor, Annie said, "I think we have to trust John and Linc — and their whole team. And if John comes up with more busywork for us, we should do it. It might seem that every hour Bella's gone means something awful has happened to her, but we have to remember that every hour, the police are putting more pieces together."

"Pieces? What pieces? It doesn't seem like they have a lick of evidence."

How she hated deceiving Earl. "Just because John isn't telling us, doesn't mean there's no evidence. We have to have faith, Earl."

He stood and started pacing the natural, buff-colored stone that they'd chosen to blend in with the landscape of Chappy.

"Have you seen Taylor or Jonas this morning?" she asked.

He shook his head. "I hope Kevin finally convinced her to go home and sleep. I'm not sure if Jonas is still in the woods. He must have walked from Cape Poge Light down to Wasque and back by now."

"That's a long way."

"Seven miles each way. But he's pretty upset."

Annie saw no need to add that they all were upset. And none of them were burdened with the guilt that Jonas was.

"So . . . ," Earl added, "did you make your list of suspects?"

"I tried. I didn't get too far."

"Is Rex Winsted on it?"

Annie winced. "Why? Do you know something I don't?"

Earl guffawed. "Not really. But Kevin told me what he's trying to do about the house. Doesn't matter how old he is; Winsted is a spoiled brat. His mother made him that way, and I always figured his father liked that his son was a tough kid. Rex could've kidnapped Bella to try and hurt his sister. For all he knows, Bella is her grandkid, as much as the new baby's going to be."

Annie hadn't thought of that. She only knew that Rex gave her the chills. He gave Rose the chills, too. But Annie wasn't going to tell Earl that both Rex and Rose were on her list.

Instead, she said, "I don't know, Earl. It's hard to picture Rex harboring a small child. What would he do when Bella started crying? And what would be his point? To hold her for ransom until Taylor and Kevin agreed to get out of the house? Legally, it's already his."

He scratched his chin. "Yeah. I suppose you're right. But I can't help but believe she's somewhere with somebody. And that somebody else knows something." Then he looked squarely at her, as if seeing her for the first time. "Do you? Do you know something, Annie?"

She turned her head slightly, so she wasn't looking in his eyes.

"You do, don't you," he didn't ask, but stated. "Like, maybe you know why John still has your cottage cordoned off with that god-awful yellow tape, like it's some kind of crime scene when he hasn't done the same anywhere else. What's going on, Annie?"

She lowered her gaze. She hated, hated, outright lying to him. Earl was a kind, caring man, and he deserved to know everything. Still, Annie had given John her word not to tell anyone about the damn note. And she really didn't want to break her promise to let him do his job without her sticking her nose in.

"Earl, please," she pleaded. "Like I said, we have to trust John."

"Bullshit," Earl said. It was one of the rare times Annie had heard either of the Lyons men curse.

She quickly stood up. "Let's get coffee. I think Lucy made fresh cinnamon bread this morning. I smelled it when I was in the kitchen earlier. Maybe we can bring a few slices to our meeting."

She could tell that he was not appeased. But he let her lead the way into the Inn and he grumbled only once or twice.

CHAPTER 30

John was late. It was obvious that Earl had been right: the tasks John had assigned were mostly meant to tamp down anxiety. And to keep everyone's hands (no doubt especially Annie's) off the real investigation.

They sat in a small circle, taking turns reporting their progress.

Claire had prepared enough provisions to keep the search teams sustained, with food, drink, and paper goods.

Earl had picked up the Stop & Shop order and distributed a "whole hunk of stuff" last night to the volunteers on the beach, in the meadow, and out in the woods. Next, he said, he'd head back to the *On Time* at noon to pick up Abigail. She'd called to say she wanted to help because her boyfriend was back in New Hampshire and she had nothing to do. Earl chuckled when he relayed that. He said he told her there would be lots to do and hoped she'd lend a hand.

Annie surmised that Abigail's actions had little to do with the boyfriend not being on the island and more to do with her father speaking to his daughter in a way Annie had not heard him speak to either of his girls; she suspected that Abigail hadn't, either.

Earl also mentioned that he was collecting the keys to every vehicle that came to the Inn so he'd be able to move anything on or off the road or the driveway in case emergency crews needed to get through.

Lucy said she'd talked to Winnie the night before and made sure Annie's booth was ready; Winnie reassured her that it would be manned all day until the Fair closed at four o'clock. Lucy had also baked eight dozen cookies and six cinnamon breads. And she'd secured extra hats and gloves and socks. She was, after all, tenacious, like her dad.

Francine didn't show up for the meeting. Claire said she'd left the Inn and gone back to their house to try to sleep because it was too hard for her to sleep at the Inn, what with Bella's bed lying there empty. The truth was, Earl had driven Francine to the house under protest; she'd been so tired and numb, she hadn't had the strength to complain.

John said the OB cops were done canvassing the Inn; they hadn't found a trace of Bella's having gone missing.

"And I checked the root cellar this morning," Annie added. "Nothing was there that didn't belong, except a chipmunk."

Earl chuckled again, sadly that time.

Then Annie blurted out, "Has anyone seen Rose? I was wondering if she joined one of the search teams." Then, so it wouldn't seem as if Rose were a suspect, Annie added, "I'm only trying to keep track of our tenants."

"She left last night," Lucy said.

Annie thought she must have heard her wrong.

"She left?" John asked before Annie could. "Where'd she go?"

"I don't know. When the cops went to search her room, she said the 'ruckus' was too hard on her nerves."

No one spoke.

Then John said, "I thought I asked everyone to stay on Chappy."

Annie didn't remember he'd been that specific. Then again, she might have been too mentally drained to have been listening closely.

"I don't think she left the Vineyard," Lucy said. "She said something about going to West Tisbury. Besides, it was kind of late.

She would have missed the last boat off the Vineyard."

"But not the *On Time*?" Earl asked.

"I don't think so. The last trip off Chappy's at eleven now, right?" Lucy asked.

"Yup, it's winter," Earl said.

"I'm pretty sure she left before eleven."

John turned to Annie. "When we're done here, would you mind checking with the captain to see if Rose went over?"

"No problem." She didn't tell him that Rose was on her list; she hadn't told him about the woman's skittishness around Rex or the supposed incident in the chef's room with the invisible mouse. What else hadn't she shared? She tried to think straight but couldn't seem to.

John told them he and Linc were nailing down a couple of leads but nothing to get excited about yet. The only lead Annie knew of was the note. She wondered what he was holding back, or if he'd thought that by saying a "couple" of leads, it would give them hope that Bella would be found soon.

She knitted and purled her fingers together, trying to calm the gymnastics in her mind.

He told them to be vigilant and, again, to call or text if they heard or saw anything, whether or not they thought it was connected. "I want to find her before nightfall. That's it for now. Thanks, everyone."

Claire and Lucy headed back to the kitchen. Earl said he'd go find Taylor and Jonas; later, when he picked up Abigail, he'd have her go with him to make the rounds to the volunteers and distribute lunches to them. Then he'd put her in the kitchen so that Claire could go home and take a nap. And maybe he'd do the same.

After they'd left and John and Annie were alone, he told her he was going to meet with the Staties.

"Do you really have a 'couple' of leads?" she asked.

He kissed her good-bye and said he'd share stuff with her later. Then he left before she had the chance to tell him about Rose and Rex and the questionable mouse.

The air had chilled; the sky was heavy with low clouds. As Annie walked to her Jeep to fulfill her latest duty, she prayed it wouldn't snow, at least until they'd found Bella. If there was a storm, she didn't think she could bear wondering whether Bella was somewhere warm, somewhere sheltered. Especially a nor'easter, like the one that had pummeled Chappy the night she'd arrived on her doorstep. When the power had gone out. And Annie could not get help for the tiny baby because the internet wasn't connecting.

Now, as she got into the Jeep, turned on the ignition, and let it warm up a bit, Annie felt as powerless to help Bella as she had that first night.

But you did it, Murphy said. *You're always stronger and smarter and more resilient than you think.*

"Only because you keep telling me I am."

She weaved around the vehicles that were scattered in all directions, then made her way onto North Neck Road and out to the main road that was blessedly paved. She reached the *On Time* almost as quickly as it took for the little ferry to cross the channel to Edgartown.

But it wasn't there; it had just left for the other side.

Annie parked. And waited.

While she sat, she glanced around the compact lot. Rose's small white Fiat with the Maine license plates wasn't there. If he could be believed, Rex did not have a vehicle on either side of the channel. Besides, the two pickups and single SUV that now sat in the lot were old and rusty — typical of vehicles that had logged lots of miles on remote island roads, not of one belonging to a former restaurant celeb from the city.

It was odd, she supposed, that only three vehicles were in the lot, Saturday being the busiest day of Christmas in Edgartown, and two weeks before Christmas itself. Annie wondered if it was because most folks who lived on Chappy were scouring the Vineyard's north side, hunting for Bella. That morning, as she'd walked through the great room, she'd overheard a man she'd recognized but didn't know suggest canvassing the vacant summer houses and cottages on Chappy — which Annie presumed were numerous.

Resting her forehead on the steering wheel now, she let herself cry a little. Not a sobbing, noisy, all-out cry, but more like a whimper of exhaustion and frustration. It was interrupted when she heard the *On Time* chug back into its berth.

She wiped her eyes, inhaled, and got out of the Jeep. She left the engine running.

Captain Joe, Lottie Nelson's husband, was working the day shift. Annie had come to know the family fairly well; they were good people, good neighbors.

"Annie!" he shouted when he saw her. "Any word yet?"

It made sense that Joe knew about Bella's

disappearance. In addition to the grapevine, he must have ferried many of the volunteers.

"Afraid not," she replied. "But I'm trying to find one of our tenants. I think we got our wires crossed. There's so much going on."

"Who you looking for?"

"Rose Atkins. She drives a little white Fiat. You know her?"

"I know the car, but not the woman. Haven't seen it today, though. Sorry." He signaled a lone Toyota that it was okay to board.

"I think she went over last night. Do you know who was on then?"

The Toyota drove onto the raft of a ferry, and Joe hooked the canvas strip across the boarding ramp. "That'd be Captain Fred. I can shoot him a text. Will that help?"

"Sure. Thanks."

Instead of heading out, Joe stopped what he was doing, pulled out his phone, and looked to be busy texting. He signaled Annie to wait in the lot; then the *On Time* engine gulped a few times and came back to life, and off it went toward Edgartown.

Annie returned to the Jeep and got inside to get warm. While she sat there, she thought about Rose. The truth was, she couldn't imagine what the woman's motive could be to kidnap Bella. Nor could she picture her actually taking the child, any more than she could picture Rex doing it. Just because their personalities were quirky, it didn't make them villains. Annie had created enough shady characters in her books to know that.

Thinking of her books, she was reminded of Trish. And of the big deal that awaited Annie's blessing. If only she had the time to think about it with a clear head that wasn't jammed up with thoughts of Bella. So jammed up, in fact, she hadn't even thought about the wedding. She hoped that John wouldn't feel slighted if he knew that. Then again, she doubted he'd thought about it, either.

By the time she looked back to the ferry berth, the *On Time* was docking again. Annie got out of the Jeep and was assaulted by a wind gust that hadn't been there three minutes earlier. She walked to the shack next to the berth and took shelter. From there she could tell that Joe had no vehicles or walk-ons on board.

Joe waved, and Annie moved from the shelter close to the pilings.

"He said yes," Joe shouted. "A woman in a white Fiat went over last night on the ten o'clock. She didn't go back on the eleven, and there weren't any emergency calls during the night. I've been on all morning and haven't seen her, so she's not back on Chappy unless she left her car at the wharf and swam across."

Annie offered a weak smile and thanked him. Then she went back to the Jeep, wondering where the heck Rose Atkins had gone. And why — unless it really had been due to the "ruckus," as she'd claimed. But if she'd gone to Edgartown last night, what would have stopped her from taking the early boat out of Vineyard Haven this morning and leaving the island completely? Annie doubted that John would have thought he needed to interrogate the entire Steamship Authority queue to see if someone connected to Bella's disappearance had been trying to escape. Besides, who would have thought that Rose, of all people, would need to sneak away?

Then another thought surfaced: should Annie unlock Rose's room and peek inside? Though Lucy and the cops from Oak Bluffs had examined all the rooms, as far as Annie knew, they'd only been looking for Bella. Annie could poke through Rose's things and perhaps find a clue, unless she had taken her belongings with her — which, of course, would suggest much more than a clue. Of course, Annie would be breaking the unwritten Innkeeper's rule not to trespass on a guest's or a tenant's space (she'd done that once before with nearly fatal results), but this wasn't about being nosy. Bella's life could be at stake.

And some things were worth taking a chance for.

Revving the engine, she drove back to the Inn faster than she should have.

CHAPTER 31

Since Rose had moved into the Inn for the eight-month, off-season stint, Annie hadn't been inside her room. Long-term guests were expected to clean their own spaces; cleaning supplies were kept in the upstairs hall closet for them to use whenever they wanted. So far, Annie hadn't had any complaints from tenants about any of the others' housekeeping habits, not that they'd know for sure. But unless there were aromas from cooking (which was prohibited in the rooms) or any dubious odors wafting throughout the second floor, cleanliness was assumed. And privacy was honored.

But Annie saw no good reason to care about that now.

Because it was nearing lunchtime, the kitchen was a cauldron of activity. Several new volunteers had arrived; she nodded a quick hello and thanked them for their help as she passed through the great room and went toward the reception area at the front door. Once there, she looked over both shoulders and up the staircase. When she was certain no one was nearby, she unlocked the reception desk, shuffled through the duplicate keys, and retrieved the one to room 2, Rose's room. She slid it into her pocket, relocked the drawer, and breathed. She felt as if she were breaking and entering into her own home.

"Stay with me, Murph," Annie whispered.

Murphy didn't respond, which was exasperating given the circumstances and the number of times the two of them had performed questionable antics — mostly at Murphy's bidding.

At the top of the stairs, Annie noted that no one was there, either: as far as she knew, all the tenants had joined the search for Bella. *Everyone but Rose,* she reminded herself.

She put the key into the lock and turned it; the door opened without resistance. Annie sneaked inside and closed it firmly behind her.

She breathed again.

That time, she closed her eyes.

When she opened them again, the first thing she saw was the dollhouse, sitting atop the desk in a corner by a window.

"Ohhh . . . ," she said aloud before stopping herself. Could the dollhouse be significant? She'd seen it the day she'd brought Rose tea and invited her to share Thanksgiving dinner. At the time, Annie merely had thought it odd, but now her legs powered her toward it, as if she were in the Martha's Vineyard Marathon and the clock was ticking.

Could the dollhouse mean that Rose wanted to be a child again . . . a child like Bella?

A small chair stood in front of it; Annie sat down and stared inside.

The furnishings were ornate, Victorian style. She remembered when dollhouses had become popular for adults, perhaps in the early seventies. Her aunt Sally had bought one; Annie had loved looking at the niceties inside. But when Aunt Sally and her husband moved to Schenectady after Sally's indiscretion, the dollhouse had gone with them.

And though Sally did not get divorced, Annie wondered if she'd felt alone, the way Rose appeared to be. And if both of the women had created an imaginary, miniature home, hoping it would somehow compensate for the pieces of their lives that were missing.

Similar to Aunt Sally's, Rose's dollhouse had wallpaper and paintings on the walls. The living room showcased settees, wing chairs, and a mini replica of a piano; a mahogany table, chairs, and matching sideboard were in the dining room, atop which was what looked like a silver tea set. A china closet on the opposite side of the room held teeny plates and cups that were painted with what looked like pink roses.

Unlike Aunt Sally's, Rose's house had a staircase that led up to a bathroom and three well-furnished bedrooms. But also, unlike Sally's, the beds had people in them. Tiny figurines: a blonde mother, a dark-haired dad, a small, equally dark-haired girl in another bedroom. A kitten not much bigger than the tip of Annie's pinkie was asleep next to the girl. Hanging from a closet door, a tiny hanger held what looked like a white christening dress, complete with a shoulder-length white veil. A chill skipped down Annie's spine as she thought of the wedding dress hanging in her bedroom in the cottage. She prayed there was not a connection.

The third bedroom was furnished, but no figurines were in it.

Goose bumps danced on Annie's arms. She had no idea what the dollhouse meant to Rose; she didn't want to think that the fantasy included a little girl who represented Bella.

Standing up again, Annie tried to pacify her nerves by believing that the dollhouse was merely a harmless pastime, perhaps one that evoked memories from Rose's childhood. Maybe that's all Aunt Sally's had been to her, too. Besides, Annie hadn't sneaked inside to judge her tenant. And she could hardly accuse her of taking Bella solely because of a toy.

Next, she checked the closet. Few clothes were there; Annie had no idea how many Rose had brought with her, so she couldn't know if she'd taken any with her, wherever she was. In the bathroom, however, there were no signs of personal items: toothbrush, comb, lipstick. Nothing. Only a bar of Annie's soap, which every tenant received.

The chill zipped down her spine again.

She moved back to the bedroom and over to the windows. Because room 2 was rented to island visitors from May through September, it was at the back of the house, with a breathtaking view of Edgartown Harbor and the lighthouse. And though Annie saw the same view several dozen times every day, she always paused to look, the same way most islanders did, whether they were at the cliffs, on the beach, or watching the big boat come or go. Some scenery was never taken for granted.

Gazing out the window now, she almost felt a sense of peace until she realized that from the windows she also had a bird's-eye view of the patio, the walkway that led from the kitchen door, and, most disturbingly, Annie's cottage halfway down to the beach.

She nearly screamed.

Did Rose stand at the window, monitoring Annie's life? Did she crack the windows and eavesdrop on conversations of guests when they sat on the patio? And, most of all, did she watch the comings and goings of those who came to and from the Inn? If so, could she have seen whoever had taken Bella? Or worse, could she have waited until she knew that only Jonas and Bella were inside, waited until Jonas was out of sight, and then taken the child herself?

Annie stood, futilely waiting for an answer. The only thing she knew for certain was that she had to tell John.

As she turned from the once-breathtaking view that now seemed sinister, her gaze moved down to the window seat. To Rose's rocks.

No longer in a heap, they were evenly displayed in a single layer. Annie calculated there were eight or nine dozen, maybe more, ranging in diameter from an inch to three or four — some gray, some white, some speckled, some with bits of color such as coral, black, and brown. At least Rose had spread a towel across the cushion before she'd put them there.

As Annie looked closely, she realized that they were all heart-shaped, which seemed sweet. Each had been lacquered and polished to a high shine and had a hand-lettered message on top: LOVE. PEACE. HAPPINESS. The thoughts seemed harmless enough. Until she spotted one that simply read: COME BACK TO ME. The words were in block letters, as those on the Post-it had been. But the paint was thicker than the ink used on the note, so it was hard to tell if the handwriting was the same.

Then she remembered she'd seen small painted rocks from time to time in random places — resting on a dune at South Beach, under a shrub outside St. Andrew's Church, tucked into a corner of the outside staircase at the Edgartown Town Hall. Many had appeared during the worst time of the pandemic; they'd been brightly colored and offered heartfelt messages with words like HOPE.

But Annie didn't think that, like Rose's

rocks, they had all been heart-shaped.

Just as she turned to leave, she noticed a small stool in the opposite corner. As she moved closer to it, she saw two cans of lacquer and one small can of black acrylic paint sitting on top. Next to them, a canning jar held three paintbrushes — all of which seemed to prove that Rose herself had collected the stones and painted them with words of love and peace. And . . . COME BACK TO ME. Whatever that meant.

She wondered if the OB cops had found them questionable, or if they hadn't bothered with them, because they'd only been authorized to search for Bella.

All Annie knew for sure was that she needed to get out of the room. And find a way to tell John — without pissing him off — that she'd been snooping.

She moved to the door and listened. Hearing nothing, she opened it an inch or two. Thank God, no one was there. So she slipped into the hallway, closed and locked the door behind her, and sneaked back down the stairs, happy that she'd dropped one of the rocks into her jacket pocket.

CHAPTER 32

Annie grabbed a cup of coffee and half a chicken salad sandwich from the table in the dining room. She asked Claire if she needed help and felt guilty for being grateful when she said no, thank you, that she and Lucy had everything under control. She added that Abigail and Earl would have plenty of bag lunches to bring to the group out in the woods, as soon as Abigail arrived. Claire also said that the folks in the meadow had combed the grid half a dozen times, and John had suggested they move on to the other properties on North Neck; they'd picked up food and drink on their way. They wouldn't be allowed inside the homes unless they saw something irregular on the property, and if they did, John would need to get a warrant.

Annie was reminded again that Francine had been squatting in the big house next to the cottage that Annie had been renting the first winter she was there. Because it was officially off-season now, she knew that lots of summer homes were regarded as fair game for intruders who were bold enough — or desperate enough — to break in and help themselves. It was especially appreciated if the heat and electricity had been left on, not shut off until the owners returned in summer.

She went out to her Jeep to have her lunch and try to think; she turned on the ignition and cranked up the heat. While she ate, Annie thought about all the things that had mattered so much only yesterday: her wedding and the ugly dress; the situation with Kevin, Taylor, and Rex; the latest announcement from her editor and the decision Annie hadn't yet made. Those things had seemed so consequential yesterday; now they were only pieces in the game of life. Her life, but, nonetheless, a game of sorts. Now, with Bella missing, nothing else mattered. Not a single thing.

Twenty minutes after finishing her lunch, Annie fell sound asleep.

She dreamed of the babies she'd never had, of the unconditional love she'd heard about but had never felt, maternal love that had escaped her, substituted by a protective love for Murphy's boys and, more recently, for Francine and Bella. She dreamed in full blazing color, of rainbows of finger paints on glossy white paper and sandcastles on the beach. The dreams were strangely happy, as if all things she'd missed out on had come full circle now, reminding her that happiness was about perception, about finding it however, wherever one could, even in sleep.

When she awoke, it was long past sunset, yet the sky glimmered pure white with falling snow. Annie was cold; the Jeep had stopped running. It had run out of gas. It occurred to her it was a good thing her vehicle was in good condition, as it didn't appear that any carbon monoxide had leaked through the floorboards into the interior.

She stretched; she rubbed her hands together, even though they still were in her mittens. She reviewed the bits she remembered from her dream and nearly laughed at how the mind could manage to be kind during the most awful times.

Picking up the trash from her lunch, she opened the door and came face-to-face with Winnie, who was dusted with snowflakes and wore a warm smile on her copper skin. Yes, Annie thought, even in the most awful times, life can sprinkle happiness.

"Where have you been?" Winnie asked as they walked through the darkness toward the Inn, the scent of wood crack ling in the fireplace beckoning them. That, and the fact there was nowhere else to go, what with Annie's cottage still off limits.

"I fell asleep in my car," she replied with a woeful laugh. "I had the engine running so I'd be warm, but I ran out of gas." She was too worn out to tell her about Rose's having left Chappy, about how Annie had stolen into her room and seen the dollhouse. And the rocks.

"You must have needed the sleep," Winnie said.

"Afraid so. There's not much of that around here right now."

They went inside and removed their boots and jackets and the rest of their outdoor gear, and Annie led her through the back hall into the reading room. They sat in the comfortable barrel chairs instead of at a table.

"No word on Bella?" Winnie asked once they were settled.

Annie shook her head. "Not that I know of." She glanced at the clock, surprised that it was after six. "A seasoned investigator probably would tell me that the longer we go without finding her, the odds decrease . . ." She shook her head again. "But I have hope. I really do."

"Good," Winnie said. "Good." She nodded as if trying to persuade both of them that having hope could change the outcome. "I'd be outside with my family looking for her, but my knees are always bad in winter." Winnie had ten years or so on Annie, and though she was very active, she once told Annie that wear and tear couldn't always be controlled. "But Barbara and Orrin are out there; Lucas and his girlfriend, Danielle, rounded up some of their old high school pals and they're searching, too. To paraphrase an old saying, I doubt that a single stone on Chappaquiddick will be left unturned."

Winnie's comment about stones reminded Annie of Rose's rock, and that she needed to find John. "We have lots of help, Winnie," she said, her fingers rubbing across the smooth stone in her pocket. "Everyone is being wonderful."

Winnie reached into her woven bag. "Which reminds me, you're a wealthy woman now. Your soap sold out in the first three hours."

"Seriously?"

"When Lucy called, she told me that in addition to the baskets you're going to put together, you're also going to donate your profits from today to island women's services. I made a sign to let people know. I hope that was okay."

Annie had meant to keep her gifts anonymous. But, like most things, it didn't matter now. "That's fine, Winnie. Thank you. Maybe it's why you sold out. You, of all people, know that making soap has become therapeutic for me, the way some people love to bake or make pottery or wampum jewelry." She reached over and squeezed her dear friend's hand. "Whatever I can do will be my modest way of trying to help. To give back, you know?"

Winnie reached into her bag and produced a cotton sack. "Well, then, congratulations are in order. Your 'modest way' now includes nine hundred sixty-five dollars." She plopped the bag on the side table between them.

Annie stared at the sack. "I'm stunned," she said. Then her emotions threatened to take over. "Thanks for taking over today at the Fair . . . and for everything you do. At times like this, it's important for people to keep their most special friends nearby, isn't it?"

Winnie put an arm on Annie's shoulder and gave it a quick rub. "Then and always."

That said, she hauled her solid body from the chair. "Now, I'm going to check on Abigail, who I understand is helping Lucy with supper duties because Claire's gone home to rest. I don't know how all of you are doing it."

"I'm not doing much of anything. John said it's best for those of us who are closest to Bella to stay the heck out of the way or, at least, out of the active search. Like he's afraid we might break down in public and scare everyone away." She did, however, wonder how his two daughters were getting along in the kitchen.

"How's Francine?" Winnie asked.

"Worse than I am. They took her back to Earl's earlier today. I don't know if she's still there."

"And Jonas?"

"He doesn't care that John wants us to stay out of the way. As far as I know, he's been looking for Bella harder than anyone."

Winnie sighed. "Call if you need anything. That includes if you only want to talk. Or share a bottle of wine." She began to leave.

"Wait, Winnie," Annie said, standing up. "By any chance, do you remember a man named Clive Atkins? He lived in West Tisbury in the sixties." It was a long shot, because Winnie would have been quite young in the 1960s.

"The cemetery guy?"

Annie blinked. "Yes. But not up in Aquinnah. Or Chilmark."

"Sure. Clive and my dad worked at the Ag Fair together — they volunteered to clean up before and after. It was at the Grange Hall then and was much smaller than today."

"Do you remember ever seeing his niece? She would have been older than you. Quite small. Or at least she is now."

"Sure. Her name was Mary."

As Earl would say, the news flummoxed Annie. Rose. *Mary Rose.*

"Why?" Winnie asked. "Did you run into her? I think old Clive died a while back."

"He did. In 1984. But, yes, I think his niece is one of our winter renters. I've only just learned that her real name is Mary Rose. Now she goes by Rose."

Winnie's eyebrows lifted. "Well. That's an awfully big coincidence. I didn't know her very well — she was only here in summers. She was a quiet, shy girl and very slight, as I remember. She might have lived in New Hampshire. Or Maine. Somewhere up north."

Quiet. Shy. Slight. Yes, that was her. "Maine, I think," Annie replied. "What was she like?"

Musing for a moment, Winnie said, "I don't really remember. I hung out with her at the hall while the men were working. We'd walk over to Alley's together for ice cream. But she stopped coming to the island when she was maybe fifteen or sixteen. I never did find out why." She hauled her bag onto one shoulder. "Wow. That's a blast from the past. I'd like to see her, though. Is she here or out with the search crew?"

"She left last night. She told Claire that the ruckus made her nervous. I don't know where she is. She might have left the Vineyard, though John had asked everyone not to."

Winnie scowled. "If she's the same person, it's hard to believe she'd go against anyone in authority. I don't think 'trouble' was her thing."

"Then she's probably around here somewhere. I'm so worried about Bella, it's hard to think straight about anything else."

"You don't think she's involved with Bella going missing, do you?"

Annie tried to offer a smile. "Like I said, it's hard to think straight right now." Then she had another thought. It was, again, a long shot, and might merely be her imagination working overtime — also again — but she decided she might as well ask because Winnie would tell her the truth and not judge why she wanted to know. "One more question, please. Do you remember what Rose's uncle looked like?"

"Oh, my friend, now you're really stretching. Hmm. He was an old guy. But when you're a kid, anyone over twenty-one looks old." She squinted, as if that would help her think. "Wait. He was a big guy. Yeah, I remember that. He was taller than my dad. Had a thick neck. Big shoulders." She smiled. "Sorry I can't be more specific."

Big guy. Thick neck. Big shoulders. *He reminds me of someone I once knew,* Rose had said about Rex. "What color was his hair?"

Winnie laughed. "From what I remember, he was close to being bald."

The pieces were starting to coalesce, though they didn't yet explain why Rose might be skittish around Rex, other than perhaps he looked like her long-dead uncle, whom maybe she didn't like. But that wouldn't have anything to do with Bella. Would it?

"I'll see you later, honey," Winnie said, giving Annie one of her generous hugs. "I hear the kitchen calling. But first, I have a five-gallon jug of gas in the van, so I'll pour some into the Jeep. No sense in you getting stranded." She waved and went out of the reading room, leaving Annie more perplexed than she'd been before.

She needed to text John. Whether or not there was any connection between Rose and Rex, it almost didn't matter. And if Rose's strange little rocks were a peculiar link, Annie could not imagine how. But she also knew that determining the level of importance of the information she'd unearthed should not be up to her. John would never forgive her if she kept it from him and it wound up being essential to finding Bella. And Annie would never forgive herself.

WE NEED TO TALK, she texted him. NOW.

She paced the reading room, waiting. Within seconds, he replied.

MEET ME AT YOUR COTTAGE IN FIVE.

She was there in two minutes; John got there in three. They sat at the kitchen table and Annie made tea, which seemed like a trivial effort given the seriousness of the past twenty-eight hours. At least John didn't lecture her for tampering with the kettle and the mugs, as if they could be evidence. Chances were, whoever had left the note hadn't gone into the kitchen and opted for a cup of tea.

He listened as Annie explained the long shot of a link between Rex and Rose.

"So my best guess is that Rex reminds her of her uncle, and that her uncle hadn't been 'nice' to her. To what extent, I have no idea."

Tenting his fingers together, John kept his eyes on his cuticles and seemed to half listen to her words. When she was finished, he merely said, "Interesting."

She pushed her chair back. "I get the feeling you don't really mean that."

"We've already run background checks on all your tenants, including Rose. My dad remembered Clive Atkins; we ran one on him, too. Nothing came up, not even a speeding ticket for either of them."

So he'd already known about Rose's uncle. Annie's agitation rose. "The current situation is hardly a speeding ticket, John."

He rubbed his hands over his face. "I know that, Annie. I'm only trying to tell you that if there's a connection between Rose and Rex, it doesn't seem to have anything to do with Bella."

It sounded as if her instincts had been right about that. But she wasn't finished. Reaching into her pocket, she pulled out the rock and set it on the table.

"And this is . . . ?" he asked.

"It came from Rose's room. I thought you

might want to see it."

He picked it up and studied the message. " 'Come back to me'?"

"It's one of many rocks, all of which Rose has painted with a word or two, mostly messages of hope. Things like 'Love,' 'Peace,' and 'Be Kind.' Like the stones that were scattered around the island early on in the pandemic. Only these are all heart-shaped."

"How many?"

"Around a hundred. More or less. I didn't count them."

"They're all in Rose's room?"

"Yes. There's also lacquer and paint and a couple of brushes, so it's pretty obvious she's doing the painting. I thought you might want to compare it to the lettering on the note."

He studied the rock a moment longer. Then he asked, "And when did you get this?"

"Today."

He eyed her as if she were a suspect. "After we'd learned that Rose was gone," he stated matter-of-factly.

"Well," Annie replied, "yes."

"And you did not have her permission to enter her room without her being there?"

So there they were: John's by-the-book morals, which no doubt served the Edgartown Police Department well, but were a big, fat pain in the neck when it came to Annie's trying to solve a crime.

"Rose left last night without saying where she was going. Because she is a woman alone, I was concerned. She's my tenant, John, and I take the health and safety of all of our tenants seriously. I entered her room for a wellness check. I don't think there's a law against that."

John sighed, then stood up. "I'll turn it over to Linc and bring him up to speed."

She stood, too, and stuffed her hands in her back pockets. "Does that mean you're blowing it off?"

He shook his head. "Not at all. But I'm going off island for a couple of days. There's another lead I need to follow up."

Shifting her stance, Annie knew that the "lead" must be important. John wouldn't leave the Vineyard for an hour, never mind a couple of days, not at a time like this. "Can you tell me where you're going? Or why?" she asked quietly. Sometimes she really did understand that he was the professional, not she. Sometimes she berated herself for forgetting that, for acting as if she knew more about crime and criminals because she'd learned a smidgen while doing research for her books.

He hesitated, as if trying to decide if she was trustworthy. She tried not to take it personally.

"No one seems to be looking for ransom money. So we've been trying to find out if someone wants to settle a score. The only person on our radar was Bella's birth father. Remember him?"

Annie pressed her fingers to her cheeks. "Stephen Thurman?" She didn't want to say she'd already thought of him, but had discounted his involvement because of the way he'd said he wanted no part of the illegitimate "kid," and he had dared them to try to do anything about it.

"As you know," John replied, "after that whole mess, he moved his family off the Vineyard. Well, now he's dead. Died last spring. Some kind of cancer."

She refrained from saying, "Good riddance to the creep."

"With Thurman out of the picture," John continued, "there's one other logical choice. Keep this between us, Annie; in the morning, I'm going to Minneapolis. We've been trying to contact Francine's aunt and uncle, but they're not getting back to us. Which is not a good sign. And before you ask, no. We did not leave a message saying we were Edgartown police officers. And, no, you can't come with me."

She stood mute. And waited.

"I have no idea what, if anything, it means," he continued. "The aunt and uncle could have planned this all along. They could have come to the island and been staying out of sight. We checked the boats and flights, and their names didn't come up. But they could have borrowed someone's ID and rented a car. They could have left the note to stop people from worrying that something bad happened to Bella. And . . . they could be back in Minneapolis by now."

Annie resisted saying that that was a lot of "coulds." Especially when John added, "And let's face it, they're the only ones we know of who actually have a motive."

"To bring Francine and Bella back."

He nodded. "And I know you won't want to hear this, but there's a chance Francine knows about it. And has agreed to it. Because it would give her a good excuse to dump Jonas, go back to the Midwest, and have her baby without him."

Annie was speechless. Did she believe it? Not for a minute. But was it possible? Well, that was the worst part. Because she could not disagree.

CHAPTER 33

John didn't stay in the cottage with Annie Saturday night. Instead, he suggested that she take a break and go to his place in Edgartown. As for him, he planned to sleep in Vineyard Haven at the home of an officer who was going with him on the trip; they'd get the early boat, hop the bus to Logan, then catch a 10:00 a.m. flight to Minneapolis, by way of Chicago. Before leaving, he reminded Annie not to say a word to anyone, including his mother and father, about where he was going or when he'd be back, not that he knew the latter.

There was no way Annie was going to stay at his place in Edgartown, though she didn't tell him that. She had too much on her mind to have to deal with Abigail if, with her father out of sight, the young woman resumed donning her challenging leopard's spots. Besides, Annie wanted to be at the Inn in case . . . in case.

She was thinking she'd sleep in Francine's room until Lucy told her that Francine was there, that she'd walked back to the Inn because both Earl and Claire were napping soundly, and hadn't wanted to disturb them. She'd worked in the kitchen for a little while, but after she'd made lasagna and salad for those who wanted a hot meal, and helped pack dinner boxes of sandwiches and chips for the volunteers who wanted to stay outside, she'd gone upstairs to her — and Bella's — room.

Which made it even more difficult for Annie to believe that Francine could possibly be involved in Bella's kidnapping. And angry with John for entertaining the idea.

Annie told Lucy and Abigail to go home; she promised to text them if anything developed. Lucy said she'd be sure to let the *On Time* captain — whoever it was that night — know that the ferry should be ready if anyone needed to make an emergency crossing.

The girls left, and Annie putzed around the kitchen for a while. As far as she knew, people were still searching, but apparently not nearby, as the grounds had become eerily quiet. Even Winnie had gone home. Kevin stopped by and said he was going to bring Taylor and Jonas home and that he'd try to nap as well.

It was clear to Annie that the first push to try to find Bella had been the strongest; people were notably weary — physically and mentally — and perhaps were beginning to feel that their efforts were in vain.

Sometime after midnight, she grabbed a blanket and a pillow from the linen room, retreated to the reading room, and hung a sign on the door that read: PLEASE COME IN AND WAKE ME IF YOU NEED ME. Then she put together what turned out to be a fairly uncomfortable makeshift bed using the barrel chairs (one for her head, the other for her feet) and a couple of end tables to fill in the middle. When she finally was able to stay in one position, she spent the next who-knew-how-long staring up at the ceiling, something she was becoming too adept at doing.

The next thing she knew, she woke up. And she was cold.

Unfolding herself from the bedding and the chairs and tables, she stood up and stretched. She checked the time: nine o'clock. Why was the Inn so still? Then a strange realization swept over her: She was cold because there was no heat in the room. She opened the blinds and peered outside; she couldn't see the sky. Instead, an all too familiar sight greeted her: blustery, swirling wind, the kind that accompanied snow. Lots of snow.

It only took another moment for her to understand that the power had gone out.

Bella, she thought. *Oh, God, where was Bella?*

Quickly shoving the furniture back where it belonged and freshening up in the downstairs powder room (where the water in the sink was predictably chilled), Annie tried not to get irritated that Earl and Kevin had put off having a generator installed last year. They'd intended to do it once the holidays were over and things quieted down. But though December was often early for a bad storm on the island, Annie knew better. She had firsthand experience from the year Bella had arrived.

She wrapped herself in the blanket she'd used for sleeping, then went the back way into the kitchen, which was silent, nearly abandoned. No dishes, no food, no thermoses of coffee crowded the big marble-topped island. The only sign of life was Claire, who was dressed in a heavy coat, flannel pants, and what looked like ten-year-old Ugg boots; her unruly hair poked out from beneath her red knit hat. She was sitting on a stool, staring out the window. Her iPad sat idle on her lap.

"Claire?" Annie asked. "You're back."

"Came back around two. You slept in the reading room?"

Folding the corners of the blanket, Annie formed small, makeshift pockets for her hands. "I did. But the power's out, right?"

Claire nodded. "Earl built a fire in the fireplace, but I'm more comfortable in here."

Annie saw no reason to question her rationale.

"Where is everyone?" Sorrow brushed her heart. The silence seemed . . . dreadful.

"Everyone but a few police went home," Claire said vacantly, not moving her gaze from the window and the white landscape outside. "Can't blame them. They left right after Earl and I got here when the storm was starting."

Annie took a seat on one of the stools. "Did you get any sleep?"

"A little. On one of the sofas in the great room. Francine's upstairs in her room. The power's been out a while. Earl and Kevin are driving around trying to find a neighbor who can lend us a generator. Lucy and Abigail are at our house; they came back from Edgartown before dawn. Lottie's husband made a special trip and brought them over.

Lucy said she was afraid nobody else would be here, what with the storm." She paused, then her voice went flat. "I wonder if we'll ever see our little Bella again."

Annie knew she would sound phony and shallow if she attempted to conjure a soothing reply. So all she said was, "Where are the tenants?" She couldn't shake the feeling that the Inn felt empty, as if even those who lived right there hadn't wanted to look for Bella in the snow. She shouldn't blame them. She supposed.

"Harlin and Greg took off on snowmobiles with a couple of cops. They're determined to check out every house and cottage on Chappy; I made sure they were bundled up and took hot coffee and Lucy's peanut butter cookies for energy. I think the teachers are still asleep. Harlin said Jenna's stuck working at the hospital. Charlie's off island on account of it's the weekend, and we still have no idea where Rose went."

Annie nodded, grateful for Harlin and Greg; thankful, for once, that Claire liked knowing other people's business, including who was where and why. She rubbed her arms and followed Claire's gaze out the window. "Everyone's been working really hard trying to find her. And John was supposed to go off island this morning to track down a lead. But I don't suppose the boats are running." She didn't think that saying that much would get her into trouble with him.

"He flew out on Cape Air last night," Claire said. "He called this morning and said he was able to get ahead of the weather. He didn't say where he's going, but he wanted you to know he hopes he'll get there later today. He wouldn't say if it's about Bella or when he'll be back. All he said was, 'Police business, Mom.' " She grunted. "You'd better get used to that if you're going to marry him."

Annie slid off the stool and headed toward the refrigerator. "Did you have breakfast? We can sit in the great room in front of the fire. I can make coffee and we can have something warm to eat." She didn't know why she sounded so coherent when her brain was fuzzy, her eyes were on the verge of tears, and her neck and back were killing her from the contorted way she'd slept.

She didn't wait for Claire to answer but started to gather what she'd need: a foldable steel grill that fit over a fire — they'd used it a few times in summer to cook steaks over the outdoor fire pit. Earl had made sure it would also work in the great room's fireplace because he'd said, "In case you need to heat a pot of chowder or make a halfway decent cup of java if the stove's gone on the blink." The stove, of course, was practically brand new, so it was more likely that he'd held off on investing in a generator because he felt the grill was more rustic, more "Vineyard natural."

She found the old percolator high above the stove, prepped it with fresh coffee grounds and spring water from a jug, and dug out a couple of pot holders. She also grabbed a couple of Francine's homemade rosemary rolls out of the freezer and a sheet of foil to wrap them in. She had no idea if she could heat rolls on the ersatz grill, but it was worth a try. As long as she was careful not to burn the whole place down.

It was unusual for Claire to stay seated on the stool while Annie — or anyone — shuffled around her, clattering and clanking pots and pans. But Annie knew that all of them were acting justifiably unusual after the past hours . . . hours that now had turned to days. Nearly two of them, by her calculation. Two days, and still no Bella. So far, the only concrete thing Annie knew was that there had been a note. And that John was off on what might be a wild-goose chase and a waste of precious time. And that

Francine had apparently severed ties with Jonas.

Which gave Annie an idea.

She stopped shuffling. She set down the grill and percolator. And she set the pot holders and the rolls on top.

"I'll be back to get this started," she said to Claire, not that Claire was listening.

Fast-walking through the great room, Annie stopped at the reception desk, snapped up the spare key to Francine's room, and sprinted up the stairs. She knew she couldn't offer any substantial information but, whether John liked it or not, she damn well could try and give her hope.

HOPE. Like one of the words printed on Rose's heart-shaped rocks.

When Annie was a third grade teacher back in Boston, long before moving to the island, she'd seen a lot of images that had brought her emotions to the surface: a little boy sitting outside on the steps after school, waiting for a parent who'd forgotten him; a shy girl named Bonnie whose science fair project (a classic erupting volcano made of flour, water, baking soda, and vinegar) was smashed by two bratty girls who'd laughed at her and said she was no Sheldon Cooper. Both the boy and the shy girl had pretended they weren't crying, but their puckery cheeks and tiny, downturned mouths had been heart-wrenching.

So when Annie unlocked the door to Francine's room and saw the twenty-two-year-old woman curled up like the fetus growing inside her, her eyes open and staring into space the way that Claire's had been, Annie's heart splintered. What made it worse was that Francine wasn't curled up on her own bed but on Bella's tiny one.

She sat down on the edge of the mattress because she suddenly felt weak. She reached over and rested her hand on Francine's head and gently combed her hair with her fingers, which were trembling.

"Have you had any sleep?" Annie asked, barely above a whisper.

She knew Francine had heard her by the subtle shaking of her head.

"It doesn't matter," Francine said. "Sleep's not going to bring her back."

As tempted as Annie was to say, "Neither is staying awake, and not sleeping might harm your baby," she deferred. Instead she slouched down and half curled up beside her. "I think she's safe," she said. "Bella is safe."

"You don't know that."

"Yes. Yes we do." Annie sucked in a small

breath. No matter if John never forgave her for what she was about to do, it wasn't right to keep this from Francine. "There's been a note," she said.

Francine sat bolt upright, her narrow shoulder catching Annie under the chin, sending a sharp, smarting shot to Annie's jaw. Her body jerked; she cupped her hand over the pain.

"What note?" Francine demanded. "When?"

Annie didn't want her to know when, because Francine would be furious that she hadn't been told sooner.

"I only know it was found outside my cottage door. And it said that Bella's fine. And safe. And that she's with whomever wrote it."

Francine looked at Annie and squinted. "What?" She sounded like a kitten.

Annie nodded. "I saw the note, honey. She's safe. John and Linc are following it up. They didn't want you to know until they have a concrete answer. But I thought it might help . . ."

Francine started to cry.

Annie reached over, held her in a long hug, matching her tear for tear.

After a few minutes, she whispered, "If John finds out I've told you, he'll never speak to me again. Or to you, either, if that means anything."

"But why?" They both were sitting up now, raw feelings now abated. "This is about Bella, Annie."

Annie gave her half a smile. "I'm so sorry, honey, but it's a cop thing. Or at least that's John's way of telling me to 'let the professionals do their job.' I think he thinks I'll butt in and somehow screw things up."

"That's ridiculous."

"Maybe. Maybe not. But I do have a way of getting too involved."

Squaring her shoulders, Francine said, "So there's nothing we can do? Does he have any idea who has her? And where? And, for God's sake, why? Do they want money? If they do, they sure picked the wrong kid to kidnap."

"I only know she's safe. And fine. And that I trust John. And so can you."

They sat quietly.

Then Francine asked, "Can't we please tell Earl and Claire? And Kevin? They're as upset as we are. If they promise not to say anything . . ."

Annie noticed that Francine hadn't mentioned Jonas. She wondered if, indeed, she had squashed him from her life, the young man she'd loved only two days earlier now no better than a tick plucked from John's dog and ground into the earth. "I'm sorry, but we can't. The truth is, if I hadn't inadvertently seen the note, John most likely wouldn't even have told me. And he swore me to secrecy. For real."

"Well, that sucks."

"I agree."

Francine wrapped her arms around herself. "Geez, I'm cold. Isn't the heat on in this place?"

Annie laughed. "Put your coat on and let's go downstairs for coffee. Claire's there, and I think it would do her good to see your beautiful face."

As they left the room, Annie glanced back over her shoulder; Bella's small bed now stood empty. She knew she'd done the right thing by telling Francine about the note, and also that she hadn't told her about Rose, the heart-shaped stones, or the mysterious mouse that supposedly had skittered into the same cabinet where Bella's toys were kept. She was glad she hadn't told her that she thought Taylor's brother was weird or about the creepy way he'd looked when he'd been standing on the dune when the rest of them were working desperately to find Bella.

Most of all, Annie was glad she hadn't told

her that John was in Minnesota, tracking down Francine's aunt and uncle to see if they'd arranged for Bella to be kidnapped. And that he'd suggested that Francine might be involved.

If she was, Annie thought as they made their way down to the great room, she was putting on one hell of an act.

CHAPTER 34

By mid-afternoon, the snow had stopped; for all its bravado, the accumulation seemed to be only four or five inches. Hardly more than a "dusting," Earl called it when he arrived in his pickup with Lucy and Abigail, the plow blade having carved a swift path on the seven-minute drive from Earl and Claire's house to the Inn. Kevin was close behind, with two borrowed generators in the bed of his truck. They were not enough to heat the whole Inn, but at least the downstairs would have power. The victory was something to be grateful for, but not as grateful as Annie would be if Bella showed up at the door. Or if John would call. Or text. Or do something to give her an update.

Easy, girl, Murphy railed from the rafters in the great room. *He's doing the best he can.*

Annie slipped into a corner of the great room, away from the rest of the troops who were clustered together, making small talk. "Are you sure it's not because he doesn't want to tell me he's found nothing?"

O ye of little faith, was Murphy's only comment before Annie sensed her spirit vanish.

Still, the remark almost made Annie smile. The last time her red-haired friend had chided her for having too little faith had been when Murphy suggested that Annie move to Martha's Vineyard and start a new life. "It's a perfect place for a writer," she'd said. "There's inspiration all around. The beaches! The water! The cliffs! Why do you think so many creative types live there?"

"Maybe they don't like the real world," Annie had suggested.

"Or maybe you're a chickenshit," had been her friend's reply.

But Annie had gotten the point. So she'd conjured up a little faith and made the leap. And now she must have faith in John. Or at least in God, whom she suspected might have a more essential hand in bringing Bella back to them.

Come back to me. She wanted to shout the message on Rose's heart-shaped rock to Bella from the top of the lighthouse.

But just as she decided to rejoin the others, she felt a tap-tap on her shoulder. And turned to see Abigail.

"Can we talk?" the girl asked. "Alone?"

Annie decided not to correct the "can" to "may." She wondered if she'd ever learn to let go of her grammar hat.

"Sure," she said. "Let's go into the reading room." She was becoming more familiar with that cozy place than with her own cottage. No matter where, however, she did not want to have to deal with Abigail right then. She did not want to have to deal with Abigail . . . well, truthfully, ever, the wedding dress notwithstanding. The girl was challenging enough for Annie on a good day, despite the fact she'd made a halfhearted effort in the search for Bella. Albeit at John's insistence.

Annie walked ahead of the clomp-clomp of the heels of Abigail's ankle boots. She wondered why the girl had no clue that Chappy wasn't a place for fashion footwear.

Sitting at the table, Annie felt her muscles tense in preparation for whatever comment was going to be tossed her way. The only things Annie was sure of were that she didn't know her future stepdaughter well enough to be able to assess her skills at manipulation, and that John would be devastated if he learned that Annie felt so defensive about her.

She sighed. Right now, Abigail should be

at the bottom of the list of the least of Annie's concerns.

"Have a seat," she said, motioning to the chair across from her.

Abigail sat. Though her long blond hair was gathered into a ponytail, she'd apparently left her trademark makeup home in Edgartown, so she looked barely twelve instead of eighteen. She kept her hands in her lap, but Annie sensed that she'd started to fidget. Perhaps the girl was uncomfortable. Good.

She focused on the green-shaded lamp, not on Annie. "Lucy told me that you hate the wedding dress," she said.

Of all the words Abigail could have said, Annie would not have predicted those. But because she was feeling edgy, she laughed. "I wouldn't say I hate it. It's just . . . well, let's say it's not a good look on me. I'm not sure the fit is right." Of course, the "fit" was fine. It was the rest of the dress that was marginal.

Abigail hesitated. "I know something about sewing. And fashion. Would you like my help?"

Annie wanted to say that would depend on whether or not Abigail would confess to having slashed her tire or having goaded her boyfriend into doing the deed. But she decided she should act like the grown-up in the room. "That would be really nice."

"Okay. Can we look at it tomorrow? I won't be great at walking through snow trying to find the little girl. I hate snow." Apparently, still the diva, she stood up then and turned to leave.

"Thanks, Abigail," Annie said. "But maybe we should wait until Bella's found, okay?"

With a quick glance over her shoulder, Abigail said, "Sure, whenever you want," and strutted from the room, leaving Annie to wonder what the heck had happened. Maybe Claire had had a long talk with her granddaughter about family sticking together. It often amazed Annie how people could dispose of grudges over long-forgotten conflicts when someone they loved simply asked them to.

Somehow, the rest of the day passed without joy or incidence, enveloped in a haze of quiet conversation. Earl mentioned that he'd heard a long-range forecast of unsettled weather across the top of the nation for the next several days. Annie couldn't imagine how he could have bothered to listen to a weather report at a time like this. But by now he, too, must know that John was away "on police business," and that he'd gone by air. Maybe he was worried about how or when John would be able to return.

All Annie knew for certain was that John had made it off the Vineyard last night and hoped to make it to Minnesota later today. But he hadn't called her, and he hadn't texted, and it was now more than fifty-something hours since Bella had disappeared. And there hadn't been any updates from Linc or any ransom call — not that she knew of, anyway.

Around ten o'clock, Taylor arrived with sleeping bags and said she and Kevin would camp out in the workshop. Annie sent Claire home with Earl and their grand-daughters. Then, no longer caring about how things looked to the tenants, an hour later, she dragged a couple of blankets and a pillow from the linen closet and nested on one of the sofas in the great room as Claire had done the night before. She would have preferred to stay in Francine's room, but Annie needed her phone nearby in case John called, and she didn't want the ring to wake Francine.

But there was no call. And now it was morning.

Monday morning.

Day three since Bella had gone missing.

Traipsing through the snow, Annie made

it down to her cottage, where she showered and dressed in fresh clothes, which helped her feel a little better. But that time, she made the mistake of looking in the mirror. Her eyelids were swollen, her cheeks sunken. In the past couple of days, she seemed to have developed more lines on her face. She wondered if the current situation was now etching itself on her skin.

"Every loss brings back every other loss," she remembered reading somewhere. If that were true, Bella's disappearance had heaped all of Annie's losses smack onto her face.

"With or without a nice wedding dress, you're going to be a very old-looking, odd-looking bride," she said into the glass. But that was no longer a priority for her to waste time caring about.

Moving back through the bedroom, she bypassed the garment bag that held the dress and went into the living room, careful not to contaminate the scene of the mysterious note, even though the note had been outside, not in. What would Linc do if he caught her? Arrest her? And what would John do when he found out? Call off their wedding? She wondered why that thought wasn't as unsettling as she might have expected.

She returned to the Inn around eight

o'clock. Inside, it was so still again, she might have thought everyone was asleep. But that morning, an urn emitted the aroma of coffee, and what had been a stanchion of empty thermoses lined up on the kitchen counter had dwindled. The tenants — probably Harlin, the teachers, Greg the carpenter, and maybe Jenna the nurse — were gone. Maybe they were scouring Chappy, looking for Bella. Now that it had snowed, skimobiles would make their trek easier.

Then Annie realized that — wow! — the power had returned during the night; the loud racket of the generators had stopped and the central heat was humming.

Plugging in her phone, she checked her messages again: none. Maybe John had no information yet, or he was lost in the wilds of Minnesota, or he hadn't made it there at all. She took an island-made pottery mug from the cabinet and filled it. While reviewing everything she needed to do, she was struck with a serious thought: despite what John might or might not say if he learned that she'd been in the cottage, she honestly doubted he'd cancel the wedding. But with all that was happening, and all that still was unknown, should they postpone it? She popped another of Francine's rosemary rolls into the microwave, counted down the thirty seconds, and tried to decide.

The wedding wasn't as important as helping Francine get through this, as being there for Kevin when he needed to vent about where he and Taylor were going to live, as Trish and the damn TV deal that was still looming out there in outer space.

Annie wondered about Jonas, too, and whether or not the young couple could survive Bella's disappearance and remain a couple. She couldn't blame Francine for her withdrawal from him, yet over the years Annie had learned the importance of forgiveness.

If Francine wasn't part of Bella's disappearance (Annie was still sickened that John had posed that possibility), she would most likely freak out if she learned that John was in Minneapolis, interrogating her aunt and uncle who had done so much for her. And if the couple alone was in this, and if they really loved Francine, they would never have kidnapped Bella. They would have known how much it would upset both of them.

Annie had never met Marty and Bill, but they seemed to care about their nieces.

So . . . who else, who else, who else? Who else besides Francine's relations had a motive to steal precious little Bella? What would someone have to gain?

Money, Annie thought, was so often at the root of crime. She'd learned that when she'd started writing mysteries and had done her homework on the primary motives for committing evil deeds. Money. Sex. Power. Those were considered the big three. But without a ransom demand, and with the other two motives seeming negligible, she truly was stumped.

John had now added the possibility of having a score to settle as a motive. But even if the kidnappers didn't want money, wouldn't they have wanted to let someone know they had her? Maybe. Maybe not.

She wished Murphy would show up so that they could have a conversation since no one else was around.

In lieu of Murphy, she had to rely on her own skills, such as they were.

What else had she learned from behavioral research that helped her carve out her characters? Trish once said that what she loved most about Annie's novels was how she wrote believable, sympathetic characters — even when they were aiming a gun and pulling the trigger. She'd said that, though she'd been around a long time, she'd found few mystery authors as accomplished at that. Which Annie might have chalked up to schmoozing bunk, except that Trish truly was a terrific editor. Even more, she was equally adept at building her authors' brands, no matter what it took.

Then Annie remembered the publicity stunt last summer that Trish had sworn she hadn't set up but had applauded.

Annie blinked at the winter-white landscape out the window. Was it possible her editor had found a way to boost Annie's visibility in order to jump-start the buzz about Museum Girls Mysteries if it was to become a TV series? Would her editor stoop so low as to steal a child?

Her heart started to race. But how could Trish have pulled it off? She was in New York City, with few flights on and off the island now that it was off-season. Besides, she'd have needed IDs to fly, which would be easily traceable. The only other option was the boat. But would her editor have known how to navigate all that? She'd once told Annie she rarely left Manhattan, that she hadn't even attended her mother-in-law's funeral because it was in Hoboken, New Jersey. She didn't trust a ferry to get her across the Hudson. And forget trains or buses: Trish did not drive or take public transportation, and she only traversed the island of Manhattan on foot or by private car. It was amazing that she'd flown to L.A.

Still . . . it was possible for her to have paid someone to do the deed. Annie supposed it depended on how important this TV deal was to her. She must be nearing retirement . . . could such a triumph provide a dazzling swan song for an exceptional career?

As Annie felt a mass of anxiety beginning to press against her chest, her thoughts were jogged by the scrape-thump, scrape-thump sounds of someone shoveling snow. Through the window, she saw her brother clearing a path from the workshop up to the Inn. She couldn't remember when she'd needed to see someone so badly, someone she trusted whom she could talk to. Maybe it was Murphy's way of helping out because right then she wasn't available.

As Annie reached for another mug, she realized that she'd already drunk her coffee and eaten the warm roll, though she didn't remember doing either. Maybe her mind was too boggled to think straight. She closed her eyes and waited to hear the back door open. It took less than a minute.

CHAPTER 35

I didn't count on the snow. At least I made sure that I stacked enough wood inside the cabin to keep the fire going for a few days. But I'm getting tired of being cooped up.

Yesterday I wondered if I could go out without her. I found a key hanging on a peg by the front door. It didn't look like anyone had used it in a hundred years, but it fit the lock. I thought if I locked her in at least she wouldn't go roaming around outside and get lost. Or worse.

But then I thought about the fire in the fireplace, and knew it would be stupid to leave her by herself and not expect that she'd get hurt.

So I kept telling myself it won't be much longer. And I wrapped her in an extra blanket and lit a few candles to make the place look cozier. More like a real home, like the one I grew up in before everything got so screwed up. Then I took out one of the books that I'd bought on the Cape and I sat on the floor in front of the chair that she's kind of glued to. I read her a story about the stars in the sky and the big yellow moon, and she seemed to like it.

She's really a nice little girl. I am so glad that I found her.

CHAPTER 36

"Taylor went home during the night," Kevin said as he peeled off his boots and parka and put them in the mudroom. "She said I was snoring from sleeping on the hard floor." He stepped into the kitchen and sort of growled. "I think she was more worried about Jonas being alone in the house with Rex, though I have no idea why I even said that." He spotted the empty mug on the counter and helped himself to coffee. "Power came on a couple of hours ago. I take it there's been no word on . . . anything?"

Annie shook her head, plucked the pitcher of cream from the refrigerator, and handed it to him. She decided to wait until he poured a little into the mug, then stirred and sipped before launching into her doubts about her editor.

"By the way," he said before she had a chance to tell him about Trish, "where's

John? A few more cops have come back, and some volunteers, though not as many as on the weekend. I suppose some had to work today . . ."

Annie couldn't bring herself to say: *And others have doubts that if Bella hasn't been found by day three, then she won't be.*

"John's in Minnesota," she blurted out before stopping herself.

Kevin must have been mid-swallow because he coughed a little, went to the sink, and spit out a mouthful. Once he recovered, he turned back to Annie. "Please don't tell me he's there to see Francine's aunt and uncle. Or that he thinks they're behind this."

"I can't tell you that. In fact, I already told you more than I should have. Please, Kev, don't ever tell John that I told you. And don't breathe a word about it to anyone . . . especially not Francine."

"It's too late for that." That time, the voice wasn't Kevin's. It was Francine's.

"Crap," Kevin said.

"Is it true?" Francine asked as she stalked into the kitchen. "Does John think my aunt and uncle have Bella? Does he think they came here and abducted her? Even though, next to me, they probably love her more than anyone?"

Annie was stunned. She didn't believe that

anyone — other than Francine — could love Bella more than Annie did. Or more than Earl and Claire. Or Kevin. Or Lucy. And yet Marty was Bella's blood relation, and she and her husband wanted what they perceived would be best for her — living in Minneapolis. It was absurd, but, allegedly, they believed it.

Francine's jaw was set firm, her dark eyes had narrowed. If she'd been a dog, Annie supposed her teeth would be bared. "Did John go to Minneapolis to get a handwriting sample? To try and prove that one of them wrote the note?"

As badly as Annie wanted to respond, she didn't want to confirm — in front of Kevin — that there had been a note. *Please, God,* she thought, *no.*

"What note?" Kevin asked before God had a chance to stop him.

"The one that said Bella is fine," Francine asserted. "And that she's safe. The one that was most likely written by the same person who kidnapped her when Jonas was too wrapped up in himself to be bothered with paying attention to her."

Kevin set down his mug and looked over at Annie. "What's she talking about?"

"Oh," Francine said, "she won't tell you. John won't let her. She only told me because

374

she felt sorry for me." She'd formed a shawl out of one of the blankets from her bed; she pulled it tightly around her now. Then her lower lip jutted out. And Francine started to cry.

"Honey . . ." Annie finally spoke, then stepped toward her, arms outstretched, ready to wrap them around the blanket that was wrapped around her.

But Francine pivoted sharply and marched toward the doorway. Then she stopped. "I'll be in my room," she said. "In case anyone decides I deserve to know what's really going on." Her feet marched again until the sound faded, and Annie heard them ascend the stairs.

Annie closed her eyes.

"Annie?" Kevin asked. "Please?"

The pressure gripped her chest again. "Come with me to the cottage. I don't want to talk about it here."

Kevin didn't mention that in order to get inside Annie's cottage they had to duck under the strip of yellow tape that still encircled the place.

The cottage was cold. Annie decided to build a fire in the woodstove because it would give her something to do while she talked and because she'd be able to focus on that and not have to look her brother in the eyes.

She crisscrossed a few logs, added kindling, and ignited the fire while she explained. She didn't tell him John's harebrained idea that Francine might be involved because Annie refused to say those words out loud. When she finished her abridged version of the story, she closed the iron door to the woodstove and shrugged.

"So that's it. And if John knows I've told you, he'll divorce me before we are married." She stayed close to the stove and rubbed her palms together.

"Jesus," Kevin said for the third or fourth time since she'd started. By some not-so-small miracle, he seemed bewildered instead of angry. "I met her aunt and uncle when we went out there, but they didn't act like vindictive people. Or that they thought Jonas wasn't good enough for Francine. Or that Taylor wouldn't be a supportive grandmother."

"Or you," Annie added. "You were there, too. As a step-grandfather."

One corner of his mouth twitched up in a smile. "Is that a real word?"

"I have no idea. Actually, I have no idea about a lot of things anymore."

He went to her and hugged her. "Well,

you know me, Annie. I'm a real fixture now. On the island. In this family. I'm also committed to finding whoever has taken Bella — for whatever their stupid reason — and slamming them into the nearest wall."

She rested her head against his shoulder. "Stop trying to make me laugh. It won't work, but I do appreciate the gesture."

"Okay," he said, stepping away. "But maybe the note is good news. Like maybe she's really safe."

"John warned me it could be a prank. Which is why he doesn't want anyone to find out and get their hopes up."

"Yeah, I get it. Maybe he's right. But let's not believe that, okay? Let's think it's a good sign, that maybe she's not out there somewhere hungry and scared and freezing."

"There's something else," she said, trying to deflect the image his last comment had painted. "It's about Rose."

"Rose? As in our winter tenant?"

Because Annie had said that much, she knew she had to keep going. So she told Kevin she'd sneaked into her room, found the dollhouse and the heart-shaped rocks. She told him about the one that read COME BACK TO ME.

He said "Jesus" again, which must have been a record because Kevin wasn't irreverent unless he felt that it was warranted. "What else?"

"Isn't that enough?"

"Where is Rose, anyway?" he asked. "I haven't seen her helping out."

"I have no idea where she went. Or why." She told him that Rose left Chappy Friday night. And hadn't returned.

He slouched down into the rocking chair. "Is she still on the Vineyard?"

"I don't know that, either. I guess Linc is following that up while John's in Minnesota. They sent the note out for fingerprints. It usually takes three to five days, but I hope they put a rush on it because a child is involved." Annie was surprised that her voice didn't crack when she said "a child."

Kevin stood again, that time tugging his hat over his ears and pulling his big gloves back on. "I'll find her," he said.

The world continues to be filled with surprises, eh? Murphy's voice came from out of nowhere.

"Rose?" Annie asked.

He sighed. "I already know about the rocks. A couple of weeks ago I was walking on the beach, trying to sort out what to do about this stupid Rex thing. I ran into Rose. She was collecting them. I asked her why. She told me."

"So . . . what's the reason?"

"Let's just say I'm pretty sure it has nothing to do with Bella's disappearance. More than that is her story to tell, not mine. And ninety-nine-point-nine percent not connected to Bella." He paused. "At least, I don't think it is. But I'll find her. Don't worry."

He left the cottage, and Annie took his place in the rocking chair. She closed her eyes, felt the warmth from the fire on her cheeks, and, surprisingly, fell asleep. Again.

She dreamed she was back in her cottage, the first one, the one that had belonged to Jonas's grandparents. In her dream, Annie was in bed; in the bottom drawer of the nightstand next to her, a baby silently slept. At that point, all Annie knew was the baby's name: *Bella.* Rolling onto her side, Annie reached down to be sure the soft blanket was tucked warmly around the tiny bundle. It was winter, after all. And there'd been a cold snap on Chappy.

But the blanket was gone; the drawer was empty. Annie jumped from her bed and flipped on the light switch; yes, the drawer was open, but it was empty. Bella wasn't there.

She yanked the lamp from the nightstand

and dropped to her knees. She shined the light under the bed, thinking the baby might somehow have fallen out of the drawer and rolled under there. But the only thing under the bed was her mother's old banjo clock, which Annie hadn't yet hung up in the cottage. The clock, and a little dust.

She cried out in her sleep. She felt herself rousing. And trembling.

"Annie?" It was a small voice, a timid voice. "Annie?" The voice grew louder.

Her heart quietly racing, her brow perspiring, Annie struggled to open her eyes. Finally, she focused. She was still in the rocker, but Kevin was standing in front of her. Next to him stood Rose. She was bundled in a gray down coat that made her look three times her size and a pink-and-red scarf and matching hat, both of which looked hand-knit. For a moment Annie wondered if she was still sleeping.

"I'm sorry," she said once the cobwebs cleared. "I must have fallen asleep."

"I've been gone three hours," her brother said. "It's almost lunchtime."

She tried to sit up; her back, her shoulders, her neck were stiff. "Rose? Where have you been?"

Rose lowered her eyes. "Kevin said you thought I left because I'd taken Bella."

There were a number of ways Annie could have responded. She chose to say, "We were worried about you."

"He told me you went into my room."

There was no denying it. Not if, more than anything, Annie wanted to hear the truth. "I did. I'm sorry, Rose. But everyone is so upset . . . and we still don't know where Bella is . . ."

"It's okay. I only left because I get so nervous when too many people are around. I've never been good in a crisis."

Kevin suggested that Rose sit on the small sofa across from Annie. The woman complied.

"I was also scared to death of that big man," Rose said. "Rex?"

Annie sat up straight now, fully awake. "Yes. Kevin's brother-in-law."

Rose rested her hands in her lap.

Annie thought that, like with the down coat, the bulky mittens could have been hiding anything. Like a knife or a small handgun. She tried not to look nervous.

"Can you tell me why you're afraid of him?" she asked. "Does he look like someone who . . ." She paused, flashing back to her days teaching third grade and choosing her words accordingly, as if she were speaking to an eight- or nine-year-old. "Does he look like a man who once . . . touched you?"

Shifting on the cushion, Rose looked at Annie, perplexed. "No! Why would you think that?" Her gaze shifted to Kevin as if he knew the answer.

Kevin shrugged, then said, "You've got the wrong impression, Annie. Go ahead, Rose. It's okay to tell her."

Tightening her thin, pale lips until they were barely visible, Rose hesitated. When she finally spoke, the words came slowly. "Years ago, I had an uncle who lived in West Tisbury. His main job was taking care of some of the island cemeteries."

Annie tried to look surprised.

"He died back in the eighties," Kevin interrupted, as if agitated by Rose's reluctant pace. "He left Rose his house."

Rose nodded. "He did."

"That's how I knew where she was," Kevin added. "I saw her out there right after Thanksgiving. I'd gone out to Lambert's Cove to walk on the beach. I needed to think about this business with Rex away from people who knew me. But, lo and behold, I practically stumbled over Rose. She told me her story and she took me to see the house."

"I was looking for stones," Rose said. "The heart-shaped ones. Like the ones

382

Bernie and I used to collect. I . . . I write messages on them. For him. Then I toss them into the water out at East Beach back here on Chappy. It's the closest place on the island to England. Which was where he'd always wanted to go."

Annie was confused. She had no idea who Bernie was; it sounded like he was the one Rose was asking to come back to her. She sucked in her cheeks so she wouldn't interrupt.

"Bernie was my boyfriend for three whole summers. I came to the island to be Uncle Clive's housekeeper because he had a part-time job driving a bus during tourist season, so he was real busy. Bernie was born here; his family lived down the street. That last summer, Bernie graduated from high school. I was sixteen." She stopped, then added, "We held hands a lot. I liked that. We kissed sometimes, too, but never too often. Uncle Clive warned me about island boys. He said they got excited for all the wrong reasons when they saw a girl from away. I knew what he meant. I'd had a class on sex education in school." She pulled off her mittens; Annie was relieved to see there was no knife, no gun.

"Maybe at first Bernie did get excited about me because I wasn't from here. He wanted to leave the Vineyard. His father and older brothers were fishermen; he didn't want to be one. He wanted to join the Navy and see the world from a big ship. Especially, like I said, England. It's where his ancestors came from. Anyway, we fell in love. And that last summer we went too far. Nearly 'all the way,' they called it back then. It was early in the morning. I'd sneaked out of the house and met him at Lambert's Cove. I had no idea that Uncle Clive had followed me."

"And he saw you and Bernie . . . ?" Annie interjected.

Rose nodded. "We were behind a dune. In the beach grass. Just like in a movie."

Annie didn't mention the celebrated Vineyard film *Jaws,* or that it was a good thing Rose and Bernie had not been in the water.

Lowering her head, now intent on Annie's Grandma Sutton's braided rug, Rose added, "Even though I was a virgin, it was so nice. And I really loved Bernie. But we never got to finish because Uncle Clive shot him."

In spite of her best intentions, Annie gasped.

Kevin leaned against the kitchen table and folded his arms.

"He . . . killed him?" Annie managed to ask.

Rose nodded. "He buried him in the West Tisbury cemetery. The one right on the curve on State Road, just before you get to where Edgartown–West Tisbury Road comes out, if you're heading up-island from Vineyard Haven. I guess nobody would have thought it was weird if they'd seen Clive digging a grave. After all, it was his job." Her voice was so low now, Annie barely could hear her.

"So . . . your uncle was never caught?"

"I don't think so."

"What about Bernie's family?"

"At the time it was terrifying. People were looking all over for him; police cars were everywhere. Just like they are now. Clive slapped me around . . . called me a slut and told me to shut up if I knew what was good for me. Then he made me pack my things — I remember shaking the whole time. He shoved me into his Boston Whaler, brought me to the Cape, then put me on a bus back to Maine. I never saw him again. I always figured he told Bernie's family that Bernie and I ran away. They probably would have believed that."

The wood pop-popped in the stove.

It often amazed Annie that people were

rarely as others perceived them, that everyone had layers of stories filled with good and evil, twists and turns.

Kevin walked to the sink, poured a glass of water, and brought it to Rose. She thanked him, then drank. Annie wished he'd brought her water, too. Or, better yet, a bottle of wine.

"Bernie had kind eyes . . . they were green, like your brother's," she told Annie. "You have the same eyes, Annie. Sometimes it's hard for me to look at either of you on account of that. It's probably why I trusted Kevin enough to tell him my story. And now, to tell you."

Annie didn't correct her by saying that Kevin's eyes, and hers, were hazel, not green. Then she had a thought. "What about your uncle? What did he look like?"

Rose sighed. "He looked a lot like Rex. Which is why Rex terrifies me. When Uncle Clive shot Bernie, I was afraid he was going to shoot me, too."

"Oh, Rose," Annie said, thinking about how the fragile woman had spent the past few months painting messages on heart-shaped rocks for Bernie, then tossing them into the sea, hoping his spirit would find them. "I'm so sorry."

Rose folded her hands. "It was a long time

ago. The real reason I came this winter was to put Uncle Clive's house on the market. I didn't want to stay out there because I was afraid someone would recognize me. And that they'd ask too many questions. I hired a woman to clear some junk out of the house so it would look better for potential buyers. While I waited for her, I went to the beach and was collecting stones. That's when I ran into Kevin. And, by the way, my real name is Mary Rose; folks here knew me by Mary."

Rose's story seemed plausible, though Annie thought it would be a stretch to think someone would recognize her after fifty years.

"Bernie's parents are long dead," Rose continued, "but he had a brother who might still be here. And I knew I couldn't . . . face him. For all I know, he'd show up here to help search for Bella. So I left Chappaquiddick and went back to West Tisbury. Some of the furniture is still in the house, including the rickety bed I used to sleep on. It was risky to sleep there, but less stressful for me than being here."

While the facts were logical, Annie felt there were a few holes in Rose's reasoning. But she decided she had no way of knowing how she might have felt, what she might have done, if she'd been in Rose's shoes then. Or now.

Rose set down the glass. "Did you really think that I stole Bella?"

Annie shook her head. "I didn't know what to think. Especially since it seemed like you'd run away . . . and I remembered that I'd seen you looking for a mouse where we kept Bella's toys . . ."

"But there was a mouse. I saw it. I really did. The house in West Tisbury is rustic. I spent enough time there to know a thing or two about mice."

Annie believed her. She also decided not to ask Rose about the dollhouse. Not all memories needed to be unearthed.

"I have an idea," Annie said as she stood. "Let's go up to the Inn and have lunch. There aren't as many people here today. We can eat in the reading room, where it's quiet."

"I'd like that," Rose replied. "I'd like that very much."

Annie glanced at Kevin. "Rex is at your house with Jonas and Taylor?"

"As far as I know. I think he's afraid if he leaves, we'll change the locks and claim squatters' rights."

Which meant there were now two people — Rose and Rex — Annie could cross off her list of suspects. They had no doubt been too occupied with their own agendas to resort to kidnapping Bella.

And there was Abigail. Annie knew she could cross her off, too, as the girl had been spending too much time on Chappy, trying to be helpful. She would not have had the time to be with Bella. Eliminating Abigail felt liberating.

But without Rose, Rex, and Abigail on Annie's list, it meant that if John got nowhere in Minnesota, and if the note came back without identifiable prints, there would be no answers. No answers at all.

Which brought Annie back to wondering about Trish.

Chapter 37

John finally called. Annie had served lunch and was cleaning the kitchen. Kevin had gone to the workshop to resume the renovation now that the Fair was over, though they didn't know who — if anyone — would end up living there. Rose had retreated to her room. So Annie was alone. Thank God.

"Yesterday was a long freaking day," John said. "We didn't land in Minneapolis until two o'clock this morning. We got here by way of an eight-hour layover in Nashville. And, no, please don't ask how that happened."

She thought of his long legs and his broad shoulders crammed into a seat in coach and of him sitting in a waiting room far too long. "Oh, John. I'm sorry."

"Hey. It's part of the job. We managed a few hours of shut-eye. We're at the police station now, waiting for our local escort. I arranged it yesterday, but no one's available for a while, thanks to the snow. Or I should say, the blizzard, 'cuz they got almost two feet." He sounded worn out.

"You can't jump in your rental car and make your way to Marty and Bill's?"

"Nope. Not protocol. At least if they have Bella, chances are she's safe, so we're not under the gun."

Annie wished he had expressed that differently.

"Anyway," he continued, "I talked to Linc. He hopes to hear back today about prints on the note."

"Good."

"He said not much else is happening there."

"Unless you care that I've eliminated two suspects from my short list. Rose Atkins and Rex Winsted. It's a long story, but neither one is involved."

"I do care about that. And I trust your judgment."

"Thanks."

There was a long, Martha's Vineyard–to–Minnesota pause.

"How are you?" he asked.

"Okay. Fine. Grappling. We had snow yesterday morning, too. Power went out. Volunteers went home."

He didn't ask her to elaborate. She could

have told him her concerns about Trish, but she, too, was mentally done in. Besides, she intended to investigate Trish on her own, because it might involve a blockbuster can of worms that John didn't even know about yet. And it might affect Annie's future if law enforcement showed up in Manhattan and banged on Trish's door the way he was going to bang on Marty and Bill's as soon as protocol allowed.

"Are my girls behaving?" he asked.

In truth, Annie knew he meant Abigail, because Lucy was never a problem, not where family was concerned.

"They are," she said. Suddenly, she felt an urge to say good-bye. It wasn't that she didn't love him or wish he were there or that she did not want to marry him. She just did not want to talk about any of this anymore. Not to him, not to anyone. She wanted, she needed, to do something constructive to help find Bella. "I'm so glad you called," she said, "but I'd better go. Our tenants have been out all morning on snowmobiles, looking for Bella. But you probably know that. I want to have lunch ready for them. Your dad convinced your mother to go back to the house and get some proper sleep."

He told her he loved her and that he'd

keep her posted. Then they rang off, and Annie stood in the kitchen, alone again, wondering what the heck to do next.

What you should do is stop procrastinating, Murphy said. *Follow your gut. You know how to do that.*

And, suddenly, Annie knew precisely what her old friend meant.

She hoped that, true to past history, Trish would not pick up her phone but would respond to Annie's voice mail when she could. Annie had never begrudged her that; she knew that her editor juggled way more projects than Annie's. Which was why she was startled to hear Trish's real voice, not her recorded message.

"Annie!" Trish said after less than two rings. "You're ahead of schedule. I hope this means you're ready to say yes."

Oh, God, Annie thought. *The deal* was the last thing she wanted to talk about. "Not quite, but I'm getting there," she replied. "First, I have another question."

Trish groaned. "Fire away."

"Okay. Are you in Manhattan?"

The pause wasn't lengthy, but it was there. Annie knew she'd caught the woman off guard.

"Where else would I be?"

"Right. Well . . ." Her words formed slowly, surprising even her. "I can't sign any kind of a deal right now. Bella — remember her? The baby who showed up on my doorstep a couple of years ago during a nor'easter? Well, Bella has gone missing. I can't focus on anything else. I can't make a decision until I'm sure she's safe. And home again."

There, she thought. If Trish was involved in any way with Bella's kidnapping — which, Annie had learned while doing research for one of her novels, was punishable in Massachusetts with up to fifteen years in prison because Bella was under sixteen — she would understand that Annie was serious, and would see to it that the girl was returned posthaste. If she'd moved her across state lines, the punishment might even be greater, but Annie didn't know about that.

"I'm surprised," Trish retorted. "I'm sure you know this is the deal of the century. It's what you've been working so hard to achieve for your future. I'm sorry about the little girl, really I am, but I'm not sure the producers will take that into account. There are too many other authors out there these days who don't let personal issues get in the way of their careers. But you no doubt know that."

Personal issues? Had she really said that? Annie's anxiety began to simmer into anger. Intellectually, she knew that Trish was using the best sales pitch she could muster. But Annie's emotional response didn't care about that. "Trish," she said, "I'm sorry if my 'personal issues' don't agree with your agenda. But we're talking about a little girl. Someone I love very much."

"But, Annie, darling," Trish taunted in a lackluster tone, "it's not as if the child is yours."

The comment cut deeply. "I wouldn't have expected you to stoop so low," Annie said, regretting that she'd once confided to Trish her heartache of not having had children.

"Sorry. But don't get me wrong. I'm sure it's difficult. However, to be blunt, the girl's situation will be resolved one way or another — and probably soon. The TV deal, however, will be gone — probably forever — if you can't give me an answer in time for the deadline. This is business, Annie. If you aren't up to the task, say so."

Annie's cheeks flared. "Since you put it that way, my answer is no."

And though it was unlike her editor, the woman abruptly hung up.

The rest of the day went by quickly, too quickly, as it passed the seventy-two-hour mark since Bella had disappeared. Annie worked in tandem with Earl and Kevin, Lucy and Abigail, tending to the needs of the volunteers, many of whom had come back since the storm. Earl had ordered Claire to stay home and rest because she "wasn't getting any younger," as if he was. She must really have been tired, because it wasn't often that she obeyed one of his so-called orders.

Lucy had taken the day off from school and announced that she'd take the next year off — no matter what her father said — if it took them that long to find Bella.

Kevin said that Taylor and Jonas were going to stay home and sleep so that they could relieve the volunteers later that night.

Francine stayed in her room, only appearing for a snack around dinnertime.

People came and went in and out of the Inn, grabbing full thermoses of coffee and brown bags of food. Everyone had fallen into a somber, efficient rhythm, zeroing in on the mission. Annie supposed that, secretly, they all hoped that while they were busy, Bella would be dropped off on their doorstep, safe, well, and glad to be home. Or maybe that was wishful thinking on Annie's part.

Rose helped out in the kitchen a few times, retreating upstairs now and again when there were too many people and too much going on.

As for the way Trish had dismissed her, Annie felt nothing. Of course, the woman hadn't confessed — Annie hadn't expected that — but her potential involvement was one less thing for Annie to have to think about. She'd made her decision heard, and if Trish had Bella, or knew where Bella was, Annie felt sure she'd soon be returned — while there would be time for Annie to change her mind and still meet the deadline. If Trish wasn't behind the kidnapping, so be it. Annie had said no, and she couldn't think of a single reason why she should change her mind. Maybe she simply wasn't cut out for the Hollywood scene; maybe she wasn't destined to be very rich. And maybe she'd just saved herself a whole lot of grief.

She also was mindful, however, that she might not be thinking too clearly right then.

You're a survivor, Murphy had once told her. *You know how to bounce back no matter what.*

She hoped Murphy had been right.

Around nine o'clock, just as Annie was feeling worn out, Taylor and Jonas arrived. Annie showed them where everything was and explained their system, such as it was. Then she decided to go to bed — in her own bed at the cottage. It was silly not to; she'd sleep better there than on a couch or crammed between end tables and chairs. And if the kidnapper dared to return in the middle of the night, she could defend herself. Or not. Either way, she needed to be in her own little house.

As she fastened her parka, Taylor walked into the mudroom.

"Kevin and I want you to take a break tomorrow," she said. "So you and I are going to Edgartown for lunch. Kevin's treat."

Annie almost asked if Taylor had lost her mind. There was no way Annie was going to leave the Inn to "do lunch" until Bella was back.

"Um," she replied, trying to be tactful because sometimes she still felt off balance with her sister-in-law, "thank you for that. And thank Kevin. But there's too much to do here."

"Not tomorrow. Lottie and Georgia Nelson have offered to take care of the food. And Kevin and Jonas will work with the cops to make sure they know what turf the volunteers are covering. So no excuses. Especially since I don't want to have to tell your brother that you turned me down." Her long, thick auburn hair was wrapped tightly and pinned atop her head, her amber eyes were lasered at Annie as if they were advising, "Do not argue with me."

Annie laughed — it felt good to laugh. Maybe Taylor was right; maybe Kevin was, too. And a lunch outing might help soften some of those lines that were now carved deeply into her face.

And when they returned from Edgartown, Bella might be back.

So she agreed. Then she grabbed her phone and headed to the cottage. Halfway there, her text alert sounded.

Standing there in the snow, Annie froze. The message was from Linc.

NO DECIPHERABLE PRINTS ON THE NOTE. SORRY. WE STILL MIGHT GET SOMETHING FROM THE COTTAGE.

Her mood quickly soured as, in the shadowy moonlight of the winter sky, another glimmer of hope evaporated. And, once again, Annie's world crumbled a little.

CHAPTER 38

John called Tuesday morning, waking her up. She'd almost forgotten about him, though she refused to analyze what that meant. Maybe she, not Taylor, had lost her mind.

"We waited all day yesterday, but no one was at the Gardners' address."

Annie rubbed her eyes. It took her a second to remember that Gardner was Francine's aunt and uncle's last name.

"So we staked out the house all night. The cops here are great. They relieved us at midnight. No one came home."

"Could they be here? On the Vineyard?"

"I have no idea. But Linc's checking every inn and hotel. We'll stick around here another day unless we hear something different from him. He said he told you there weren't any prints on the note. I'm sorry."

"Me, too."

They fell into silence, the sounds of their

breaths the only things passing between cell towers.

"They still might get something from the cottage."

Annie might have felt hopeful if John hadn't used the same words that Linc had texted, as if the pair had agreed on "how to tell Annie."

"Right," she replied. "We'll see." She could tell that her tone was as flat as John's had become. Loss of hope, she thought, was an awful thing.

He promised he'd update her as soon as he knew anything. Then they rang off, and Annie sat on the edge of the bed, wondering if there was any way she could cancel her lunch with Taylor. When she decided that there wasn't, she hauled herself up and wandered to her closet, trying to decide what to wear that day, not that, like everything else, it mattered anymore.

But she was doing okay or, rather, okay enough. Until her phone rang again.

As an innkeeper and a landlord, Annie knew it was important to answer every call. Even when, like this one, caller ID simply read UNKNOWN.

But she couldn't deal with anything else right then. Later, she could always say she was sorry, that she'd been in the shower, that her battery had died, or something equally lame.

So she decided to ignore it. Until she felt a slight nudge on her arm. Which felt a lot as if it had come from Murphy.

On the third ring, Annie sighed. Then she picked up her phone.

The connection was snowy, reminding Annie of the old TV reception on the island back when she'd been a kid and had vacationed there with her parents. Snowy, crackly. She was about to hang up when she heard a small voice.

"Ammie?"

Her heart stopped, if that's what hearts did when they went into shock.

"Ammie? Happy Cwistmas."

A knife shot through her, CPRing her back to life.

"Bella?" Annie quaked. "Bella, honey? Is it you?"

Then the line crackled again. And disconnected.

Taylor picked her up at eleven thirty. She said she wanted to beat the Christmas-shopping crowd to the restaurant, even though it was a Tuesday. She suggested they eat at the Newes from America — the old, cozy pub that was close to the ferry. She also said she had a couple of gifts left to buy, so she wanted to take the truck off Chappy, maybe drive over to the shops in Oak Bluffs that weren't yet closed for the season. She didn't seem to notice that Annie was on the cusp of catatonia, that her only responses were silent nods.

They bumped along the snowy ruts of North Neck Road in Taylor's old pickup and headed toward the *On Time*. "Looks like snow again," Taylor said.

She was right; the sky was gray, the ceiling low, and overall there was the kind of stillness that foretold an impending storm. At least when it snowed, it wasn't bitterly cold.

"Let's hope it isn't too bad," Annie forced herself to say. Her mind, however, was fixated on Bella. The little girl had sounded okay. Which told Annie that she was safe. Warm. And dry. Or maybe it had been Annie's imagination, that she'd wanted — no, needed — to think those things.

She had almost called John.

She had almost texted Linc.

But Annie had been shaken, uncertain about what to do. Had there been a reason the call had come to Annie and not Francine? Or the police? Would Bella be in jeopardy if Annie reported it?

She wondered if she should have Taylor

403

drive her to the station as soon as they reached Edgartown. She wished she felt more in control of herself. But her mind was immersed in the sweet sound of Bella's voice: *Ammie.*

They crossed the channel and Taylor found a parking space and they were seated inside the Newes, menus presented, before Annie realized they'd arrived.

She looked around. A small arrangement of logs crackled in the Revolutionary War–era fireplace; fresh green boughs, tiny white lights, and colorful handles from a variety of beer taps stood upright across the wide mantel, creating a clever holiday display.

Their server was a young man with dark, curly hair that reminded Annie of Bella's.

"Jonas is barely holding up," Taylor babbled. "He looked so tired last night."

Jonas, Annie thought. *Taylor's son. The one who started this.* She struggled not to blame him as she had in the beginning, which had been four days ago.

"He doesn't eat," Taylor continued. "He barely sleeps. It hasn't helped that Francine wants no part of him. Even after I told him I might have done the same if I were her."

As always, Taylor was direct, which Annie suspected made it difficult at times for sensitive, artistic Jonas to connect with his mother. Yet they'd developed a bond that both of them seemed to value.

There, Annie thought. *I thought about someone else for a few seconds.* Maybe her mind wasn't gone, after all. She swiped her eyes from the fireplace up to the timbers. "I'd like to say I wouldn't have blamed him," Annie said, "but I have to agree. Francine and Bella have gone through so much in their young lives. And with the new baby . . ." As soon as she'd said it, she wished she could take it back. The new baby, after all, would be Taylor's grandchild.

"I don't want to talk about that," Taylor said.

Fortunately, the server returned to take their order.

After he left, Annie asked if Taylor had made any progress with Rex. It felt like a safer topic.

"I think he's biding his time until the current crisis is resolved. Then, for all I know, he'll have us evicted."

"I'm so sorry, Taylor. Have you thought about what you'll do?"

"I've started caretaking houses again. Maybe we can find a seasonal family that will let us rent their garage apartment or something. But in all honesty, I can't think of anything else except Bella. Even if I tried to make a decision, it would probably be the wrong one. I've always been better off if I don't let my emotions get in the way of being smart."

The comment stung Annie as if Taylor knew what Annie had told Trish. Had her decision to turn down the deal been a mistake that she'd come to regret? Straightening the fork and knife at her place setting, Annie toyed with her napkin. *No,* she thought. She absolutely, positively, could not think about that now.

"How are John's girls?" Taylor asked. "Well, never mind about Lucy. I know she's okay. She takes after her dad. It wouldn't surprise me if she becomes a cop, too. She'd be a good one. But what about Abigail? I saw her at the Inn; she and her sister are polar opposites, aren't they?"

A small snicker escaped Annie's throat. "That they are. Abigail's quieting down, though. She goes to college on the Cape and plans to transfer to RISD next year. Her heart's set on fashion design."

That's when Annie knew she couldn't keep this up. She could not sit there and act as if everything were fine. She could not pretend things were under control when Bella had called out to her. Had *called* her, for God's sake.

Annie opened her mouth to ask Taylor if they could leave, if she would drive her to the police station. She needed to report the call to Linc. Maybe there was some way they could trace the number. She set her napkin back on the table and started to stand when Taylor spoke again.

"Even as a little girl, Abigail liked prancing around in frilly dresses with shoes and hair things that matched. She was a prima donna by the time she was six."

Annie squirmed, feeling an unaccustomed need to defend her soon-to-be stepdaughter. "She's come a long way. She has a nice boyfriend; maybe he's helped her mature." She didn't feel a need to mention her suspicion about how her tire might have been sliced. She really needed to chalk that up to a roadside mishap. She picked up her bag from the empty chair next to her.

"Is he an island boy?"

Annie didn't want to keep talking, but she still felt a need to be polite for Kevin's sake. "No," she said. "He lives in New Hampshire."

As she was about to leave, even if it meant walking to the station, the server returned with their lunches: a veggie burger for Annie, fish stew for Taylor. If Annie hadn't just been talking about the *boyfriend,* as Lucy still called him, she might not have had an epiphany when she glanced up to thank the curly-haired server. When she'd been in Granite and had seen Abigail with her new beau, Annie now knew why the boy had looked familiar — and it had nothing to do with the idea that once anyone had lived on the island a while, other year-rounders tended to look familiar. The truth was, the boyfriend looked like Bella's half brother . . . one of the two sons of Stephen Thurman, Bella's biological father.

Taking a quick bite of the burger, Annie nervously chewed, trying to reorganize her thoughts, trying to contemplate what to do next. According to John, Stephen Thurman was dead. But had Abigail's boyfriend found out that his girlfriend was in some way connected to his father's unwanted baby? Had he remembered Annie from when she'd arrived unannounced at the Thurmans' house, first with Earl, then with John? Had he come back to the island to claim Bella? He must not want money — there still was no ransom request. But if he'd wanted to see Bella, why hadn't he simply shown up at the Inn and asked?

Then Annie had another disturbing thought: Did Abigail know he was involved? And . . . did she have something to do with it? Could that be the real reason she was being so nice? Helping to keep the searchers well fed and offering to alter the wedding dress? Was Abigail feeling . . . guilty?

When Annie tried to swallow, the bread stuck in her throat. She took a long drink of water. Then another. And then she knew what she had to do.

She touched Taylor's arm. "I need a favor. And I can't tell you why."

Taylor frowned.

"I need to borrow your truck. Can you take the *On Time* back to Chappy and have someone pick you up there?"

"Seriously? I wanted to go shopping."

Annie reached into her purse and threw down a twenty that would more than cover her share of the meal. "I'm sorry. But please trust me, Taylor. And tell no one. It's got to do with Bella." She pulled on her jacket and hat while Taylor fished out the keys and handed them over along with the twenty.

"This was on Kevin, remember?"

"Oh," she said, hurrying into her coat. "Thanks."

"Can I go with you? Whatever it is, I know how to keep quiet."

Annie knew that, too. And she was grateful. But she also knew she had to do this by herself. Until she was certain. For now, every instinct she had was telling her she needed to talk to only one person — the woman who had helped her untangle the story of Bella's birth. In order to do that, Annie had to go up-island.

And maybe along the way, Annie would text Linc. Just in case. Though, in case of what, she wasn't sure.

CHAPTER 39

The air had chilled in the short time they'd been in the pub. Maybe it was only Annie's nerves. Or maybe a storm was really on the way. She decided not to turn the truck radio on; she did not want to hear about inclement weather or any gloomy local updates about Bella that wouldn't really be updates because there was no news. Yet.

She'd driven a pickup only once, nearly two years before, when Claire had had a stroke and Earl was in no condition to make his way home after showing up at the hospital. His truck was newer than Taylor's and did not smell like the jasmine cologne that Taylor favored.

She managed to start the engine and back the truck up without ramming into anything or anyone. Her first stop would be up-island because Winnie's nephew, Lucas, had known the Thurman boys back in high school. Annie didn't recall the boys' names,

411

only that one had a dimple in his chin, the same way his half sister, Bella, did. It had been one of the first things that had directed them to their father.

Abigail's boyfriend might or might not have a dimple; his neatly trimmed beard would have camouflaged it.

Navigating the one-way streets of the village, Annie kept to the speed limit so she wouldn't get pulled over and lose time. However, after she passed the library and the elementary school on Edgartown–West Tisbury Road, she floored it. The pickup, however, didn't have much get-up-and-go. When traveling the back roads of Chappaquiddick, get-up-and-go was rarely warranted.

While putt-putting toward Aquinnah, Annie reconsidered sharing her epiphany with Linc. If she was wrong, she'd be wasting his time. And if he was tracking a lead that she didn't yet know about, her interruption might divert him from something that would turn out more successful.

And yet . . .

And yet . . .

She decided to wait until she could ask Lucas if he'd seen either Thurman boy lately. It might be a slim chance, but she had to stay positive.

If she'd called Winnie and asked for Lucas's phone number, it might have been smarter. But she wanted an in-person conversation with him, not one on the cell-service fly. Maybe she'd be able to learn more that way. If only the damn truck would move faster.

She drummed her fingers on the steering wheel, twisted this way and that on the seat. She started to turn on the radio, then remembered she'd decided not to. She did not dare check her phone. Not even when she remembered she'd silenced the ring when they'd gone into the Newes and hadn't turned it back on.

Passing the transfer station and the airport, the truck was doing forty at best. By the time she finally made it to the fork at State Road and went left, she pulled into Alley's parking lot. Her one consolation was that it wasn't July or August, when, in addition to the pokey mobile, she'd have to contend with the god-awful traffic.

She pulled her phone from her purse and checked for texts, messages, voice mail. Nothing appeared. She supposed she should turn off Wi-Fi, although the little wheel was going to rotate over and over, groaning with frustration while seeking a signal as she drove into the wishy-washy, up-island connection area, which was on par with that of Chappy. But if she turned off Wi-Fi and anyone had news — or if another call came through from Bella — Annie needed to know right away.

So she turned on the ringer and set the phone on the seat, its roaming feature already spinning fruitlessly.

She drove out of the lot and headed southwest. She used to be confused as to why Aquinnah was referred to as "up-island" when to get there one did not travel north. But Earl had explained that the "up" had come from the old sailors' orientation of the vertical, global lines of longitude and had nothing to do with where Aquinnah was in relation to Tisbury or Edgartown. She supposed it made sense, but all Annie was sure of was that the road was predictably windy in winter, with the air currents made worse by the hills, dips, and curves that defined the terrain. The sky seemed more overcast than it had been in Edgartown; the clouds looked more threatening, and light drops of wetness began to dot the windshield. Annie hoped it was salt spray off the ocean, which at that point was near her on one side or the other. Sometimes both. Whatever those directions were.

She passed the Allen Farm and, finally,

the Wampanoag Tribal Headquarters, and made it to Winnie's in less than an hour, which might have been a record for Taylor's old truck.

But when she turned into the driveway, there were no vehicles parked anywhere, not even on the lawn. Annie stopped, got out, and hurried to the back door. But when she knocked, no one responded.

And then the wind picked up, and the sky started to sleet.

It didn't occur to you to call Winnie first to find out if anyone was home?

Murphy's chastising words weren't helpful. Especially since she damn well could have suggested that when Annie still had been in Edgartown. Trundling back to the truck, she got in and slammed the door.

What? Murphy added. *I have to do all your thinking for you?*

Rather than dream up a retort, Annie muttered something she knew was neither fair nor useful. Murphy was right, of course; Annie was a big girl and shouldn't have acted so hastily. She wouldn't have if there had been a way to clear her head. But her brain wires were clearly misfiring, thanks to the echo of Bella's voice.

Ammie.

Happy Cwistmas.

With a heavy sigh, Annie started the engine again and turned on the heat, what there was of it. She wondered if she should wait to see if someone came home; after all, several of Winnie's "clan," as Winnie called them, lived in the big house. But the weather was troubling — more troubling than snow, because sleet could quickly turn to ice, and the winding roads up-island could become treacherous. With any luck, Annie would see some of the clan on the way and be able to flag them down. In the meantime, she needed to get ahead of the storm, or whatever the fine shards of icy water turned out to be, which she might have known had been predicted if she'd turned on the radio, which she still would not.

But as she backed out of the driveway, her text alert dinged. She slammed on the brakes. It was John. Thank God he'd gotten through.

F'S AUNT AND UNCLE DON'T HAVE HER, he'd typed. THEY'RE COMING TO MV WITH ME TO HELP SEARCH. CAN'T FLY OUT TILL TOMORROW — TOO MUCH SNOW.

That's all he wrote. It said a lot. But not enough.

With her hands now shaking, Annie went to her recent calls and hit John's number.

"Hey," he said.

"They really don't have her?"

"They do not. They were at a restaurant north of here yesterday but got snowed in last night. I'm told that happens a lot here."

Annie decided not to tell him where she was. Or why. Or that it was sleeting. She looked at the fine slivers of frozen stuff that were now coating the windshield too quickly.

"What?" John asked. "I can't hear you."

She decided it would be better to let him think they had a bad connection than to tell him she didn't know what to say.

"No more news?" John asked, raising his voice. "Can you hear me?"

Annie held her breath. She knew it wouldn't do any good to tell him about the phone call from Bella. Or to share her instinct about Abigail's boyfriend. But, again, it would have been doable if they were face-to-face, not held hostage by precarious cell service, especially since he was so far away. "I hear you now. And no. No news that I know of." She hoped she'd become a convincing liar.

John said something again, but the connection wavered, that time for real.

"What?" Annie asked.

"Ten days," he shouted over the gravelly connection. "Ten days till our wedding."

417

She wished she hadn't heard him. "Let's hope this is over by then. And that everything turns out well."

"That's what's keeping me going right now."

John could be sweet. She knew that about him; she cherished that quality. But right then, she did not want to talk about their wedding.

"I've got to go," she said. "Kevin's looking for me." She gulped her guilt and told herself it was for the greater good. For her good, actually, as he'd be angry if he knew she hadn't alerted Linc about the call from Bella, and that she'd driven to Winnie's to start her own probe. He'd also be upset that she was driving Taylor's old truck in the sleet.

"Let me know when you get a flight," she said, then added, "I love you," which was a small consolation for not having told him the truth.

If he responded, his words were lost to a gust of wind.

She clicked off and finished backing out of the driveway. Then she drove out onto the road, deciding that to make amends for her disobedience, on the way home she'd stop at the police station and tell Linc everything.

With her eyes drilled on the pavement, Annie gripped the steering wheel, her hands set at ten to two. "A steering wheel is like a clock," her dad told her when he'd taught her to drive several decades ago. "If you keep your hands at ten minutes before two, you'll always be in control."

She wasn't sure if the same theory applied when roads were slick and sleet was rapidly turning to ice. So much more hazardous than snow. The constant curves of the hilly terrain made the driving extra-precarious. As did the fact that the icy windshield was now clogging faster than either the squeaky wipers or the rumbling defrost fan could clear it. And, despite its cranking, slap-slapping sounds, the old heater was losing its battle for effectiveness, thanks to the wind that had picked up speed and was blasting the truck from all directions.

If she had her Jeep and not Taylor's pickup, things might go more smoothly. But she did not have her Jeep. So she knew not to waste time feeling sorry for herself but to concentrate on getting back to Edgartown, and on what she'd say to Linc.

She could always lie and say the connection between Abigail's boyfriend and Stephen Thurman had occurred to her only when she was up-island at Winnie's. But he'd be bound to ask why the heck she'd made a mad dash up there with a storm on the way and in someone else's vehicle, Taylor's especially, since, as John's close friend and coworker, he no doubt knew that Taylor had not been one of Annie's favorite people, though Annie tried, she really did.

Shut up, she told her brain and went back to fixating on the road.

Reaching the top of the hill that descended past the road that led to the tribal offices, she lightly tapped the brakes — her dad had taught her that, too, though she couldn't remember if she should do that only on snow, not ice.

But just before the bottom of the hill, the vehicle didn't slow; she tapped again . . . the bed of the truck swayed to the right . . . to the left . . . and skidded. She held her breath and forced her eyes to stay open.

Turn into the skid! Murphy shouted from wherever she was.

Annie obeyed, and the pickup instantly righted itself. That's when she remembered that those words had also been part of her dad's driving instructions. She eased her foot off the gas pedal and continued more slowly, smiling at the thought that maybe her dad and Murphy had come together in the heavens in order to help her out.

She half considered turning back to Winnie's, but the memory of Bella's voice calling out kept her moving forward.

Hill after hill, curve after curve, Taylor's truck inched toward Annie's destination. The ice bombarded the steel and the wind grew angrier, but instead of being more afraid, she grew more determined.

Just before Squibnocket Pond, she realized she was going faster again, faster than she should. As she started down another hill, she lifted her foot off the gas . . . too late. The truck skidded again. Worse than before. It picked up speed, accelerating as if a ghostly demon had stomped on the pedal. Annie's throat started to close. Her hands clenched in the ten-to-two position. And yet . . . the skid turned into propulsion. Steering into it was useless. The truck kept going, going, veering to the right . . . then taking off — airborne — from the icy pavement . . . smashing through a stone wall . . . hurtling toward the pond . . . crashing into a cluster of scrub oaks . . . and . . . finally . . . stopping dead.

Annie's forehead smacked the steering wheel. She wondered why the airbag didn't inflate . . . or if Taylor's vehicle was too old to have one. Then she wondered . . . nothing.

CHAPTER 40

An annoying sound was making her head hurt.

Rap-rap-rap.

Then the passenger door of the pickup was being yanked open.

"Jumpin' Jehoshaphats, is that you, Annie Sutton?"

She struggled to open her eyes. She turned her head toward the voice that sounded familiar. A man's voice. But his face was blurry, either from her vision or the snowflakes coating his dark hair.

Snowflakes? she wondered. Was it snowing now?

"Christ, woman," the man's voice said, "you're bleeding."

The blurry figure shut the door.

Annie sighed and rested her head back on the steering wheel.

Then the driver's door — her door — opened. The man reached inside and unclicked her seat belt. Her vision cleared. Her savior was Orrin, Winnie's brother.

He pulled a phone out of his pocket. "I gotta call Tri-Town. We need an ambulance. You need the hospital."

"No," Annie said, surprised that her voice worked. She squared her shoulders, leaned against the back of the seat, and touched her forehead; her fingers came back red with blood. Her blood. "Is Winnie home yet?"

"Yeah," he said. "We were in Menemsha at my trawler. I expected snow, not ice. Had to prep the engine block so it wouldn't crack. You okay to make it to my truck?"

"I think so."

She was dizzy and her head hurt, but obstinacy kicked in. That and Bella's little voice resonating in her mind.

Annie leaned on Orrin as they walked gingerly up the slope, through the stone wall where Taylor's vehicle had careened, and into his truck that he'd pulled onto the roadside.

"I saw the break in the wall and figured somebody was down there," he said.

She nodded, grateful.

He turned over the ignition and eyed Annie again. "You sure you don't want the hospital?"

"Maybe after I see Winnie. It's really

important. And Lucas. Is he there, too?"

"I expect so. He went with Winnie in her van. In case she slid off the road or something." He then uttered a "huh," steered onto the icy and now snowy pavement. And he carefully guided his truck toward Winnie's.

In spite of nasty road conditions, they made it without incident.

Winnie made tea while Orrin's wife, Barbara, tended to Annie's wound. Barbara was a nurse, so when she told Annie that she needed stitches and an X-ray to rule out a concussion or worse, Annie took her seriously. First, however, she asked to see Lucas. Her head was pounding then, but it didn't matter.

Winnie hustled from the room. Seconds later, Lucas appeared.

"Geeez, Annie," he said, "what happened to you?"

Annie shook her head. "Nothing serious. But I have a question. You were in high school with the Thurman brothers, right?"

"Uh, sure."

"Have you seen either of them lately?"

"Funny you should ask. I saw Caleb last week. I was driving to Edgartown. He was heading toward OB. I blew the horn, but he didn't wave or anything. Maybe he was in a hurry."

Caleb. Hadn't Lucy said that Abigail's boyfriend's name was Cal, but that his real name could be Calvin, like in the old cartoon? Maybe it wasn't Calvin. Maybe, just maybe, it was Caleb. Annie stood up, got dizzy, and slid to the floor.

"Lucas," she heard Barbara's voice, which sounded as if it were somewhere in the distance. "Call the ambulance."

Annie wanted to ask if someone could drive her. She hated ambulances, hated the lights, hated the siren, announcing to the world that a person was in crisis. But though she hadn't passed out, she felt too groggy to speak.

Barbara and Orrin got her back onto the chair; Barbara checked her vitals and had her sip water. Winnie and Lucas quietly watched.

By the time the ambulance arrived, Annie had found her voice; she told them that the pain in her head had eased, though it had not.

The EMT who rode in the back with her insisted on yakking all the way down State Road toward the hospital. Annie wanted to ask him to please be quiet, but she suspected

426

he was trying to keep her alert.

Finally, they made it. The EMTs whisked the gurney out the back door and into the ER. Within seconds, Annie was wheeled to a separate room, where she received twelve stitches. Then it was on to radiology. While she sat in the dark room, waiting for the technician to adjust the camera angle, she wondered how she was going to look as a bride wearing an ugly dress and sporting a battered face.

After she was moved back to the first room, the doctor came in and told her she needed to stay awake until the X-rays were read. Annie, however, was tired. Very tired. As she was struggling not to nod off, Winnie came into the room with Lucas.

"You drove all the way here?" Annie asked. "But the roads . . ."

"Never mind the roads. Lucas didn't finish telling you everything about Caleb before you landed on the floor. I decided you should hear the rest. Traipsing up-island on such a nasty day seemed a bit much, even for you, so maybe this will help." Winnie's smile warmed her copper skin and instantly put Annie at ease. "The truth is, we would have called to tell you, but the damn service went out."

Annie almost laughed. Then she looked at

Lucas. "What else?"

"You asked me if I'd seen Caleb recently, so the first thing I thought of was when heading toward Oak Bluffs, like I told you. But I saw him earlier. Back in September. On the boat."

It was interesting but did not seem important. "Was he coming to the Vineyard?"

He shook his head. "Heading to Woods Hole. I was surprised 'cuz, like I said, I'd heard they left the island. Anyway, we said hi; he told me he'd been here to see the headstone that was finally put on his father's grave. He died, you know."

Annie said yes, she knew. Again, it did not seem important. Or relevant. Until Lucas continued.

"Anyway," he said, "just when we started talking, we saw Abigail. John's daughter?"

Annie blinked. She sat up, ignoring her pain. "And?"

Lucas shrugged. "She's younger than we are, so he didn't remember her in school back when she went to school here. Before her parents got divorced. But I know who she is, because our family's always been close to Earl's. Anyway, I told Caleb that her father's going to marry a famous author. That would be you."

Annie hated that Lucas had called her

famous, but knew he'd meant no harm. "And?" she asked again.

"And that was all. Until about a month ago, when I heard he'd been on the island again. And that he was dating her." His chin dropped. "I should have remembered it earlier. Maybe it would have helped. But when I told him about you in September, he asked me if you were the one who found a baby . . ."

Annie stopped breathing. She wondered if she was imagining this conversation, if her head injury had put her in a coma and she was dreaming now. Stephen — Caleb's father — hadn't wanted Bella; his wife had socked him in the jaw when Annie revealed the truth.

Then Winnie reached over and took Annie's hand. Despite the doctor's instructions, Annie closed her eyes. She had to think. And she could think more clearly if she wasn't sitting in a hospital with a dozen stitches in her head.

"Where's Caleb now?" If he had Bella, having her talk into the phone might have been a kind gesture to let her know that Bella was alive. And *fine,* as the note had read. Maybe he wasn't all bad.

But how did he get Annie's number?

Abigail. Or, at least from Abigail's phone

— though Annie had no idea if she had her number. Unless, for some reason, John had put it there.

"I don't know where he is," Lucas was saying. "I haven't heard that anyone's seen him."

"Lucas, please. This is important. Do you know where his friends live on the island? Anyone he might be staying with?"

He thought for a moment. "He really only hung out with his brother. Once in a while they came up to the Winsted house, but . . ."

Annie felt as if someone had filled a bucket with icy water out of Squibnocket Pond, where she'd almost just landed, and dumped it over her head.

"What's Taylor got to do with this?" Then she realized, maybe it wasn't Taylor but Rex. "And why would Caleb be at their house?"

"Not their house on Chappy," Lucas replied. "The one up-island, not far from the reservation. The old man won it in the derby a long time ago."

An image of the clipping from the *Gazette* flashed into Annie's brain. "But . . . but he won land, didn't he? Not a house, right?"

Winnie stepped into the conversation. "You're right. He won the land. But over time, he built kind of a ramshackle place. More like a fishing shack, I think. I never saw it, but my father told me about it."

Annie struggled to think. Was Rex involved, after all? But why? And how? Hadn't Kevin said that Rex was on Chappy the whole time since Bella had gone missing? Then again, with Kevin and Taylor — and Jonas — spending so much time looking for her, would they have noticed if he'd left?

And how was Rex connected to Caleb Thurman?

Her head hurt now, in more ways than one. "Do you know where the place is?"

"Sure," Lucas said. "And I hate to disagree, Aunt Winnie, but it's more than a shack now. It's a neat little cabin. A bunch of us used to hang out there sometimes. You know, high school stuff. It even has a woodstove where we heated up canned stew and baked beans."

Annie and Winnie exchanged looks that said they were sure a group of high school kids did more in a cabin than heat up canned food. Then Annie slid off the bed. "Take me there. Right now."

On the way out of the ER, she signed herself out, against the doctor's wishes, but made sure the nurse had her number so they could contact her with the X-ray results. Not that Annie cared about that.

CHAPTER 41

Once again, the trip up-island seemed to take forever. The roads were even slicker now, with several inches of snow piled on top of the ice. It was slow going in Winnie's van; Annie tried not to be impatient.

Lucas finally took a right onto a bumpy, narrow side road. In addition to the snow, it was dark, thanks to the day having turned to twilight. Annie tried hard not to wonder whom they'd find — if anyone.

Then they came upon a pickup truck, newer than Taylor's, but not by much. Parked next to it was a small car. Annie also saw the silhouette of a cabin, a short distance away, up on a hill.

Then her stomach roiled. The small car. Her eyes flicked back to it — a VW Beetle. Was Abigail's car a Beetle? The compact size would be perfect for both the island and the Cape when she was in school. John had said she'd brought the car back to the

Vineyard to have during winter break. But Annie hadn't yet seen it.

Without intending to, she let out a moan.

Then she said, "Stop. I'll walk in from here."

Lucas stopped.

Annie got out. She touched the hood of the truck to steady herself, to stop her head — and her world — from spinning.

Then she walked, grasping tree trunks for balance along the way, treading through the icy snow, mindful to be quiet, hoping that whoever was inside didn't hear the van approach.

Finally, she reached the cabin. There were no curtains or blinds at the windows, nothing to block her view. Candles lit up the room; a fire glowed in the stove. She knew it was easier for her to see inside than for anyone to look out and see her in the dark; unlike the first time she'd come upon Rex, the light inside wasn't leaking out to the yard. So Annie had a clear view of Abigail, who stood in the middle of the room, dressed in a coat, a hat, and mittens. It looked as if she had been crying.

Caleb was a few feet in front of Abigail. Yes, Annie knew, it really was him. The young man she'd seen with Abigail at Granite, the one who had looked so familiar.

In Caleb's arms was . . . Bella.

She sheer-willed herself not to scream.

Moving as stealthily as possible, she went up to the door and turned the handle. Either it was locked — or stuck. Steeling her shoulder on her right side — instead of the left side where her head now sported stitches — she counted to three, as if that would make a difference. Then she rammed her body, full force, against the door. It lurched open.

Which alerted Bella.

The little girl scrambled out of Caleb's grasp faster than Annie had ever seen her move.

"Ammie!" came her happy cry as she rushed toward her. "Ammie!"

Annie held her breath and stooped down. "Hey, little one!" she called, and enfolded Bella into her arms. "We've missed you!" She held her close and smoothed her beautiful curls. She hoped that Bella could not feel her trembling.

"I didn't hear from Caleb after the weekend he was here." Abigail's words spilled out in a rush. "I thought he dumped me . . ." She cried again. "He texted me this afternoon. He asked if I could keep a secret. I was so afraid if I told anyone they'd think that I'd done it . . ."

Annie knew she had a choice: to believe Abigail or to challenge her right then — and risk losing any chance they might have of ever being friends. And maybe risk losing John, too.

But, in truth, Annie did believe her. Abigail's terrified expression that Annie had seen through the window had said it all.

"Which one of you slashed my tire?" she asked.

Caleb frowned. "Abigail said you didn't like her. I was trying to impress her."

Abigail shook her head. "I didn't think he'd do it, Annie. Just like I never, ever, would have thought that he'd take Bella. Even though I now know that he's her father."

That was something Annie hadn't seen coming. She looked back at Caleb, who looked as if he, too, were about to cry.

"Bella's father wasn't Stephen Thurman," Abigail explained. "Caleb is. He . . . he had sex with Francine's mother. When he was with his father and brother over on the Cape, supposedly fishing." Her voice quivered; she turned toward the door. "He . . . he *raped* her."

"I didn't mean to, I really didn't." The boy hung his head. "But I was drunk. I was mad at my dad . . . I thought he was fooling

435

around with her . . . it would have killed my mom . . . ." Then he added, "I'm so sorry, Abigail. It happened a long time before I met you." As if that made the current situation okay.

"We'll pretend you didn't say that," Annie said.

Caleb shook his head. "You don't understand. My father raised me and my brother to take responsibility. And, yeah, I made a mistake with Bella's mother. But when this . . . when *she* happened" — he gestured toward Bella — "he said we'd tell everyone that she was his. That otherwise I'd screw up my whole life. But all this time, I wondered where she was. I was hoping she was still here. My dad had cancer a long time . . . it's why he and Mom decided he'd say the baby was his. They knew it wouldn't be long before he was dead, and then no one would ever blame me."

"But the fight your parents had . . . ," Annie began.

"When Mom socked him in the jaw? It was an act," Caleb said. "Mom hit him harder than either of them expected, but it was fake."

"I was convinced," Annie said. She was also convinced now that Caleb, indeed, was Bella's father. The dark eyes, the thick, black hair, the little scrunch of his brow when he was upset — all along, Annie had confused Bella's features with Francine's. But, as it turned out, Bella looked like Caleb, too.

"That was the point. But I knew all along that after my dad died, I'd find a way to see my little girl. Just *see* her, you know? I finally got up the nerve to come back to the Vineyard. I remembered that Earl Lyons lived on Chappy. I got as far as the *On Time* when I chickened out. On the boat back to Woods Hole, I ran into Lucas. I made up a story about checking on my father's headstone. And then he introduced me to Abigail." He hung his head again. "When he told me her father was going to marry the famous author Annie Sutton, I remembered your name. I couldn't believe my luck."

"So you decided to take Bella?"

"No! I told you. I just wanted to see her . . . ." Tears spilled. His mind seemed to drift for a moment. Then he said, "But first I had to find her. I knew Abigail could be a key to making that happen." He looked at her then. "I wasn't using you, honest. I really liked . . . I really like you."

Annie couldn't tell if Abigail believed him.

"You pumped me with questions," she said. "I told you about Annie and the Inn. Don't tell me you weren't using me." It wasn't apparent whether she was angry or hiding the fact that she felt crushed.

"We had such a great time when I was here for the weekend," Caleb continued. "But when you brought me to the boat, I never got on. It felt like it was my chance."

"What did you do next?" Annie asked.

"I crossed the street. I rented a van and drove up here. I didn't even know if this place still existed. But I found it. That was on a Monday. By Friday, I knew I either had to go to Chappy and try and find her or forget it. So I went. And when I walked into the Inn and saw her right there, all by herself . . . I just . . . took her. Because she's my daughter. And she looks like me, don't you think?"

Annie ignored his question. She held Bella more tightly. "How did you get my phone number?"

He nodded toward Abigail. "From her phone."

Before Annie could register surprise, Abigail seemed to realize what had happened. "The morning we were leaving Plymouth, Dad called to say you'd pick Lucy up at the boat. She'd forgotten her phone, so she put your number in mine. In case the boat was running late." She turned back to Caleb. "When did you look at my phone?"

"You were in the bathroom, putting on your makeup. Lucy answered your phone, and I heard her side of the conversation. I figured out what was going on, so after Lucy left the room, I looked at your phone and wrote down the number."

"So you really were dating me just to . . . do this? Not because you wanted to be with me?"

With Abigail asking questions, Annie wouldn't be perceived as the nasty stepmother. Which pleased her.

"No. I don't think so. But then . . . when you said I should come to the island the next weekend, everything fell into place. I even bought one of those cheap, throwaway phones and put Annie's number in it in case I got up the courage to call her . . ."

Which explained to Annie why the caller ID had read UNKNOWN.

Abigail folded her arms. "Stop. Just stop. I don't want to hear any more."

Then Winnie called out, "Is everything okay in here?" She and Lucas came into the cabin . . . just as sirens blared outside and the red lights and blue lights flashed on and off across the snow. Unlike with the ambulance, Annie was grateful to see them.

"I texted my dad before you got here," Abigail said.

"It's okay, honey," Annie said. "Bella's safe now."

"Of course she's safe," Caleb whimpered. "Why would I hurt her?"

Annie didn't know how to respond, except to ask, "So I expect you also wrote the note?"

"What note?"

"The one you left on my porch that said Bella was fine. That she was safe with you."

"I didn't write a note. All I did was take her. And her teddy bear."

"Mr. Bear," Bella said, and pointed to the corner of an old plaid chair.

Then the police tramped through the doorway. Annie grabbed the teddy and handed it to Bella while Caleb was being handcuffed. She didn't know the up-island officer who recited Caleb his rights, but she figured John must have had Linc alert the Aquinnah force because they weren't far from the cabin.

None of which would have happened as fast and maybe not as safely if it had not been for Abigail.

Annie handed Bella and Mr. Bear to Winnie. Then she went to Abigail and hugged her. It was the first time she had done that; she hoped it wouldn't be the last.

"Thank you," Annie said. "You risked a

lot by coming out here on your own."

"I kept thinking about Gramma and Gramps," she said, crying again. "And how freaked out they've been because the little girl was missing. I don't know the rest of you very well, but she means a lot to them."

"She means a lot to a lot of us," Annie said. "And I hope it's not long before you know that you do, too."

Winnie joined them. "Come on, Annie, let's get you and Lady Bella home. You have a wedding to finish planning, don't you?"

Which was when the rest of Annie's world came back into focus.

On the way back to Chappy, the first thing Annie did was call Francine. Their conversation was interrupted when a nurse called Annie from the hospital — her X-rays were negative for a concussion or other complications. "The doctor wants you to stay mindful of any unusual symptoms, and he wants you to take it easy for a few days." Annie almost laughed at that.

Then she called John.

When they finally arrived at the Inn and went inside, she found Francine sitting on one of the big sofas in the great room. Jonas was next to her, his arm around her, her head on his shoulder. Annie marveled at the good news all around her.

"Mama!" Bella cried, and Annie set her down, folded her arms, and tried to watch the reunion without shedding more tears. Her attempts at staying dry-eyed did not work.

Annie had no idea if Francine and Jonas had reunited before or after she had called with the good news. But knowing the answer to that didn't matter; Annie was far too happy that they were back together.

"Blue! Blue! Blue!" Bella happily exclaimed as she opened and closed her tiny hands, mimicking the cruiser's flashing lights.

Annie laughed. "We had a police escort all the way from Aquinnah," she explained. "I didn't have a vehicle — well, that's a long story, but it's connected to the bandage on my forehead, and everything's fine now, thank God. Anyway, they wouldn't let Abigail drive her Beetle on the slippery roads."

"Abigail?" Francine asked.

"That's a long story, too. I'll tell you later. In the meantime, I'll call Earl and Claire and Kevin and Taylor. And give Taylor the bad news that her truck met with a stone wall."

"I already told them," Francine said. "Except about Taylor's truck."

"Then I guess it's time for that little girl of yours to have a cookie."

"Peanut butter cookie, pwease," Bella said.

"Lucy's been baking enough to feed all of Chappaquiddick," Jonas said as he took Bella from Francine. "And we've just been sitting around, missing our Bella." He held her close, tears brimming.

"You my daddy," Bella said in a small voice. She put her arms around his neck and nuzzled her face on his collarbone.

"I knew all along that Jonas didn't mean to leave her," Francine said to Annie. "I couldn't stand knowing how much he must be hurting. And I missed him. So much . . ."

Annie felt a swell of emotion that was so palpable, she knew it was time to turn the reunion over to them. "I'm glad for you, honey. I really am." She kissed her cheek. "But if you'll excuse me, I'm going to grab one of Lucy's cookies for Bella and one for me. And then I'm going to go home to put my feet up and call Taylor and tell her I owe her a new truck. I need to get that over with, because I've had enough excitement today to last a lifetime."

"You'll have more when John comes home tomorrow," Francine said. "And you can get back to finishing your plans for the wedding."

Annie really wished that people would stop reminding her of that.

CHAPTER 42

On Thursday, John was on his way back to the Vineyard on the six-fifteen, which every islander knew would arrive in Vineyard Haven at seven o'clock. Annie was determined to pick him up — along with Francine's aunt and uncle, who had decided to come, even though they now knew Bella was safe. Annie had no idea how long they planned to stay, but she was able to book a room for them at the Kelley House, within walking distance of the Chappy Ferry. Francine said that she, Jonas, and Bella would be in their room at the Inn: she wanted them to be together, not in separate rooms at Earl and Claire's.

As Annie sat in the parking lot at the Steamship Authority, waiting for the boat to arrive, she knew she was still numb from the past days. She wondered how long it would take for things to go back to the way they'd been, or if that might never happen.

Bella's abduction had very much been a wakeup call that an idyllic life rarely existed or, at least, was not guaranteed. Not even on Martha's Vineyard.

She was happy that neither Rose nor Rex had been involved; she was glad for Francine that it hadn't been Marty and Bill. As for herself, she was relieved that Trish hadn't been behind it, that her editor and friend hadn't hired someone to do the deed in an effort to entice Annie to become a superstar. After having worked together for years, Annie knew Trish better than that. But when Bella disappeared, her brain was so muddled, she might even have thought John had been behind it . . . which would have been as preposterous as when he'd suggested Francine was.

Still, Annie wondered if she'd ever be able to tell him that she'd walked away from a small fortune. And if she did, how he'd react.

Then the big white boat suddenly appeared, as if it had sneaked in and docked while she'd been musing.

The next thing she knew, John's arms were around her. If Francine's aunt and uncle hadn't been right behind him, Annie would have collapsed against him.

Marty and Bill were nice; Annie was

ashamed that they'd ever thought they might have tried to take Bella from Francine. She decided right then that she would never remind John of his suspicions about Francine. He'd been being thorough. And doing his job.

The officer who had accompanied John said he'd walk over to the Vineyard Haven station; John loaded Marty and Bill's suitcases into the back of the Jeep. Once again, Annie was thankful that she no longer had to be in charge.

Give me a break, Murphy suddenly whined in Annie's brain. Which, of course, made Annie laugh. Then she apologized to the present company by saying she often laughed out loud when she was happy. She had no idea if they believed her.

Still, it wasn't until she was back on Chappy, tucked into her cottage with John, with a warm fire glowing in the woodstove, that Annie felt safe enough to inhale and exhale without feeling as if her lungs were constricted. She didn't mind when he told her that the report on the fingerprints inside the cottage had come back: there were numerous ones, but they belonged to Annie, John, Earl, Kevin, Lucy, even Taylor. None that could not be identified as belonging to one of the troops. She didn't mind when he started to explain that, in addition to his arrest for Bella's abduction, Caleb would also be responsible to pay the expenses of processing the fingerprints and the extra-duty police needed in the search. Or when he said that Caleb's punishment might not be as lengthy as they might have thought — or hoped — because he was Bella's biological father. He added that the young man was lucky there had been so many volunteers searching for Bella so that Edgartown hadn't incurred more costs by having to call in law enforcement from the Cape.

Annie didn't even mind that John fell sound asleep on the love seat or that she had to coax him into the bedroom and onto the bed, where he slept not only through dinner but also through the night.

Mid-morning on Friday, in spite of the big table, two shifts were needed for breakfast: first, for the tenants; second, for the rest of them — Annie, John, Earl, Claire, Lucy, Fran cine, Jonas, Bella, Marty, Bill, Kevin, Taylor, and . . . Rex, who had made a custom recipe of eggs Florentine with tender, sweet scallops.

Abigail didn't come — Lucy said her sister had gone home to Edgartown, that she was too embarrassed about having picked a boyfriend who'd hurt everyone so badly. Annie hoped that, in time, she could help Abigail understand that no one blamed her.

The conversation was lively, the spirits were high.

"Here's to family," Earl said, lifting his mug of java in a toast.

"Of which we all are a big part," Claire added, clinking her mug against Earl's.

"Hear, hear!" Kevin said.

Then Rex stood up, a glass of orange juice in hand. "And I have another toast. To my sister and brother-in-law. Who are about to become the proud owners of the family home on Chappaquiddick."

The jovial conversation came to a sudden halt. Some eyes stared at Rex, the others at Kevin.

Finally, Kevin spoke. "Not that I want to challenge you, Rex, but could you maybe elaborate?"

Rex laughed. "I know I've probably freaked some of you out these past couple of weeks." His glance flicked to Annie. "The truth is, I'd forgotten what it's like to live on the island. When that little girl was missing, I watched everyone pull together. I walked around, just watching, maybe a little too often. But all the while I was thinking,

449

'This is the Vineyard, this is a great place. And this is my home.' " He paused, cleared his throat, and continued. "I know I wasn't too popular when I was a kid . . . ."

"You can say that again," Earl grumbled, and Rex laughed again.

"Thanks, Earl. I deserved that. But I like to think I've grown up since then. And as it happens, I'd forgotten about that little piece of property Dad won at the derby. The one where they found Bella. It turns out Dad had authorized Attorney Johnson — Sophie Johnson's father — to fix up the cabin and rent it out in summers. When old man Johnson died, the paperwork got lost, so Sophie just kept doing what her dad had been doing. She said she figured that sooner or later it would get resolved. I went out to look at it early this morning; I decided it would be a decent place to live. Maybe I'll even meet a nice lady somewhere on this godforsaken island. The last woman bailed on me — well, that's another story." He looked at Annie; she offered him a small smile.

His small audience was silent, as if awaiting his next confession.

"Oh," he added, "did I forget to mention that Dad left the cabin to my sister? It's not worth as much as the house on Chappy, but

450

I'd consider it an even swap. If you're interested, Taylor? There's even some cash from the rentals that we can split; maybe I'll use my share to open an up-island restaurant — one that stays open year-round. I think they'd be happy to have one up there. And, Taylor, you can buy a new cello or two."

The silence turned to murmurs.

Earl stood up and shook Rex's hand.

"I think those are dandy ideas," Earl said. "A house, a new cello or two, and I heard a rumor that Taylor's also getting a new truck. What more could a girl want?"

And everyone laughed because how could they not?

After Earl sat down, Jonas stood.

"I think I've said 'I'm sorry' more times in these past days than I have in my whole life."

"Without a doubt," Earl interrupted. "So, please, don't say it again. There's no need, my boy."

Jonas nodded shyly. He glanced at Francine, who smiled up at him and nodded.

"I also want to say something to Marty and Bill," he said. "Speaking for Francine, Bella, and me, we're really glad you're here. But what I'm going to say next might upset you, and we're sorry for that. We're going to stay here on the island. We both love it here. We don't know where we'll live yet, but we're going to try and get our own place. I'm going to sell the place in Hawaii; it makes no sense to hang on to it when we'd rather be here. But we'll make sure we have a place that's big enough for you to come and visit." Then he sat down.

Kevin looked at Annie; she knew he must be thinking about the workshop and how he'd better get cracking to finish fixing it into a nice little home for Francine and Jonas and their kids. Annie felt sure that Kevin wanted to say it now, but he kept silent; perhaps he'd tell them later, when they were alone.

Then John stood up. "I have no toast to make and no big announcement. Other than to say I'm glad this all worked out and that Bella's safe. But I do have to get to work now, because at least one of us has a real job." He didn't mention that Caleb had been arraigned Thursday afternoon or that no one had posted bail. He picked up his empty breakfast plate and added, "Oh, and I know I'll see all of you here a week from today for the wedding of the century."

He kissed Annie on the cheek, said he'd see her later, and soon after that, the party dispersed.

■ ■ ■ ■

A week from today wasn't easy for Annie to digest. She spread the ugly wedding dress out on her bed and tried to assess if Abigail really would be able to save the day or, at least, the dress. It was easier to think about than to wonder if Annie's agent, Louisa, was going to fire her as a client or if Trish would pull her next book deal before Annie had finished writing it. She knew she had to face that her writing career might be over and done with. "Creative differences" was the term she'd often heard when an agent or publisher cut ties with an author.

Dwelling on the dress might also be easier to think about than the actual wedding plans.

Then she had another thought: *a week from today.* Wasn't today the last day they could get the marriage license? Wasn't there a seven-day waiting period in Massachusetts?

She quickly texted John.

There was a knock on the cottage front door. Hesitant to miss John's reply, Annie brought her phone with her into the living room. Because she was busy staring at her phone, she opened the door without looking to see who it was. Besides, this was the Vineyard, where bad things never happened. Well, almost never.

It was Rose.

"May I talk to you a minute?"

"Of course." Annie lowered her arm that was holding the phone. She stepped back and let Rose inside. "Would you like tea?"

Shaking her head, Rose made no move to take off her coat or mittens. "I can't stay. I have too much to do."

Annie smiled. "Is something special going on?"

The sigh was hesitant but cheerful. "I need to tell you that I wrote the note. The one on your doorstep about Bella."

Annie blinked but let her talk.

"I saw that boy take her," Rose continued. "I was painting my rocks; I saw him from the window upstairs in my room. He was holding Bella, and she seemed to like him. I assumed it was Jonas; he had on a hood and his back was toward me. It never occurred to me that Bella was in trouble."

"Could you see if the boy had a car?" Annie asked.

Rose shook her head. "Not from my window. After that, when the police came and the turmoil began, and everyone was frantic that she'd gone missing, I panicked.

I'd been so nervous since the first day I saw Rex. And suddenly, it was like the day Uncle Clive shot Bernie . . . I got so confused . . . I could barely breathe . . . and all I wanted was to run." Her eyes darted around the room, as if she were reliving the trauma again.

Annie wanted to hug her but she knew that she should wait until the story was finished.

"I know it was stupid of me," Rose stammered, "but I wrote the note because I was pretty sure Bella was okay. She wasn't crying or anything. I doubted that she'd be washed up on the beach or left out in the woods. But after I put it under the planter on your porch, I knew it wasn't fair. I had no right to get everyone's hopes up in case . . ." Tears formed in her eyes. "By then, it was too late. And I was so scared. So I ran away from Chappaquiddick, just like I'd been forced to run when Clive had killed my Bernie. I didn't know what else to do. And I didn't want to get blamed for not telling the police about Bella when I should have."

Annie thought quickly. "Rose, John thinks the note was a prank. And there were no fingerprints on it. So I think we should leave it be."

Rose brushed her tears. "But I am so sorry . . ."

"Chances are," Annie said, "we wouldn't have found her right away, anyway. And you were right. Bella was safe all along."

Rose considered that, then slowly nodded. "There's something else," she said. "I'll honor my lease through May, but I'll be going back to Kennebunk. All these years, I rented out Uncle Clive's house year-round — the last tenant was there over twenty years. But she's old now; she moved off-island to be with her children. Her rent check paid for the upkeep and the taxes and gave me a small income. But the house has sold now — for far more than I imagined. And I don't need to be here any longer."

Then Annie's text alert dinged. Her innards groaned, if innards could do that sort of thing. She knew that, right then, Rose needed to be her priority.

Annie gave her a hug. "Oh, Rose, we'll miss you. But, please, don't worry about the lease. You're free to go whenever you want, no strings attached." It did, however, occur to her that she was a terrible landlord to let her emotions get in the way of a business contract. Still, that's who she was and, more than likely, she was not going to change.

"And as much as I'd like to stay for your wedding," Rose continued, "I'd really like to be home for Christmas."

"I understand."

"What you don't know, though, is that when I say I'm going 'home,' I mean I'm going back to Maine to be with my husband."

Annie blinked. "You're right. I had no idea you have a husband."

"His name is Fred Chapin. He owns a general store and bait shop in Damariscotta. This coming summer it will be fifty years since Uncle Clive kicked me out. I've been haunted by that. Anyway, I told Fred I needed to come down here and get the house sold and set myself right again. He's a good man, so he agreed. I use my maiden name as my middle name — I've done that since we married, I have no idea why. So when Rose Atkins Chapin opened a checking account, I had no problem simply using Rose Atkins. I thought I might need to do that in order to sell the house. I probably didn't, but . . ." She seemed to think about that for a moment, then dismissed whatever had stopped her. "Anyway, now that I have the money from Clive's house, I hope Fred will retire. Our little community isn't much different than here on the Vineyard, where folks watch out for one another. Maybe now, we'll have the time and money to do more of that."

"Oh, Rose. That's wonderful." It was fabulous to think that Rose's world wasn't the sad, lonely one that Annie had pictured.

"Before I go," Rose added, "I'm going to go to the police station and tell them what happened to Bernie. I think I can remember where Clive buried him. I don't know if he still has family around, but the island has a right to know. My attorney doesn't think I'll get into trouble for taking so long to tell the truth because I was so young and Uncle Clive traumatized me. But I still feel awful about it." She sighed.

Annie nodded, never having imagined that Rose Atkins would end up being so brave. Just as she'd never thought Abigail would have played such a big part in Bella's rescue. "I'm sure it will work out, Rose. Keep us posted, okay?"

"I will. Thank you for everything." She smiled. "Unlike Bernie's life, mine has turned out very lucky. I also have two sons who want me home. They're both married; Fred and I have three grandkids. Two grandsons and a granddaughter. Her name is Lily; the dollhouse is hers. She insisted that I take it in case I got lonely down here.

Fred and I gave it to her for Christmas last year; Lily and I decorated it." She quickly produced her phone and scrolled through photos of the towheaded children — and a kitten — that were all part of her family.

And Annie realized that the couple in the bedroom of the dollhouse were supposed to be Rose and Fred; in the other bedroom was their granddaughter, Lily. Annie pointed to the last photo and asked, "Does the kitten belong to Lily?"

"Oh, my, yes. Little girls love kittens, don't they?"

Annie wondered if life would ever stop surprising her. Or how a quiet woman like Rose would contribute to reminding Annie that sometimes it was important to "set" oneself right, in order to let new seeds of life take root and grow.

She didn't know how John would feel about it, but Annie knew that it was her time, once again, to do that.

After Rose left, Annie checked the text.

DON'T WORRY ABOUT THE MARRIAGE LICENSE, John had typed. I HAVE CONNECTIONS IN HIGH PLACES.

And Annie laughed to think that her go-by-the-book husband-to-be could still surprise her, too.

■ ■ ■ ■

"So you're sure the license will be okay?" she asked John later that night after he returned to Chappy and they had a quiet supper. Restless had come with him; they'd both agreed that the poor little dog hadn't had enough attention in the past days.

"We can pick it up — and sign it — first thing in the morning. Judd filed it under the wire today, so we'll still be seven days out." Judd, yet another good friend of John, worked in the town clerk's office.

"That's great," she said, "but I sure am exhausted."

Sitting on the love seat, John propped his elbows on his thighs and tented his fingers. Restless was nestled on the braided rug, his chin on top of John's feet.

"Yeah," John said, letting out a long breath of air. "I'm exhausted, too. It's so damn hard to stay objective and be a good cop when you really should recuse yourself. But we never have enough help. Not in season or off."

Leaning her head back on the love seat, Annie looked up at the ceiling. Her stitches still hurt, but her head felt so much better. Especially now that John had given her the perfect opening to bring up the topic she'd been dodging. "Here's an arbitrary question," she said. "What would you do if you won the lottery?"

He laughed. "Seriously?"

"Sure. I don't buy tickets, and I don't know if you do, but what would you do if you won big?"

Scratching his stubble as his father did when he was thinking, John paused, then said, "That's a no-brainer. I'd fund the department so we'd have more money for year-round cops and more special-duty ones in summer so none of us would have to work ridiculously long shifts. Ever again."

His answer did not surprise her. He would not build a mega-mansion out in Katama near South Beach. He would not want to leave the island for a tropical paradise, where he could hang out in a hammock and drink beer all day. The man Annie planned to marry did not hesitate to say that he'd help others, because that was who he was.

"Are you suggesting I should start buying tickets?" he asked.

She smiled, reached over, and took his hand. "No. I was just confirming that the man I'm going to marry has a heart."

He rolled his eyes the way Lucy often did. The genetics in that family were often hilarious examples of apples not falling far from the old Yankee tree.

"Speaking of getting married," Annie added, lightly stroking his fingers, "you were right about our big day being a week from today."

"Yup. And you were right to remember about the license, 'cuz I forgot."

She laughed, trying to maintain a happy mood. "I keep thinking how much I love you. And about how much I want to marry you."

"But . . . ?" he asked, as if sensing hesitancy in her tone.

"But is it really the right time? I'm just starting to get to know Abigail. I want to know her better; I want to have a good relationship with her before I launch into being her stepmother. I want to get back to my writing. I haven't done any since the book tour finished in October. I miss it, and I hope that Trish hasn't given up on me. And, as for our living arrangements . . . well . . ."

John laughed. "Yeah, we haven't spent much time figuring that out, have we?"

She raised his hand and kissed his palm. "Every time I try to do it in my head, I get confused. Where will we live? How will I write? Who will manage the Inn day to day?

I usually give up and find something else to worry about." Then she outlined each of his fingers, slowly, thoughtfully. "I also want to tell you about something that happened with my editor. But I can't right now, because I really am exhausted and, frankly, I'm tired of thinking."

He leaned back and put his arm around her. "You think we should postpone the wedding?"

"Only if it would be okay with you."

He scratched his chin again. "Are you thinking maybe we should do it in the spring? When there's less drama?"

Then they both laughed, because they knew there was no guarantee about that, not on the Vineyard, the most magical place in the world.

"At least it would give me time to buy a pair of proper wedding shoes," she said with a smile. "On the other hand, the flowers and the caterer are already paid, and people are already planning to come . . ."

"Hmm . . . ," he said.

"Then again, by spring Abigail will have fixed my wedding dress. And if we set the date for sometime in April, there will still be time before Francine and Jonas's baby is born . . ."

"So it sounds like you're saying you want

to postpone it."

"I'm not sure. If we have to eat the cost of the flowers and caterers, would that be okay?"

Before John could answer, Annie sat up straight, suddenly no longer tired. "Wait! I have an idea!"

Technically, the idea might have come from Murphy, but Annie decided not to share that tidbit with John.

Instead, she started to prattle while John nodded, smiled, and even laughed. She literally formed the plan while she was speaking, and John threw in a boatload of suggestions, and Annie knew that everything would be fine, it really would.

EPILOGUE

Friday, December 24
A Vineyard Wedding

On Christmas Eve, the great room at the Inn glowed in candlelight; it was filled with scents of lavender and freesia and hydrangea and was packed with family and friends dressed in their finest Vineyard attire. Before the ceremony started, Annie moved among the chairs that Kevin and Earl had set up and Lucy had decorated with white and powder blue lace bows. She greeted every guest — from up-, down-, and even off-island; from Winnie and her clan to all the folks on Chappy and other towns, all amazingly caring people who'd been part of the search for Bella. Which meant that there were way more guests than they'd originally planned for.

Kevin sat down, squeezed in next to Rex, as if they were good buddies, which maybe they now were. Taylor was in the back corner, cello between her knees, poised, ready to play enchanting music for the bride and groom.

Claire was in the front row; Francine's aunt and uncle were next to her. Annie was happy they had stayed. Their presence was going to make Christmas extra special for Francine and Bella.

Looking at her watch, Annie began to thread her way to the back of the room for a last-minute check to be sure the guests were all seated and it would be okay to begin the ceremony, when someone in the last row caught her eye: Trish. Sitting next to her was Louisa. The two women Annie had dissed by her actions. She smiled; apparently they hadn't given up on her, after all.

She gave them a quick wave, then ducked into the reading room for the final preparations. Everyone seemed ready and was awaiting the cues; Bella was positively adorable in the powder-blue dress that matched Lucy's, with its overlay of glittering silver. Both girls wore crowns of fresh flowers that Abigail had made — in between helping Lucy and Annie put together the wonderful, overflowing gift baskets and deliver them to the women's services group in time for Christmas delivery. And Annie was beginning to feel that she might make a decent stepmother, after all. Whatever the future might hold.

Poking her head back into the great room, she signaled for Taylor to start to play; the groom and his best man, Earl, walked up the aisle and stood in front of the fireplace. Across the mantel, white lights twinkled among evergreen boughs.

Taylor began the prelude; the bride smoothed her hand across the midriff of her dress and nodded that she was ready.

So Bella started walking — *toddling,* Lucy would have called it — down the center aisle, a basket of ivory rose petals on her wrist. As she had practiced, she tossed three or four petals with every step, her little teeth sunk into her lower lip, her brow scrunched in concentration. Annie was glad that she and John had decided to give Bella a kitten for Christmas. Rose had been right; little girls did love them.

Then it was Lucy's turn. Annie watched her younger almost-stepdaughter grip her nosegay of lavender, blue, and cream-colored blossoms, align her shoulders in the perfect posture of a young lady, and move in sync with Taylor's music toward the fireplace, toward the man who had filled out the necessary paperwork to be the one-day marriage officiant, toward the groom, toward her grandfather, up to the makeshift altar.

And then, the wedding march began. Annie inhaled, then slowly let out her breath. And then, with a mother's love, she watched as Francine — looking so beautiful in a sparkling white dress that Abigail had designed and made in less than a week — moved down the aisle toward her beloved Jonas.

After the "I dos" were exchanged, after the chairs were moved out of the way and the group of well-wishers mingled among their friends, the chatter was over-the-top joyous for the newly-wedded couple.

"What happened?" more than one guest asked Annie.

"Did you and John split up?"

Questions were fired from all directions, so Annie and John went to the fireplace and stood at the altar where Francine and Jonas had just exchanged vows, following the instructions of the officiant, Edgartown Police Detective Sergeant John Lyons.

"We're going to do this again in the spring," Annie said.

"And that time," John added, "we promise, Annie and I will be the bride and groom."

They had agreed not to tell anyone that they'd rushed Francine and Jonas to Judd's office late last Friday and convinced him to rewrite the license for the young couple instead of Annie and John. But even Judd could not work miracles — he said the marriage couldn't happen until Monday, the twenty-seventh, or even the day after, because he wasn't sure if they'd count the holiday as within the waiting period. They decided that because all the arrangements had been made, no one needed to know that little glitch. So, come Tuesday after Christmas, they would do this again — with only Lucy and Annie as witnesses, and Bella. John would need to do the paperwork to be the officiant again, but that, too, would be easy. And then there'd be no doubt that Francine and Jonas were legally married.

But right then, Taylor punctuated the announcement of Annie and John's spring wedding with a grand stroke of her bow, and laughter filled the room, along with many toasts to the current bridal couple.

"And Francine and Jonas are going to have their own place, after all," Kevin announced. "As soon as I finish converting the workshop into a house for them."

"I'll help," chimed in Bill, Francine's

469

uncle, who, it turned out, was a plumber.

"Count me in," Linc said. Annie had forgotten that in his "spare" time, Linc was a licensed electrician.

"Me, too!" Jonas said. After all, he'd spent a lot of time helping to build the Inn.

Then another voice bellowed from the crowd. "But do you have the proper permits?" It was Richard Sullivan, a town selectman.

A hush fell over the group until Earl spoke up.

"Hell yes, Richard," he said. "It's not exactly our first time on the island."

Laughter broke out then, because almost everyone knew that the Lyons family had been on Chappaquiddick for more generations than any islander would be able to dispute.

As the party continued, Annie walked past the newlyweds and around Lucy, who was feeding Kyle one of Claire's fabulous appetizers, and Claire, who was sharing the recipes on her iPad with friends, and meandered over to the two unexpected, yet very welcome guests: Trish and Louisa. Standing with their backs to the windows, surveying the crowd, the ladies were tastefully dressed in New York City black, which Trish had enhanced with a netted fascinator, and

Louisa with an embroidered shawl. They were grinning.

"I'm surprised you came," Annie said, returning a smile.

"Not as surprised as we were to see that the parts of bride and groom were being played by different actors," Trish said.

"When you hear the whole story, you'll understand why it's been so much fun," Annie said.

Then Trish reached over and took Annie's hand. "I'm sorry about our last conversation. I stepped over the line. I'm accustomed to having to do that with our vendors, but never with an author. Especially you."

Annie smiled. "Apology accepted. And I'm sorry I was so defensive."

"Please stop, ladies," Louisa interjected. "Next, you'll be hugging one another, which will be embarrassing."

They laughed, then Annie said, "I'm so glad you're both here. Where are you staying?"

"A place called the Kelley House," Trish answered. "The internet said it's the closest hotel to the Chappaquiddick Ferry. Which, in itself, presented a memorable experience."

By then Annie knew that while not everyone would ever understand the inner workings of the Vineyard, most people agreed it had a special charm.

"Well, thanks for coming to my wedding, even though Francine was the bride. And, by the way, I intended to leave you a message later, Trish."

"To apologize for walking away from fame and fortune?" She waved it off. "Don't bother. It's not always what it's cracked up to be."

Louisa let out a howl and said to Annie, "I can't believe she just said that."

"Will it help if I tell you I've changed my mind? That I don't want to 'walk away?' "

The women fell silent, their expressions now vacant.

"What?" Trish finally asked.

"It's probably too late," Annie said. "But I spent the past week thinking about it and talking to John. I showed the contract to an attorney. I was going to e-mail you earlier today, but we were a little tied up here."

Louisa spoke up. "We didn't come to your wedding that turned out not to be your wedding to try and convince you to change your mind."

Annie smiled. "You didn't. I convinced myself. So is it too late for our Museum Girls Mysteries to go to Hollywood?"

A moment passed, then another. Then

Louisa jabbed Trish with her elbow. "Tell her," she said. "Or I will."

Trish let out a big sigh. "I figured that once you were married you wouldn't want to be bothered with having to make a decision. So I lied about the deadline."

Annie was confused. "So . . . when is it? Or when was it?"

"January second. They're on vacation until then."

A sudden tingle coursed through her. "Then it's not too late?"

Louisa shook her head. "Nope. We just hope you have a good financial planner to take care of your earnings."

Annie's eyes darted around the room in search of John; he was busy nattering with a group of island cops.

"Oh," she said, "that will be taken care of. I have everything I need right here. So does John. We decided we don't need more money or a bigger house; after we're married, we'll live in John's town house with his girls. Francine and Jonas will be on the property; I'll keep my cottage, where I can write, which means I'll be right here if I'm needed."

Then Annie smiled again and simply said, "But you don't need to hear about the island's housing issues. I'd like you to know, though, that I'm going to set up a foundation and give most of the money to Martha's Vineyard Community Services. They will decide whatever island families, businesses, nonprofits — whoever, whatever — need it the most."

The women looked at Annie as if she were speaking another language.

Then Trish said, "But you're going to have to do a lot of work."

"Work doesn't scare me. Especially because it will help others. I have a good life here. That's what really matters, isn't it?"

In the distance, above the hum of the happy family of islanders and the gentle tones of Taylor's lovely cello, Annie heard what sounded an awful lot like applause. It was, of course, coming from Murphy, though it was difficult to hear her over the love that filled the room.

ACKNOWLEDGMENTS

Many thanks to Hilary Wallcox, librarian at the *Vineyard Gazette,* for resurrecting my memories of sifting through envelopes of old news clippings; to Jay Elliott, for reviewing what I'd thought was my last draft with his English professor's spot-on eagle eye; to mystery author Steven Cooper, for helping me untangle many mysteries in life and books; and to Paul, for letting me escape to his comfy kingdom by the sea where I composed many of the chapters in this series. And to Jim, for being Jim.

I'd also like to thank Kensington's cover artist Judy York for the beautiful cover design of *A Vineyard Wedding* and the entire Kensington team, who keep these books flowing: Elizabeth Trout, Vida Engstrand, Lauren Jernigan, Carly Sommerstein, and others behind the scenes. Thanks also to freelance copy editor David Koral.

In addition, this book requires a very

special thanks to my editor, Wendy Mc-Curdy, and to my literary agent, Loretta Fidel, of the Weingel-Fidel Agency. The year of its publication — 2022 — marks thirty years since Loretta asked "to handle my career," and since Wendy, as a young editor, took a chance and offered us a contract for my first book, *Sins of Innocence*. Three decades is a milestone that marks how much they've changed my life, and I'm honored that they still have faith in me. Over the years, they've contributed lots of great ideas that, most recently, have changed Annie Sutton's life as well. So thanks to them from me . . . and from Annie, too.

ABOUT THE AUTHOR

Jean Stone is the author of over twenty novels about contemporary women. Her book *Good Little Wives* (written under her pen name, Abby Drake) has been optioned for a Lifetime TV movie. From Germany to Japan, over a dozen countries around the world have purchased the translation rights to her novels. Jean has taught at a number of writers' conferences and has been a guest lecturer at many colleges and conferences. A native of New England, she has lived on Martha's Vineyard and Cape Cod for several years. Visit her website at JeanStone.com or her blog, JeanStoneMV.com.

The employees of Thorndike Press hope you have enjoyed this Large Print book. All our Thorndike, Wheeler, and Kennebec Large Print titles are designed for easy reading, and all our books are made to last. Other Thorndike Press Large Print books are available at your library, through selected bookstores, or directly from us.

For information about titles, please call:
 (800) 223-1244

or visit our website at:
 gale.com/thorndike

To share your comments, please write:
 Publisher
 Thorndike Press
 10 Water St., Suite 310
 Waterville, ME 04901